Black White Blur

ROSEMARY OKAFOR

'Black White Blur' Rosemary Okafor 2024

This novel is entirely a work of fiction. Aside from some locations that are used for credibility purposes, the names, characters, and incidents portrayed in this story are works of the authors imagination. Any resemblance to actual persons, living or dead, events or localities is entirely coincidental.

All rights reserved. No part of this publication may be reproduced, stored in a retrieval system or transmitted in any form or by any means, electronic, mechanical, photocopying, recording or otherwise, without the prior permission of Rosemary Okafor.

Contact Info: https://romanceanderoticstories.blogspot.com/

IG: @authorrosemary_ok

Cover Art & Design by: Bookney

Text Layout & Formatting by Agbalumo Publishing

Edited by: Titi Awobode and Glory Abah

Proofread by: Emem Bassey, Amaka Azie, TD West.

Also by the Author

STANDALONES:

One More Night.

Paradise: A Twin Bliss Romance Novel

Many Waters: The Soldier Story Book 1.

God, Michael and Me.

Akwaugo.

Amongst A Thousand Stars.

ANTHOLOGIES:

BE MY VAL: VOL 2

Healing Hearts and Hurts.

Nights at Club Nova.

Hell Hath No Fury.

COMING SOON:

Scented Waters: The Soldiers Story Book 2.

Fall: A Jubilee Ministry multi-author series.

Whispers From Home: A Dahomeyan Bride Paranormal Romance Series.

Trigger Warning

It's nice to know you chose to read this book. Before you go any further, here are some triggers inside this book:

Violence

Gore

Murders

Steamy scenes

If the above doesn't bother you, then flip to the next page.

Happy reading.

Author's note

You may find the prologue unnecessary as you progress into the story, or you may be glad that I didn't yank it out. Whichever one, my aim is for you to connect it to the main story at a rather slow and gradual speed rather than instantaneously.

Also, I'd love to emphasize that though the character, Abdulrasheed, is a Muslim, he is not a judiciously practicing one. None of the characters are overly religious. So, meet them with an open mind.

Prologue

DAURA, KASTINA. 1997

IT WAS DURBAR, the festival that marked the end of Ramadan.

The boy, fair—almost pale-skinned, sat on the steps to the terrace, eating a piece of fried meat he fished out of his pocket while going through the pictures he took a while ago with the digital camera his father gifted him on his last birthday. Occasionally, he would look up to greet a passerby with a smile that wrinkled his eyes and flaunted his modesty and humility, then he would return his attention to his camera. After a long moment, he got tired of the device, hung it around his neck and his face assumed a faraway gaze.

It was late, and he should be going home, but he feared that Inna Shatu, his father's elder sister, would lash him severely with her bulala, and there would be no one to come to his rescue no matter how loud he cried. His parents weren't home. If they were, Inna wouldn't dare lay a hand on him. Inna hated that the boy's parents never used the bulala on the boy. She said they were making him useless by always allowing him to get away with so much. So, Inna looked forward to when the boy's parents would make business trips like the one they embarked on two days ago, so she could discipline him the way a mischievous twelve-year-old boy should be disciplined.

"I don't like Inna," the boy muttered in frustration, taking a bite from the piece of meat and chewing it slowly. With a face so strong like Baba Gaji's farm tractor and the temper of a pregnant *saniya*, the elderly woman was nothing like her younger brother—the boy's father.

Inna wouldn't allow the boy to go out and play when his parents were away.

"Who are you leaving the house to go meet?" she would ask with her hands on her waist and a bulala hanging on her skirt's waistband. "Responsible children don't gallivant around like homeless *marasa gata*. You have a home, *gidan ku kake*, Sit in your room and study!"

Today, Inna had refused to let the boy go to see the colorful horse parade at the Emir's palace. The woman had locked him inside so he wouldn't sneak out when she wasn't looking.

"Read your book, or sleep. Those would be more beneficial to you," she said.

But the boy snuck out eventually, disconnecting some window louvers in his room to make his escape. His first stop was at his friend's house, where his friend's mother gave them a bowl of delicious *tuwon shinkafa* and *miyar taushe* before they headed to the Emir's house to watch the *hawan Sallah*.

Sometimes the boy envied his friend, whose parents knew how to do proper celebrations—they celebrated both Christian and Muslim festivals with music, dancing, and lots of delicious foods, unlike the boy's parents.

Now, as the boy sat outside his friend's house, eating the meat given to him by his friend's kind mother, he wondered if

Inna was looking for him or just swearing and stomping around the house like she always does when angry.

"I have to go home," the boy said to himself. He put the last piece of meat in his mouth, licked his fingers, and fetched another piece from his pocket.

Darkness had descended, and night creatures were sending out their twilight songs. Behind the boy, a conversation was happening. His friend and his friend's mother were talking in steady tones. The boy sensed his friend's mother was drunk again. She was a little loud, and the slurs in her speech gave her away.

The boy wondered why a woman would want to get herself drunk often. Why would she even want to take alcohol in the first place? In Islam, drinking alcohol was haram.

"This is the right time to do it."

"I know, Mother, but don't you think people will suspect?"

Why will the mother and son choose to speak in English instead of their local dialect? The boy thought. They always had serious conversations in their dialect.

"I have everything planned out. Just do as I say, and everything will be fine."

"But, Mother—"

"Nobody will notice he is gone until tomorrow morning."

The boy sat up a little to listen keenly.

"I know how hard this is for you. He's been a good dad to you and his other children," the woman said. "But this is your future. I overheard his conversation with his lawyer. They are planning not to give you anything."

"We can meet his lawyer and make him change it. Let's not kill anybody, please."

The last statement was like a douse of cold water on the boy.

"What if the lawyer refuses? What if he tells your stepfather? We have to do this."

The conversation between mother and son drifted into a melancholic silence. But the boy wasn't feeling melancholic. He felt alert, more awakened and present than he'd been in years.

After half an hour later, the boy watched mother and son disappear inside the bush in front of the house. He slipped the remainder of the fried meat back into his pocket, got to his feet, stepped away from the terrace, and moved down into the darkness of the bush.

The boy had no torchlight, but as he advanced in a slow footfall, inside the bush following the contours of a sloppy path like an animal track snaking through the undergrowth, shapes began to define themselves.

Soon, the boy could hear water clapping against rocks, and birds chirping in their nests, and he knew he was about to come out at the bank of a river. But as he proceeded, lightning broke into the darkness and the boy saw...

There were two figures near the river's edge. One a female —his friend's mother. And from the boy's distance, he could make out the stooped form of his friend's stepfather pushing his face close to his wife, articulating his point in a sharp burst of language, hand gesticulating, voice strained, while his wife had her hands folded across her chest, staring ahead, refusing to make eye-contact with him. The man animatedly articulated his point, his hand gesticulating and his voice strained, while he kept a whispered hold on it.

There, in the shadow hidden behind a tree, the boy observed the exchange. He could feel the charge in the air between the two. The man seemed agitated. He shook his head, then dropped it briefly on his cupped hands for a while.

There was someone approaching the man from behind. Someone...The boy's friend? He had in his hand a long pole, walking with precision.

The boy moved a little closer now, painfully aware of each crackle of grass beneath his feet, aware of every dislodged stone. Releasing his breath in shallow bursts, he watched.

"No, no, no," the man said in English emphatically. "How can you even suggest that?"

The man was about to say something more when he became aware of a presence behind him, as he turned, his son lifted and swung the pole, sending the man face-first into the wet ground.

The urge to scream fought like a squirrel trapped in a paper bag inside the boy's lungs. Covering his mouth with his hand, he watched mother and son deliberate over the unconscious man's body for a while, then they bent down to drag the man by hand to the river.

"Do it now or he'll regain consciousness!" the woman shouted and began to walk back to the edge of the river.

Her son hesitated. Looking back.

The boy was going to hide properly behind the tree, or even run, but there was a movement—a creature under the bush's growth that made him gasp and jump and made the woman and her son turn their heads towards him. At first, everything stood still, and in the silence surrounding the boy, he felt a nudge of fear.

They had seen him.

The stillness in their pose told him a lot.

Instinct told the boy to turn away, to run, yet there was this fear in his brain that told him he would not outrun them. They would pursue him and would kill him. The best thing was to beg them to let him go. So, he took frightened steps towards them.

"Did you follow us?" his friend's mother asked. There was an edge in her voice. Any trace of kindness was gone from her.

It was as though the unconscious man had regained consciousness and had inhaled the bitter coldness of the river. Instinctively, he began to fight the water and the panic that must have flooded his brain.

"Go in there and finish him off!" the woman ordered her son.

The woman's son went back inside the river and grabbed the man by the neck, forcing his head down.

"No!" the boy shouted. "Stop! Stop!"

In a few strides, the woman moved to jam her knee on the boy's stomach. "You stupid child, we keep welcoming you into our home while your irresponsible parents tour the world. What we ask of you now is to keep your mouth shut or I will kill and bury you here."

Burning pain seared from the boy's stomach to the rest of him and he dropped to his knees. "Please," the boy sobbed. "Let me go."

"So you can go and snitch on us?"

"*Walahi*, ma. I won't say a thing."

"Mama, he's still fighting!" the woman's son shouted from behind.

"Hold him down!" the woman echoed back. "One little thing I asked him to do and he's going to mess it up?" she muttered, lowering her head. Then she looked up to stare hard at the boy trembling before her. "You know, cute boy, you can buy your freedom."

"Eeh?"

"Get in there and help your friend."

The boy started to sob, shaking his head as pee began to leak out of him.

"Listen to me you little privileged imp. You must do as I say now, or I'll strangle you and throw you into the river. Is that what you want? Eh?"

The boy shook his head.

"Get in there and help your friend, now!" She commanded, roughly snatching the digital camera from his neck. "Come on, get in there!"

And so, the boy staggered to the river and pressed his knee on the man's back to pin him firmly inside the shallow river, looking back now and then at the woman, who was recording the total horror with the camera she took from him.

He didn't know how long it took, but in a short while, he felt someone—his friend—pulling him out to the bank of the river. He shrugged himself off his friend's grip, collapsed on the sand, lowered his head on his bent knees and began to cry.

"Stop...people will hear you," he heard his friend say.

But he didn't care. He'd killed someone. He'd killed a man. As he lifted his head to slap his friend's hand off his shoulder, he witnessed his friend's mother pushing the body deeper into the river, presumably to let it float away and never be found.

"He's not even your father...why are you acting as if this is a big deal?"

"Because it is!" the boy shouted back.

He'd never watched anyone die before. Never imagined killing anyone, not even Inna whom he didn't like much. Now he'd murdered his friend's father. The worst part of the whole situation was that he could never speak a word about it to anyone.

EIGHTEEN YEARS LATER...

"I will lie to save my life and I will lie even when I don't have to. Tell me about 'look me in the eye and...' Girl, don't even put me on the spot to get something out of me, for I'm gonna lie to your face."

But how I felt that first time I saw you in that auditorium where I'd come to deliver lectures wasn't a lie. You were sitting amongst other girls, drinking. I was the man beside you, pretending to be minding my business, but my attention was on you and what you were talking to your friends about.

I felt faintly disappointed when I heard one of them call your name. Your luxurious hair and glossy brown skin gave you a rich kid look, so I had expected your name to be something a little classier. Sandy perhaps, or Chelsey. You were, however, the prettiest of your group. The others were rather too brash, too obvious.

I guessed all of you were of the same age, but you had maturity that showed on your face even then. Your simple-mindedness excited me, and I wanted you to turn around so you could see me, but you didn't.

It pained me that you didn't, and I had to leave to go prepare for my lectures a few minutes later without exchanging a word with you.

I had agreed to deliver four lectures: part of your Vice Chancellor's drive to integrate real-life business experiences into your department's scheme of work. The lecture that day was easy enough, with the students either half asleep or keenly attentive, leaning on every word I uttered about entrepreneurship.

Not bad for someone whose business was sinking.

As I spoke, I made a habit of pausing mid-sentence to make eye contact with you. At first, you didn't notice what I was trying to do. You just gazed back at me the same way other students who were paying attention were doing. Then you realized, and started blushing *under my gaze, returning my smile before dropping your eyes as I continued with the lecture.*

It pleased me that you got the message I was trying to send to you.

The message wasn't a lie.

One

ABUJA, NIGERIA

"THAT MAN HAS MORE red flags than a Chinese military parade —"

First, Ifechukwu Ojukwu didn't miss the red flags. She looked at them and thought, *'yeah, I can bleach them and dye them pink.'*

Who would blame her? The Abuja dating market was like a crocodile-infested river. Here, the pool teemed with men with red hues, screaming like the siren of an ambulance. Determined ladies had to walk with care. And that was what she did. She'd taken her chance in the sea of red-stamped men and caught one who wasn't so bad. Apart from a few stains here and there, George was okay, near-perfect even.

Her mother was vehement when she brought George to her.

"Of course, you can't marry him," her mother had said. "He has no money, no position, no house. Your father won't hear of it."

Her father did hear about it; about her wish to marry

George because she made him listen. But he reiterated everything her mother said.

"Crazy. Throwing your life away. I will not allow that. You must marry properly, Ifechukwu, into your own class. Someone who can keep you and support you reasonably."

Ife didn't want to marry properly. She wanted to marry George because she loved him. Not the deep, head-over-heels kind of love, but the kind that convinced her he was the one for her. George had a brilliant future. He had once run a successful online radio station and would soon be opening a TV station in Abuja.

"Successful, nonsense. If the online radio was successful, he wouldn't have closed it, would he? No, pumpkin," her father had said. Because he adored her.

She was his youngest, a late flower in his life, the only child who had chosen him instead of their mother when his thirty-seven-year-old marriage ended.

"I'll help you find someone suitable that you can marry straight away. That's what you want, I know. A home, husband and babies. It's natural. I won't dream of stopping you. But it's got to be someone who's right for you. This fellow can't do much for you."

Well, she didn't mind if George could do much for her or not. What mattered was that she wanted George, and finally, she'd gotten what she wanted.

Her phone buzzed again, and she lowered her gaze to it. Her sister had sent her another message:

"Ifechukwu, I still feel you should have waited a little longer. Dad is really mad at you. You know how he feels about you not listening to him."

Really? So, they were going to start this again?

Ozioma, her sister, had watched her accept George's ring and had even whispered 'Congratulations, kid sis,' into her ears while giving her a hug. Yet she chose to send her those unsure messages?

"Too late," Ife replied, dropping the phone on the bed. She pushed strands of hair away from her ear to fasten a crystal-long drop earring—the latest collection George added to her already overflowing stash. Picking the other piece from the bed-stand, she fastened it on the other ear and strolled across the exquisite marble-floored room to stand in front of the full mirror by the wardrobe.

Dad is really mad. Ife harrumphed. Why should she care what her father thought of her? She wasn't going to give her father the honor of emotionally blackmailing her into rethinking her decision. Besides, it was already too late. She was now officially engaged to George, irrespective of her father's efforts to stop her. She had done it, and with no regrets.

She looked down at her sterling silver engagement band and a slow smile worked its way up her face and into her eyes. It was worth it. All the crazy moments with her father, the impassioned arguments and her stubborn insistence on going back to George after their second break-up. A break-up her father had partially encouraged.

Her father, the man who had clutched her too tightly to his big chest and given her love, for the first time in years, was disappointed in her the day she announced that she'd made up her mind about marrying George and that nothing was going to make her change it.

Things got much worse between them after that day. She'd shouted, raged, sworn she would never marry anyone else, and threatened to move out. Her father had shouted back at her and told her she was being stupid, that she had no idea what she was talking about or what marriage was. He said that marriage was a serious matter, a considerable undertaking, not some stupid notion about love.

When she moved out later, and her father realized that she was hell-bent on going ahead with her decision, he'd tried to berate her over the phone, but she wouldn't take his calls. He then bombarded her with text messages and emails she didn't read.

Oh...daddy...

Sometimes her father acted more like an overindulged, selfish boy than a father. It was obvious that the old man was spoiled and capricious. Ife spoiled him as much as he did her. But she still loved him all the same. Their bond would have been tighter if only he could learn how to stay out of her personal life and if he would come to terms with the fact that who she dated or slept with or indeed married was her business and hers alone.

George might look a little rough, aggressive even—but life had not been fair to him. He was a great guy who, for the past three years, had been proving himself to her father, doing things he hated so much—she knew he hated them because he would complain to her after, and would groan the next time she suggested they go visit her father—just to get her father to like him. Yet the not-so-easy-to-please Chief Ojukwu never spared him a little acceptance.

Her mother wasn't any better. The former beauty queen—turned cosmetologist—had turned up her nose in disdain the first time Ife introduced George to her. She couldn't even mask her disapproval. Same as Ozioma, her elder sister.

But Ife had had enough of them all and was glad that they had watched her publicly accept George's engagement ring before they left without posing for pictures. Only Ozioma had stayed behind.

She wouldn't pretend it didn't hurt—the way her parents

left the party, especially her father, who had not hesitated to tell her how disappointed he was. Months ago, Ife would have given everything all up to put smiles back on her father's face, but not now. Not in this case. George said the old man was trying to trick her into backing out from marrying him.

That seemed to be true.

Her father was used to getting things done his way. He made her study business administration so she could be part of his company. It was also because of him that she attended lectures from home until her final year, when she had to lie so he could allow her to move in with Fatimah.

But she wasn't going to hand over to him the power to decide who she got married to. And that was okay. It was time he began to understand that she was no longer a child. Besides, it felt good to stand up for herself for once, to be free from the old man's overprotective clutch.

Ife abandoned that thought and concentrated on the flawless beauty staring back at her from the mirror.

Perfect. She smiled, stroking the delicate silver-plated crystals which dropped from her ear to her shoulder. *Kenneth Jay Lane* design. This one must have cost... how much? George didn't say. He never said. So, she had stopped asking and was now resigned to relaxing and enjoying being treated like a delicate ornament. George didn't have much, but Ife loved that he could buy her things out of his little savings.

Her phone rang as she finger-combed her honey-blond weave curls—one of the hair pieces that came in with her last shipment from Korea for her shop. She cast another appraising glance at her reflection in the mirror, then hurried to get the chiming device. It must be George checking on her. She wasn't one to arrive late on occasions, but today was different. It was their engagement party and she had to look perfect for it.

For him.

"George—" she started without checking the caller ID.

"Pumpkin—"

"Oh." Ife's heart sank immediately, and she flumped on the bed. "Dad."

"I guess... congratulations are in order," the man said in resignation.

Relief brought a smile to Ife's lips. "Dad." She didn't realize how much she craved to hear him say those words until now. "You left in a hurry."

"I have some important things to attend to."

"Important things? Dad, you know you are lying."

"Okay, okay. You caught me." His laughter filtered into her ear. "But I mean it when I say congratulations. I'm happy for you."

He's happy for me? That's another lie, but she'd rather not argue. "Thanks, dad." She shut her eyes and inhaled deeply. "Thank you so much. And thank you for bringing your friends along. Honorable Nasir and Senator Bosun are still here." The old man had promised, after a lot of pleading, to make some of his friends grace the occasion, and they did.

"Glad to be of help to you and your man..." the old man trailed off.

Ife imagined him running his large palm over his face and tapping his feet repeatedly on the floor the way he always did when he was uneasy.

"I pray he treats you right."

"George is so sweet, dad."

Though George tended to lose his temper at little provocations, Ife had learned to rein him in. She couldn't even remember the last time he hit her.

It had taken them a long time to get to where they were now. Years of misunderstanding, bruised faces and egos. Twice, they had taken the decision to stay away from each other. Twice, they had gotten back together again because they were meant for each other. They both knew it.

"He's a good man."

There was a silent beat. Ife knew her father was trying to pick the right words.

"If you say so—"

"I know so."

Another silent beat.

"Tell you what?" Energy returned to her father's voice. "Why don't you both come over to the house sometime so I can properly welcome him to the family?"

"Dad, I... uhm...that will be great."

The door opened, and George walked in, shooting her a questioning stare.

'My father,' she mouthed, and his face fell. "I'll speak to George about it," she replied to her father, her eyes still on George.

"About what?" George asked in a hushed tone, taking her by the arm and pulling her up. "You are as beautiful as the first day I met you," he said, looking her over.

Ife giggled. "Dad I—" She giggled again as George made a face. She turned her back on him and continued her phone conversation with her father. "George would be glad..." To rather count the cars passing the street than spend a single minute with her father. But she was sure that with time, both men would learn to tolerate each other.

"I assure you," she said to her father.

Grabbing her from behind, George rubbed his hands across her small breasts—braless beneath a cosseted strapless blue dress, her second dress for the occasion. The first, the one she wore through the first half of the party, was a floating top embroidered with gold on top purple harem pants, and a pair of low heel gold embellished sandals.

She didn't push George away as usual, rather she stood still and allowed him the feeling he had been waiting months for. They weren't celibates per se, but four months ago, she suggested they abstain from sex. She wanted a break. But the truth was that their sex life had degenerated into a routine. Nothing fun. His foreplay skills were practically nonexistent. And that was because his passion for owning a media station had grown to a self-consuming level.

But she still loved him, and she was sure he loved her much more than she did him.

"Yes..." Ife tried to continue her phone conversation, but George's hard-on chafing to escape his pants while he parted the slit of her dress and slipped his hand underneath to reach her butt cheek was a little distracting.

"Dad...dad..."

George's hand moved to the front, shifted her thong to stroke the entrance of her cove.

"Dad, can I call you back later?"

George took the phone from her and ended the call. "I don't want to share you with anyone now. Not today at least," he muttered, pocketing the device.

"Dad said we should—"

George's hand came up to squeeze her breast. "We are not going to talk about your dad," he said softly, but she could hear the note of finality. "This evening is about us."

He kissed her neck. "You know that, don't you?" He pulled her even closer to his body. "Maybe we should have a quick one," he said, leaving her breast to run his hand up and down her curves. "You don't need to remove everything, just lift your gown and..." another kiss on the neck.

"You are already dressed," Ife murmured.

"I don't mind removing everything," George replied, slipping his hand back inside her dress to find her cove. "For this here, I can even cancel this party," he murmured, tapping two fingers on her labia.

"We can't do that, George. There are a lot of people waiting."

The idea was to kill two birds with one stone. Celebrate their special day with friends and family, while pitching George's business idea to potential investors. For months now, George had been trying to get people to buy into his plan of opening a television station which would cater for rural community dwellers, and he didn't want to start small.

Her father had called it a stupid and lofty idea that would fail just like his online radio station, and the adult learning center he started nineteen months after the online *thing* failed. She sponsored that. And it failed because... well, the covid-19 pandemic happened. However, she was ready to help him raise the money he wanted for this latest project. She would have single-handedly sponsored it had it been that the money involved was decent. It wasn't. So, the only option left for her, when her father refused to spare even a kobo, was to apply for a loan from her bank. She wouldn't want to do that either. She'd rather leverage her relationship with some of her father's friends who were financially heavyweights.

"All these preparations—and you want to cancel?"

"It's my party." Letting her go, George said with a hint of edginess. "I can decide to send everybody home now. After all, we are done with the important aspect of it."

"Dad will not like that he invited his friends here for us, and—"

"You think I still care about what he likes?"

Getting her father to invite his friends to the party so George could sell his proposal to them was a difficult task. He would rather she returned to his company—which she resigned from a month after she moved out of the house because she could no longer stand him reminding her, every day, how accepting George's marriage offer would be her biggest mistake.

"You'll earn your own money and live comfortably," her father had tried to cajole her.

But she didn't want to earn her own money while George struggled. She wasn't asking her father for anything more than pulling some strings for her and her fiancé. In the end, her father only promised to make the men attend the party, the rest would be left for her and George.

"We need those men," Ife sighed.

"I don't need any help from your father."

She would forgive George's stubbornness because she understood he was tired of her father treating him like scum. "Nobody is asking you to accept help from my father...just grab this opportunity."

"That your father is offering me?"

"That I've worked so hard to get for us."

He stared her hard in the face. "Okay," he said grudgingly. "But come on, Ife. I want to make love to you. Okay, let's have a quick one—won't take time, I swear," he said, looking down at the bulge in his pants.

"George. Oh, baby." Ife would have wanted them to wait a little longer, till the wedding night perhaps. "You know you'll eventually have it."

"Then let me have it now, I can't go out like this." He lowered his gaze to his bulge. "With an unspent erection."

"George, please."

"We are practically living together now."

He slept in her large house more than he did in his one-bedroom apartment because, according to him, it was better they stayed in each other's faces. That way, they would be inseparable.

"We are like a married couple, Ife. Yet, you keep torturing me."

"I don't want to do this now," she persisted, staring into his rich brown eyes.

"Ife, you're killing me," he said, getting up. "So you know, I'll never take this from any other woman.

Two

"YOU ARE BEAUTIFUL,"

Beautiful and ready to pose for paparazzi and entertainment rag hunters. They would be present, and Ife didn't mind at all. In fact, she was beginning to enjoy the media attention. While growing up, her father tried to shield her from the desperate clutches of sensational news scouts, but that became almost impossible as she got older and began to make friends with ladies who didn't know the definition of keeping a low profile. Fatimah first; back then in school. Later, Awele; a crazy daughter of Eve who relocated to Lagos with her husband two years ago. Habibah: a customer who forced herself into Ife's life and soon, both of them were touring clubs where they would dance most of the nights or watch Abuja babes get high. Fola joined the *girls' gang* much later. She was the only introvert among her friends.

With George's palm on the small of her back, Ife swept down the stairs, acknowledging Bashiru, her housekeeper, with a nod. The party was going well, Lionel Richie's *Stuck on you* filled the air.

"Everyone is here," she whispered, allowing George to lead

her to the guests, while her eyes roamed for any sign of Habibah. The mischief-maker was one among her remaining friends who had not moved out of Abuja in search of love or greener pastures. And they'd agreed, weeks ago, that she would be her right-hand woman tonight.

"Your parents left," George said. They had stopped to shake hands with some guests and moved on. "As usual, they abandoned you on a special day like this. All because of what? You chose me, a wretched guy who will stain their personality," he added, taking her hand.

She glanced over her shoulders and caught uncle Ekwuozo —her father's elder brother—sitting with two other men, his face fiercely stern. Obviously, the man shared her father's sentiment about George. *The old hypocritical man.* Ife still remembered the many holidays she spent in the man's house when she was a kid. How pretty housemaid after pretty housemaid was banished from the house because the man had a crazy penchant for sleeping with maids. Odogwu Mmadueke was present too. The kinsman who came from the village was leaning on his cane. By his side was his sister Maggie. And just behind them, Ozioma her sister was standing rather stiff, formal and bored, her absurdly handsome husband, Okwuchukwu, was talking with a group of people.

"Ozioma and her husband are still around," Ife said, still scanning the place for more familiar faces. She must admit that there weren't as many guests as she wanted. Just her parents' friends, some extended family members, the people from the estate that of course wouldn't miss her engagement party for anything, some faces she didn't quite recognize. Her own friends weren't even present.

"You know why she stayed."

"Who? Oh, Ozioma. She is my sister."

"She is protecting the family name. When the press notices

your parents' absence, who will be the person to give excuses? Ozioma, the perfect image maker."

As much as Ife wanted to debunk George's claims, she knew he was right. Her father had made it to the party because she pleaded—almost cried— on the phone. Her mother too decided to grace the occasion because she heard her estranged husband would be attending. The former beauty queen didn't want her ex-husband to tag her as uncaring. And Ozioma— though it was obvious she too didn't like George, came probably because no matter what, they were still sisters who had each other's backs.

"What about you? I can only see your uncle," Ife challenged, summoning up a smile as they walked towards a table where a slightly portly man was nursing a glass of alcohol.

"He's the only close relative I have left. You know already."

"Sorry," Ife apologized.

George's parents died years ago, he told her. He had no siblings, and no grandparents—those were dead too.

'His life is filled with misfortune,' her father had said when she told him George's story. *'That's not good, Ifechukwu. A man without a family is too dangerous to get involved with.'* But her father was being…himself— a traditional conservative. People no longer needed a community to get married. If the two people involved loved each other, that was enough.

"I'm really sorry, George," Ife said again.

"Don't be. I have friends I invited. I'd like you to meet them."

Friends? George never spoke of friends. And why did it take him this long to introduce them to her?

"You will be amazed when you see them."

"They are here already?" she asked, stepping ahead to greet his uncle.

"You are a princess," the man said.

"A queen," George corrected.

The relationship between them wasn't a cordial one. George hardly talked about the man, and Ife doubted if it was George who invited him. The man might have read about their engagement from an online blog site.

"Congratulations, my boy," the man said.

George made no effort to take the man's outstretched hand.

"Have you had something to eat...drink?" Ife asked, uncomfortable with the unspoken animosity between the two men.

The man relaxed back on his chair with a sad smile on his face. "I don't mind more of this." he said, twirling the drink in his glass and pouring it inside his mouth. "Scotch."

Ife beckoned a waiter.

"You'd better make it a double," the man said.

They continued their stroll, leaving the man to enjoy his drink.

"You should consider mending your relationship with him," she said, plucking a grape from a bunch on top of a table and eating. She picked another one and offered it to George.

"Can we not talk about him?" George grumbled, opening his mouth wider so she could push the grape in.

"Okay," she said, laughing.

She didn't know she would enjoy playing hostess, she'd never done it before. As she walked from table to table, greeting and smiling, giving witty responses to the press and making sure everyone, especially her father's friends, were well taken care of, she realized how much she loved everything about the event. George was also having a good time networking and showing her off like a prized possession. But he wasn't comfortable with the press. Their constant questions were beginning to annoy him.

Two hours later, Ife wanted the evening to end. Fortunately, people were beginning to depart. She couldn't be more pleased.

"Bashiru, keep your eyes on the remaining guests," she instructed her housekeeper and began walking back into the house. The sound of a vehicle pulling into the compound made her stop. She sighed and turned graciously, ready to meet another power broker—another of her father's friend perhaps, but the man she saw stepping out of the black, sleek Lexus SUV that just parked some distance away left her gaping.

He had a mixture of silver and black beards that shockingly complemented his face that was as fair as the fire-gold glow of dawn. His white thobe must have been made from one of the finest of cottons. She could smell the richness of the ankle length robe that was embellished with black embroidery. The red and white checkered headscarf on his head, held in an Emirati men's pattern with two black ropes, fitted like a band around his head and gave him an aristocratic look. ...E*gal*! She got to know what they were called from one of her father's friends who'd traveled to Dubai.

He wasn't perfectly handsome like George, but *Eish*! He looked like a deity. Exuding the perfect balance of danger and charm.

His eyes lowered to his wristwatch for a split second and when he lifted them again, they landed on her and stayed for a while. She could swear she saw something, a hint of...shock? It was as if the guy was trying to recollect where he knew her from. He gave up and began to walk towards the poolside where George was sharing a drink with Senator Bosun.

Ife concluded that the new guest didn't know her, and obviously, he wasn't there for her but for George. However, he was their guest and she had to keep him busy until George was done with whatever business discussion she presumed he was having with the Senator.

Ife took tentative steps towards the guest. "Welcome to our party," she said, summoning a smile to her face.

He stopped abruptly; Now it was his turn to stare at her.

A Muslim, Ife thought, noticing the dark spot on his forehead— a prayer mark.

"I know you," the man said.

Okay... deep voices were Ife's catnip, and when garnished with a Hausa accent like this man's own was, she was sure to give up all the coffee in the world just to listen to the auditory caramel for the rest of her life.

"I swear I've seen you before," he repeated, looking at her like she was a marble puzzle she had to piece together.

"Definitely." Hers was a familiar face on social media and news blogs. "My father was once the junior minister for petroleum. Chief Nelson Ojukwu. He served under—"

"No, not that. I mean...I've met you somewhere before. I'm sure I have. I never forget a face."

"Uhm...I don't know...maybe...I don't remember," Ife gave off a strained laugh. "I meet a lot of people every day." she said, looking down to brush an invisible lint from her dress. His eyes were utterly attractive in an enticing and forbidden way—dark, wild, crazy, like some animal peeking out from a burning forest. And the way he was staring at her was rather disturbing.

Clearing her throat, she said, "anyway, welcome to the party."

"Thank you," he replied, gazing around, allowing her the chance to give him a proper perusal.

She was right to describe him as not perfectly good-looking. He's was a dark kind of handsomeness. Fascinating and somehow suspicious.

"It's like I'm late," he said with that trace of local accent that shifted the tone of his English.

"At least you still made it," Ife replied lightly, wondering why her heart was starting to beat at an accelerated rate.

"*Kai*, I hate coming late to functions." A frown crossed his face and disappeared almost immediately. "*Subhanallahi.* Anyway, you are right. At least I made it."

"Better than not coming at all," she said with a satisfying smile, while trying to interpret his Arabic exclamation—*Subhanallahi*—in her head. She was neither a Muslim nor from the Hausa/Fulani region, but she'd lived in Abuja and had mingled with a lot of indigenous people long enough to understand most Arabic and Hausa words. She could even engage in a long conversation using the Hausa language. Unlike George who, unbelievably, couldn't say more than a few words of the local dialect even though he'd stayed in the North longer than she had. "So, George invited you?" she asked.

"Uhm...Kind of." He paused to observe her. "*Masha Allah,* you are beautiful."

His eyes, filled with interest, locked with hers. For some reason, she found herself almost lowering her gaze. Thank goodness she didn't, for that was what shy girls who got all squishy inside while standing before men like this would do—looking away or lowering their heads. But Ife wasn't that kind of girl. She wouldn't lower her head, or this strangely good-looking man would think he was discomfiting her with his intense gaze. It was even funny how she was already having this...this tingly sensation all over just because he was looking at her like a man would look at his woman of interest. She had to watch it so she wouldn't join the thread of shameless Abuja ladies who would be engaged to a guy and still got soaked under on seeing another, especially if the latter seemed cuter and richer. That was always ridiculous to her—instantly getting attracted to a man because of his smoothness or looks. It was like picking one's breakfast cereals based on color instead of taste. In this case, she didn't want *the breakfast* at all. She already had a three-course meal to herself, George.

"There you are," George said, appearing out of nowhere as a paparazzi zoomed into action, flashlights popping nonstop.

Ife dragged her eyes away from the stranger.

"Hey... hey... get out, now!" George shouted at the camera guy. "And you—" George grabbed the guest's arm and pulled him into a bear hug, slapped his shoulder and released him. "You are the man I want to see right now."

"I wouldn't have forgiven myself if I didn't make it to your engagement party today."

"I wouldn't have forgiven you too." George let out loud laughter. "Come on in. You shouldn't be standing."

"Your—this good lady has been a great company since I arrived here," the guest said, redirecting George's attention to her.

"Oh." George slipped his hand around her waist and pulled her closer. "Ifechukwu is special."

Once more, their eyes met, and Ife had to silently warn herself to be careful. This man might not be deliberate with his flirtation but his instant interest in her wasn't hidden, and she wasn't going to encourage him. No. She had an important person in her mind—George, and this man here was turning out to be an unnecessary distraction.

"And beautiful too. *Kyakkyawa ce*," he murmured, lowering his gaze to her neck. "Look at her skin—smooth, deep bronze like *Joan Miro* Sculpture on Jeddah Corniche, Saudi Arabia."

"Rasheed," George interrupted. Rudely, she must say. "Enough now—"

"Oh, I'm sorry," the guest looked up to meet her eyes. "It's again my pleasure meeting you, Ife. My name is Abdulrasheed." He offered her his hand. "People call me Abdul or Rasheed. But it's always better to call the name in full. Abdulrasheed. Servant of Allah who is the right minded. Shortening the name takes the meaning out of it."

"Nice to meet you too, Abdulrasheed." Ife withdrew her hands as soon as her fingers touched his. "And I'm Ifechukwu, George's fiancée—"

"You are what?"

His sudden response, the shock on his face which graduated into a deep frown took Ife aback.

"George's fiancé?" She carefully replied, glancing at George and back at the man. "I thought I mentioned it?"

"No, you didn't. Neither did this man here." He cast an accusing stare at George. "Anyway, it's fine. So, your name is Ifechuku..." he picked out the sounds like a child learning how to pronounce a new word. "What does it mean?"

Ask Google, she would have snapped had it been someone else wanting her to explain her name. But for some funny reason, she felt the urge to not just interpret her name but also do so much more. "Light of God," she said. "And there is a 'W' after the 'K'. Chukwu, not Chuku."

"Light of God, I like it," he said, a smile playing on his lips. "Can I call you Ife?"

"Sure, everyone calls me Ife."

"Good. Ife it is then," he said, then turned to George. "My friend, you sure have an eye for good things. Your...lady is such a beauty."

"Thank you—now the introduction time is over," George said impatiently. "Rasheed, you are going to invest in my TV station."

"You're starting a TV station?"

"It has always been my dream," George enthused.

"Thought I told you when we chatted on Facebook? Anyways, you'll want to put in your money once you hear what I have in mind."

"I don't think I would want to throw money into any business that is not tech related now."

"But you will love this project," George near-cried. "It's about doing good, and I know you sponsor things like this. Your Facebook page suggests that you are into charity."

"Is it a kind of charity thing?"

"No... not really," Ife stepped in. If George felt that Rasheed would be one of the investors they needed, then it wouldn't hurt to add her convincing power to this conversation even though she was having a bad feeling about the man himself. "It's a community TV station. It will help the poor get help from the government, in a way."

The look on the man's face was discouraging. It was as if he wanted her to shut up or change the topic. But she chose to do neither. If George wanted his money for this project, she would do anything to get it. Anything except, of course, throwing moral decency to the wind.

"Please," she said. Hating it that she had to resolve to beg for the attention of a total stranger, just to get George this one thing. How she wished her father wasn't being strong headed, that the old man would be reasonable enough to see how much this meant to her, and just give her the money. "At least let's pitch the project to you first, I promise you would want to invest."

She smiled inwardly as Rasheed's face softened. Who said she'd lost touch with her convincing super-power? "So, you think you can sit and hear us out?"

"*Insha'Allah*—" Rasheed muttered. "If you want me to."

"Of course, Ife would want you to. Don't you, honey?"

"Yes." She breathed. "Yes, I want him..." Sparing the guest

—Rasheed, a glance, the shocking look on his face confused her at first. Then...*Oh...Oh!* Embarrassment ran through her when she realized...*such a dirty scoundrel*, he must have thought she meant that she wanted him...like...sexually wanted him. *Eish*. "I mean I'll appreciate it if he gives us an audience," she corrected.

Got you, she thought as his face came down in an embarrassing frown.

"That's okay. I will. But not here. It's your engagement party, man." He slapped George's shoulder. "I like your fiancée, George," he said, as George led him to a table. "She's got brains I tell you. I'll sit for hours and even more to listen to her."

Three

WHEN IFECHUKWU MET Fola in an all-women's conference that Habibah took her to, three months after her first breakup with George, she didn't know the lady had a history with George. It was months after she was back with George that she felt it wise to introduce her new friend, Fola, to him. Ife was pleased to learn they both attended the same university. That knowledge tightened her friendship with Fola so much that even when she got to know Enitan—Fola's husband—their bond didn't loosen.

With time, Fola became more like a sister to her as she was the only person from George's past she had met. Apart from her, George had nobody else: no formal work colleague, not even a childhood friend. But tonight, George had introduced her to some rich looking guys he said were his school mates.

Ife picked a glass of cocktail off a waiter's tray and walked towards the bar. Again, she thought about George's friends and a frown crossed her face. She didn't understand why George would have such important people and not leverage them to get himself to the top. Why was he comfortable scrambling at the bottom when he had people like Rasheed...

And just as his name slipped into her thoughts, she found herself looking around in search of him. He was standing a distance away, laughing heartily at what a snap-snap one with face full of makeup was saying. Another lady was standing by his side, craving his attention. Ife wondered which of her father's friends the ladies had escorted to the party because she was sure she didn't invite them.

Ife brought the glass of cocktail to her lips, observing the lady by his side. She had on her head the funniest spongy wig Ife had ever seen and was looking at Rasheed as if he was a perfect dinner.

But he is.

Who cares?

Miss Spongy-Wig was laughing hard now, an unladylike kind of laughter that made the whole of her body shake. Ife set her drink down and held her breath behind pursed lips to steel the slice of envy that just gripped her throat as she watched the lady push her boobs which were straining to be set free from the shirt that would have fitted a twelve-year-old girl perfectly, to Rasheed's face while toppling with laughter.

Miss Heavy-Makeup-Face must have told a lame joke because the three of them seemed to be bonding over it.

Ife took a sip from her drink, her eyes shifted to Miss Heavy-Make-up who had fished her phone from the pocket of her ripped jeans and was tapping on the screen with an extra-extra smile on her face while Rasheed was muttering something. His phone number? The other lady had her hand inside her purse, searching for something with a frown masking her face. Ife watched as she spilled the contents of the purse on the table behind her.

Now the game is on, Ife smiled. Soon the lady would claim to have lost the money she kept for *Uber* and would need a lift back home. Then Rasheed would offer to either pay for her ride or drive her home himself, and they would eventually end up in a hotel or something. Either way, this was Abuja, and ladies hustled to grab and secure rich men the same way politicians struggled to keep ministerial appointments.

Eish!

Rasheed just caught her staring.

She quickly looked away, swearing under her breath, as a flash of anger ran through her. Since their first encounter, she had been unable to stop searching him out among guests. At first, she had convinced herself that it was because she didn't want to lose sight of him since she was hoping they could have that business talk before he left. But now she wasn't sure. Whenever he locked gaze with her, she felt this sensation... like weightless baby feet dancing in the pit of her stomach.

Ife gulped the remainder of her drink all at once, pushed her glass to the bartender, and sat down on one of the bar's long stools.

"Ma. We are running out of drinks," the young guy with a tinted Mohawk haircut said while refilling her glass.

"How come? We planned for fifty guests. I'm not even sure we have up to that number of people in attendance."

"Ma? we have more than that number!" the boy said in amazement. "They didn't come all at once, but I assure you, people have been coming as others were leaving. It's like someone made an announcement that there's a party going on here. I think some of the enlisted guests also came with a friend or two."

Some came with escorts like the two ladies she just watched sampling their assets for Rasheed.

"I can call for more supplies *sha*, if you want," the young guy added.

Ife shook her head. "It's late already. People should be thinking of going back to their houses." She sipped from her refilled glass and turned fully to observe the handful of guests; Ozioma and her husband were heading to their car. Mama Joe was shoving *jollof* rice inside her mouth as if it was her last meal on earth. George was walking Fola to the gate.

Taking another sip from her drink, Ife watched the duo until they disappeared, then she sighed and brought the drink to her lips again. Tonight, there seemed to be something off about Fola. Something that was not quite there. Ife had even asked her earlier if she was sick, because she was looking so...washed out, so faded. Maybe that was why she had deliberately avoided her for the rest of the night.

Ife yawned, rubbed her eyes and yawned again. Her body was gradually shutting down. *Eish*, she could pay anything to get a back rub—which George was good at—and a good night's rest. But she was by no means done for the night. She still had appreciation calls to make. She wouldn't leave that for tomorrow because she hated carrying tasks over. She also had to check with her Korean hair supplier to know if her orders had been shipped, then she would bathe and fall into bed, ready for tomorrow's early start.

Gradually, she was becoming a workaholic. But who would blame her? She needed to recoup the chunk of money she took out of her savings to buy her house—a modest four-bedroom duplex inside *Mary Slessor* estate. The house wasn't quite as big as she wanted, but it had a sizable compound, a pool and a garden. She had also parted with another chunk to purchase the 35-meter office space she was using as her hair shop. The rest she had invested in the business, determining to put away enough money to buy a place for George's TV station. It would be her gift to him.

Fortunately, she was well on her way to achieving her goal, proof that all her hard work had been worth it. If George was able to get investors tonight, it would be a double win.

Ife allowed a fleeting smile on her lips while she glanced around. The number of guests had thinned down to just a few. She was about to return her attention to the bar when she caught Rasheed leaning against the coconut tree by the poolside, watching her. Feeling a sudden giddy roiling in her gut as he tipped the glass in his hand towards her with a cocky grin on his face, she looked away fast, drank the remainder of her cocktail and beckoned the bartender for a refill.

The guy gave her a *'are you trying to get yourself drunk'* look but went ahead to do as she wanted.

"I'll be fine," she said to the guy who only shrugged and busied himself with his phone. Ife pushed hair away from her face, lifted the glass and took a sip. Even though she had been off alcohol for years, she didn't think a few glasses of cocktail would get her head swinging.

"Hey, beautiful."

The sound of that deep, sexy, tone shifting voice, like warm black coffee down the throat, caught her unprepared and made her sputter drink out of her mouth.

Abdulrasheed.

"Sorry," he said, settling on the stool next to her. "I didn't mean to startle you."

Ife wiped her mouth and lifted her face. Her shocked gaze met his.

"Are you okay?" he asked, picking a napkin up from the bar.

His breath of warm air tickled her bare arm as he leaned forward to wipe a splash of the drink off her hand, making her tense. He smelled so good, like a perfect addiction. What was that perfume? And the way he was looking at her too—like that moment before a kiss, or a longer time after.

"I'm fine," Ife sighed, taking the napkin from him while willing herself to relax. His fingers, which brushed through her skin as he was wiping the splash, had robbed her of a few breaths.

He leaned back. "Hope you don't mind me sitting with you? I can make the rest of your evening memorable. I have been told by some pretty ladies that I'm fun to be with."

"You mean—" she swallowed down nerves. "The two ladies I saw you with a while ago?" she said, running a burgundy polished manicured index fingernail over the rim of her glass.

"Which...oh...those ladies," he paused to get his phone out from his thobe's side pocket. His fingers tapped fast on the screen. "Funny bunch," he said, placing the device back inside his pocket and facing her fully.

"Jealous?" he asked with a hint of humor in his voice.

"Jealous? Me? Oh come on." She scuffed. Refusing to meet his eyes, her gaze settled on his lips instead. It was too beautiful for a man. Full and sensual, yet masculine. There was something rather erotic about the contrast between them and his salt-and-pepper beard. Something which almost made her run a finger over his skin, stroke those lips, feel the layer of his chin and jaw hair—would they be softer to touch than they looked?

"Let me assure you, the struggle is mutual," he cut into her thoughts with a grin.

Struggle? What strug...Oh! Ife was aware that she had been staring at him for too long, but for some silly reason she didn't think he would notice.

"I get it. I too, I'm struggling not to act on the stirring inside me since I set my eyes on you," He added so casually.

Ife clicked her tongue, ready to fire back a snarky comment but the titanic clash of emotions in his eyes rendered her speechless for a moment. His stare was guarded yet exposed.

Challenging yet submissive. Unwilling to bend yet impossibly vulnerable.

"You know what? I'm actually enjoying you looking at me." His jaw twitched. "So long as you promise not to break the golden rule."

"What golden rule?"

"Look but don't touch." He laughed. "I saw you from over there—" he pointed backward. "Staring at me, and I thought...maybe it'd be nice if I'm with you instead of—"

"Of course not," she interrupted. "I have a man." *Yeah, never forget that, Ifechukwu.* "You...I was only looking around and saw you. Besides, I don't want to lose sight of you. You mustn't leave without first hearing about our project."

"About that..." he started so nonchalantly. "I'll tell George when I'll be free for a meeting."

"My man will really want you to invest in this," she said.

"You mean George?"

"Yes. George, my fiancé."

"What do you want?" he asked, leaning forward.

"Me?"

"Yes, you."

Anything George wanted. She wanted anything that would make her man happy. But she wasn't going to explain that to Rasheed because, like her father and Habibah, and everyone else, he wouldn't understand. Maybe he would. If he had ever been so committed to someone so much that he would do anything to make the person happy.

"I want George to be happy," she said.

They slid into silence. The *thump-thump* of her heart became louder. God, she hoped Rasheed wouldn't hear that sound.

He broke the silence. *"Kai, Yan Mata.* Why do you want to do this for George?"

"He is my man," she replied. "And please don't get it

twisted, I would do anything to get this for George, but I will not...uhm...give in to any form of sexual seduction."

He narrowed his eyes at her as if she just said the most ridiculous thing. "You think..." he barked out a laugh. "Lady, though I'm struggling to rein in my attraction for you right now, but trust me, my intention is not to seduce you. I think you are the one nursing ideas in your head."

That hurts. The embarrassment that came with those words slapped her so hard and almost made her cry. Jesus Christ! How could he say those words as if every flash of naughty thoughts were closed-captioned on her face? She looked around to be sure no one was within earshot. "I'm not nursing any idea," she said, wishing her voice wouldn't tremble the same way her inside was doing. "I have a man already. Why would I nurse ideas with you in them?"

He held her gaze a moment longer then started tracing a pattern with his finger on the slab. "You love him?" he asked.

"What?"

"It shouldn't take you a second to answer my question if you really love George."

"It's not taking me a second—"

"You are being defensive."

This was bad, allowing Rasheed to steer the discussion towards a direction she wasn't comfortable following him in. The man was a fox. He had figured her out so quickly and was now capitalizing on her discomfort to devour her. But what scared her the most was the fact that being under his uncanny presence excited a little part of her.

"I love him," she said. "I love George." She did love George. She had to...why was she even second-guessing her love for her man? "I love him," she said with finality.

Rasheed looked like he was going to laugh, and Ife had this

strong urge to throw the remainder of her drink at him to wipe the naughty grin off his face.

"There, there...trying to convince yourself again," he said.

"You are despicable," she retorted.

"I agree. You also like me." His grin broadened. "Don't deny it."

"Keep flattering yourself," she hissed.

The sudden feeling of sobriety around them made her look his way and her heart began to beat faster again.

"I like you, Ife," he said, a little...serious.

Even when those few words made her smile irrespective of herself, she knew she wasn't going to allow them to mean anything to her. "It's natural. I'm likable," she said.

"Abdulrasheed!" George called from behind, approaching them. "I have been searching for you everywhere." Turning his attention to Ife. "And you, honey. I thought you'd retired," he said.

Ife summoned a smile and stood up.

"Your woman is a great hostess, and an amazing company too," Rasheed said, getting up too. He held her gaze as he lowered his head toward her. "Thank you for giving me such a memorable night. I hope to meet you again, soon."

"Soon. Of course," George said breathlessly. He was suddenly uncomfortable. Ife knew. She also knew that later, when everyone was gone, and everywhere was quiet. He would ask her if Rasheed had acted inappropriately with her. He always asked. Because he was quick to jealousy.

"What of...the business. The proposal?" George asked Rasheed who was already taking steps towards his car.

"I'll schedule a good time! Rasheed replied without breaking his stride.

"Fine," George called back.

They'd walked a distance towards her apartment when George asked, "what was he telling you?"

"Nothing, just some old stories about himself and... you know." Ife wasn't going to tell him that for a moment, under Rasheed's interrogation, she had second-guessed her love for him.

"You would want to be very careful with Abdulrasheed."

Ife nodded her agreement.

The following day, you were there again with your friends. When I walked to seat beside you, you looked at me, smiled, and returned your attention to your friends as if yesterday never happened.

Your conversation moved from coursework to relationships. Boys, I supposed, although you called them men. Your friends spoke in lowered tones I had to strain to hear, and I braced myself to hear your part in this litany of one-nightstands and careless flirtations. But I had judged you correctly. All I heard from you were peals of laughter and good-humored digs at your friends.

You weren't like them.

It pleased me.

But I was saddened that you didn't give me the attention I wanted that day. Not even when I climbed the podium and tried making eye contact with you like I did the day before. It was as if you were throwing my truth to my face, and I was scared. I hated being rejected. I even took a walk through your university grounds after that day's lecture, hoping I would bump into you. I saw one of your friends instead, the tall one with blue tinted hair, and I walked behind her for a while, but she disappeared into the library. I couldn't follow her inside to see if she was meeting you.

On the day of my fourth lecture, I arrived early and was rewarded for my efforts by the sight of you alone, in the same chair row I've seen you on the previous three occasions. You were reading a message from your phone, and I suspected you had been crying. Your mascara had smudged beneath your eyes and although you would not have believed it, you were far more beautiful that way.

"Do you mind if I sit beside you?" I asked

You pushed your phone into your bag. "Go ahead, sir."

"We've seen each other before, I think." I said, sitting down.

"Have we? I'm sorry, I don't remember."

It was so irritating you would say that to me after three days of me showing you myself and my truth. But you were upset, and perhaps, not thinking clearly.

"I am a lecturer." I didn't know why I had to tell such a lie. Maybe because I discovered earlier on that being a teacher in the school of higher learning held immediate appeal for young girls. "From the University of Nigeria Nsukka." The lie flowed smoothly, and it worked on you.

"Really?" Your eyes lit up. "What subject?"

"Economics."

"Oh." The spark in your eyes disappeared, and I felt a burst of resentment that you couldn't reward my lies with enthusiasm. Or maybe I should have said medicine? Or law?

"You look too young to be a lecturer though," you said.

Younger than your professors, I know. But way older than you—must be ten years older—so I deserved the kind of reverence you gave your lecturers. But it was like you didn't care.

"So, what do you do when you are not giving lectures?" you asked.

It shouldn't have mattered what you thought but it was suddenly important to me that you were impressed. "I own a tech company." I watched the spark return to your face. "We create and sell software all over the world," I continued, liking it that my lies pleased you.

"You are a final year student?" I changed the subject.

You nodded. "I'm going—"

I held up my hand. "Don't tell me, let me guess."

You laughed, enjoying the game, and I took my time pretending to think about it, letting my eyes run over your Lycra dress, the swell of your breasts stretching the fabric tout across your chest. I could see the outline of your nipples and I wondered if they would be huge or small.

"You're doing banking and finance," I said finally.

"Yes!" You looked amazed. "How did you know?"

"You look like someone in that field."

You didn't say anything, but two darker shades of brown appeared high on your cheeks, and you couldn't stop the smile spreading across your face.

"So, what's your name?" I asked without giving mine. You must have known mine from the many times I introduce myself before each lecture. If you've forgotten, you should ask me so I can tell you.

You told me.

I repeated the name. I told you that I loved it while in truth, I hated it. I would have asked if you had another name, but I didn't want to offend you.

"People tell me, a lot of times, that they love my name." You gave a careless laughter. The last trace of your tears had disappeared and with it, the vulnerability I found so compelling.

"I like it." Gosh, I hated it. "I couldn't help but notice you were a little upset earlier," I pointed at your bag, hoping you would understand what I was talking about. "Have you received bad news?"

Your face darkened immediately. "It's from my mother."

I said nothing, just tilted my head slightly to one side, and waited. Women rarely need an invitation to talk about their problems, and you were no exception.

"I told her about my birthday party next week and she said she will not be coming. That I should understand she had 'a lot of things occupying her time' and wouldn't keep attending all my functions."

You sketched quote marks in the air and effected a sarcastic air that didn't hide your bitterness.

"That's terrible," I said. "I can't imagine a mother not wanting to be around when her daughter is celebrating her new age."

You softened instantly. "Her loss," you said, although your eyes were glistening again, and you looked down at your fingers. "Don't blame her though. My brother's death did this to her. She can't stop blaming dad for it." You went ahead to tell me how Uche your brother was kidnapped and killed when your father delayed paying the ransom required for his release because the police promised they would nab the kidnappers and set your brother free. Your mother had pleaded with him to ignore the police and pay the money so your brother could return home, but your old man was being selfish and stupid.

I wanted to tell you that it served your father right. I had no pity for him that his son was killed, or that your mother left. Like my stepfather who had clung to his wealth even after his death, your father deserved every pain that came consequently to his foolishness.

"Can I get you something to drink?" I asked.

"Coffee would be lovely," *you said. When you saw my brows go up in confusion, you added,* "Nescafe has a spot outside the auditorium, just by the left before you get to the palm groove."

There were not many coffee shops around town, and I wasn't expecting to find one in your school.

When I got back, your friends had joined you. I recognized two of the girls, but the third one was new, and there was a boy with pierced ears and bushy hair. They had taken all the chairs. I had to hand you the beverage and go fetch another chair.

I waited for you to explain to them that we were in mid-conversation, but you just thanked me for the coffee and introduced your friends, whose names I instantly forgot.

One of your friends asked me a question, but I couldn't take my eyes off you. You were talking earnestly with the bushy-haired boy about some departmental assignment. Your hair fell across your face, and you tucked it impatiently behind your ear. You must have felt my gaze on you because you turned your head. Your smile was apologetic, and I quickly forgave you for the discourtesy of your friends.

My coffee grew cold—I wasn't a coffee person but that day, I wanted what you wanted. I didn't want to be the first to leave, and have you and your friends talk about me, but there were only a few minutes before my lecture, so I stood up and waited until you noticed me.

"Thanks for the coffee," you said.

I wanted to ask if we could see each other again, but how could I with all your friends around?

"Tomorrow, perhaps?" I said, as though it really didn't matter to me in the slightest. But you had turned back to your friends, and I left with the sound of your laughter ringing in my ears.

Four

"YOU WERE SUCH A SHOWBOAT OUT THERE."

George began as they stepped into the sitting room, with total disregard that the housekeepers were within earshot. He was furious, plus he'd had too much to drink. "Carrying on and on about the project like it's your idea. You made me look like a fool before those men—you had the words, the ideas. And my job was to follow you around while you do the talking."

His harsh words shocked Ife into a stunning silence. An outburst like this was not unlike George, but he was forcing her to accept that she overdid things when all she did was water the ground for him.

"And what's that you did in front of Abdulrasheed, my guest? Trying to flirt while I..." George stopped to grab Bashiru who was passing by. "You," he said sharply. "Get me a bottle of beer. Very cold."

The frightened housekeeper glanced at Ife. "I can't serve you beer, sir. It's against my religion."

"Get me anything to drink! Malt, juice...anything!"

"Yes, sir."

"Bring it now!"

"Yes sir."

"You disrespected me," he continued as soon as Bashiru left. "You made me look stupid."

"George, I'm sorry. You must understand—"

"Oh, I understand so well." He took the malt drink from Bashiru who returned almost immediately, opened it with his teeth, guzzled and frowned. "This thing always tastes like rat piss," he muttered. Then returned his attention to Ife. "You like Rasheed, don't you? He has the looks, the money, and you being the attention seeking queen, the celebrity who mustn't be ignored, you decided to throw yourself at him."

"But he's my guest too. I was only trying to make him comfortable."

"Flaunting your skin for his greedy eyes to feed on was making him comfortable, I see." George hissed. "Let's not even talk about your father's friends. You chose to talk to them about my business instead of allowing me to do the talk. I'm not grand enough. Isn't it, Ife? I am not damn rich enough for them. I don't own big, important companies, so why on earth would they bother with what I have to say?"

"It's not like that, George."

"What is it like? You'd rather talk to them because...because you are ashamed, I'm not bright enough to hold a conversation with any of them. You've always presented yourself to everyone as the one controlling everything."

Oh, goodness. George wouldn't want to do this. Not on her engagement night. "This is not fair."

"I'll tell you what's not fair." He drank what was remaining of the drink and wiped his mouth. "You showing off like you know anything about opening a media house while you know nothing."

Ife wanted to tell him that she knew enough to sell his

proposal to potential investors, that she spent most of her spare time reading up how to run a TV station because she also wanted to be part of it, but she knew this wasn't a good time. "I'm sorry," she said, kicking off her shoes and bending to pick them up.

"Screw you, Ifechukwu. You're full of shit," he shouted, walking up the stairs.

"Look," she said in exasperation. "I was trying to help."

"For *chrissake*, save your dumb excuses," he shouted back, entered the room he always slept in whenever he came around and jammed the door.

Reluctantly, she made it up the stairs, into her own room. This wasn't the way she'd planned on ending the evening. George's behavior was inexcusable. How dare he assume she was disrespecting him while all she was doing was helping?

She stepped out of her dress, took two analgesic pills to take care of a sudden throbbing head, and dived into the remaining tasks for the night.

George was waiting for her when she came out of the bathroom. Sober enough to realize that he probably wasn't thinking straight, and that he certainly shouldn't have said all those things to her.

"Baby, honey...you know I didn't mean any of those things I said to you."

She met his apology with mixed emotions: anger first because there was no place in all the things he said that he fixed the words *'I'm sorry'*; then guilt because George was right: she had felt something for Abdulrasheed—like her heart was burning a hole in her chest. The overwhelming attraction she felt, especially when he sat beside her at the bar, was so thrilling that she'd forgotten, for a moment, that George might be watching. But she didn't flirt with him as accused by George. By God! she didn't.

"But you know how much I hate being treated like I'm a man of straw," George tipped her chin up. "You shouldn't have allowed Rasheed to look at you like that," he said, stroking her lips. "And you should have allowed me to introduce myself to your father's friends. I didn't need you to do that for me."

She nodded.

"You know how much I love you."

"Yes." They might have their fallouts every now and then, but one thing was sure; George loved her so much and he'd done enough to show her. He wasn't perfect, nobody was. All she had to do was to try not to be controlling. He hated it when she took over things without him wanting her to. It reminded him of her father.

He kissed her lips. "You are my life, Ife. These past years, you have brought me nothing but favor."

"You've said that a million times," she managed to say, inhaling his scent of soap and freshness. "You make me feel like I've given you so much—"

"But you have!" His voice rang.

He was excited again. Something told Ife he'd got some news.

"Today, you brought me the biggest of luck!" Steering her towards the bed, he made her sit on his lap. "How do you do it?"

"Do what?" she asked, chuckling.

"It's like an enchantment. Every man that sets his eyes on you falls in love with you."

"I don't know." She shrugged and tightened the towel around her chest. She should choose her words wisely, or she might trigger him again. "Maybe I have an invisible magic wand or a pixie dust."

"Maybe. Not that I like it that you are attracting unnecessary attention but..." He gave her a deep kiss. "Tonight, you made me the happiest man in the world." He gave her another kiss and eased her off him. "Someone has finally agreed to invest in the project!"

"Wow, this is amazing." She sat and leaned her back on the bed's headboard, placing her legs on his thighs. "Really, George, this is great news."

"Don't sound surprised. You already know who I'm talking about. Rasheed."

And just like that, her heart galloped. *How convenient.*

"He called me a few minutes ago. He has agreed to meet with us."

Irrespective of how she felt about the man in question, knowing that he was ready to give them a chance brought hope and excitement to her. "Mm-hm?"

"He's willing to give me the whole money if our proposal is convincing enough!" George enthused.

"What?" Now she could hardly sit still. *Eish!* It was like the news was going to make her throw off sparks.

"I tell you. He's going to give me all of it."

"Did you send him the proposal... feasibility study... you know?"

"Not yet."

"Why?" For Christ's sake, that should be the first thing: get the man's email address, send every necessary paper to him and then wait for him to schedule a meeting.

"I know, I know...but," George paused. Gave her a long stare. "That's where you come in, Ife."

She noticed he was fidgeting.

"I want you to be the one dealing with him."

She allowed a long silence. Then, "I don't think this is a good idea," she said.

The shock on George's face made her look away.

"Wha...why?" he stuttered. "What do you mean it's not a good idea?"

Ife glanced up at him and lowered her head again. How could she tell him that the man made her uncomfortable? Yes, she wanted him to invest in their project because it meant so much to George, to her. But she thought it would be George and not her dealing with him because, somehow, she knew the man was stricken by her, though he was modest with his feelings. She saw it—his struggle not to say too much, stare too much. Not to touch her. Even as she thought of it now, her heart was fluttering like a flapping cloth on a clothesline, which was even more disturbing.

"Come on, honey. This is what we've always wanted—someone to pick interest in this dream."

"But it would have been better if you did this yourself, George. He's your friend."

"You are the one with the super brain." It was like he didn't mean for those words to come out because he bit his lip and hung his head. "I can do it, you know—I mean, I can go to him. Just that...I think he likes you and that's good. He will do anything you ask of him."

Like her. That was the problem. She didn't want Rasheed to like her. Or rather, she knew that what Rasheed felt for her that day was much more than liking. She'd been with men and could read their body languages. This Rasheed was taken by her. It wouldn't have been a problem if she hadn't felt a stir—a persisting tingle all over her while she was with him.

"My father's friends—most of them already gave us their promises."

"Waiting for them to make up their minds will take a lot of

time. I don't have such time," he retorted. "Come on, honey. A few moments ago, you seemed awfully interested in this guy. Now he's picked interest and all you have to do is to add a little push, why are you going cold?"

Awfully interested, ehn? "And you accused me of flirting with him a few minutes ago."

His eyes hardened. "You think I don't know he has his eyes on you? If I could get this money anywhere else but from him, you think I won't consider that option?"

"But we can—"

"Your father and his friends," he groaned. Lifted his head, sighed, lowered it again. "I don't have time, Ife. I don't. Please, honey. Do this for me, for us." He shifted closer and palmed her face. "Just tell me when you will be ready, I will tell him to book the appointment and then you both will meet. It's not that hard nau."

"Or we can do this online." That way, she wouldn't be in close proximity with him. "The proposal can be sent to his mailbox," she said. "He has an email, doesn't he?"

"Who doesn't have an email in this time and age?" George asked, massaging her shoulders like he hadn't lost his temper some moments ago. "But you know it will be better if you meet him in person even after sending the papers."

Why her? "This guy—I don't trust him, George." Or rather, she didn't trust herself around him. Won't her steady composure evaporate at the sight of him?

"I don't either, especially with you. But I can trust you, right?" He pinned her with eyes filled with a desperate plea. "You'll not do anything to hurt me, will you?"

"No, I'll not." Anything for George. Anything.

"Good." He leaned forward and kissed her, moaning as his lips trailed down to her collarbone. "Let me stay here tonight," he whispered, his hand tugging on her towel.

"No." She gently pushed him away. "Not today."

"Not today? This is our engagement night, honey. We should celebrate."

Ife didn't feel like celebrating. And sex with George was the last thing on her mind.

Five

MOSQUITO BITES *on the fingers could give one a crazy kind of itchiness.*

"Eish!" Ife muttered, abruptly sitting up. She'd slept off on the couch again. She had been doing that lately. "Shish." Her body hurt like a locomotive train had run through her, and had a rat crawled into her mouth and died there? Oh, she didn't brush last night, she just remembered.

She got up, scratched the itchy spot on her finger and made her way into the guest's bathroom to pee and rinse her mouth. She caught her reflection in the mirror and realized how crappy she looked. Not only crappy, but there was also an unsatisfying look about her. Truth was, she looked miserable. No, she was miserable, and she knew why.

Life with George had become unbearable.

After the argument they had the morning following the party and he stormed out of the house, he had not returned. Or called. Or even returned her calls. That morning, George met her as she was about to leave for business, asked if she had sent the proposal to the email address he forwarded to her WhatsApp, Rasheed's email address. He had also wanted to know when she would be going over to see Rasheed. He had erupted like pus from an abscessed wound when she told him she'd sent the proposal but still thought that he should go for the physical meeting instead of her.

To pacify him, she had promised to stop by her father's. "I can tell him to remind his friends—"

"I don't want you to meet your father on my behalf," George screamed. "I found someone who's ready to help out. All I'm asking is for you to please go mesmerize him with your intelligence."

"Me, mesmerize him? I thought you hated me doing the talking and making you look like a fool? Why are you sending me to this man now when you can do it yourself?" she said stubbornly.

The way his jaw dropped, and his gaze narrowed at her told her that she'd said too much. "You're mocking me."

"No, please..."

But he was already walking to his car.

"I'm sorry," she shouted, running after him. "George, wait!"

He slammed his door and turned the ignition on.

"George please, where are you going!"

"Away from you."

Reluctantly, Ife had stepped aside and watched him drive off, swallowing the anger that was about to erupt inside her.

Damn George for not seeing how much she was trying to help him. She'd gone to great lengths to make her father put in a word for him and his TV dream, and this was how he was repaying her.

Damn him.

Ife wasn't bothered when he didn't return that night and the nights after, but after two weeks of not hearing from him, she became worried and had gone looking for him in his house. He wasn't there. One more week later, he was still absent.

Then last weekend he showed up, refusing to talk about anything. The study and his room became his coven. It was a torment staying up half of the night listening to him scraping pencil on paper or having a low conversation with himself. Sometimes there would be a roar of rage through the silence, he would slam the door and then there would be heavy silence again.

Two days ago, he disappeared and when she dialed his number, he kept busying it.

Ife hissed, threw more water on her face, and came out from the bathroom. She walked over to the table and picked up her laptop. She was halfway to her room when a roar of rage boomed up George's room, stopping her in her stride.

George.

When did he come in?

Maybe she should go check on him. *Naaa,* she dismissed that thought and walked into her room which was opposite his, changed into her nightie and got into bed. It was some minutes past eight a.m., but she didn't feel like starting her day early.

In a short while, there was a long diatribe coming from downstairs, clearly accusatory in nature, punctuated by an occasional silence during which the accused was clearly endeavoring to defend himself. Or at least to speak. And then a loudly slammed door and then— blessedly— silence.

Ife heaved herself over onto her side and closed her eyes in relief. But her peace was short-lived as her bedroom door opened and George came in.

"Stupid, moronic, incompetent idiot. And to think you're paying him. Paying him! It's an outrage—"

"George," Ife said mildly. "This is no way to start the morning." It was no way to start anything at all. He should first explain to her where exactly he had been spending his time. After his adult learning center shut down, he'd not found anything engaging to do, he wasn't even interested in the many job offers she had brought his way. So, where could he be disappearing to these past weeks?

"No way to start the morning alright. But I assure you that Bashiru shouldn't be working here. He ought to be locked up with animals! I've told him so."

"George, this is outrageous of you."

"Why? The moron can't get anything right!"

"Funny. I've never found anything wrong with his service."

"I don't care."

"I have developed a considerable faith in Bashiru. The way he handles the house... and he never gets impatient and angry." Ife kicked the duvet off her body and sat at the edge of the bed. "He's a nice man, maybe you've not figured out the kind of person he is."

"It's his job to figure me out, not the other way round." George removed his shoes, kicked them aside and collapsed on the chair in front of the dressing mirror.

"What is going on with you? What is going on with us?"

He ignored her, stood up to wear the shoes again, and walked back to sit down.

"This is not about Bashiru, is it?"

"No, it's not! It's about you not seeing things from my angle."

Now that—why was she not surprised?

"You never see things from my angle. You've stopped understanding me. I sometimes wonder if you were the same woman I met years ago. You used to do things for me."

"Stop sounding ridiculous, George." Ife got up, walked

across the room to stand in front of him. "You know I'll do anything for you. That hasn't changed."

"That hasn't changed? Ife, how can you say that when you have only fought every idea I've brought concerning this project?"

"It's not true." That he would insinuate that she had been unsupportive while all she'd done since she met him was assist and encourage him was preposterous. "You know it's not true."

"What's not true?"

Ife observed her thirty-three-year-old- fiancé sounding like a whiny teenager. "I've always helped you." She wasn't in the mood to indulge his childish fit.

"Always putting me at the mercy of your father—you call that help?"

She was not ready for this today. In fact, she was tired. But it was obvious George was on the warpath, looking for a fight, and she was the perfect target—it wouldn't take a genius to figure that out.

"You are about to become my wife," he said with a baleful look. "For Christ's sake, you should be doing what I ask you to do."

"I'm sorry for not realizing that being your fiancée entails jumping at your demands without thinking," she said, tempering. It drove her nuts when he pulled the perfect relationship standard card on her—as if she wasn't trying her best to make things work between them. "I simply don't feel like meeting this Rasheed guy."

"Not even when I tell you it's the best for me? You can't do it for me?"

"Dad is already helping us. His friends—"

"Yeah. Daddy. The almighty Okwute Nelson Ojukwu. Oil

magnate, business mogul, political kingmaker, Egocentric pain in the ass—"

"Shut up, George."

"Do not tell me to shut up!" He stood up, pinning her a glare. "And so you know, you are nothing different from your father...no wonder your mother left you both."

That was the height of it. Jesus! Maybe they should have remained the way they were—lovers without further commitment. It was as if their engagement had turned them against each other.

"Oh God," he muttered under his breath, pulling up his pants. "Oh God, Oh God." He walked up to her and gripped her shoulders. "I shouldn't have said that."

But he did. And it hurt that he would draw that straw.

"Ife, honey..."

Jesus Christ! Why did he always say such horrible things when angry? Why did he go out of his way to make her feel like she was not doing enough for him—for them?

"I'm sorry. I swear I didn't mean all those things I just said."

"I'll do it."

"See, you don't have to keep pissing me off like I'm..."

"Book an appointment with Rasheed and I'll go see him."

His eyes widened in shock, then his face softened to a childish smile. "Oh, darling." He kissed her hard on the lips. "I'm so sorry... so, so sorry for all the things I said to you. I've been so selfish."

His sudden tenderness was disarming and once again, she was rebuking herself for regretting the engagement. George was a great lover. He had his weaknesses, but she was sure they were meant to be together.

"Okay, I'll call him so he can book an appointment with you." He searched his pocket for his phone. "Let me send you his phone number, in case." His fingers typed fast on his screen. He was done in a few seconds. Then he pulled her into his arms. "See, I know how hard it is for you to accept this, but this is my ticket to hitting it big."

Without the help of her father, of course.

"Let's prove to your old man that we can do without him and his connections."

Of course, of course...

Six

CLAD in a polka dot chiffon blouse and white pants, heads turned when she walked into the *Blucabana* Restaurant, Wuse. Conversations stopped and she was sure eyes on her. Slowly, pockets of low voices rose and of course, some of the discussions were about her.

Reactions like those no longer bothered her. She was an Abuja *big girl,* a social media sensation, the spoiled daughter of the great Nelson Ojukwu, and more importantly, a successful entrepreneur.

"Thank you," she said to the waiter that welcomed her, while she scanned the cozy restaurant.

"Any reservation, ma'am?"

"Uhm, yes. Table twenty-two."

One-hour max. That was what Ife had agreed with George that she was going to spend with Rasheed. After that, she would go to the Federal House of Assembly to meet senator Bosun.

Bosun, whom Ife was sure had not been able to get *it* up for his wife in a long while but kept making advances at her each time he had the chance, wanted them to meet after the day's *house sitting*. He said he would be taking her to a convenient place where they could talk about George's business proposal.

What an asshole.

He must be thinking the meeting would be his chance to get her into his bed. Ife wished she could report the man to her father, but she needed all the money she could get, so she must apply wisdom. She gritted her teeth at the thought of listening to the senator's obscene ramblings and hoped she could convince him to have the meeting in a public space where he wouldn't dare do anything that would attract the undue attention of the press.

"Okay ma'am." The attendant looked at his notepad and back at her. "Come with me."

Rasheed chose here because, according to George, he didn't want to choke her with the ambiance of his workspace. But Ife knew Rasheed's decision to have her come to this place was made from that part of his mind that was lusting after her. That part that wanted her but was being cautious, lest he overstepped boundaries.

What was wrong with men? Or rather, what was it with her that made every man she'd come across hunger for her? When she was in school, her friends had always joked about her exuding subtle sex appeal like a low wattage light bulb in a romance filled room. Years later, the media began to use her as a symbol of feminine sexiness, even when she was not the type of woman who wore clothing that left little or nothing to the imagination. In fact, she hated any dress that showed a lot of flesh.

Well, she was done getting bothered about shameless men who wouldn't see her and not think of sex.

And she shouldn't allow herself to get so uneasy about this

meeting which was supposed to be a business appointment in every sense. A business meeting she shouldn't have honored because just the thought of setting her eyes on him again was giving her a kick to the stomach.

Eish! The truth hurt like a bone stuck in the throat. But Ife was in the restaurant already. She would try to stick to business.

Ife took her seat at the reserved table which was in an enclosed booth by the window. Checking out the plush interior of the café, she imagined how nice it would have been if she had been there with George for a romantic dinner.

"You want to order anything now?"

"No. I'll wait."

The frown that crossed the attendant's face didn't go unnoticed.

Ife changed her mind. "Okay, get me water."

As the attendant left, Ife dialed George. "He's not here yet," she said.

"He's running late then."

"He's not supposed to be running late." Her water arrived and she poured herself a glass.

"Calm down, honey. He may be held up in traffic or something."

"George, this is past six." The meeting was scheduled for 6 p.m. "He should have called to tell me he was running late if that was the case. For God's sake, you gave him my number."

"Give him a little time. Okay, let me call him, but I still think you should calm down."

When the call ended, Ife turned her face to the window and settled her gaze on the blue pool outside. It was so beautiful. It reminded her of the time she took George to Clayton Hotel in Dublin, for a vacation. It was her way of apologizing for their second break-up.

She couldn't remember what led to the fight that brought about them going their separate ways, but she knew she snapped at the point where he accused her of wanting him out of the way so she could *'hook up with some tootsie guys and play around.'*

Oh, George.

Three years they'd known each other. Three long years and not once had she cheated on him, although the opportunities to do so came in abundance. She was twenty-four and had the kind of vibe men found most attractive. She got hit on all the time by men. Celebrities, young executives, other women's husbands, but she always turned them down. She was committed to George. And though their relationship sometimes turned out to be a nightmare, it did not mean that she should cut and run, although they did break-up twice. It also didn't mean she should cheat the way most of the girls she knew were doing. She had principles and staying faithful was one of them.

They had started out so well. George was handsome, sweet and caring. Their first lovemaking was a bit of a disappointment though. Ife was pretty sure George hadn't guessed at that time— he got to know later. She'd worked awfully hard at being grateful and telling him how wonderful it had been, especially *it*. But— well, maybe she just kept telling herself it would get better. Of course, she had nothing to compare *it* with but from everything she had heard and read. So she wasn't too bothered. At least it didn't hurt— or not too much anyways— which her friends had implied it would. That had been a relief. That and the kiss which was lovely. He was quite good to her that day and hadn't rushed her as she was twenty-one and a virgin. He had stroked her small breasts and told her they were beautiful, and he loved them. But now, oh dear, now…

The sound of the restaurant's swing door opening forced her back to the present. Someone walked in but it wasn't Abdulrasheed.

Ife hissed, picked up her phone and began browsing through pictures, stopping at the photo of George and herself in bed.

It was funny how they had become sexually bored with each other. In those early times—after they'd gotten a grasp of how it was done—they were wild and adventurous. Now sex with him had become a hassle. Yet she loved him still. Only that she no longer felt excited about having sex with him.

Habibah said it was *see finish*. That it happened between her and Ahmed, her ex-husband.

Ife hated this *see finish thing*. She hoped it would change when they got married.

"Apologies for keeping you waiting," Rasheed's voice interrupted her reminiscing.

And as she looked up... *Oh...Oh!* Her heart skipped a beat.
A beat. Not bad.

He walked across the table to take the seat opposite hers and her heart did a full somersault. No, it sank into her stomach. Curse him for looking as good in a black two-piece slim-fit suit as he was in a thobe.

Remember, it's a perfectly innocent business dinner with a potential investor, she tried to convince herself. *Remember that Ifechukwu, Remember.*

"I was delayed in the office by a client. I'm so, so sorry," he said.

Most people gawked at Ife because of her exotic appearance, or stared with envy at her beauty, but the way Rasheed was looking at her, the way he was watching her, it was like he'd been enchanted by every breath that came out of her. It was simultaneously beautiful and scary.

Unable to speak, Ife grabbed her glass of water and drank while managing a quick calculation in her head to work out how old he must be. Thirty. At most, thirty-two.

"Kai, Ife," she heard him mutter. *"Kin hadu, ga ki kyakyawa dake."*

There. He'd said it, and like a dirty old man coming on to her with such an obvious line; *you look so sweet.* This should be the part where she shot him a glare. But she couldn't get herself to do that as she was busy calming the flush that was moving from her neck up to her face.

"It's like the creator airbrushed the hell out of you and ran out of paint for everyone else."

Even though she didn't want to, she laughed. He laughed. The sound of their laughter together was like happy feet on a dance floor.

Then he sobered up, still looking at her in awe.

"What?" she asked, giving him a questioning stare before lowering her gaze.

"Your laughter," he said. "Like a little girl getting tickled."

And his words were like feathers stroking her sides and her thighs. How was it that he knew the right things to say to get her flushing all over?

This is dangerous, Ife. You have to get in control now.

"Did you read the proposal I sent to you?" She quickly changed the topic.

His silence made her look up. He had a cocky grin playing on his lips— And she began to feel a sensation in the pit of her stomach which wasn't sickness or hunger, but something close to that excitement that comes with anticipation.

Sitting there, facing such a cute stranger with unfathomable dark eyes that contrasted his light-toned face, eyes so deep and expressive that one could get lost in if one stared long enough, Ife could swear that she saw a hint of pain which disappeared as quickly as it emerged with his slightly crooked smile—a smile she knew could be her undoing, yet he had the audacity to always flash it.

He looked like a man that was in-shape. His body beneath his perfectly made suit got her thinking about doing some crazy things. And oh yes, he had great hands with long, artistic, ringless fingers. *Damn it!* No band on any of his fingers meant he was free.

Or not. Abuja married men rarely wore rings.

"I'm hungry," he said as a waiter came over with the menus.

Ife accepted one of the two menu books, buried her face behind it while she tried to get a handle on exactly what was going on with her.

"Anything you fancy?" he asked. "Local or any of the intercontinental dishes?"

She heard herself mumbling something about how chicken mushroom soup might be nice. He agreed, so a double order of chicken mushroom soup it was. He added a bottle of wine she'd not heard of, but he promised she would like.

"Do you know what I fancy more than what we ordered?" he asked, a few seconds after the waiter left.

She didn't want to know. Oh shit, she did want to know.

"I fancy you," he said, putting down his menu. Their eyes met across the table. For a moment, time stood still. Then she broke the gaze and refilled her glass of water.

"And I think you fancy me too. Unfortunately, we can do nothing about it because you are already taken."

"You don't know what you are talking about," she said, lowering her head again to hide the embarrassment that had washed through her.

Was he right? Of course not! George had her. Sex might not

be working for them now but as soon as they had the project behind them, that aspect of their relationship would be fine again.

Their food arrived and she escaped into it, wishing he would do the same. But he suddenly started talking about things... books, movies, politics, arts. And she was forced to listen, and chip in a few words every now and then.

He knew plenty about everything, and she was able to keep up because she made time, every morning, to scan the daily papers—something she learnt from her father—so that she would have plenty to converse with her father's business partners about. She was also a bit of a CNN junkie and a Discovery Channel addict. It turned out he was too.

She told him she spoke Hausa, though she wasn't very fluently in it. That impressed him. He asked what other languages she could speak.

"Just Igbo, English and Hausa, unfortunately."

When he told her he spoke five languages: Fula his native language; Hausa because he spent his early childhood in Daura before his father moved them to Abuja; English the official Nigeria's lingua franca; he learned French when he left Nigeria to Brittany with his mother; and a little bit of Arabic—because he was a Muslim, it was her turn to become awestricken.

Out of excitement, she asked him to say something to her in French. He stared up as if the words he was searching for were written on the restaurant's artistically designed ceiling, when he brought his head down, she noticed, with awe, that his eyes had become softer than she knew eyes could be. What she saw in them removed her ability to comport herself, and she instantly sensed her doom collecting around her like a malevolent cloud of static electricity.

"*Depuis je t'ai vu, j'ai toujours su que tu es pour moi, pour posséder et protéger,*" he said.

Some words were statements of intense longing, his—though she didn't know what they meant— sounded like they were that and more. His tone, low and sober, enclosing her in his emotions.

"You are an immense beauty, Ife," he added.

She bit her lip, eyes everywhere but on him. She'd never seen anyone so *villainy handsome*, and never had so many warning bells pealing in her head at the sight of a man. Yet, when he leaned forward to cover her hand with his, her breathing became shallow as she watched his pensive look melt into a smile as calm and honest as the morning light.

"Ife, your voice, your smile, everything—you are the beginning of my demise, *yan mata.*"

She felt relief sprinkled with sadness when a waiter broke into the moment with a bottle of wine.

"I forgot I ordered that," Rasheed muttered, withdrawing his hand and leaning back so the waiter could fill their glasses. "Non-alcoholic. I don't drink alcohol. My religion. You know...hope you don't mind?"

She just nodded and continued with her food. To save herself from acting awkward further, she asked him to tell her about the many places he'd visited. That gave her several minutes' breathing space to regain something approaching comportment, while she kept eating, sipping wine, nodding and smiling.

By the time they were done eating and were ready for business, it was as if there was never any sexual tension between them.

"When do you want the money paid?"

"Ehn?" She only spoke for thirty minutes, and he'd already made his decision?

"Would you want me to call my account officer now so he can initiate the transaction?"

"I'll suggest you take your time and think about—"

"Nothing to think about. It's a go for me. As long as you want it."

Dumbstruck, she stared at him for a moment. "Are you sure?"

"Don't you want me to help your boyfriend?"

Boyfriend. The way he spat the word. "Okay. George will call you in... let's say... tomorrow?"

She was on her feet, reaching out to pick up her bag when he grabbed her hand.

"Why are you with him?"

"I had...uh...excuse me?" she said, taken off guard. Again.

The tension she thought was gone returned like a sudden strong wave, his dark eyes intense as he continued staring at her, stealing her breath and the heat from her skin. Suddenly the hard-as-bricks-defense she thought she'd built became just paper, paper soaked by rain drops. "I don't know what you are, uh, on about but."

"You have to leave him."

"Leave him?" She wanted to get angry, to tell Rasheed how disgusting he was, but he was on his feet now, a hair length away from her, forcing her to take in all his formidable form, his thrilling smell– like a blown-out birthday candle, sharp and smoky.It was that smell in one's nostrils when one closed the eyes and made an impossible wish while one's mouth watered for something sweet.

"At that party, seeing you both—all I wanted to do was wrench you away from him."

Before she could draw in the air her body needed for her mouth to speak, he had taken her other hand. Though she wasn't supposed to, she allowed him to pull her into an embrace, and like a child craving the comfort of warm arms, she melted into his form, feeling his firm torso and the heart that beat within. Her brain shut down as his hands folded around her back, drawing her in.

She didn't know how much her body needed this closeness... this feeling of lapping against this stranger's form until now. And it felt good. Weirdly good. And super relaxing.

So much for *'this is a perfectly innocent business dinner with a potential investor,'* she thought as a shiver of excitement tore through her, and she swallowed a baffled squeal that could have been either delight or indignation. It had been so long she felt this deprived just by the mere brush of her body against a man's. Allowing him to lure her into his arms was a mistake. Now, she must free herself before she disintegrated in his hand. This man... Rasheed... he must have been sent to shatter her perfect life. Maybe not so perfect a life, but... this feeling.

"Yan Mata" he sighed. "You must leave George, please."

She tore herself away from him, fighting off a feeling of disappointment, anger even, for losing herself this way to his charming deceit. "I've known George for years, I'm perfectly fine and safe with him," she said, picking up her bag.

"Are you sure?"

Her voice faltered into unintelligible croaks when she tried to reply to him.

"*Kai*, Ife. Why did he have to find you first? Why?"

Again, she said nothing. Because her head refused to produce a suitable reply.

"*Ya Amar*," he murmured. "George is not good for you, he's poisonous. Believe me."

Ya Amar...what language was that? Definitely not Hausa because if it was, she would know the meaning. It sounded like Arabic.

"You can't be with him. Don't feel bad about leaving him."

"I am not—why should I leave George?"

"Because he is bad. I know him."

"How long have you known him?"

"Since childhood. I've...he's...you'll not understand if I tell you all that I know about him."

"Then don't tell me."

"Please, Ife."

"I am George's fiancé!"

"Do you love him?" When she didn't respond immediately, he said. "I thought as much. Even your body—when I held you—confirmed my conviction."

"I don't...you can't..." Ife sighed. "I don't know what you are talking about, alright? You pulled me into your arms—you shouldn't have done that. I have a man."

For a moment he simply gazed at her, as if he was saying *'there you go again, trying to convince yourself about what you feel for George.'* Then drew a deep breath. "When do I see you again so we can explore this burning desire we have for each other? We can have sex. Just crazy, brain freezing, intense sex. No strings attached. I would love to have the strings though because I doubt if I would want to let you off my grip after just once, but..." he shrugged, "That'll depend on you."

What the... "You know what? Fuck you."

His lips curled up in a naughty smile. "I'll love that so much," he said, leaning a hip on the table, his hands folded across his chest. "Imagine you riding me for a long awesome night. Or should we have it the other way round? I'd like that too. In fact, I'd love that so much." He sucked in air from his clenched teeth, rolling his eyes up like a man lost in the throes of sexual pleasure. "I would enjoy nothing more than thrusting into your—"

"You are a crazy son of the devil."

"Crazy, yes. But you are wrong with the son of the devil part. I'm just a man who's trying to help you. See, I'm offering a solution to the attraction we have for each other. Even though you are denying it, I know it's there."

"So you know, I'll never have anything to do with a northerner. I would never date—not even have a fling with them even if I'm single."

Ife didn't see the hurt that descended on Rasheed's face early enough to stop those words from flowing out of her mouth. Once she saw it, she couldn't help the rue that gripped and clung to her like a bitter pill that refused to go down the throat.

She shut her eyes and took in air, when she opened them, she felt herself shrinking under the flecks of amber in his stare.

"I'm..." Sorry? *After the damage is done? No, Ife. 'I'm sorry' would never mend what you just said.* "I... should go now...Excuse me."

He didn't stop her when she began walking away, willing herself not to look over at him because she knew if she did, he'd see the regret in her eyes and how much she was sorry for what she just said to him.

Ife decided to go home straight instead of keeping her appointment with the senator. She doubted if she would be able to pay attention to anything the old man would say. Not with the weakness in her stomach. The brief and uncomfortable meeting with Rasheed had convinced her how much she needed her father's friends to come through for them. It was the only way she could distance herself from Rasheed.

She thought of her father and hissed. The old man could single handedly sponsor George's project. But he didn't want to because he didn't like George.

So, Ife would do what she had to do. She would call Bosun

and plead for him to reschedule their meeting for tomorrow morning.

Your friend's laughter the previous day stopped me from coming to you the next day, even though I saw you. But when we met again a day after, the relief on your face showed me that I'd done the right thing by staying away. I didn't ask to join you this time, just carried across two cups of coffee.

"You remembered I like coffee!"

I shrugged, as if it meant nothing, although I had noted and saved it, together with other things I observed about you, in my phone.

With your friends not anywhere near, I took time to ask you about yourself and watched you unfurl like a leaf seeking moisture. You prattled about how you would be working in one of your father's companies and wanted to know what I thought about it. Of course, I told you it was a good idea, couldn't get myself to tell you how nauseous your decision made me, and how you kept slipping your father in every sentence made me want to scream.

When your friends finally arrived, I was about to stand and fetch more chairs, but you told them you were busy; said you'd join them later. At that moment, any concern I had about you disappeared, and I held your gaze until you broke off, flushed and smiled.

"I won't be seeing you again," *I said.* "Today is my last lecture."

I was touched to see disappointment cross your face. You opened your mouth to speak, but stopped yourself, and I waited, enjoying the anticipation.

"Perhaps we could go for a date sometime?" *you asked.*

I hesitated, as if the thought had not occurred to me. I would have even asked you myself, but I was glad you asked first. "How about next week? Dinner next week. I know this new place in town."

Your undisguised delight was endearing. I thought of Fola—my ex girlfriend now married lover, and how she was so coldly indifferent to everything; so unfazed by surprise and bored by life, I had not previously thought it down to age, but when I saw your childish pleasure at the thought of dinner with me, I knew I had been right to look for someone younger who wouldn't run into another man's arms at every little act of discipline I melted on her, someone less worldly-wise. I knew you were not completely innocent, of course, but you had at least not become cynical and untrusting like Fola.

Next week, I picked you up from the flat you shared with one of your friends, Ignoring the interesting glances from students walking past as I kept my eyes on you. You were so elegant in a long dress, your feet encased in black heels.

You surprised me with the food you ordered when we got to the restaurant—two wraps of garri with egusi soup that had more pieces of meat. I never imagined someone as small as you could finish that in one sitting. "You shouldn't be eating this heavy at night," I said. But you did not care.

"I don't diet," you said. "Life is too short."

"It's rare to find a woman who doesn't care about putting on belly fat." *I smiled to convince you that I was making light of it, but I would die if you shoved one more thing inside your mouth.*

When the waiter came with the dessert menu, I waved it off. "Just water, please." *I saw your disappointment. You'd love to taste their chocolate cake, but I wouldn't allow you stuff fat-laden pastry inside your system. Lacing my fingers through yours, I stroked my thumb across the smooth skin between your thumb and forefinger.* "You are beautiful," *I said.* "I wish my parents were still around to see you."

"Your parents... where are they?"

"They're dead." *I had told that lie so often I nearly believed it myself. It might even have been true—how would I know? I did not send my new address to my biological father. My relationship with* him finally crashed six years after my mother died— alcohol and drug overdose. She went into too much drinking and periodic use of pills a year after she found out that there was no wealth left for me after we killed my stepfather, the man used almost everything he had as collateral for a huge bank loan. I couldn't imagine my biological father losing much sleep over my disappearance from his life. He never cared about me, not even when I finally connected with him after many years of him not knowing about my existence.

"I'm sorry." You squeezed my hand and your eyes shone with compassion.

I felt a stirring in my groin, and I dropped my eyes to the table. "It was a long time ago."

"We have something in common then," you gave me a brave smile which showed you thought you understood me. "We are both missing our parents. Mine, my mother. She's alive but... I hardly see her now."

It wasn't clear if your ambiguity was intentional, but I let you think you had worked me out. "If your mother doesn't want to make herself available for you, then forget her," I said. "You are better off without her."

You nodded, but I could tell you didn't believe me. Not then anyway.

You expected me to come home with you, but I had no wish to spend an hour in a student's house, even though you were a rich student. I would have loved to take you to mine, but I had another lady's things in there and I knew you would object to that. Besides, this felt different, I didn't want a one-night stand with you. I wanted you.

I walked you to your door.

"Chivalry isn't dead, after all," you joked.

I gave a little bow, and when you laughed, I felt absurdly pleased to have made you happy.

"I don't think I've been taken out by a proper gentleman before."

"Well then." I took your hand and brought it briefly to my lips. "We must make it a habit then."

You flushed and bit your lip, lifting your chin a fraction ready for my kiss.

"Sleep well," I said, turning to walk to my car, not looking over my shoulder. You wanted me—but you didn't want me enough.

Seven

"GOOD BUSINESS," Senator Bosun said, balancing his arm on the rail of the Federal House's gallery. His voice was a little louder like his mission was to stop Ife from hearing the voices of the protesting Labor Union members outside the building. They wanted an upward review of the minimum wage to meet up with the inflection of goods and services biting the country.

"I like this idea."

"Thank you, Senator."

"I'll put my money."

"Oh, thank you so much," Ife said. She wanted to ask when to expect his financial commitment but decided against it. It wouldn't be wise to rush the man, or he would think she was desperate. She was desperate, alright. Desperate to get the funds that would force George to reject Rasheed's offer and save her the brewing trouble she feared might escalate if she ever met with Rasheed again.

"You know I was a little disappointed when I saw the man you are engaged to," the Senator said. "He looks like a boy to me. You need a man, my dear, not a boy. I mean a man who knows how to touch your—"

Ife tuned him out as he began pontificating about the joy of sex with older men, at which he was, according to him, the absolute master. The very idea of Senator Bosun having sex with any woman was repugnant. However, Ife kept a smile on her face while praying that the man would stop talking so she would say her goodbyes and leave.

"See, what you need is a real man—"

For no justified reason, her thought drifted to Rasheed as the words *'a real man'* began to take form in her head. Rasheed with his devastating, rakish kind of handsomeness. The way he talked; fast, smooth, as if he was just opening his mouth to let air out. His English tainted with accent, though subtle, but it was there. Letter *P* coming in the way when he wanted to pronounce words that had *F* in them. His native language creamy like a rich *fura da nunu*. His face lightening up with excitement when he chose to flirt with her, his lips curled in a smile... and his laughter, that beautiful smooth sound, unlike George's that sounded like an old engine steeped in nicotine-laced catarrh, turning over on a frigid cold morning.

Ife mentally shook those thoughts out of her head and fixed her gaze on Bosun's face, smiling as if she'd been listening all along. The thought of Rasheed, to her amazement, had become stronger since she left him at Blucabana. And with those thoughts came a strong desire... an insane longing that she had tried to push back with the constant reminder that she was in a serious relationship with a good man whom she had invested so much in. Yet Rasheed had recently become the star of every sexual fantasy she'd had after the day they met—

"You are not listening to me," the Senator complained. He didn't like it when he wasn't receiving full attention. "What are you thinking about?"

"Nothing that will interest you, Senator." Bag in hand, Ife was ready to make her escape.

"Ah, but everything about you interests me," the Senator said with a toothy leer, adjusting the waistband of his pants that bound him in a way an inventive hooker couldn't dream of.

"Senator, let's not get carried away," she interrupted him before he could say another word. "Frankly, I thought that you will be afraid that I may tell my father about your advances."

"Will you tell him?" the Senator, slightly leaning forward, asked.

"If you keep bothering me, Senator."

"Oh," relaxing back, the man gave off a nervous laugh. "Your father isn't a saint either. I know the small-small girls servicing him in this Abuja."

Ife cringed inside. Although her old man had always been discreet in his affairs with young girls same age with her, some of the younger, she knew about them still. And as much as she had chosen to ignore it, after all, her father's sex life was none of her business, she still felt hurt each time anyone pointed it out to her.

"My father's dealings with *girls* doesn't make flirting with your friend's daughter right."

"The girls calling him *zaddy* and rubbing his stomach are also people's daughters."

Gush! Daddy, this one is on you. You set me up for this embarrassment. Had her father agreed to provide all the money needed for the TV project, she wouldn't be listening to Bosun's *dust yarning.*

"See, forget all these *chin-gum* boys, let a man like me handle you—"

"I'm engaged. You will stop with the chauvinistic talk."

She spent some few more minutes listening to the old man objecting to her calling him a chauvinist while stating how much he loved and adored women. Out from the building, she avoided the group of protesters who seemed to be getting agitated because nobody had come out to speak to them, got to the canteen beside the main house and bought a takeaway coffee, burning her tongue in her impatience to satisfy her morning addiction. Her phone beeped as she walked down the steps. It was George wanting to know where she was. She typed a quick reply, sent it, and resumed walking. She was jolted by a woman who bumped into her, and her coffee seeped through the ill-fitting plastic lid and on to her hand.

"Sorry," Ife said automatically. But when she stopped and glanced up, she realized that the woman had stopped too. The woman was holding a microphone. A sudden flash of light made Ife look up to see a photographer a few feet away. "Jesus," she muttered under her breath, rebuking herself for getting so lost in her phone conversation with George and not hearing the approaching protesters.

"These protesters have been here since morning, and nobody is coming to speak to them."

"I'm not a member of—"

The microphone was thrust so close it almost brushed her lips.

"We know who you are, madam—" someone shouted from the crowd.

They did? Then they should know she was not one of the people they were itching to meet. She was only here to convince one old idiot to invest in George's dream. She had nothing to say to the Labor Union Congress protesting members.

"Can you go in there and tell those men that we will not leave here until one of them comes and address us?"

"Sorry, ehm, I—" Ife tried to speak. She was now at the center of the aggrieved protesters, and they were beginning to push her from every angle as if she was the sacrificial lamb who would bear the brunt of the whole situation. The voice of the woman who was asking her questions rose over a chant she couldn't decipher. There was so much noise it was like being in a football stadium, or a concert arena. She couldn't breathe, and when she tried to turn, she was pushed in the opposite direction.

She really had to leave the place but, how?

The protesters were around her, locking her inside, chanting into her ears like she had committed a crime which they would make her atone for.

"Your father is one of them!"

"You fly first class to every country of your choice with taxpayers' money, while we are left to suffer!"

Someone pulled on her cloth and she lost balance, letting go of the coffee cup as she fell heavily against another person who pushed her roughly upright. Shielding her face from camera flashes, she turned again and tried to push her way out, but felt an arm grip her shoulder. She tensed, twisted away and looked frantically for a way out.

"Come with me if you want to leave here unharmed!"

Rasheed.

It was Rasheed!

His face was grim and determined while he pulled her firmly back up the step and into the canteen. He let go of her once they were safely past security without saying a word to her. Not even acknowledging her 'thank you.' Ife swallowed hard and followed him mutely through a set of double doors and out into the quiet yard at the back of the building.

"Follow here," he gestured towards a gate. "It will lead you out. You can come back for your car later, when this whole thing calms down."

She expected him to turn around and disappear as unannounced as he had appeared, but he stood staring at her.

"Are you okay?" he asked, his gaze moving, not unblinking but slowly, down to her feet and up again to her face. The effect was soft and inviting. Perhaps it was his lips that gave away his own feelings, not quite smiling but tilting as if they meant to.

"Yes, yes. I'm fine, thank you."

"Good. I was having a business lunch with a… friend in there," he pointed at the canteen, "when I spotted you from the window. I should head back now."

He was at that canteen when she went in to get a cup of coffee? Why didn't he *hola* at her or something? Was he still angry about the other day at Blucabana?

"Rasheed?" she called.

"Hm?"

"Thank you."

"For?"

He looked taken aback, and for a moment Ife wondered if no one had ever appreciated him before. Then it occurred to her that he hadn't expected an appreciation from her, and she knew why.

"For…" What she said to him before abruptly ending their meeting at the Blucabana must have given him an unpleasant impression of her. "I've never been this relieved someone showed up in a place at the right time. I would've been mobbed you know."

His face broke out in a half-grin. "I'm glad I was able to come to your rescue," he said.

"About what I said to you the other day…at Blucabana…I'm sorry." She waited for him to speak, but he only slipped his hands inside the pockets of his jean pants, bopping his head.

"I didn't mean to…that was so insensitive of me," Ife added.

His lips parted. Instantly, a thousand possible responses began to form in her head. His responses.

"Ife?"

"Hmm?"

"We are not all bad people—the northerners, I mean. We are not all terrorists. We all don't kill people."

"What...no... I don't..." What was she going to say to make him not to think of her as a... a

What does it matter what he thinks of you?

"Rasheed I've never classified all northerners as terrorists. It's just that—"

"It's okay, Ife. And it's good to know that you don't think such of all of us. I don't want you to be scared of me."

"I'm not scared of you."

"Good," he allowed a short pause, then added, "I didn't get the chance to also apologize for the sexually suggestive stuff I said to you too. I guess I was thinking with my groin instead of my head."

She managed to let out a laugh. "It's okay."

"I must tell you, I enjoyed our date. You are a very intelligent, and beautiful lady."

"It wasn't a date, Rasheed," she said, her face heating up because of his compliment.

"It wasn't?" he asked, wearing a gorgeous frown.

There was this thing he did with his face each time he feigned sadness, it was so cute that Ife swore a hen could hand her eggs to him for breakfast, if he gave the hen that look. "It's just business," she said.

"Okay, agreed. But I still enjoyed watching you eat yesterday." A slow grin tugged on his lips. "I love women that eat well. Nowadays we have women that would rather eat a piece of chicken out of a whole dish and that's it."

"Well, I'm a different kind of woman. Before you say good morning, I've taken three cups of coffee."

"Coffee is no food though."

She was sure he would have continued talking had her phone not rung.

"It's George," she said, lifting the device to her ear. She spoke with George for some seconds and ended the call. "I told him about the protest."

"I heard."

"He's coming to get me."

"Good for both of you." He shrugged.

"Rasheed, I—" why did she have this sudden urge to explain George to him? "George is a great guy. We have our ups and downs but…he's really nice to me."

Rasheed squinted at her through eyes that, a few seconds ago, were a delight to gaze into, but now carried the unfounded accusations of a… jealous…lover? Their color, which had only reminded her of the poetry of the universe told in moments, moments that weave together to form lives' fabric, were now simply chilling, every muscle in his face tense and with these very few words; "good to hear," he walked back into the canteen from the same backdoor he led her out, leaving her wondering if there was anything that happened between him and George in the past–an ugly incident that he hadn't gotten over?

"I'm already outside," Ife spoke into the phone as she walked down the road. Behind her, protesters shouted their anger, with placards raised up high. It was either the security inside had succeeded in pushing them out or that more people who had come to join the protest weren't allowed in. Whichever was the case, she was relieved that she got away when she did.

"Senator please," she interrupted the old man who was at the other end of the line. The man always chose the wrong time to talk trash, not that there was ever a right time. "My car is still in there; can you get a security personnel to keep an eye on it? Okay...thank you...no, I won't be coming back...later today, maybe."

She ended the call. A few seconds later, her phone rang again.

It was George.

She looked up, scanned the area, and saw him leaning on his car parked in front of the bank across the road. She slipped her phone back into her bag and headed towards him.

George's car reeked of coconut. "New Car-Freshener?" she asked, wrinkling her nose.

"Hmm."

"Okay." Not one of her favorite scents but she could afford not to show any displeasure. She bent to pick up a half-empty bottle of *Gordon's Gin* from the floor, gave George a worried glance and laid it back.

"I've not been drinking too much, I promise," George said.

Determining not to start a sermon, Ife swallowed her discomfort, leaned back and shut her eyes.

She didn't know there was someone else in the car until George said, "How are you feeling now?" and a mousy voice muttered, "fine," the same time she responded.

Fola?

Ife wouldn't mistake that voice even if she was just waking up from coma. Yet she opened her eyes and looked behind to satisfy her curiosity. Fola was cowering at the back seat—almost perching, as if the leather of the seat would disintegrate if she relaxed well on it. She was looking out of the window, her arm protectively wrapped around her midriff.

"Fola?" Ife said.

Slowly, Fola turned, gave her a weak smile. "Ife, hi."

"Fola said she's not feeling too well," George chipped in. "I met her on my way to this place and offered to give her a lift home."

That was okay, Ife thought. But she felt an inkling that something wasn't right. She didn't know what it was, but she couldn't get herself to push the feeling out of her head.

"I'm so sorry, girlfriend," Ife said. "Maybe you should come stay with me for a while, until you get better."

Fola shook her head.

"Come now, babe. Let me take care of you—"

"No!" Fola snapped, widened her eyes in shock of her outburst. "I am sorry… I didn't mean to snap at you, just that…I'll be fine. Really, Ife. It's nothing."

Yap. Something wasn't right. Ife could feel it like a tight knot around the neck. Fola used to be bubbly. Her smile brightened any room she walked into. Then, one day, she stopped being all that. Her smiles gradually ceased, or if they did, they looked dead. Like that of a plastic doll.

"It's nothing serious, ehn?" Ife asked.

"Yes… I mean…" Fola stuttered, like someone who was afraid to speak so as not to attract punishment. "I will let you know if… it—nothing, I can't handle—"

Then it occurred to Ife, maybe the lady was… "Girlfriend, are you pregnant?"

"Pregnant?" Fola managed a giggle.

Maybe Fola was in her early stage and didn't want to divulge it to anyone yet. It's a Nigerian thing—not announcing one's pregnancy until it became visible, for fear of *village people* harming either the mother or the fetus.

"You'll be the first to know if I'm pregnant *nau*," Fola said.

Okay...if Fola wasn't pregnant— "Then what's the problem?"

"Honey, give the poor lady a break, will you?" George interrupted with an air of finality.

They rode in silence for a while. Then George drove off the road, slowed in front of an estate and Fola stepped down.

"Poor woman," George sighed. "She must be missing her husband."

"You think that's the problem?"

"I don't know," he said, pulling the car back on the road. "How did you manage to get yourself in the middle of angry protesters?"

"I didn't. They found me and decided to make me a scapegoat."

"Peaceful protesters don't make passers-by *scapegoats*. Except, maybe you said something—did something that triggered them."

"If walking out of a canteen with a cup of coffee is a trigger, then I'm guilty."

"It's not that. Those guys must have seen your privileges," George said, giving her a sidelong glance. "You can afford fuel for your car even if the price climbed to a thousand naira per liter. They can't. And you..." another glance, "are damn rich. You can afford anything. You don't understand their pain."

"In other words, the mere sight of me triggered them."

"The poor will always be pained by the privileges of the rich. Especially when it seems like the rich does not care."

Ife didn't expect that George's statement would anger her that much. But it did. Maybe because nobody had ever called her insensitive. She could pass for an upper-class Nigerian, but she also had a heart. She had children she was caring for, women she had helped, Bashiru and his family had been recipients of her benevolence for years now.

Everyone close to her knew how generous she was. Everyone but George.

They made the rest of the journey back to her house in silence.

"What is it?" George asked, killing the engine of the car.

"Nothing," she settled a lazy gaze on him. "Just—"

"I have something that'll cheer you up," he said with lilt, got something from the backseat and tossed it on her lap. "For you." A large grin splitting his face.

"What—" She slipped her hand inside the cellophane bag, came out with a jewelry box and almost rolled her eyes. Some months back, having another piece of gem added to her overflowing collections would have gotten her elated. But now she felt like dropping the box on the ground and stomping on it, probably because she was having a bad day that started with almost being mobbed by some protesters and glided into her heart skipping a thousand beats at once on meeting Rasheed again.

"Thank you," she murmured, putting the gift inside her bag.

"Aren't you going to open it?"

Ife murmured an apology and brought out the box.

It was a *Pamela Card heavenly flight amulet* necklace. "Thank you," she said with all the excitement she could muster.

If George noticed her coldness, he didn't show it. "You deserve much more. I tell you, honey— when I finally get this TV station running, and start making enough money out of it, I'll choke you with gifts."

What she wanted was something to take her mind off Rasheed, and this gift talk wasn't doing it. She couldn't stop thinking about that moment when he pulled out from the angry mob and guided her back into the canteen. And his stares when they were finally safe and alone, that was so penetrating, like he can read her mind and see into her soul all at the same time. She would have found it offensive if it was some random man that stared at her like that, but it was Rasheed. He didn't even need to try hard to rattle her core the way he did. She would have wanted him to stay a little longer with her so he could continue looking at her *that way*, and never stopped talking because she loved to watch his lips move. But George had called when he did.

Maybe it was George she was angry at for calling when he did. Or herself, for falling like ninepins for Rasheed's innocent lecherousness.

"So, I got a call from Rasheed a few minutes ago."

Just a mention of his name and she felt blood rush to her heart with a thud. "What does he want?" She prayed her disorientation remained unnoticed to George.

"Not what he wanted, but what he said and did!" George said with excitement and grabbed her hands. "My love. How do you manage to stay amazing?"

"O...okay..." She let out a nervous chuckle.

"Rasheed isn't just going to give me the money, he's introducing me to a company that will supply all the equipment I need to start up."

She should be excited. This was the breakthrough they'd been waiting for. But why did she feel that Rasheed was trying to compensate for something? Like he was making up for a wrong, offering an atoning of some sought?

"I can't believe he knows a lot of people. You see, I knew he was that man we needed to make this work!"

"Yes." *Smile... make your eyes light up with excitement. Do something other than sitting here like a cold fish!* Her conscience chided. *Be happy for your man.* "I'm glad he's doing all that," she muttered. While she put a grin on her face, uneasiness rocked her inside.

"And I have you to thank," George continued.

"You've thanked me enough."

"No, I've not. I owe you my life!" George gave her thigh a squeeze. "I mean it."

"George..." She managed a giggle.

"Rasheed is doing this because of you. When he called, he said you remind him of his late wife."

Wait a minute, "He had a wife?"

"Yes." George gave her a mocking glance. "You think a man like that wouldn't have a woman?"

"No, I—" In her wildest dream, she wouldn't have thought that a man like Rasheed would care for something permanent with a woman, something other than hot sex a few times and—

"I'm shocked he's not gotten himself another woman nine years after Salma."

Salma, that's her name?

"Back then, Rasheed's biggest problem was women." George said, picking a copy of *Feminine beauty* on top of the dashboard and began studying the bikini-clad models on the cover. "He was shy but damn flirtatious. He didn't need to talk much to get the ladies falling for his weak ass. I wondered what they saw in him to make them want to lick his uncircumcised dick—"

"George!"

"What! Dude is a bloody Fulani immigrant that feels he's more Nigerian than every other citizen."

"How do you know that?"

"Don't be so dumb, Ife—I grew up with this guy, I know his family."

Giving George a disapproving stare, Ife tried to tuck in the sudden spark of anger that had grabbed her chest. "Knowing his family still doesn't prove you right. And calling him uncircumcised...Come on George, what is wrong with you? It's like...do you have unsettled beef with him?"

George stared back at her. For a moment she saw the question in his eyes, the mixture of shock and uncertainty.

When she thrust her chin up stubbornly, he sighed. "Okay, sorry. I shouldn't have said that."

"You shouldn't have."

"That's why I'm apologizing, alright? See, he's never serious with any of those girls. With any girl at all. He wasn't even serious about his studies. Dude dropped out of school in his second year. I heard his father cut him off because of that. But you know *nau*, as an only child the man couldn't totally forget him. He was later sent abroad. He came back years later with this woman, Salma and—" George dropped the magazine. "Introduced her as his wife."

"I don't see anything wrong with that."

"I was shocked."

Shocked? That a man returned from abroad with a wife shouldn't be George's headache. Except there was something more to the story, something George didn't want to tell her.

"She died eventually."

"Eh?"

"His emotions shut down that day. Long after her death, he still had difficulty getting his interest up for the parade of women who were throwing themselves at him. That was then though. Can't say if he's still that way now."

"His wife, when did she die?" Ife felt a lump in her throat, imagining the pain and heartache Rasheed must have gone through.

"Less than two years after they came back."

"What?"

"Suicide. She hung herself."

"Jesus!"

"Depression. At least that's what's the police concluded was the reason. But something didn't add up."

Ife thought of the story that once trended years ago, in Abuja. About a woman that hung herself. They had even discussed it in her shop. She, Fola and Habibah. While checking out new stock arrivals.

Could that be the same story George was talking about?

George wand down the glass and spat out. "Salma didn't strike me as someone who was depressed. I rarely visited them then but the few times I saw her, I don't think she is capable of taking her own life."

"So, you are saying—"

"It's not suicide. She was murdered and was later hanged so it looked like it was suicide. But you know Naija. Issues like this don't get properly investigated."

Ife felt a deep sense of uneasiness holding her rigid as she tried to imagine the scenario. "You suspect...know anyone that could have...uhm...done this to her?"

George thought about her question for a moment. "Rasheed," he said, half turning to gaze back at Ife who had her eyes fixed on him in shock. "The marriage was already over from what I heard. Salma wanted a divorce, but Rasheed didn't want that. He didn't know how to deal with the shame."

As Ife absorbed the shocking revelation, an outburst of emotions surged within her, leaving her feeling like a bird caught in a violent storm. Her thoughts raced, her heart pounded, and a maelstrom of uncertainty engulfed her. Jesus!

"He had every reason to want her dead," George continued.

Jesus, Jesus! Rasheed, a murderer? Unease settled in the pit of her stomach like a heavy stone. "She cheated on him?"

"No. I don't think so. In short, I don't know."

"Bu—" Ife felt an invisible knot around her neck. a knot that got tighter and tighter with each bout of fear. "Why didn't you say anything? Tell someone about your suspicion?"

"Why should I? The night of the murder, I met him at a friend's party. We even left there together."

"The police would have investigated more."

"That's wistful thinking. Rasheed is from a powerful family. If the father wants nothing to be investigated, trust me it won't."

A powerful family. Was his father a political office holder? Or a bastardly rich multi-businesses controller? Ife's curiosity flared.

"He disappeared from the country before the *yeye* investigation the police were carrying out was concluded. None of us heard from him until recently. I was shocked to get his Facebook message."

"What of his kids?" sure he must have had one or two with his wife. "What happened to them?"

"They had none." George sighed. "Please let's not talk about this now."

"Yes, yes." Her voice trembled slightly. The air in the car had suddenly grown stifling even with the windows down. It was the news. The realization that she'd taken a liking to Rasheed and had even gone beyond just liking him to slightly being sinfully drawn to him.

"I want us to celebrate tonight. You and I."

"That, that will be nice." She answered carefully. She wouldn't want to have him in her bed yet—if that was what his definition of tonight's celebration meant. She was still shaking from the revelation. Even without that, she wasn't still up to having sex with George. God, how did she get to this point with George? Imagining sex with him was no longer sexy. He no longer turned her on in any way, shape or form.

"You know, I feel something is bothering you, are you worried about something?"

"Everything is fine," Ife lied. "I just haven't gotten over what would have happened to me inside that state house if Rasheed—" the name slipped out of her mouth before she could stop herself. When she glanced up, George had a frown on his face.

"Rasheed was in there with you."

"No. Not in that way. I didn't even know he was there until those protesters almost stamped me."

"Why didn't you tell me?" George said, visibly irritated. "I spoke with him earlier today and he didn't mention anything about him being at the state house either."

They sat there in silence for a long moment.

"You know how much I love you, Ife?" George finally said.

"Hm."

"Rasheed—I'm sure he committed that murder. I may still be rolling with him because of the money but I'm careful. You should too."

George didn't follow her in to celebrate like he said he would. He didn't even step out of the car when she did.

"I'll be meeting with Rasheed later in the evening," he told her.

She didn't walk into her house immediately, rather she leaned forward and spoke to George through the window. "Be careful when you are with him."

"Don't worry, honey. I know this guy very well."

She nodded, straightened up and watched him drive off, then she headed inside her building.

George's warning about Rasheed might have come from a

place of suspicion more than it came from a place of safety. But Ife was grateful. If George's suspicion was true, then Rasheed must be avoided at all costs. In a saner environment, he would be incarcerated forever!

She walked into her room, sighed in disbelief and checked her phone. There was a message from Habibah, an apology for not making it to the party. Her excuse was that she'd traveled with Ahmed—her ex! —to Dubai. The offer just came up and she couldn't resist. She would be coming to the shop to see her when she returned from her trip.

Ife typed a quick reply and sent, dropped her phone on the bed and was about to hurry downstairs when it started ringing again.

It was one of her impatient but faithful customers. Ife had totally forgotten her appointment with the woman. And it was almost time.

Some minutes later, as Ife sat in the cab, her mind still reeling from the shocking revelation about Rasheed, her phone buzzed with a WhatsApp notification from him. She hesitated for a moment before double-tapping on it.

"I told myself after our brief meeting at Blucabana today that I was going to forget about you. Then we met again, and it became impossible to stand by that decision. Please, Ife, leave George. He will mess your life up, trust me. I know him so well. He is damaged. He can explode like a time bomb when threatened...

The message, accusatory and defiant, sent jolts of confusion and anxiety through her. A while ago, George warned her to be careful with Rasheed. Now Rasheed was telling her to be wary of George—actually, he'd told her that the two times they'd met. Was there something going on? A dark secret both men shared? And had she inadvertently been caught in the middle of their beef, forced to fight the inner battle of deciding which of them to take seriously?

She should hold on to what George told her about Rasheed and dismiss Rasheed's claims as a lie because she'd been with George long enough. Besides, Rasheed might be playing her like a wild cat playing a 'separate and devour' game with potential prey. But her heart wasn't sticking to her conviction. It had begun to waver. The unfaithful organ started wavering since Rasheed showed up at her party and made her second-guess her feelings for George. She felt like her brain cells had been randomized. One moment it was strong on George, next minute it would be thinking of Rasheed, analyzing everything that happened since the night he showed up, considering his subtle revelations. What was making Ife's head spin were the transitions. Like now, after she'd agreed with George that Rasheed could be a dangerous man, her heart was now considering that...maybe...George might have some deadly secrets too.

Ife bit down her lip and went back to the message.

"You don't have time, Ife. Leave him now. I'm not asking you to come to me, although I would want that so much. I can't seem to forget about you after our first meeting. Your scent lingers in my head, keeping me restless, your eyes haunting me. And your lips, I want to suck on them so bad that most times I find myself licking mine while imagining the taste of yours..."

It was about him, Ife sighed. She was right. Rasheed knew nothing about George. Or rather, he was lying just to separate her from George so he could fulfill his shameful lust, his raging desire. She knew. She had known long before now. But why was her heart still considering him, still thinking that maybe he might be right and good and sincere, and incapable of committing such a cruel crime?

The fact that you are also dying to have me isn't helping our situation, is it? Ife, I want to touch every part of you, to bury the whole of me deep inside you and never let you go until both of us figure out this madness. But above all, I want you to be safe. I fear that something bad may happen to you if you don't leave George..."

That was enough, Ife thought, closing the app. Rasheed was the dangerous one, the wild card. And for the love of all that was just and holy, she wasn't going to leave George for a sly pickup artist with charm to spare and a mystery surrounding him.

Eight

SIX MORE CUSTOMERS and *Hair Heaven* was closed for the day. But Ife had, by no means, wrapped her day up. She still had to go through the sales record, then she would book a ride to go get her car from where she left it that morning, and if she was lucky, she would meet up with the 7 p.m. appointment she had with her father. Not that the old man wouldn't forgive her if she ran a little behind time, but she wouldn't want to get there late and be forced to sleep over. She got up and walked to her mini-fridge to get the ginger flavored tigernut juice one of her workers gifted her that morning, unscrewed the lid, guzzled down and walked back with what was left of it to her desk to begin the second phase of the day's job.

She didn't know how much time she'd spent cuing numbers on spreadsheets when something made her straighten up. A sound like a rasp on the door. She listened for a while, then sighed. It was nothing. Some passers-by must have carelessly touched the door. She picked up her phone and groaned when she checked the time. Past seven already? And she'd gotten three missed calls from her father.

Her old man must be worried sick by now. He was always apprehensive whenever she didn't pick up his calls. When she was younger, having her old man fret about her made her feel special, but now she wished he would stop. She was no longer a baby.

The sound came again. A knock on the front door. Ife was sure she heard it loud and clear.

Who now? She thought, getting up. A customer? A friend? George? Or her father.

Laughing at the thought of Chief Ojukwu driving down to her shop to check up on her, Ife left her office to go check the door. The day's active business hour ended about an hour ago, and she was sure her workers placed the 'closed' sign before leaving. Whoever it was knocking must be aware she was still inside, working her ass off.

The cadaverous figure standing outside the door, chewing on her nails, had Ife frozen and her heart on a hair trigger. Ife narrowed her gaze at the figure for recognition, but it was dark outside, and the hair that had fallen over the woman's face in heaps made it impossible to recognize her until she called out Ife's name.

It was Fola, and the panic in her voice was jarring.

What happened? Ife thought, unlocking and opening the door. "Were you robbed?"

Fola shook her head, gathered the hair that was on her face and moved it back. She was chewing on her bottom lips so hard that Ife feared she was going to draw blood.

"Can I... can I speak... to you?" Fola asked.

"You know you can always speak to me." Ife stepped aside for Fola to walk in, and then shut the door. "In fact, I was wondering when you would come. I know there's something going on with you. Please sit." She ushered Fola to the only cushion in the store and sat beside her.

For some minutes Fola didn't speak, but was staring blankly at somewhere over Ife's shoulder, her thumbnail digging into the flesh of her index finger. When she turned, Ife noticed that her lips were trembling and there was a cloud of tears in her eyes.

"Ife, I'm in trouble," Fola said in the faintest voice Ife had ever heard her speak with before. "Someone is after me."

"Jesus! Like...blackmail?"

"Yes...no....It's more than that," Fola said, paused for a while to catch a breath, then began to tell the scariest story Ife had heard in years. It was like something conjured from a mystery book.

"My Ex. We dated back then in school before, before something happened and we...I couldn't keep up with his demands. I met him again years after—you remember the day I told you I met someone I used to know? A guy from school?"

"He was in the same plane with you." Ife remembered. Years ago, Fola had hinted her about a guy, an ex she met on her way back from Canada where she went to spend time with her husband. "I know you mentioned something like that."

"Yes." Fola affirmed.

They had exchanged numbers and promises. A month later, the man paid her a visit. He wanted them to catch up on old times. Fola was skeptical, but the man told her that he lost his wife—the woman committed suicide or something. Fola felt it would be insensitive of her to deny him what he wanted. After all, it was just a harmless catch up.

Ife didn't give the story any serious thought that time because she was emotionally unsettled herself. She had just broken up with George for the second time and wasn't holding up well.

"One thing led to another, old flames were aroused and before I knew it, we were having sex." Fola brought out a hankie from her bag, blew her nose into it, stared at the mess for a while before folding and putting the piece of cloth back inside her bag. "I tried, Ife. I tried to stop after some time, but he wouldn't have that. He said I'm his and he would rather die than let me go again."

"Hold on, Fola. You slept with this man?" Ife said in dismay. In her wildest dream, she'd never believe Fola would do this. "You cheated on Enitan?" Married women sleeping with other men wasn't news in Abuja. Married women that were not Fola. Fola was a different breed of woman; calm, decent, she loved her husband so much. If it was Habibah telling the story, Ife wouldn't be taken aback because she knew what Habibah was capable of. But this was Fola. Ife didn't even know what to say. And to think that Fola kept this to herself all these years.

"Please don't judge me," Fola murmured. "I didn't plan it."

"Yet you did it. And didn't even tell me?"

Fola frowned. "How do you tell a friend that you cheated on your husband with—" Fola clamped her mouth and looked away.

"You're right." But goodness, of all the strangest things Ife had heard in her life, Fola cheating on Enitan sat proudly at the top. Ife would have sworn Fola wasn't capable of something like that. "Did you tell Enitan?"

"Are you kidding me? I cannot...I couldn't tell him. He would die," Fola sobbed, wiping away tears from her eyes with the back of her hand. "Later, that same year, I finally got the courage to stop going to him. But he resolved to carry out an onslaught on me, on my common sense, my sanity... the same thing he did to me when we were in school. He telephoned me several times a day, sending me pictures of us doing it in that hotel."

Jesus! What kind of psycho person was the man?

"Can you imagine that? He had videos of me naked—of us having sex!"

"Fola, that man is sick!"

"He was having endless flowers and gifts delivered to me. He would pack his car outside my house, waiting for me to come out. For four months I stood by my decision of not seeing him again even though he was driving me insane. Then he hurt someone, a woman I know. He said I made him do it. When I still didn't budge, he started sending me emails, cold, harsh–blood chilling messages like this one." Searching inside her bag, Fola came out with a crumpled piece of paper and offered it to Ife.

"I'm sure it's nothing," Ife said, carefully unfolding the piece.

"'I say when we are done, not you.'" Ife read aloud. "I don't understand. Where did you get this from?"

"It was stuck at the entrance door frame of my house this morning. I don't know how it got there."

"Did you ask your gateman? Maybe he mistakenly left it there." Even as the words left Ife's mouth, she knew it didn't make sense. Why would a gateman write such a thing and leave it for his madam to see?

Fola shook her head. "It's not my gateman. I'm sure. But I asked him." She grabbed Ife's hands so tight, as if her sanity was hanging on them, and said, "He didn't open the gate for anyone this morning or last night. Ife, only one man can let himself into my house without being seen!" Raw panic was in her voice. "I was glad when he stopped bothering me and... I thought I was free. I could rebuild my life and my marriage."

Her palms over Ife's were cold and clammy, and in less than no time, Ife began to feel her fear transporting into her own body, coursing through her veins.

"Fola, you can't be too sure."

"I've never been this sure in my life. That writing…I can recognize it anywhere. He's back, Ife. He's after me."

"But what does he want?"

"Me! He wants me."

"After how long?"

"He doesn't let go, Ife. Once he has something with any woman, he'll always come back."

Nearly a week after our first date, I didn't contact you. And I could hear the doubt in your voice when I finally did. I guessed you were wondering if you miscalculated my gesture, if you'd said the wrong things or wore the wrong dress.

"Are you free tonight?" *I asked.* "Can we go out on a date again?" *As I spoke, I realized how much I was looking forward to seeing you. It'd been surprisingly difficult, waiting a whole week to speak to you.*

"I'd love that, but I already have plans, sorry."

There was regret in your voice, but I knew the tactic of old. The games women play at the start of a relationship are varied but largely transparent. You had conducted a post-mortem of our date with your friends who would have dished out advice like hairdressers in an only women salon.

'Don't make him think you are too desperate.'

'Give him a hard time.'

'When he calls, pretend you are busy.'

It was tiresome and childish. "That's a shame," *I said casually.* "I've managed to get hold of two tickets to go see 'Wakanda Forever', and I thought you might like to come."

You hesitated and I thought I had you, but you held fast.

"I really can't, I'm so sorry. I promised Fatimah that we would have a girls' night out at Krystal bar. She just broke up with her boyfriend and I don't want to leave her by herself."

It was convincing, and I wondered if you had prepared the lie in advance. I let a silence hang between us.

"I'm free tomorrow night?" Your upward inflection turned into a question.

"I'm afraid I'm already doing something tomorrow. Some other time, maybe. Have fun tonight." I hung up and sat on my bed for a while. A muscle flickered at the corner of my eye, and I rubbed it irritably. I hadn't expected you to play games, and I was disappointed that you thought it necessary.

The anger boiling inside me couldn't allow me to settle for the rest of the night, so I resolved to cleaning the house, and sweeping up all Fola's things—things she left in my room several years ago when we dated in school. She never came back for them, and I had to bring them along with me when I moved into this place because they reminded me of how much she hurt me when she left without notice, and how much I'll love to make her cry for doing that to me. I gathered them in a pile outside my door. They were more than I thought, but I couldn't give them back to her now. I stuffed them in garbage bags and took them out of the gate where some trash scavengers would find them.

At seven o'clock, I thought of you again as I sat with my feet on the table, watching some silly show on the television. I contemplated ringing you and hearing you tell me that you didn't go to the bar after all. I couldn't imagine you having fun without me. Just with your girlfriend whose boyfriend left because of her unfaithfulness maybe.

How was I even sure you were going to be there with just your girlfriend?

What if there were boys?

By eight o'clock, I decided to drive to the bar, sat in the car for a while, watching people walk in and out of the door. The girls were in *the skimpiest and flimsiest of dresses, but my interest wasn't in any of them but in you. I was so disoriented by how much you occupied my thoughts even then, and how important it suddenly seemed that I knew whether you had told me the truth. I had gone there to catch you, to walk through the crowded bar and see no sign of you. But I also realized that wasn't what I wanted. I wanted to see you walk past me, ready for your girls' night out with your miserable, dumped girlfriend. I wanted to be proven wrong. It was such a strong desire that it almost made me laugh.*

Getting out of the car, I walked into the bar, bought two bottles of beer and began weaving my way through the packed room.

Someone jostled against me and sloshed drinks on my shoes, but I was too intent on my search to demand an apology.

Then I saw you trying to get the bartender to sell you some soft drinks. When you saw me, your face went blank for a second. Then you smiled.

"What are you doing here?" you said as soon as I pushed my way through to you. "I thought you were seeing Wakanda Forever?" You seemed a little cagey. Women said they like surprises, but the reality was that they would rather know in advance so they can prepare.

"I gave the tickets to my neighbor and his wife," I said. "I don't want to go there alone."

You were embarrassed to be the course of my change of plans.

"But, how come you ended up here? Have you been here before?"

"I bumped into a friend," I said, holding up the two bottles of beer I was wise enough to buy. "Went to the bar and now I can't find him. I guess he got lucky."

You laughed.

I knew you were not a fan of alcohol. You told me you stopped drinking after your brother died, but I wasn't going to give up on getting you a little tipsy. So, holding up the bottles of beer, "Let's drink. We can't let it go to waste, can we?" I said.

"I should get back," you said without taking the beer. "I'm

supposed to be getting drinks for us. Fatimah is saving a table over there." You glanced over to the corner of the room, where the tall girl with dyed crimped hair was sitting at a small table, talking to a guy in his mid-twenties. As we watched, the guy leaned forward and kissed her.

"Who is she with?" I asked.

You paused and shook your head slowly. "I have no idea."

"Looks like she's gotten over her broken heart so fast, then," I said, and you laughed.

"So…" I held the beer up again. You grinned and took it, clicked it against mine before taking a deep swallow and then licked your bottom lips. It was intentionally provocative, and I felt myself harden. You held my gaze almost challengingly as you took another slug of beer.

"Follow me to my house," I said suddenly. Fola's things were no longer there to make you uncomfortable.

You hesitated for a second, still looking at me. Then you gave a tiny shrug and slipped your hand into mine. The bar was heavy with people, and I pushed my way through, keeping a tight hold of your hand so I didn't lose you. Your keenness to come with me both excited and worried me. I couldn't help but wonder how many men you'd gone home with like this.

Back home you walked around the sitting room, picking things up and looking at them. It was disconcerting. And I brought more bottles of beer from the fridge as quickly as I could. You said you didn't want any more drinks, neither did I, so I placed them on the glass-top table and made you sit next to me on the sofa. Tucking your hair behind your ear, I leaned forward and began kissing you. Your response was instant, your tongue exploring my mouth and your hands running over my back and shoulders. I pushed you slowly backward, still kissing you, until you were lying underneath me. I felt your legs wrapped around mine: it was good to be with someone so eager, so quick to respond. Before Fola stopped coming, she became so unenthusiastic about sex with me, at times it was as if she was entirely absent, her body going through the motion but her mind somewhere else.

I slipped my hand up your leg and felt the soft, smooth flesh of your inner thigh. My fingers brushed against your lacey panties. You pulled your mouth away from mine, and wriggled up the sofa, away from my hand.

"Slow down," you said. But your smile told me you didn't mean what you said.

"I can't," I said. "You're so sexy—I can't help myself."

A flush spread across your face. I pulled you close with one arm and with the other I rolled your skirt up to your waist. Slowly, I ran my finger under the elastic of your panties.

"I don't—"

"Hush," I said, kissing you. "Don't spoil it. You are the loveliest thing, my love. You turn me on so much."

You kissed me back and stopped pretending. You wanted it just as I wanted it.

Even though it was your first time, you still wanted it so much, I wondered if I should be bothered that you were eager.

Nine

IFE THREW her shirt with the rest of the dirty laundry inside the washing machine, then removed her denim trouser, searched the pockets—a habit she formed when she was staying with her father—and came out with a few naira notes, her bank app's token, and a scrunched piece of paper, the note Fola brought to her shop that evening.

She dumped the trousers inside the machine, closed the lead and turned it on, placing the items on top of the washer. On second thought, she picked up the piece of paper and unfolded it.

I say when we are done, not you.

Whoever wrote it must be the messiest writer in the world; it was like a chicken scratch on paper, all the letters were crawling all over each other. Yet, there was something unsettling about it. Earlier, Ife had tried to convince Fola and herself that it was probably a prank by someone who was trying to scare the shit out of Fola. But the more she read the crawly words on the paper the more she felt discomfited.

Her discomfiture didn't start now though. Her father had noticed how off she was when she drove over to his place that evening. He had wanted to know what was bothering her.

"The protesters roughhandling you, is that it?" her father had asked.

She told him about the incident with the protesters only because he wanted to know how her meeting with Bosun went.

"I can't say I didn't see my whole life flash before my eyes. I have never been scared like that before."

"Poor baby," her father had said as his chef walked into the sitting room to place a plate of barbecue fish on the mini table beside Ife and walked away. "But that's not what is bothering you, Ifechukwu. What is it?"

"I'm fine, dad. Having some drama in my life right now," she dismissed.

"With that...boyfriend of yours?"

"Dad, he is my fiancé."

"Boyfriend, fiancé, what's the difference? I just wish he'll leave you alone."

"Sorry to disappoint you then. And no, I am not having any drama with George."

It was past nine when Ife made it home even though her father had pleaded that she stay over for the night. And thank God she insisted because the old man wouldn't have spare her an hour of peace if she had stayed. He would either be talking about George or his desire to have her back in one of his companies where he thought she belonged.

Ife gathered the items that were on top of the washer and walked —in her underwear—back to her room the same time her phone beeped. She threw Fola's note inside a trash can by the wardrobe, wrapped herself in a towel, and went to check her phone.

She'd gotten twelve messages, mostly from customers who

wanted this or that type of hair. One from Habibah, she was back from her trip and would like to come around tomorrow to check out the new stock that came in and also gist her about the Dubai trip. There was another from Senator, the idiot wasn't sure he would want to invest in George's project again.

"Stupid moron," Ife muttered and was about to drop the device when it rang.

"We are heading to your place right now," George said as soon as she picked.

"We?"

"Yes... I'm sorry I didn't tell you... I'll be coming with a visitor. It's no big deal. Just something ready food, you know."

"George, it's late."

He paused. "Since when did my coming to your place by this time become a problem?" he finally said in a subdued voice that drove guilt deep into Ife's heart.

"No... not that..." Why was it getting harder every day for him to understand her? "I mean the food part—"

"But you are not the one making the food. Just tell your cook to make something."

"She's retired for the day."

'Wake her up. You are not paying her every month to sleep!"

That's harsh and inconsiderate, Ife wanted to tell him. But she knew, from the tone of his voice, that he wouldn't get it. Such an entitled egocentric man. She didn't blame him though. She made him that way. From the day they met, all she'd ever done was give him everything he asked for, make everything easy and accessible for him. Now he felt he had a right over her staff too?

"I'll see what I can do," Ife sighed, clenching her teeth at the ill-feeling that knotted her stomach. She hated calling any of her staff up before and after the official duty hours, which were 7 a.m. to 8 p.m.

"Please... and, honey?"

"Hm?" Ife loosened the towel to unhook her bra with her free hand and pulled it off. She rolled her panties down her legs, kicked it off and walked into the bathroom.

"You know how much I love you, right?"

"Hm," she mumbled, waited for a few seconds and ended the call. She placed the phone on the sink, filled the tub and stepped inside.

"You know how much I love you, right?" George had said those words to her so many times that they were beginning to lose their magic. During their early dating years, hearing him tell her how much he loved her made her feel like a kid who had just won a pack of lollipop in a game shop. Everything about those words was so perfect. Now the excitement that once accompanied those words seemed to be gone. Perhaps it was the *see finish* syndrome. Ife had seen George do the same thing, use the same words to describe his love for her, kiss her the same way and... all of those were beginning to bore her.

Even irritated her a little.

Maybe they should just get married. Or separate for a while. No, they should get married as soon as possible. Marriage might bring back the lost spark. Ife had seen that happen to couples. Awele, her friend, had countless break-ups with her man to the point that everyone became sick of them. It came as a shock when they announced they were getting married. Now, two years down the road, Awele and her husband had become so inseparable.

That could also happen to her relationship with George.

Out from the bath, she dialed her cook, "I'm sorry for waking you up...okay...yes please I'll be having some guests tonight, do you think you can prepare something...oh, that's nice. Thank you."

Twenty minutes later, she was downstairs, decently dressed and ready to play host to George and his—

Her heart developed wings and flew in scattered directions when George walked in and beside him, in an unexpected twist, was Rasheed—a possible murderer that she'd been warned about. A cold shiver of shock ran down her spine, and her heart thudded with a sense of dread. Her gaze swept across the two men, then settled on George, hoping he would read her feelings through the look she gave him. He had explicitly cautioned her about Rasheed and yet here they were like nothing was amiss.

Then her gaze shifted to Rasheed, her heart pounded loudly in her chest, her inside a tumultuous mix of confusion and...and something else.

Why didn't George tell her it was Rasheed he was bringing along?

What difference would that have made?

Did her mind just ask her that? She wasn't prepared for the meeting. Setting her eyes on Rasheed sent panic inside her like a snowball in the stomach. And when he gave her an intent stare while walking past her to take a seat at the dining table, gripping the arm of the sofa was all she could do to steady her weakened legs.

※

Ife knew George was still talking from the rise and fall of his voice, but the words themselves were pushed out of focus even though her eyes were fixed on his face, and she was nodding and shaking her head at intervals, the clicking sound of cutlery on plates reminding her of the uncanny but tasty man sitting next to her who had become a great distraction.

"I'm not interested in becoming a shareholder in your media station," Rasheed replied to something George said, something about drawing up a contract. "I have a lot I'm handling right now."

The clicking sound had stopped, but Ife was still as aware of his overwhelming presence as she was of her heart jumping right into her throat each time he spoke. And his perfume...it must be the same one he wore during her engagement party, so thrilling, serenading her heart.

"What about partnership? We can be partners," George said, saving a few grains of rice that dropped from his mouth with his palm.

"I can't do that either," Rasheed replied. "Here's what I'll do. I'll give you time to make some profit—let's say...a year? Then I get my money back."

"A year? That's not enough time to make the kind of profit that will sustain the business when the capital is pulled out," Ife finally found her voice to speak, directing her attention to Rasheed. She wished she hadn't done that because the depth of his gaze was mysteriously attractive, like a magical portal calling her to crave the flavorsome darkness lying in wait.

"One year is more than enough to make enough profit," he said, holding her gaze. "What it'll take is proper planning and a great strategy."

"Not every business yields a reasonable profit in one year. This is a media firm we are talking about."

There was a long pause, and she sensed he was weighing her words.

"Hmm," he said, nodding. "Interesting."

She didn't realize her gaze had descended to his lips until he licked them and gave her that cocky grin. Washed with shame, she returned her attention to George, watched him eat from the big croaker fish-head inside his pepper soup, then lowered her gaze to her own soup.

"So, how many years will be enough for you guys?" Rasheed asked.

"Three—"

"Four—"

She and George echoed simultaneously.

"Four," she re-echoed.

A long pause followed.

"Four years it is," Rasheed said, shifting, with his chair, closer to hers.

From under the table, he placed his hand on her thigh, and she swore she heard her blood sing. It was beautiful—his hand so soft and warm on her skin. The touch was like wildfire through her veins, kindling her, heap of ashes that she was, into fire.

For all you know, he could be his late wife's murderer, Ifechukwu. You mustn't allow him to melt your brain. Slap his hand off now.

Ife would have done just that, but he began to stroke her skin. Gently. Sending her brain into a scattered and distracted pattern. Perhaps, it was the way his touch was making her feel like one who'd taken a dangerous dose of alcohol, that feeling of dysfunctional excitement, that made it impossible to heed to the voice in her head.

"Enough of business talk, George," Rasheed said, taking his hand off her thigh. "This is a very delicious meal, Ife. I have not had rice and fish pepper soup this tasty in a long while. You made it?"

"She can't cook to save her life," George retorted. He must have noticed her embarrassment, because he gave her hand a squeeze. "It doesn't matter, honey. I love you regardless."

Still under the delirium Rasheed's touch placed her, Ife could only nod. She picked up her spoon and resumed eating.

"There's nothing difficult in cooking," Rasheed said to her so casually. His voice so soft and close and suggestive, it made her shiver "You can pay me to teach you."

"You can cook?" Ife asked, attempting to crack the discomposure that was still heavy on her.

"Insha'Allah," Rasheed replied with a modest grin.

"I would rather be disappointed if you said you can't cook. Your auntie was a wicked witch. She tortured you until you learned how to cook for yourself, didn't she? You told me yourself," George commented, his voice tinged with sarcasm as he sucked on a bone. "That wasn't really bad. You were a spoiled silly boy then. The poor woman knew you needed an iron fist. Look at how you turned out now? Nice, domesticated. I guess you were the one cooking for your wife—before she passed."

Quietness descended, a silence so consuming that even time ceased ticking. Maybe it wasn't really silence so much as it was the weight of something unsaid, words that should have been kept away by talking about other things.

Then Rasheed shrugged. "She... yes, I cooked for Salma," he said, drumming his finger on the table.

Ife had expected a range of emotions—perhaps grief, guilt, or at least a hint of sadness when he spoke. But, to her astonishment, he seemed remarkably calm, almost detached. It left Ife feeling even more unsettled.

"You're right, George. I learned how to cook from my *Inna*." Rasheed stopped drumming on the table and looked at George. "I'm grateful I learned. Now I find pleasure in cooking, like I do in some other things."

"Really?" Ife pushed cold pepper soup away and faced Rasheed. "That's nice. What else do you find pleasure in doing aside from cooking?" she asked, suddenly wanting to know more about this intriguing in-a-suspicious-way man.

"*Walahi*, you don't want to know," Rasheed muttered, leaning back on his chair.

"But I do want to know."

He gave off a leisurely laugh, picking a stick of dental floss from the dispenser and began to pick his teeth.

"Rasheed, come on," George pressed. "The lady wants to know the other things that you occupy your time with when you are not working or cooking?"

Shaking his head, "I'd rather we drop this topic," Rasheed said, a little edgy.

"Why? You don't want to talk about yourself?" George insisted.

"It depends."

On what? You're afraid you'll spill some secrets?"

"I don't know what you're talking about.'"

"Now I'm curious, man." George snickered. "What's up with you?"

"Drop it, George."

"No, man," George, with a mischievous glint in his eyes, leaned in closer towards Rasheed. In his eyes was this burning curiosity coated with malicious intent. "I want to know what you have up your sleeves now."

Looking from one man to the other, Ife immediately sensed that there was more to the conversation, a secret they didn't want to let her into.

"You want to know what I enjoy doing other than cooking or what's up *my sleeves*?" Rasheed asked, stressing the latter, his gaze remaining locked with George's.

"Both," George propped his jaw with his hand and said.

There was a horrible, swelling, billowing silence that sent

dread crawling all over Ife's body as she felt rancor, like dense air, hanging over them.

"Why are you acting as if you've been asked to reveal a horrifying secret?" George added.

"Horrifying. Hmm." Rasheed muttered. A suspicious smirk appeared on his face. Why did Ife feel that the next thing he was going to say would be spiteful, nasty rather, and that the consequences could be disastrous?

"Ina son shan labanon ki," Rasheed said.

Pow-powww! His wanton confession knocked the breath out of her. W-what? She hadn't imagined that he would…he could…*Eish!* This would be one of the many times she was grateful that George did not understand most Hausa words because, goodness Lord!

"Eating a woman out," Rasheed repeated, this time spitefully.

"Eh?" The shock on George's face would have made a hilarious social media meme had anyone cared to take a picture of him. The toothpick hanging loosely on his lip had fallen off and his jaw was slacked.

"*Walahi,*" Rasheed affirmed. "That and making money," he continued unperturbed. "I love developing new apps and selling them to the highest bidder. Oh, the feeling of that is next to riding a woman all night long. Exhilarating."

The *ridding a woman all night long* part must have deepened George's feeling of repulsiveness. His face had crumpled up more. Ife wanted to feel disgusted too. But for some sick reasons, she her clitoris went on speed dial as if someone was touching her center so perfectly, just the fingertip upon the entrance, moving slowly. *Eish!* She'd never heard anyone describe *smuttiness* so deliciously.

As George's frown deepened, a childish confused look

colored Rasheed's face and he looked from George to her. "What did I say wrong?"

"Everything! God, Abdulrasheed!" George shouted.

"I still don't understand," Rasheed frowned. "I only gave an honest answer to your question."

"So shamelessly?"

"You mean eating a woman out or development apps?" Rasheed corked a brow up. Then he added, "okay, let me assume you are referring to the former. What is shameful about me admitting to it? I'm a man, and I love—"

"Don't say that again!" George spat, downed a glass of water, and coughed fitfully. "Jesus," he croaked, leveling his watery eyes on Rasheed who sat like a satisfied fox, watching him. "Not in front of my woman."

"Calm down, will you? You asked me a question, I answered you. It's not serious," Rasheed replied casually.

"You should have been cautious... Christ! We have a woman with us, my fiancée!" More coughs tore through George's throat, and he grabbed the bottle of water on the table, hissing on realizing that it was empty. He got up, nudged his chair backward, murmured something about needing a drink and left the table.

An awkward silence followed his departure.

Rasheed cleared his throat. "*Walahi*, that escalated rather fast. What I said wasn't that offensive nau. We are all adults." He paused, probably waiting for her to respond, she didn't. "You think what I said was bad?" he asked.

Ife ignored him and started scrolling through her phone. Perhaps she should run after George. But she wasn't sure she would be able to take a few steps without faltering.

"Ife, did I say something wrong?"

He must be a bad actor if he wanted to sit there and

pretend that he didn't know how nasty his words were. He didn't deserve a response from her, not even a sound.

"I'm sorry." His voice was low and soft. "I didn't know being this honest would hurt you both. I mean it, Ife. *Ki yi hakuri*. Please forgive me."

Ife gave him a sidelong glare—the type Nigerian TikTokers christened *the bombastic side eye*. She almost sputtered out laughter irrespective of herself. *Bombastic side eye*, ha! Whoever it was that came up with that tag must have been under the influence of a substance.

"Not sorry for getting on your man's nerves, though."

"Why?" she asked.

"*Na Rantse da Allah*, he's an asshole. What was he trying to do reminding me of Salma, my late wife? I wish he would piss off to *pissfinity* and beyond."

She should be infuriated, especially because Rasheed just called George an asshole right in front of her. She wasn't. Instead, there was a tugging sensation brewing inside her, tickling her throat and forcing her lips into a grin. Before she could stifle it, she giggled and then burst into laughter. "Where the hell is *pissfinity*?"

He laughed too. "I don't know. Anywhere assholes like him are meant to be."

The blatant disregard in his voice aroused an awful feeling inside her and made her sober up. She should bury her head in shame. Really, how could she condone Rasheed insulting George in her presence?

George started it first. He shouldn't have reminded him of his late wife.

But you know why George did it. For you. He did it for you.

"Yanmata," Rasheed interrupted her thought.

She withdrew her hand before he reached for it. "Stop," she snapped.

"What did I say wrong—this time?"

Again, she should be angry at him for feigning ignorance of how contemptuous his words were. But she was rather worried that she felt just a little offended by his outright disrespect. And that was some minutes after she'd laughed. "You shouldn't have... you shouldn't have spoken about him like that."

He didn't respond. Probably, he was humored by her sudden defensiveness. After all, she'd *kikied* when he said George should piss off to wherever.

"I'm sorry," he finally said.

She didn't reply at first, because she hadn't expected his apology. "I'm sorry too for what George said about your wife," Her words laced with an uneasiness that she couldn't hide. What if George was right? What if he was truly responsible for his wife's death? In that case, he deserved every bit of disrespect and torment that came his way.

But when she looked at his face, a flicker of doubt crossed her mind. He could be innocent—. It was an inkling, a seed of doubt that gnawed inside her belly. Perhaps it was because she was helplessly and dangerously getting attracted to him.

"It's okay," he said, shrugging. "Seriously, Ife, if what I said to George hurts you, I'm sorry. He's your man. I should learn to respect him—for your sake." He scratched his chin, gave her a long stare. "Truth is, I don't like him that much."

"He's your friend," she said, her voice trembling slightly as she braced herself for his response which might be a layer of the secret he'd been trying to hide. In the silence that followed, she could feel her heart racing with a mix of trepidation and anticipation, unsure of what might come next.

"We are not friends," he said, looked down at his fingers for a moment, and looked up again. "We used to be. A long time ago."

She wanted to ask what happened to their friendship but decided to take it slow. "I feel you hate him," she observed, choosing her words carefully. "Then I'm not sure again because you've been nice to him also. One moment, you are giving him everything he wants—everything he ever dreamed of, and the next…" She hesitated, unsure of how to put her question into words. "What do you want?" she finally asked.

He allowed a long silence before replying, "What makes you think I want something?"

"Isn't it obvious?"

"Is it?"

He looked around, as if he wanted to be sure no one was in sight, then leaned closer, his face a breath away. She felt he might move to brush his lips against hers. The thought of it sent her heart thumping faster. And oh, if there was a master class where people learned the act of staring into a woman's eyes, Rasheed must have graduated with first class. Each time he looked, like he was doing now, into her eyes, she felt vulnerable—naked before him.

"You really want to know what I want?" he asked, his warm spicy breath stroking her face, knotting her core. There was an intensity in his eyes that was impossible to ignore.

"I want—"

Her. Ife's heart pounded harder as the truth became clear. Rasheed wanted her in a most vicious way. The realization left her breathless. He had desired her from the very first moment they crossed paths, and despite his attempts to suppress those feelings, he had never stopped wanting her. Now, it seemed he had decided to be shameless about it. She didn't need him to give voice to the desire in his eyes that was like a palpable force, a magnetic pull that stirred her emotions and increased her anxiety.

"You can't have me, Rasheed," she said, her words breathy but firm.

"Did I say I want you?"

"You don't need to give voice to what is obviously written all over you. But know this, I don't want the same thing you want. I don't." *Liar*. She got drawn to him the first day she set her eyes on him.

"You can't be with George. You can't love him," he gritted, his eyes making a quick sweep around the room and back to her. "Let me help you, Ife."

He was angry. She could see it in his face. "Jesus! Rasheed. I'm not going to be a toy you can play with." That was what she would end up being to him, a toy. "I am NOT going to be the fool-heady girl you can use as a distraction, a puppet—"

"What if I tell you I don't want you to be fool-heady or a toy—whatever you mean by that." The edge in his voice got tighter.

"I am not going to be anything at all to you. For Christ's sake, I am not leaving George. And even if I decide to do that —which will be stupid of me, we can't work. You could be a—"

"Terrorist? I could be a Terrorist or a suicide bomber because I'm a northerner?" he interrupted.

Murderer, she was going to say. He could be a murderer.

"Let me ask you, Ife, are you rejecting my help because of what you think you have with George or because I'm from the north?"

Both and more. Even if she wasn't engaged to George, there was no way she was going to give herself—no matter the temptation—to this good-looking, possibly dangerous man. It was...it was not going to happen. Still, every time she found herself this close to him, she allowed him to fan her emotions without putting up any resistance.

"You didn't reply any of the WhatsApp messages I sent you."

"There's nothing to reply."

"Ife, *kina tafiya da hankali na*, you're driving me crazy. Your silence—you don't know the danger you are in... okay, forget about that for a while. I wanted to hear your thoughts, to have you admit your feelings for me."

"I don't feel anything—"

The *'I know you're about to lie'* stare he gave her sent embarrassment up to her face and made her look away from him.

"George is—"

"He doesn't give a damn about you."

"You don't know that."

"I know you are not safe with him," Rasheed blurted, then leaned backward. "I guess he told you about..." he paused, sighed and stood up. "I have to get out of here." Without waiting for her response, he headed for the door.

He was almost out when a question popped into her head. And before she could quench the absurd curiosity, his name had already left her mouth. "Abdulrasheed?"

He turned.

Don't ask him, please, don't!

"Did you..." *Ife, don't do it!* That was enough warning to make her change her mind. But now she had his attention, how was she going to dismiss him? He was waiting, his head cocked to the side, his brows lifted in a questioning gesture. Should she just say to him; *'Never mind...I've forgotten what I wanted to say?'*

His brows had come down in a frown. She had to say something, ask him anything no matter how absurd.

"Down there…" making a hand gesture towards his groin, she gave a nervous shrug. "Did you…are you, I mean. George said you are not circumcised."

Confusion crossed his face. *Oh God*, among all the reasonable questions in the world, she chose this to ask him? *Ah, Ifechukwu*, how could she be this outrageously embarrassing? She admitted that she'd stupidly been thinking about *uncircumcised dicks* among other things since she had that discussion with George. But *God, God!* Why would she ask him that?

She watched his confusion shift to humor.

"I am circumcised, Ife. A lot of northern men are."

The way he said it, patient, forbearing—like he was teaching a child—made her hang her head, a rinse of shame going through her. "Sorry," she said. "I'm so sorry—"

"No need to apologize. I understand you want to know if my dick is worthy of your *labano*. I assure you, it is. I can show you."

"Oh...ptuu." Swatting off his preposterous offer. "I don't want to see your—" she let off a discomfiting chuckle. *What in the world!*

He'd already stepped out of the house, his laughter still echoing in her head, when George reentered.

"He left?" George asked.

"Yes."

"Such a shameless idiot," he said, sitting down and placing the bottle of beer he returned with on the table. "What did he say to you when I left?"

You don't want to know, Ife thought, mentally giggling. "Apart from your suspicion of him killing his wife, was there something that happened between you both in the past?" she asked, reluctantly pulling her eyes from the door Rasheed exited from to look at George. "He said you both used to be friends but not anymore."

"He's an annoying son of a bitch," George swore under his breath. "What else did he tell you?"

A dirty lot. The most insane of them was him offering to

show her his dick. *Eish,* what a man! "Nothing to bother yourself with." But something she would have a hard time wiping off her mind—imagining what his penis would look like, that is.

"I'm worried, George," she said, pushing the *dick thought* to her mind's backseat. "This thing between you two." She didn't realize it earlier, but tonight it was clear. In the glances they threw at each other was this expansion of cold contempt, a subtle disregard. It made her wonder why George insisted on Rasheed funding his project and why the latter had no issues with that. "There's something going on, George—"

"Let's not do this now, please," George gave her a disapproving look while tapping on the gold Rolex around his wrist. She got it for him on his last birthday. "Okay, we have a past," he grumbled and looked away. "Rasheed isn't a nice guy. You know that already. I told you."

"Because you think he killed his wife?"

"You think he didn't?" He stared at her in disbelief. Lowering his gaze, "Bastard," George muttered under his breath, then looked up again. "What did he tell you that is making you think of him as a saint? He convinced you, didn't he?"

"No," Convinced her how? Of what? She and Rasheed didn't speak about his wife or his past at all. However, her instincts told her that there was much more beneath the surface, a web of secrets that George had yet to reveal.

"Then you believe me when I tell you he is not a good man," George probed.

"I want to...I mean, I am trying to but you...why are you letting him in—"

"I need money." He reached for the beer on the table, his hands shaking. He caught her watching him and lowered his hand to his lap, stared at it as if it was a foreign object.

"We had other means of getting the money you need," she said.

He didn't reply. He Just sat there looking at his hand, forcing her to wonder why she felt so lonely and out of place with him this close. Was Rasheed right about him?

"I'm going to bed," he murmured finally and stood up.

"George?" she called as he reached the staircase's down landing. "Is there something I should be bothered about? You know...you and Rasheed?"

"As long as you stay away and let me handle him, you have nothing to be worried about," he replied.

Her eyes followed him up the stairs, returning when her phone beeped.

Fola;

He knows Enitan is coming home in a week's time and he's threatening to harm him if I don't meet with him soon. I don't know what to do...

"Oh Jesus," Ife muttered. She took a deep juddering breath and continued reading the text message she just received;

...I must do what he wants or he will harm my husband. I'm so scared, Ife.

"Still here?" George said from behind her, making her jump a bit. "Are you okay?"

"I'm fine. I thought you...I didn't hear you walk back in," she muttered, glancing at her phone. The screen had gone dark. She contemplated telling George about Fola's visit to her shop and the message, but decided against it when his face warmed up and he placed his hand on her shoulder.

"You're worried about Rasheed and me, isn't it?"

She nodded and took a deep breath. "I'm sorry. I don't know why what happened this night is making me this uncomfortable." Her voice cracked, the tightness in her chest returning and she couldn't point out if it was Rasheed's visit or Fola's message or the both that were turning her into a nervous wreck.

"I understand. That's why I'm here." George pulled her up and wrapped his arms around her. "Come to bed with me, honey. Let me make you feel better."

That night, he led her into his much smaller room, and they had sex. But it turned out to be as disappointing as a lost lottery ticket. At least for her. The excitement that came with having it after months of denial made George not notice that she was faking her own response. Her mind was in a hamster wheel.

And then, her reality diminished, giving room for images that started like flickers and grew into bold motion pictures playing on a loop in her head. She and Rasheed were the actors. In a blindfold, she felt every minute motion of his hand as it crossed her body, his fingertips finding secret places, his palm on her bare buttocks, his hard shaft nudging at her clitoris. Then he was kneeling astride her, ready to thrust into her...*labano*, he had called it *labano*, and she thought it sounded naughtier, sexier. In that split second before he slid in, every nerve in her body and her brain became electrified.

Somewhere between the act, she moaned. Not out of George's humping that tasted like hopelessness and disintegration, but of the eruption of pleasuring tingles that followed her mental porn—Rasheed pushing through her entrance to reach her titillating cove.

Rasheed the dangerous man.

Rasheed the possible murderer.

She knew...Ohh God, she knew all the wrong things he might likely be. Yet her body went wild at the thought of him trashing her so recklessly.

A few minutes later, George grunted.

"How was it?" George asked, rolling off her.

"Good."

"Did you cum?"

"You know I always do," she said, smiling brightly and hoping he wouldn't see, through her stretched lips, the unsatisfied hunger she was trying to hide.

Ten

FIRST MONDAY MORNING'S *SHEGE*, successfully seen.

Wearing a white dress had seemed like a nice idea earlier, but her menstrual cycle was a heartless bitch that appeared when she was busy slaying and maintaining steeze. Obviously, nothing made the sadistic monthly visitor happier than shaming happy women.

And why was she feeling so hungry this early morning when she didn't fight a war last night in her sleep?

Ife pushed away a strand of wet hair that the wind flicked across her face, and screwed up her eyes against the rain as she braved the heavy downpour to walk the distance from the grocery store to her shop. Weather like this made unfortunate people that had no umbrellas scurry past slippery roads with chins lowered. Ife had an umbrella in her office, but she was in a hurry to get to the store nearby so she could get a pack of sanitary pads and a pair of panties she was going to change into. Now she was forced to run like a jack rabbit avoiding a prairie fire. She didn't want to get more soaked than she already was and further escalate her predicament.

A passing car sent wet sand spray over her shoes just as she crossed the road to get to her shop, and she swore loudly.

"You look like a worn out, time-tested slipper," someone said behind her as she stamped off wet sand from her legs.

Habibah. The rascal was finally back from her Dubai rendezvous.

Ife thought of ignoring Habibah and going into her office to clean herself up. That would also show the unapologetic hedonist—Habibah— that she was still angry with her for not showing up at her engagement party. Too late. Habibah grabbed her from behind and pulled her into an embrace.

"Leave me joor!" Ife protested, stifling laughter.

"Ife. *Kar ki yi fushi mana.* Don't be angry nau."

"I shouldn't be angry? Biba, tell me why I shouldn't be angry. You left me on my own that day, Fola came late too—I understand her explanation though, she had gone to pick some of George's friends. But you...my partner in crime!"

"*Kai, Kawarta.* I tried to make it to your engagement—"

"Really?"

"Yes nau. I even had my dress ready. You know nau."

"And what happened? You didn't even tell me you weren't going to make it, until the D-day. You also couldn't call to tell me. Babe, I only got an SMS from you. An SMS, Biba!"

"Ife, honey—" Habibah reached for her again.

Ife rolled her eyes, pushed Habibah away, hissed and walked into her store.

Habibah followed.

"I couldn't resist when Ahmed asked if I would want to accompany him to Dubai," Habibah said relaxing on one of the seats inside Ife's office. "You know how I am with vacations."

Ife knew. Habibah would jump at any all-expense paid trip offer, even if the destination was the Bermuda Triangle, and the person offering was a dead-beat idiot.

"You are so decadent, Biba," Ife said, disappearing into the bathroom. She didn't know why Habibah would salivate at every swanky offer. It wasn't like the lady grew up in poverty and was making up for years of lack. Habibah was the daughter of a one-time attorney general of the federation. An author of crap biographies filled with information gleaned from newspaper files, all out-of-date and totally inaccurate. The celebrities she'd written about regarded her as a pathetic joke who couldn't write her way out of a corner, but she kept trying. "If vanity had a face, it would look exactly like yours," Ife added as she reentered the office space, fresh in the juncture between her legs.

"Me, decadent? *Kai*, Ife. I'm not that bad," Habibah dismissed with a hand gesture. "I just love a good life."

"That's the point. You are made for the street, girl."

The ladies burst into laughter.

"I don't even know why you got married in the first place. You were never meant to get married."

"Ahmed was madly in love with me."

"You people didn't last up to a year though."

Habibah wrinkled her nose. "He was expecting too much from me."

Too much? Ife would never understand it when women spoke about their men as wanting too much, especially when the men were anything like Ahmed, Habibah's ex-husband who practically worshipped Habibah. The day Habibah announced she was divorcing Ahmed because *he was too demanding*, and not because of the alleged adultery with one TV host, Ife was angry. She had called Habibah a spoiled brat that harbored nothing but thoughts about herself. Their friendship would have ended that period had Awele and Fola not stepped in.

"Biba abeg, no bring that talk back." Ife pulled her wet wig off, hung it on the suit hanger behind her chair and sat down. "Ehen, wetin you carry come from Dubai?"

"*Barawo*, thief. Oh, now you want Dubai souvenir?"

They burst into another fitful laughter.

"Leave me o," Habibah said, sobering up. "You told me your orders came in last week."

"Changing the topic because you don't want to share your Dubai loot, abi? Okay o. Anyway, I have Peruvian double drawn—"

"That's for washout ladies," Habibah muttered. She fished a pack of bubble gum from her bag, popped two into her mouth and offered the pack to Ife. "I need something real and very expensive. Something only a few ladies in this Abuja can afford. Ahmed is paying."

"Your Ahmed?" Ife checked the label on the pack of gums, then popped one into her mouth.

"Who else?"

"Ah, Habibah! What brand of *Kayamata* did you give to this man?"

"Kaya wetin." Habibah blew a bubble and sucked it back into her mouth. "*A'a, ba ruwa na da kaya mata,*" she mused, playing with one of her gold hoop earrings. "I don't do love potion, honey."

"Then why is he so into you even when you broke his heart?"

"A man never gets over a good *punani*, you know. Once he tastes it, he will be coming back for more."

"So, it's just sex."

Habibah shrugged. "Ahmed is obsessed. And me, I don't think sex without thinking of him, the way he fills me up with his strong overpowering *bura*—penis."

Why would some ladies have it all, less relationship hassle, great sex, great life, while others had to live off the bottom pot of life's goodness? Listening to Habibah talk about her ongoing sexual relationship with her ex-husband made Ife think of George.

Falling in love with him was sudden, easy, and fun, like a child going down a playground slide. But losing sexual interest in him was slow, difficult, and painful. She'd thought that staying celibate would bring back the flair. However, last Saturday, as he humped her, all she could think of, all that ever came into her head was if it would have felt better with another man.

With Rasheed.

Eish, Ifechukwu!

There was a thin line where strong attraction ended and obsession began, Ife swore she had crossed that line. And that baffled her. More disturbing was the fact that she just met Rasheed, she didn't know *jack* about him except the things George told her, blood curdling things. Yet every nerve in her stood any time she thought of him.

"Are you still paying attention to me?" Habibah asked, pulling her mind back to the conversation.

"Uh, eh, yes. Sorry." Ife hissed. "Did you ever cheat on Ahmed when you were married?"

"Once." Habibah laughed as if cheating wasn't such a terrible thing. "I wanted to get back at him for shagging that ugly presenter."

"You know he didn't do it."

"It was hard to believe him then. He insisted he only shared a few WhatsApp messages with the lady and didn't go further, but the lady was loud. She posted their conversations on twitter."

The rumored affair between Ahmed and Amanda, the TV presenter, made a huge buzz because Habibah and Ahmed were regarded as the golden Abuja celebrity couple. Both were so bronzed and tall and beautiful, so crazily in love with each other.

"He wants us back together," Habibah said dismissively.

"Ahmed?"

"Hmm. But I said no. It's better this way. Just sex and him lavishing money on me. No marriage hassle, just comforting, wild sex."

Just comforting, wild sex. Where did Ife hear that before?

From Rasheed, at the *Blucabana* restaurant.

He didn't use Habibah exact words, but something close;

"Just crazy, brain freezing, intense sex. No strings attached." She remembered that moment and shivered. Maybe she should try it. Just once. One date and that would be it. But she was not a fling or a one-night-stand kind of girl. She had come close, during a truth or dare game they had during the last birthday party Awele had before relocating. Awele had dared her to make out with one of the guys in attendance. Ife had kissed the guy long and hard. The guy, on the other hand, was full of enthusiasm, ready to take her into one of the rooms in the hotel and shift her panties. But, as thrilling as it was, Ife couldn't go further. She was a one-man woman, had always been.

Now, watching Habibah speak about sex with her ex as if the man was presently under her *abaya*, giving her a brain-distorting *head*, made Ife seethe with envy. *Eish*, she too needed to experience a long, fierce, rutting that would be crowned with a grand climax.

You know what you want, and it's not just sex with any man. You want Rasheed, period.

So crazily true. The fact that the last time they met, the day he had dinner in her house, he was reckless with his own desire for her, added to this craziness. Ife still thought of his audaciousness and shivered with excitement. His salacious response to George's question had taken her aback, yet desire curled through her in hot tendrils that insinuated itself in deep private places each time she remembered it. Even now, thinking about it made her knees weak and her bones fluid.

They said there was a time in every good girl's life when the urge to do the most unthinkable, nasty thing comes so strong. Ife didn't know if these past few weeks were a slice of that time for her because, every day, since the first time she set her eyes on Rasheed, she lost concentration in virtually everything; including putting more work on her stalemate relationship. She didn't even know there was anything wrong with what she had with George until Rasheed came along and though he scared her a whole lot, she had started comparing him with George. It was crazy because she'd never compared George with any man before. That was because no man had ever measured up. George was a beautiful man who had loved her in his own way all these years. Though he had his annoying moments but…which man didn't?

"So, are you going to show me something more to my taste?" Habibah said, again, yanking Ife back to the present.

Three hours later, Ife had two Vietnam raw hair and one Brazilian deep curl packaged for Habibah. The rain had subsided, and she was seeing Habibah off to her car.

"Again, congratulations on your engagement," Habiba said, settling inside her car. "I really would have loooved to attend—"

"Eh-eh, abeg, don't even say it. You simply didn't want to be at my engagement, so let's leave it at that."

"*Haba*, Ife." Habibah gave off a dramatic gasp. "Forgive me nau. Anyway, I got something from Dubai for you. I'll bring it over to your place."

"Why do I feel you are lying?"

"*Amma da gaskiya na samo ma ki wani abun a dawowata.* I'm serious. I forgot to bring it along."

Ife folded her arms across her chest, lips downturned. "Hm-hm?" she said.

"I'm serious."

"I believe you." Ife didn't, and Habibah knew.

"Ife I'm not lying."

"Did I say you are?"

"I don't know. You are looking at me as if I'm lying to you. Anyways, congratulations again. So, when is the wedding happening? Oh, wait..." Habibah cut in without break. "Don't tell me that man of yours is dragging his feet."

"Actually, I—"

"He had better wake up and do the right thing before someone takes you from him," Habibah said, reaching for the nail file on the front passenger's seat. "This is Abuja, no man owns any woman until he puts a ring on her finger."

"He already has."

Habiba raised her chin and gave Ife an amusing stare. "I don't mean...that." she gestured with the nail file trapped between beautifully manicured fingers. "I'm talking about a proper wedding ring."

"That will be happening soon," Ife's heart sank a bit and she wondered why. Thoughts of marriage and a lifetime with George used to get her all excited. Why was she feeling this unfounded doubt and fear now?

"*Toh.*" Habibah shoved the file into her bag and faced Ife fully. "You want to hear the truth, girl? I don't think I like that your guy. That's why I didn't think too much about your engagement when Ahmed asked me to go to Dubai with him."

"Biba!" Ife shouted, aiming a slap on Habibah's arm. "You deliberately avoided my engagement party?"

"It's not that...I didn't know how to tell you what I think about that guy."

"I don't care what you think, you should have at least showed up for me!" And in the name of God's sweet son, why was everybody complaining about George? First, it was her family, then Rasheed, and now Habibah—a woman who didn't even know how to keep a man.

"Ify, be reasonable."

"Biba, Biba...George and I are fine," Ife interrupted. "Ehen, that's reminds me, have you heard from Fola lately?"

"No. We spoke twice when I was in Dubai. I called her again yesterday and she didn't pick up."

"Hmm." Ife sighed. "She was here some days ago. She also called me this morning. I feel there is something going on with her."

"Did she tell you what it is?"

For a moment, Ife felt like telling Habibah, but then she remembered, Habibah had a mouth as loose as a loosely woven basket. She didn't know how to keep a secret. "No. She didn't say," Ife said instead.

Habibah eyeballed her for a while, shrugged, "Then leave her alone. She'll tell us when she's ready. And get out of that wet dress before you catch a cold," she said and drove off.

Ife's first thought, when she stepped into her office after Habibah had left, was that the gate of hell had been opened in her office. Either that or someone had brought a stove in and left it on. The atmosphere, which was cold, almost chilling before she left with Habibah, was now dense.

It didn't take her time to notice that the heater had been turned on and its regulator increased to a flesh-roasting point. "Jesus Christ!" she muttered, grabbed the remote and turned it off. One of her staff must have done this in a bid to warm the office. But increasing the temperature heating appliance up to such an alarming level was crazy. Was the person trying to set the office on fire?

She was shocked when none of her workers admitted to being responsible. But it was useless trying to figure out how the heater got switched on when she had more pressing issues to think about, like the hunger gnawing in her stomach and the desperate need to change into something dry before she would set off to Fola's place.

It occurred to her that she should dial Fola first, to confirm if she was home before setting out for the visit. She was greeted with the automated; *the number you are trying to call is currently not available* crap. She dialed again and got the same result. She gave up, walked to her makeshift kitchen and fixed herself a cup of coffee. She was halfway finishing the strong black beverage when she received a text from George.

"Finally," she sighed and double tapped on the notification.

Been busy with a lot of things. I have paid for some of the equipment needed, but still have a lot more payment to make. How far with the location you talked about? Have you been able to secure it for me?

Ife read it twice, then gave in to the anger swelling inside her. The insensitive whiny baby had gone incommunicado since he left her house the morning after the night they had sex. His phone line had been unreachable too. Now he was throwing her this message like he never left her worrying.

She attempted calling him but couldn't connect to his line. Did he blacklist her number again? Probably. Typical of him to get her worrying about him and then making sure she never reached him for a period of time. And each time he did that, she found herself being so scared that something had happened to him, or that he'd gotten fed up with her and had walked away.

For a moment, Ife wondered whether there was some truth

in what Habibah said about George not being good enough for her. That couldn't be true. She was sure it wasn't. It was just that she had been engrossed in life so much that she stopped giving George the kind of attention he was used to. Maybe she should use some part of the money she was saving and buy him something extravagant. His birthday was coming up soon. It might be a good time to party.

Ife dialed his number again. This time, it rang but he didn't pick. Frustrated, she pushed the phone away and rested her head on the desk, abhorring the fact that she would go look for him at his place this evening when all she wanted to do was to get a manicure, a pedicure and a facial before heading to Fola's place.

At least hours of maintenance would take her mind off things. Temporarily.

Sipping from the cup of coffee that had gone cold, she thought of the possibility of George having a girlfriend on the side whom he was spending time with each time he shut her out like this.

Then she decided, no, absolutely no way. One thing about George: he was no cheater.

Or was he?

Again, doubt began to creep into her mind.

Her father said all men cheat. That was the way of the world.

She shook the thought off her head and dialed George again, hissing when he didn't pick. She would have to go look for him in his house. Fola had to wait. On second thought, she decided to go home and change out of her wet clothes first.

The smell of something disturbing gripped her nostril when she stepped out of her car. It was almost like tragedy had just walked by. Had Ife imagined it? That feeling of someone lurking around in the dark, watching her as she took steps towards George's doorstep. She slowed her gait, and she looked over her shoulder. For a moment, she thought she saw a shadow disappear behind the huge water container adjacent to the gate.

She narrowed her gaze to the spot but there was nothing. She let out a sigh and continued walking, then looked back again. There was no movement, no shadow. She had felt so strongly, just for a moment, that she was being watched; and there was a silhouette of a man. Her face came down in a frown as she got to the front porch. Maybe she was beginning to have a nervous breakdown. She'd been apprehensive lately, seeing things that weren't there. It must be her latest involvement with Fola's issue.

That was it, of course. The whole boogeyman story was getting to her. Ife chuckling softly, turned the door handle and pushed. To her surprise, the wooden leaf gave way. This meant only one thing; George was around. Had he been in town all along?

Oh George, George...

She shook her head and let herself into the brightly lit sitting room.

"Of course, I would like to meet with him," George was saying to a man who was hunched over a laptop on top of his dining table. He straightened up when he saw her, a broad smile on his face. She didn't need to guess who George's visitor was; she could recognize that back view anywhere, and his hair—with no covering— had the same mixture of rich noir and silver scattered beautifully in places like a black and white bouquet.

"Honey?"

"Ife."

Both men started simultaneously.

Unbelievable. How was it that these men were here, seriously talking business as if they were fraternal friends who would bury a dead body for each other, after the animosity that passed between them the last time? Looking from one man to the other, Ife wondered if she wasn't the one being misled, if both men weren't conniving to make a fool of her.

"I wasn't expecting you."

"And I wasn't expecting to meet you present." Ife walked across the room to stand beside George. She gave him a look over. "You didn't call me. Two weeks and—I was worried sick. All the while you were here, and okay."

Ife found herself checking Rasheed out when all she wanted to do was just glance. He had a white collarless short sleeved knit shirt over a pair of khaki shorts. Her eyes made a stroll down his legs. Impressive, she admitted, lowering her gaze further to his white sneakers. So... uhm...cute and well congregated.

"I've been busy," George said, pulling her attention back to him. "I didn't know starting this project is this draining, but Rasheed is being of great help."

Ife saw something in George's eyes when he spoke of Rasheed, a quickly vanishing look of contempt. They were not friends. They were just tolerating each other because of this project. But why? What was Rasheed's stake in the project? If, according to him, he wasn't interested in any financial gain, why was he helping George?

"We were checking out camera models when you walked in. We must decide the one to go for, place the order now so I can—"

"Actually, George. We are done here—for tonight," Rasheed interrupted, giving Ife a quick look over.

"But we are still going to make the—"

"Whatever remains can be done online." Rasheed insisted. "Your fiancée is here to see you."

Nothing prepared Ife for the shocking sense of abandonment that came with the coldness in Rasheed's tone. He was indifferent, his eyes lacking their familiar charm when he settled them back on her. In fact, his voice was less caring, almost irritable. Maybe he'd decided she was not worth his interest.

Ife picked a toothpick from the dispenser on the table and began to fiddle with it, thinking about how nice it would be if her suspicion was true, if Rasheed had decided to back down. She could then concentrate on working on her relationship. That was if she would be able to get him off your head. Of course, that would be simple. All she had to do was focus on George and Rasheed would be forgotten like an outdated almanac. Sparing Rasheed a glance, she agreed it wasn't going to be easy, not when she was already throwing a mental fit because he wasn't paying her any attention now.

God, she felt so silly. And angry for feeling silly.

"But I must make the trip tomorrow. We need to send this order tonight so it will be added to the others I'll be bringing down," George said.

"What trip?" Ife asked, turning to George. "Are you travelling?"

"I have to be in Lagos tomorrow to bring the equipment down."

"But you mustn't go to Lagos. The company can waybill them—"

"What happens if what were sent weren't exactly what I ordered?" George interrupted with irritation.

"Your fiancée has a point, George. You mustn't go to Lagos. Besides, the company has a free return shipping policy so you will not be losing money." Rasheed said.

"Don't be ridiculous, Rasheed. Ife is just being a pain." George retorted, shooting Ife a reprimanding glance. "Even when she knows how important this is to me."

Ife would have managed the embarrassment had she not connected gaze with Rasheed and the look on his face even when she forced a smile, made the weight of the humiliation heavier. Hot tears burning her eyes. He noticed the tears and tightened his jaw.

"You don't call a woman you claim to love 'a pain,' George," Rasheed muttered. From his tone, one could surmise he was trying to contain his emotion.

"Come on, man." Nervous laughter screeched out of George's mouth. "Ife is just being unreasonable. You know women—"

"The only ones I know so well are my mother and Salma. And Salma died long ago." An uncomfortable silence followed Rasheed's words.

"I'm so sorry," George muttered, grabbing his phone that had just rang. He picked, spoke to the caller for a moment and dropped the call. "I have to meet someone outside," he said, brushing past Ife and hurried out. Grateful, maybe, for leaving the room that had suddenly become murky.

With George gone, Ife suddenly felt claustrophobic, breathless. Leaving the room should be the safest thing to do. But she didn't. Rather she pulled her phone out from her jeans and started checking messages. When she looked up, Rasheed had his eyes on her, urging her with his gaze to say something.

"How long have you known him?" he asked.

"More than three years." Ife drew the bowl of fake fruits

that was at the center of the table closer and began fiddling with the objects inside.

"Pity."

She ignored him.

"It's either you're stupid, or he's done a very good job keeping you in the dark."

"I'm not stupid."

"You're not?" His gaze slid down to the fake apple she was fiddling with and came up again to observe her. "Then you must know you shouldn't be with him. You don't know him."

"And you do?" Her voice was halfway between a whisper and a shout. He was doing it again—stoking fear in her heart. Fear for a man she'd been with for years.

"I've known George since I was ten. Such a selfish bastard," he deadpanned.

She wanted to insist that he didn't know what he was talking about, but he was right about George being selfish. George was the definition of selfishness that came in a sack. And greedy and... inconsiderate. And irrational like a cow. But he had been nice to her multiple times. He loved her in his own way.

"Leave him now that you've got the chance."

The urgency in his words sent a sense of foreboding entangled with fear down her spine. "Abdulrasheed," she said. "Is there something you think I should know? Or are you trying to make me doubt my man so you can take advantage and...and sleep with me?"

He stared her hard in the face, then shook his head. "*Kar ki bani dariya mana. Duk da dai ina Kaunar ki, amma ban yi tunanin wanna maganar daga bakin ki ba*. If this is just about me fucking you, Ife, we would be having this conversation on my bed or any other comfortable place."

"That will never happen."

"*Yan mata,*" He stopped. All semblance of the serious, controlled man who was all about business earlier had vanished. His expression had softened. Ife saw the exact moment when his self-restraint snapped. Alarm jolted through her and oh dear...whatever he was going to say next would be wild and nasty.

"I have this strong feeling that I'll one day make love to you." He broke off again, a flush crossing the crests of his cheeks and the bridge of his nose. "I don't know how or when, but it will happen. I assure you." He glanced over his shoulder, probably to be sure George wasn't within earshot. Satisfied, he continued. "*Kai,* that day I'm going to drive you crazy, change your breath with every thrust, then stop, then do it all over again until you beg me to finish it. Even then, I won't. I would just do every naughty thing to you until your mind and body explode." The rather cocky smile he gave her was breath hitching. "I'll time your moan to my movement—every deep thrust would draw a moan out of your mouth."

A prickly silence sat between them. Instinct told Ife to save herself from the embarrassment of having him notice how much his words had affected her by fleeing, but stubbornness told her to stay. Stubbornness won. She stayed put, staring back at him while the weight of his words pulsated between them—the heat from it sending desire as tingles down to the juncture between her thighs, the wrongness of it being spoken in that space that held the not-so-recent memories of her many times with George pricking her heart with guilt.

He glanced behind again. "I feel it, *yanmata*, you will come to me yourself," he said. "And I'll have fun playing with every part of your body, the right kind of play. I must warn you. My imagination is wild. But you'll enjoy every bit of what I'll do to you."

"Never," she whispered.

"Never say 'never'. The future may not seem—"

"I'm so sorry I took so long." George said, walking in with a box. "I had to be sure what I ordered was what I got," he dropped the package on the table. "Don't touch that!" he barked as Ife reached for it.

"What's in there?" Ife asked.

"It's delicate."

She would have probed more but a phone on the table, which she didn't notice until then, started ringing. Rasheed picked it up and walked out, but not before she caught a glimpse of the caller ID;

Fola!

You spent the night with me that first time, and I was happy. So happy that I pulled the duvet over us both and lay beside you watching you sleep. Your face was smooth and unbothered. When you slept, I didn't have to pretend that I hadn't fallen for you. I could smell your hair; kiss your lips; feel your soft breath on mine. When you slept, it was perfect.

You smiled before you even opened your eyes, reached for me without prompting, and I lay back and let you make love to me in an almost laughable way. Laughable because you were trying too much to please me when I knew you weren't that good. But I was glad to find someone in my bed in the morning, I didn't want you to leave. If it had not been absurd, I'd have told you right then and there that I loved you. Instead, I made you breakfast, and took you back to bed, so that you would know how much I wanted you.

I was pleased when you confessed that you would like to see me again. I wouldn't have to spend another week on my own, waiting for the right time to call you. So, I let you think you were in control. We went out again that night, and again two nights later. Before too long you were coming over every evening, even when you said your friend wasn't happy that you were mostly absent from the house. I wondered why that should bother you. I wanted you with me and that should matter to you more than anything in the world.

"You should leave some things here," I said one day.

You looked surprised, and I realized I was breaking the rules: It was not the man who fast-forwards the relationships. But when I returned from work each day and only an upturned mug on the drainer told me you'd been there at all, I found the impermanence unsettling.

Then one night you brought with you a small bag; dropped a new toothbrush into the glass in the bathroom; a clean underwear in the drawer I had emptied for you. The next morning, I brought you coffee and kissed you, tasting you on my lips as I drove to the office.

I was so excited that you were in my house, and afraid too. I didn't want to return and not see you there. I called home and could tell from the thickness of your voice that you had gone back to sleep.

"What's up?" you said.

How could I tell you I just wanted to hear your voice? "Can you make dinner today?" I said. "You never do."

You laughed and I wished I hadn't called. Now you knew that I was missing you.

You shouldn't know.

You mustn't know.

When I got home, I went straight upstairs without removing my shoes and found you gone. But it was fine: your toothbrush was still there.

I made space for you in the wardrobe and gradually you moved in more of your clothes.

"I won't be staying tonight," you said one day, as I sat on the bed to put on my tie. You were sitting up drinking coffee, your hair tangled and last night's make-up still around your eyes. "I'm going out with some of the guys from my department."

I concentrated on tying the perfect knot in my dark-blue tie.

"That's okay, isn't it?" you asked.

I turned around. "Do you know it's exactly three months today since we met in your school?"

"Is it really?"

"I booked a table at Jevinik for tonight," I said, thinking it was the only way to stop you from going out with the guys from your department. "I'll like us to celebrate alone." I stood up and put on my jacket. "I should have checked with you beforehand, but I thought that...there's no way you would appreciate something as silly as the remembrance of the day—"

"I do!" You put down your coffee and pushed the duvet aside, climbing across the bed to kneel next to where I stood. You were naked, and when you threw your arms around me, I felt the warmth of your breast through my shirt.

That day, before I left, I gave you my house key and hoped you would appreciate how much I was trying to make you not to leave me.

"I have to go to work," I said, gently pulling you away. "Please let me know if you are still going out with your classmates."

"No, I'll cancel."

I didn't know such small words could bring me so much joy. 'I'll cancel.' I loved it. And I loved you for choosing me over a bunch of idiots.

"You've gone through so much trouble," you continued. "I'd love to go out for dinner with you. And now that I have this," you held up the key, "I'll be here when you get back from work."

My worries began to lift as I drove to work, but it didn't go completely until I called Jevinik and booked a table for that evening.

Eleven

THE TIME on the dashboard said it was some minutes past two p.m., a long time to when she was supposed to go pick George from the airport. Ife depressed her car seat, relaxed her back and began juggling options; it was too early to go home, and she was not in the mood to go back to *Hair Heaven* or pay a return visit to her father who, she was informed, visited yesterday evening when she was away.

But wasn't going to her father's place better than sitting in her car, waiting to see Fola who, obviously, was avoiding her? However, she wasn't going to let Fola be, like Biba suggested. The many disturbing texts and WhatsApp messages Fola had been sending to her after that evening she showed up at her shop had given her shuddering nightmares and panic attacks each time she remembered them.

And just when she thought she was overreacting, Fola's name popped up as a caller ID on Rasheed's phone. Ife never got over that shocking exposition. She worried about it all the days that went by; as she made and drank her coffees, as she washed herself and got ready for each day, as she attended to her classy customers, as she went for waybill pick-ups.

That was why she wanted to see Fola. She'd been on this quest for the past five days, dialing Fola's number without success, and *determinedly* driving up to her house only to be turned away by her gateman with the dismissive words, "Madam no dey."

The sound of Fola's gate being opened made Ife sit up. A woman with a pair of dark sunglasses covering her eyes stepped out of the house.

Fola?

There was a shawl cloaking part of the woman's face, partially hiding her identity.

"Fola!"

Ife hurried out of her car and went after the woman who glanced over her shoulders every now and then.

"Fola!" For Christ's sake! "Hold on. Wait! It's me!"

Of course, Fola knew it was Ife calling, yet she kept moving fast. Only slowing her gait to grope inside her handbag.

"Fola, I've been looking for you," Ife said breathlessly, drawing near.

Fola looked at her, her lips parting as if she was about to let words out, then she snapped her mouth shut and continued searching furiously inside the bag.

"Fola we have to—"

"I can't talk." Fola whipped her head up, her face contoured with despair.

"What? Why?"

Silent.

"Fola?"

"No!" Fola flinched as Ife reached out to touch her. "He said not to talk to you again."

"Who said?"

"I am not supposed to speak to you."

This was where it started getting confusingly weird. "Who said you shouldn't talk to me?"

A sob escaped Fola's throat. "Stop asking me. He'll kill Enitan if he knows I'm speaking to anyone—to you!"

Weird.

Weird, weird, weird.

Ife was beginning to feel the heat of the scorching sun across her forehead and cheeks, and the searing knot of a headache announcing itself at the back of her eyes, but the chord of urgency in Fola's words struck the worst feeling. Fear. "It's him," Ife stuttered the only reasonable explanation to this whole apprehensive drama. "This man you spoke about, he's the one doing this to you?" There were approaching voices and footsteps, but only a few passers-by slowed their steps to observe them.

"It was a mistake," Fola said.

"What was a mistake?"

"Coming to you with that note. I shouldn't have. Now he's going to punish me for that."

"Fola, you are scaring me."

Fola let off a laugh…or a sob? Could be a mixture of both. "It's useless, Ife. Useless. I should have listened and not come to you."

"Fola please tell me—who is he? Give me a name, his name." Then it started, the stream of frightening possibilities. This man could be anyone; Ibukun, Fola's husband's younger brother; or maybe someone from the past. A childhood friend. A school mate. An ex whose wife committed suicide…Rasheed's face popped into her head as she continued weighing possibilities. His wife committed suicide. And he knew Fola.

Jesus! Could it be?

"What is this man's name?" Ife asked.

The silence she got from Fola morphed into warning sounds in her head. Telling her to hold steady for what was to come.

"Rasheed. Is his name Rasheed?" she added. Fola remained mute. "You know Rasheed—he was there at my engagement party. You called him, I saw your name on his phone."

"I don't know what you're talking about," Fola said and broke into a run, crossing to the other side of the road.

Perplexed, Ife watched Fola walk to a pitch-black tinted glass red Nissan Altima and slip in.

It started as a thought that Thursday morning, while Ife still had last night's make-up slipping off her face; her hair, the kinky collapsed up-do she did a few weeks ago that she hadn't yet brushed out, still spiky with grip, and three customers squatting around five cartons of hair.

Ife was only half present with the women, the other half of her wished the women would hurry up and leave so she could jump into her car and high tail it to the one location she'd been itching to go to since that absurd meeting with Fola.

Rasheed's workplace.

Getting the address was a challenge. But yesterday, after a week or so had passed since George returned from his trip, she casually brought up Rasheed in-between their conversation. "What's up with your friend?"

"Who, Fola?" George mentioned impatiently, snatching the cup of dice from her hand. They were in his house, playing a Ludo game. "I thought I told you she has a lot going on with her now. I'll rather not talk about it."

"Fola is your schoolmate. And you don't talk so much about her."

He gave her a very direct look. "I don't talk about her because there is nothing about her you don't know. She's more of your friend now than mine."

Ife ignored his attack and tried again. "I meant Rasheed, the one with no solid bio-data—no notable business and business address."

"Did I say he had no solid bio-data?"

"You sound as such when you speak about him."

"I doubt that," he said, shaking the dice. "Rasheed manages his late father's software company in France—Hantech. They develop and sell apps." He rolled the dice and hissed at the poor numbers that surfaced. "They have branches here in Nigeria—Lagos and Abuja."

And that was that. She didn't ask further so she wouldn't seem too interested in Rasheed and aroused George's suspicion. He wasn't exactly dumb.

After she left George's place, she drove home fast. Without taking a shower, she sat down in front of her computer and googled Hantech software company.

There were plenty of entries: their official website, their LinkedIn and Instagram links, Awards and Newspaper reports about them. Ife clicked on the official website, went straight to the company's *about us* and read. His full name was Abdulrasheed Rabiu Lawal, the company's second CEO. He took over the prestigious seat after his father died a year ago. The site still had the picture of his old man and not him, which didn't make sense. It also didn't make sense that Rasheed's picture wasn't anywhere on the site. Only his name and very brief details. Ife absorbed every detail. She wanted to search for him on social networking sites when there was nothing else to read about him on the company's website, but it was midnight and she would be having a long day, which involved paying Rasheed a visit, tomorrow.

She dozed off almost immediately and was plunged into a dream where she saw herself fall off a cliff into a river. She tried to wake up but only her eyes obeyed, the rest of her remained numb. Soon, she was struggling to breathe and to scream because there was something pressing her neck—large hands, like a knot, squeezing tighter and tighter. She'd had sleep paralysis before, a very long time ago, but last night's experience was the scariest.

Ife thought of that terrifying ordeal while she watched her three customers make small talks over the cartons of hair, answering the questions they threw at her every now and then. She wondered if last night's horror was because of her disoriented state of mind—the panic that had kneaded webs in her head. She thought of Fola, then Rasheed. Rasheed with his uncanny kind of handsomeness that morphed into modest beauty each time he smiled.

What if she was wrong? What if he was not the man after Fola? Maybe, his wife dying the same way Fola's ex's wife did was a coincidence.

Her conversation with herself was halted by the entrance of Habibah, accompanied by another lady.

"Oh, my. This place is full already," Habibah exclaimed, handing Ife a nylon bag. "I told you I got something for you from my trip." She pulled Ife closer and whispered into her ears. "We're travelling again today."

"Ah! You and who this time?" Ife asked.

"Ahmed of course. Our flight leaves in three hours."

"Kai, Biba you've finished this man o. He's no longer thinking straight, true."

"It's not my fault." Habibah moved towards the women that were now stuffing their stock inside their different shopping bags. "He won't leave me alone."

"He still loves you."

Habibah picked a twenty-inch bone-straight hair, looked it over and dropped it. "Tell you what. I think he's jealous. He doesn't want to see me with another man. That's why he's bent on taking me with him everywhere."

"Swear you no longer feel anything for him. No, aside from the money and his attention you are enjoying, Habibah, you still love this man."

"I don't know." Habibah picked another hair. "I never stopped loving Ahmed. And I think he knows. That's why he's not remarried. He's waiting for me to come back to him."

It took another extra hour for Ife to be finally free and she was speeding in and out of traffic to get to Rasheed's workplace: a magnificent building situated in the bustling epicenter of the city. She was directed to the lot where she parked her car behind a Pajero SUV. At the entrance of the building, she took the landings up to the terrazzo-floored porch and was about to walk into the reception when her eyes caught something that made her stop in her stride.

There was a red car parked by the building, almost hidden. Anyone could have walked past without noticing it. Anyone but her. Something about it triggered a memory and made her approach it.

It was the same Nissan Altima with tinted glasses.

Or was it a look alike?

She pressed her face to the window and peered. There was a pile of books at the backseat, a laptop, a *Tangaran* hat, and an object lying on the floor; a hammer—metal head with a long wooden handle. A faint twitter, and a sound like the flutter of bird wings made her move from the rear door window to front glass. Balanced on the passenger's seat was a cage that had a little bird in it. It had silky soft feathers and a flare of blue on its throat—

"Looking for something?"

The unexpected voice jarred her into straightening up and looking back. She was more shocked to see him—Rasheed standing just at arm's length. Watching her keenly. How in God's sweet son's name did he know she was there?

"Are you looking for something?" he asked again, his voice slightly gritty.

"I, uhm." In her perplexed state, and with her heart racing like a train pounding down the tracks, she stuttered. "No, uhm…how long… how long have you—"

"Long enough." He heaved. "Why are you here?"

"To see you," she replied, glad he'd dropped the previous question.

"To see me?" His disbelief was evident on his face.

"Yes. I wanted to…was sent to…" Think. Think! Damn brain. Why was it so hard for her to cook up a believable story now? "I just feel there's something—unfinished discussion." At least that was true. He was hiding something, and God! She was dying to know who this man really was.

Maybe I am dying to prove that he's as clean as a newly appointed Nigerian minister on his first day on the job.

"Unfinished discussion," he repeated, balancing his weight in a hip-thrust stance and Ife thought that even with all the mysteries surrounding him, he was still sexy.

Her gaze lowered to his chest and… She never thought she would be drawn to a hairy masculine upper body in her life. But damn him. Did he sight her from wherever he was and decide to come meet her looking this indecent—his shirt half-buttoned up, and no inner vest? All that swirled hair that disappeared into his cloth was extremely unsettling and thrilling. She longed to run her fingers through those curls, to stroke them down to his…

You are getting off track.
Oh, yes. That I am.

He may be the man after Fola.
Yes, yes...
Never forget that, Ifechukwu. Never lose your guard.

Yet she allowed her eyes to roam: his sleeves were rolled up, his whole look ruffled— like he was just coming out of a brawl or a wild sex section with some woman—Fola?

"Come with me," he said, and began walking into the building without sparing a glance back to be sure she was coming along.

Twelve

AS THEY PASSED the reception hall into an elevator which took them to the fifth floor, and as they walked through the long corridor that led to his workspace, Ife realized two things: One, every female staff they walked past gave him a smile which he responded warmly. Two, they greeted her with a pretentious half grin. Twice, she'd turn to catch a lady they walked past staring at them—at her with what looked like a scowl.

It soon became patently obvious to her that even though some of them seemed married, every woman in that place felt that she had a strong claim on Rasheed, and given half a chance, most of them would be willing to hop into bed with him, were he to ask.

Had he asked any of them?

The question should be, *'How often does he ask?'* And which among them was his regular?

The thought of him with any of these women made her stomach knot.

Jealous?

She had no reason to be.

"What are you thinking about?" he asked, interrupting her conversation with herself.

When she didn't reply, he got off the edge of his desk where he'd sat and watched her, and with that cocky grin she didn't know she missed, he made his way towards her. Her decision to remain tough around him vaporized in a puff of steam. Every foot he put forward made her heartbeat beat faster like rain on a metal roof.

Unable to continue holding his gaze, she lowered her eyes to...a mistake! Why did she allow her eyes to move this low...down to his nipple that was like little baby perma-boners poking through his shirt? Now all she had to do in order not to allow the spittle that had gathered inside her mouth to spill was swallow. Swallow and look away. Nothing seemed out of place in his office, there was no sign that he was previously engaged in some kind of *disturbing* activity there. Except the dagger on his desk. It was forged in gray steel, fixed on a rich dark metal hilt. It appeared medieval, like an antique.

"You said we have an unfinished discussion," he said.

She couldn't make out whether his smile was genuine or he was better at covering his discomfort than she was.

"I hope you're okay. Are you in any kind of trouble?" he asked.

"I'm fine." The cold air emanating from the AC in the room did nothing to dispel her uneasiness.

"Oh." He was standing close now. "Then you've finally made up your mind to satisfy this raging ache we have for each other."

"I'm not going to sleep with you, I told you already." Yet, she could feel, for a moment, something titillating, taking possession of her whole being.

They looked at each other. She was sure he was feeding on this *looking*, because his breathing changed, and his eyes became softer. She had never wanted to admit there was a pull stronger than sexual attraction between them, but now she couldn't help it. She knew he was aware of it too, just as she knew he was equally aware of her burgeoning fear of him. Even their most casual encounter seemed to be charged with apprehension or some elusive emotion.

"Yes, you did say so," he said. The softness, the anxiety in his voice was a wild tonic in her brain. "I should respect your decision. But it's not easy controlling my desire for you when you are here, alone with me. I wasn't prepared for your visit. I thought you'd keep your distance."

He was right. She should have kept her distance. Wasn't that what her mind advised her to do? Yet, with the laughable excuse that she was into finding something big, something to prove that he was evil, her legs had led her to him.

He held her gaze for some uncomfortable moment, and she thought he was going to kiss her. He didn't. He just leaned *kissably* close and asked, "Why are you really here?"

"I... to see you." She shut her eyes as he took a curl of her hair between his fingers. He was close enough for her to take in his overpowering oceanic scent. Yes, he smelt like the ocean. Deep, mysterious ocean with huge surge of waves. "To know if—"

"What would you do if I kissed you right now?" His unexpected question shocked her. "Tell me, *yanmata*. What will you do?"

Ife opened her eyes and stared at his face, her gaze slid down to his sensual mouth, and she wanted nothing more than to taste it. "I would kiss you back." *Just a kiss, right? Just a kiss and nothing else.*

"*Ke ce rayuwata,*" he swore under his breath and without warning, his arms were around her, pulling her to his body and his mouth came down to hers.

Everything went oddly quiet at first, like the moment of silence between lightning and thunder.

Then bang! The sky was torn open.

She didn't know if it was him or her that swooped in, but all the self-control she'd exerted over the past weeks went, like water crashing through a broken dam. She was up on the tip of her toes, and her arms came up around his neck as he pulled her against him. She was kissing him as fiercely as he was kissing her. His tongue was flicking all her sexual switches. In his kisses, she heard him telling her all the things he could never say out loud.

She let out a whimper and pulled him even closer, feeling the heat building around them like amber being fanned into a chrism coal. She knew he felt it too, because a groan escaped his throat, and his kisses became even more earnest.

He surfaced for air, allowing her some time to breathe too. "*Masoyiata*," he said

Did he just call her *Masoyiata—My love*? This man must be thinking from his testosterone right now because...why in God's sweet son's name would he call her that?

"You want me." The words left his mouth in helpless groans.

Of course, no.
Of course, yes
This is ridiculous.
And you want it.

"Rasheed we can't—" She was here to find out the truth about him. To know if he was the same man blackmailing Fola. Not to lose herself to his lust. "We can't—"

But when he claimed her lips again, she welcomed him, giving up her mouth for his pleasure while greedily drinking him in. Her fingers were on his face, touching and stroking his beard, then they moved to the nape of his neck, and she heard him hissing as if she'd shot electric currents through his body. She could feel him hard against her pelvis and it was turning her on.

Another hiss escaped his throat. In a flash, he whipped her off the ground, balancing her— legs wrapped around his waist —and coursed them through the floor to crash her back against the cold wall of his office.

"Ife—see what you do to me." He rushed the words and recaptured her mouth, forcing a moan out of her as she found herself melting like an ice cube in a heated pan.

This felt good. He felt good.

And you like it.

Very much. Her veins were throbbing, and her heart was about to explode.

Get some sense, woman! Do you know how many times he's done this?

How many women he's fucked and abandoned?

You could be one of the hundreds, or thousands.

Who cared? He was a great kisser, so much better than George. And he tasted like she had imagined he would—like a sweet strong wine. The warmth of his breath and the heat from his body were filling her senses in such a way that left her wanting more of him.

From the farthest part of her mind, George's warning drifted into her head. *Rasheed's biggest problem was women... Shy but damn flirtatious. He didn't need to talk much to get the ladies falling for his weak ass... his wife didn't commit suicide, she was murdered.... I may be rolling with him, but you must be careful with him.*

Ife gasped when she felt the straps of her white silk camisole slipping off her shoulders, and cold air kissing her skin. Tearing her mouth away from his, she looked down to find her bare breast—a sizable apple cupped in his hand.

"Beautiful. Dark and hard," he murmured as his thumb and forefinger began to work on her nipple with great deal of expertise.

She felt electricity all over her body, her higher brain shutting down and her animal self—passion, intense and intoxicating—awakening.

"Just the way I love them," he muttered. Grabbing her waist with his free hand, he pressed her against the bulge of his pants and began to move–stroking her groin with his arousal, making love to her with clothes on.

It felt so good. Made her brain curl up like wilted leaves, and all she craved now was for him to carry her to his large desk so she could spread her legs for him. No, she wanted him to spread them himself. She wanted him to sink into her and rut her until his flesh was all that would be in her mind. And he wouldn't stop. Because she wouldn't want him to, not until she also became the only thing in his head while he rode her to that point where she would be floating in space surrounded by streams of bright colors.

"Ife, *ba wani sai ke*, you are my undoing," he groaned against the skin of her neck.

Desire brought another moan to her lips, as he pushed her camisole further down and began to fondle one breast after another, while his other hand traveled down her ass to squeezed hard and came up again to her waist.

"Rasheed...Oh." The heat his touch was transporting into her, his warm breath on her face...her neck...her shoulders. She was sure that in her state of intense arousal, she wouldn't object to whatever he wanted to do to her—with her. There would be nothing she could do to stop him. Just his groans were sending her into a heady trance, one she doubted would end until their bodies were joined, and flesh began to slap against flesh.

But, out from nowhere, George's warning filtered into her head again, reminding her who this man might be:

A sexual psychopath.

A murderer who killed his wife and is after Fola.

The wet flat of his tongue was dragging over her collar bone… moving lower…and lower, licking its way to her areola…Oh…oh… The warmth of his breath around her nipple was sending frisson of exciting sensation from the hardened peak down to her cove. When his tongue finally touched the tip, she didn't recognize her voice when she let out a whimper as a bolt of pleasure punched her core. Had he not pinned her firmly against the wall with his weight, she would have crumbled to the floor.

He made a sound of pure hunger, took one nipple into his mouth and sucked, gently at first. Then he sighed as her fingers dug into the flesh of his back and began to go faster, doing everything at once: sucking, licking, flicking, while fondling the other breast and giving it mild pinches in between touch.

"Rasheed please…" she moaned.

"I know, I know." *Lick. Flick. Suck.* "I love the way you shiver," he murmured. "You're so easy to please."

Was that humor in his voice?

"Ra…sheed, I can't…" Oh Jesus. "We can't—"

"We can." His free hand had left her breast and was settled on her triangular region. She heard his breath hitch and realized he had just discovered the dampness down there. *Truly, Ovulation is shameless.* The bad bitch had set her estrogen on overdrive, and her wetness into an unhinged stream. The fabric of her chinos was the receptor.

Pressing his thumb hard against her entrance, "Ife, *Idan ban danne ki ba yanzu zan iya shiga mummunan hali.*" he gritted.

Immediately, embarrassment brought some sense into her head, "No." she murmured. "Rasheed, no."

"Please, Ife. I want to make love to you." His hand had found the hook of her trousers' waistband, and he was struggling to get it loose. "Just this once...Okay, the tip. Just the tip of my dick in your pussy, I won't go deep, I promise."

Summoning the willpower she had left, she pushed him away, panting as hard as he was. "I'm not having sex with you—"

"*Astaghfirulla.*" he said, husky voiced. "Ife, you want this as much as I do."

"Speak…" her un-even breath was making it hard for her to talk with composure. "Speak for yourself."

His desire-laden eyes journeyed down to her aching breasts. "What we feel for each other is strong. Even your body can't deny it. Look at these." He pointed at her nipples.

"You are shameless," she spat, awkwardly slipping back the straps of her camisole while looking around for her shirt. She saw it some feet away—lying carelessly on the floor. She hurried past him to pick it up. Refusing to give a thought to how it ended up there, she threw it over her shoulders. "Oh God," she muttered, her feverish fingers fussing buttons inside holes.

"I wish you'd stop fighting this thing between us," he said, cupping the bulge in his pants with his hand.

"And I wish you go to hell for...for..." *Taking away my sense and leaving me trembling like a... a soft hair in the wind.* "For murdering your wife and framing it to be a suicide."

Shit!

"I'm sorry." Apologizing was inadequate but she meant it. She didn't plan on starting this probe this way. Now she didn't know what to do with the man standing expressionless in front of her.

"George told you." It wasn't a question.

"I'm sorry."

"What for?"

He was going to let her off so lightly? "For speaking so senselessly. I shouldn't have accused you of…"

"Killing my Salma?"

She closed her eyes. When she opened them, Rasheed had gone to look out the window. This could be where he saw her from earlier. He shut the window, drew down the blind and sat behind his desk.

"Tell me, *yanmata*. You think I killed my wife?"

"George said your wife wanted a divorce, but you couldn't stand her leaving you." Her response fell over themselves in her hurry to speak. "I wouldn't have given it a thought if Fola —" she searched his face for any expression. He remained stoic, "Fola was receiving threat notes…and… she called you and… I know, I saw her name on your phone that day we were at George's house and… I was frightened when—"

"Suddenly everything clicked," he interrupted. He wasn't denying not knowing Fola. *He wasn't concurring to the fact too.* "The same man accused of murdering his wife, got a call from a woman who's receiving threat notes." He shook his head as if he didn't know what to make of her. "Enough reason to go Sherlock Holmes on him—"

"What would you have done if you were me?"

Before his response came, there was a knock.

"Please get the door for me, will you?"

She did.

One of the women they walked past earlier on their way to his office, walked in with a man that resembled a rumpled grocer. The woman introduced the man, threw Ife a careless glance and excused herself.

"Christ! It's cold in here," the man exclaimed, coming

towards Rasheed, who was now on his feet, to give him a handshake.

"You. Is it—"

Ife looked up at the rumpled grocer-looking man who seemed to have spoken to her.

"Okwute's daughter?" the man asked.

The way that man was giving her a look over made Ife wonder if he suspected anything odd. Her hair...she lifted her hand to smoothen it. And her pants... God, she dared not look down or the man might glimpse the damp patch on the juncture between her thighs. "Yes," she said, her voice a little above whisper. "Yes," she reaffirmed, louder this time.

"You must be feeling cold, Miss Ojukwu," Rasheed cut in, so formally.

She was confused at first, then she realized he was trying to tell her something other than...oh... The movement of his eyes down to her chest drew her attention to her unabashed nipples that were still hard from his touch, and perky from the fabric of her shirt.

"A lot of people complain about how cold my office always is," Rasheed said.

Biting down the urge to burst into tears as embarrassment gripped her, Ife nodded.

"Why don't you turn your damn AC off?" rumpled grocer-looking man retorted.

Rasheed did as the man said, then grabbed the jacket hanging at the back of his chair and came to her. "Here," he remarked, throwing the garment over her shoulders, his fingers brushing her arms as she slid her hands inside the sleeves.

Uncomfortably aware of how close his face was, she tried not to look at him. He still smelled of wild sexual desire.

"I hope this will keep you warm," he said, then leaned close to whisper, "relax."

Their eyes met and for the briefest of moments she forgot they weren't alone anymore. All her nerves responded to the heat she felt around them. When the rumpled grocer-looking man cleared his throat and broke the spell, Ife was aware that Rasheed caught the blush that crept up her face before she turned away from him, because he had that cocky grin on his lips as he walked back to his chair.

"Still selling wigs?" the rumpled grocer-looking man asked.

"A girl has to make a living somehow," Ife replied. On impulse, she ran her tongue over her lips that were swollen and sensitive. And when her eyes caught Rasheed grinning, she flushed.

"Good. Good. I hope you're making a lot of money. Not that you need it anyway. Your father has enough to last you for a lifetime," the man said, and without waiting for her response, he faced Rasheed.

For a while, Ife listened to them talk about politics, and the latest bandits' attack on the *Kuje* prison. Then she decided it was time to leave. She pulled his jacket off, folded it and placed it on the sofa. Without interrupting their conversation, she walked out of the door and closed it behind her.

Her phone vibrated while she was walking down the long corridor.

"Where have you been?" George shouted immediately she picked. "God! I've been calling your number since morning. Don't you check your phone?" he said without pausing to breathe. "I was even at your place a few minutes ago. Where are you?"

"I... I stepped out. I needed to get something done," she said.

"And you couldn't pick your calls?"

The phone had been in her pocket all the time. She didn't even hear it ring.

"Are you okay? Is there something wrong?" There was a wrinkle of concern in his voice.

"I'm fine," she replied, a little remorseful. "So, what's up? How is the TV station coming up?"

"Oh that? Fine, I wanted to even ask if you've paid for the space you promised me."

"Not yet. But I'll soon do that." Once she had the money complete.

"We don't have much time, Ife. I don't want someone else to take that place."

"I know. I'll try and get the money completed by the weekend." Why wouldn't he make the money up from the one Rasheed gave him?

An awkward silence passed between them.

"There's something else," he said. "Enitan. Fola's husband."

The way he said it made her mouth dry and she stopped walking. "What?"

The hesitation in his voice sent a jolt of alarm right through her.

"You haven't heard?" he finally spoke.

"Heard what?" Her heart was pounding.

"I'm sorry to be the one to tell you, honey," he said softly, "but Enitan is dead."

Momentarily, her shock drained away as she reeled from the impact. It lasted but a second. Then the shock was back, followed by the full realization of what the news meant. She started running non-stop until she reached the elevator.

You finally moved in with me, against your girlfriend's disapproval and your father's threats, on the last day of your final exam. Showing up at my door with one of your daddy's cars loaded with stuff. It was fun helping you unload.

"I'll get the rest of my things from the house anytime I go there," *you said with excitement.* "Hang on, there's one more thing in the car. It's a sort of surprise for you. For us."

You ran back and opened the passenger door of the car where a cardboard box rested in the footwell, carried it back to the house so carefully that I thought it was something delicate, but when you handed it to me, I noticed it was far too light to be a glass ware.

"Open it." *You were almost bursting with excitement.*

I lifted the cardboard flap on top of the box and almost screamed on seeing a tiny bundle of fluff staring up at me. Finding my voice, I said, "It's a puppy." *The one you carried around like a baby. I had always wanted to tell you to put it away each time I visited the house you shared with your friend, but I didn't want to offend you.*

"It's May, my puppy!" *you said.* "Isn't she adorable?" *You scooped it from inside the box and held it to my chest.*

"Did it not occur to you to ask me before bringing this thing to my house?" *I said without tempering my tone. You began to cry. I knew it was a tactic to get me to accept this animal that would leave hair on my sofas and eat my shoes. A pathetic, obvious tactic that made me even angrier.*

"I thought you liked May," *you said, still crying.* "I thought it would be company for me while you're away—she can watch me do things around here."

It occurred to me that you might be right. The puppy might as well be entertainment for you while I went to my crumbling business. Perhaps I could cope with the damn thing, if it made you content.

"Just make sure you keep it away from my things," *I said and* walked into the room. When I came out again, you had laid out a dog's bed and two bowls in the kitchen, and a litter tray by the door.

"It's only until she gets used to this place and can go outside on her own," you said. Your eyes were sad, and I hated that you had seen me lose control. To salvage that, I bent and stroked the puppy on the head, and you sighed with relief, came up to me, and snaked your arms around my waist. "Thank you." You kissed me in that way that was always a precursor to sex, and when I gently pushed you away, you sank back to your knees and without as little as a word for me, you began playing with the animal.

You became obsessed with it. Its food, its toys, even its shitty litter tray were more interesting to you than tidying my house or cooking for me. Far more interesting than talking to me. You spent entire evenings playing with it, dragging stuffed toys across the floor on pieces of string.

You told me you were working on your final year project but when I came home from work, I'd find your stuff strewn about the living room, as it had been the previous day.

Two weeks or so after you moved in, I came home to find a note on the living room table.

Out with Fatimah. Don't wait up!

That day, we spoke, two or three times, like we always did, but you hadn't thought to mention that you were going out with your friend. You didn't leave any food, so presumably you were eating with Fatimah and hadn't bothered yourself with what I might want to have for dinner.

As I entered the kitchen and reached for a beer in the fridge, the puppy whined and tried to climb up my trousers, digging its claws into my leg. I shook it off and it fell on the floor. I shut it in the kitchen, went to sit in the living room and turned the television on. But I couldn't concentrate because all I could think about was that last time you and Fatimah went out: the speed with which she disappeared with a guy she had only just met, and the ease with which you came home with me.

"Don't wait up," I harrumphed.

I hadn't persuaded you to come live with me for me to spend my evenings alone. I had already been taken for a fool by three women—add Fola and that would be four—I wasn't about to let it happen again.

Finishing up my beer, I got up to fetch another one. I could hear the puppy as I neared the kitchen. It skidded across the floor as I pushed the door open sharply. It was comical, and cheered me momentarily, until I returned to the living room and looked at your scattered books. You'd made a half-hearted attempt to stack them in one corner, yet it infuriated me that you couldn't do that right.

My ears captured the whining of the puppy as I took a swig of my beer and returned my attention to the television now showing Dogs Odyssey on Net Geo Wild. I turned up the volume, but I could still hear the dog whining. The sound twisted itself into my head until each cry tuned up my anger level by level; a white-hot rage I recognized but had no control over.

So, I got up and went to the kitchen.

You found her prone and immobile on the kitchen floor when you got back. "May!" Your hands flew to your mouth, and I thought you were going to be sick. "Oh. God! What happened?"

I was by your side to comfort you. "I don't know, I came home and she threw up in the living room. I looked online for advice, but I was too late. She died within half an hour. I'm so sorry. I know how much you loved her."

You were crying now, weeping into my shirt while I held you tightly.

"She was fine when I went out." You looked up at me, searching for answers in my face. "I don't understand why it happened. It must have been the food...I changed her food to a new one I saw in the supermarket. I killed her."

"Darling, you mustn't blame yourself." I pulled you into my arms and held you close, kissing your hair. "It was a mistake, you were trying to give her the best treat," I added, taking your bag from the table where you'd dropped it. "Come on; let's get you into the room; I'll be up before you in the morning, and I'll deal with May then."

In the bedroom you were quiet while you went about your night routines. When you were ready to come to bed. I allowed you cuddle up to me like a child.

I loved that you needed me so much.

"Do you mind if we do it tonight?" I asked, stroking your back in circles, and kissing your neck. "It'll help. I want to make you feel better."

You nodded. But when I kissed you, there was no response. Ignoring your rigidness, I pushed myself inside you and thrust hard, wanting to provoke a reaction—any reaction—but you closed your eyes and didn't make a sound. You took all the pleasure out of it for me, and your selfishness made me smack your face as I thrust harder.

I saw tears ran down your cheek, but again, you didn't make a sound.

Thirteen

"I CAN'T BELIEVE IT. Enitan is dead," George said for the second time since he walked into her room later in the evening. For a moment, everything fell away—George, her surroundings, even the throb in her head seemed to still itself for that instant.

Then George spoke again. "At least he didn't get to see the monster that did this to him."

"What?"

"He was murdered while he was asleep. His wife came home early in the morning and found the house had been broken into, blood everywhere, and his mutilated body was —" He couldn't get himself to continue.

"Jesus, George!" A wave of nausea came over Ife, and she gripped the dressing table to steady herself. Someone had been murdered. Enitan, Fola's husband. It didn't matter if he was asleep or wide awake when his life was gruesomely taken!

"I'm sorry, honey." George grasped her shoulders, steering her towards the bed and making her sit down. "That was insensitive of me. I had no idea you'd take this news this hard."

"Enitan is Fola's husband," Ife said quickly. "He's a great guy. I can't believe anyone would want to murder him." She got up and mumbled something about changing into another dress so she could go see Fola.

"I'll go with you."

"There's no need—"

"Fola and I, we are friends too."

"I know."

"So I need to go see her."

Leaving George in the room, she stepped into the bathroom, stood in the shower, and cried a little. Afterwards, she put on a boubou gown, and soon they were on their way to Fola's place.

The coconut scent in the car made her stomach rebel, so she tugged down the car freshener hanging on the rearview mirror and shoved it into the glove compartment. George observed this without protest. It was only when she picked up the Bible on top of the dashboard that he held up his hand. "Sorry, honey. It stays on that dashboard."

Irrespective of the devastation she was feeling, her eyes widened in surprise. "You now have a Bible in your car?"

"Yes." A grin of pride brightened his tired features.

"And you...you discarded that raunchy magazine?"

"Mm-hm."

"Why?"

"To cleanse my mind, of course."

She regarded him now, taking him in properly for the first time in weeks, and noticing a new leanness. He had always been slender and fit, but there was something added to him now. He looked neater somehow. "You've lost weight," she said in a speculative manner.

"I've been fasting," he said, keeping his eyes on the road,

and biting down on an embarrassed smile. "Stop eyeballing me, Ife. It's unnerving."

But she couldn't help it. George had a Bible, and he was fasting? "Is it just your decision or did something happen to you?"

"What do you think?"

Wait! Did he...had he met... "Don't tell me you've met God."

He shifted his shirt collar and flicked out the crucifix on a chain. Grinning, he said, "Attended one of those open field crusades while I was in Lagos, out of boredom. The word of God found me, and the rest is history."

"This is...unbelievable, George." She managed a half smile and lowered her gaze to her fingers.

They rode in silence for a while.

"I met him a few times," George said. "Enitan. Some years back, before he traveled out. Such a great guy."

They got to the estate, and he slowed the car to a crawl. Two police pickup trucks were strewn haphazardly down the street; lights throwing blue and red glow on top of them every other second. George parked some meters away, and for a moment, they stared at the house.

"You ready?"

Ife nodded, but the truth was she was feeling like shit. "Thanks for not allowing me to talk you into not coming along," she muttered, leaning across to plant a kiss on his bristly cheek.

They joined others at the gate where a young lanky police officer was holding up his hands and imploring those gathered there to disperse. Dealing with all those people looked like penance to him.

"Who are you?" the officer asked when they pushed their way to the front.

"Friends to the family."

"Any ID?"

"Who carries ID when going to see a family friend?" George retorted. "Tell her Ife and George are here."

"It's an ugly situation. I've been instructed not to allow anyone in."

"Fola will be expecting us," Ife said.

The officer stared at her for a while. "Don't I know you? The daughter of that big man...what is that his name again...ohhhh I've forgotten, but—"

"Officer," George snapped. "Can you allow us in?" he said matter-of-factly.

The officer gave him a cautious stare. "Your friend dey for one of those houses," he said, pointing down to a row of duplexes down the street. "The fourth house. Abi una wan see the husband body fes?" came his muffled afterthought.

"No—"

"Yes." George interrupted, squeezing Ife's hand.

Ife swallowed hard and nodded her agreement.

"Who are you?" another policeman asked when they walked in.

"We—family," George answered.

The police man nodded. "Come," he said and led the way to the bedroom.

The first thing Ife felt was the anger in the room. The violence. Whoever did this must have been deranged with fury. There were broken glasses and broken frames. Blood splatter above the bed's headboard gave Ife a heart attack even before she lowered her eyes to the body.

"Whoever did this was deliberate," the policeman said, spitting into the hankie in his hand. "He wanted to make a statement."

The policeman was addressing everyone in the room, but

Ife had stopped listening. She couldn't drag her attention away from the man with a squashed skull on the bed. His eyes were open and unseeing, his badly beaten mouth frozen into an O of surprise. Ife moved her eyes down to his stomach that had several stab wounds, and she felt the beginning of nausea.

"I don't think he was hit while sleeping. He must have fought his attacker. But he was overpowered. The idiot put him out with that sledgehammer, dragged him to the bed, before stabbing him."

The weapon was propped against the wall. It was a metal-headed hammer with a long wooden handle.

Someone reminded her it was time to leave, but she kept staring at the hammer, her mind transported back to where she'd seen that object before... yesterday, inside the red Nissan Altima... or wasn't it... *Oh my God!*

"Ife," George called.

An urge to throw up came stronger over her, and she ran out of the room. Outside, she tried to breathe but couldn't. Someone was clutching her throat, stopping her from taking in air. It wasn't someone but something. A picture.

It was the hammer. Black metal head. Yellow long handle.

Her phone beeped, and she took it out from the pocket of her gown. It was her mother's message, reminding her of her brother's burial memorial service next Saturday. She wanted to text back but couldn't. A cold shiver was swimming inside her, and her fingers were shaking uncontrollably. She closed her eyes and waited for this feeling to pass—the fear that she might know who it was that had killed Enitan. She had kissed his lips even.

"Terrible, eh?"

She looked up and saw the young officer approaching her.

"First time seeing something like this?" the young officer asked. "I remember when I saw my first dead body. The man's death was pedestrian, except for the fact he was hanging upside down. There was no blood like this one. But I was terrified." When it was obvious to him that she wasn't ready for a conversation, he asked, "Do you want to see your sister—friend?"

Ife bobbed her head, and without waiting for him to lead the way, she started walking.

Every step was a struggle.

Fola was sitting on a small sofa when Ife entered, her gaze lowered to her hands that were on her thighs.

"I am so sorry, Fola."

Fola looked up, twisting a rope from her dress so tightly around her hand that the cord gouged red grooves in her skin. "He shouldn't have come back," she said. "I told him not to."

"He wanted to come home to you."

"Then it's my fault. I killed him."

"You didn't." Ife sat beside her. She tried to relieve Fola's hand from the rope around it, but Fola wouldn't allow her.

Sitting on a kitchen chair next to the sofa was another police officer who was speaking rapidly into a cellular he was holding to his mouth.

"I was out that night. It was a vigil... you know... I've not attended in a while," Fola said, the words a release of emotion. "Then I came back and... I only left him for a few hours." She pulled the rope tighter around her hand, and Ife watched the color drain from her fingers. "I shouldn't have gone out."

Ife could feel it coming. The tightening, like a belt around her neck. Since that day Fola brought that note to her shop, Ife had been feeling the belt tightening by a notch each time she set her eyes on the woman. Like that day she watched Fola slip into the red car—notch. And every time her phone beeped with Fola's messages—notch. With every thought about Fola and the note, and the possibility that she'd also gotten herself roped into the whole mystery—another notch.

Most times, when Ife tried to remind herself that she had no reason to feel the notch, that Fola's situation had nothing to do with her, something would happen, like the red car that took Fola away resurfacing at Rasheed's company premises; the hammer she saw inside that car that was similar to the one used in beating Enitan to death, that was when she would begin to feel the tentacles of fear reaching out to grasp her so that she couldn't breathe.

There was a grunt behind, and the scrape of wood on tiles. Ife turned to see the policeman walking out of the room.

"Habibah called this morning," Fola said. "I didn't pick up. She sent a message. She's in France."

Ife nodded. "She told me you've not been picking her calls."

Fola didn't reply, so they slid into silence.

"Where are Enitan's people?" Ife asked after some time.

"Not here yet. But I've called them."

They slid into silence again. Then, "he did it," Fola said.

"Rasheed?" Ife didn't mean to mention the name, but as she saw a glimpse of something... fear... shock... in Fola's eyes, her curiosity quickened. "Is it Rasheed?"

"I can't tell you."

She can't tell me. What did Fola mean? Ife wanted to scream at the other woman, to shake her until she would give her a name. Any name. But Fola had a weepy air about her now, and Ife wouldn't want to upset her further.

"He did it to punish me—he said he'll make sure I hurt so much."

"Fola... talk to the police."

"No!" Fola whipped her head up to look at Ife. "He will kill more if he feels threatened."

"You have to stop him."

"Not talking to anyone will make him stop."

"You think so?"

Fola lifted her butt cheek and searched underneath. When she pulled her hand out, she was holding a crumpled paper. "When I went into the room this morning and found that—his body, I also found this." She uncrimped the paper. "Someone placed it on his chest."

Fola took one look at it, then handed it to Ife.

As soon as Ife's gaze fell upon it, she felt the belt around her neck.

Apart from the bloodstain on some parts of it, Ife recognized the chicken scratch handwriting.

You pushed me. Each time you disobey me, I get mad and do terrible things. Now you'll make me do another terrible thing. You didn't stop speaking to her even after I warned you.

You didn't stop speaking to Her... Ife knew who the "Her" in the note was referring to. Yet she didn't understand why she was marked for...for murder. What had she done?

"Did you show the police?" The air in the room suddenly felt chilly.

"Hm-mm."

"But, why?"

"You don't get it, do you? I can't tell the police—what will I tell them?"

"I don't know... tell them something... anything," Ife said briskly, thrusting the note back at Fola, but the other woman refused to take it.

"Keep it, please," Fola said.

Ife walked out of the house a few minutes later, stood on the granite step—where the sun found her feet and traveled up her face. Then she headed out of the gate.

George was waiting in the car.

"The security guy said you went to see Fola.

"Hm," she said, settling inside the car.

"How is she? What did she say to you?"

She couldn't answer immediately, just sat there trying to get a grip on herself.

"Did they allow you to speak to her?"

She shook her head.

A while later, as they made the silent journey home, she wondered why she had lied to George.

And why didn't he come to see Enitan's widow?

Fourteen

IFE GRABBED the chiming brass alarm clock on her bedside table and was shocked it was 10:30 a.m., already. She'd gotten into bed immediately after George left, but had remained awake, her heart pounding in rhythm with her fear. Enitan's death affected her the way nothing else had ever done. But it wasn't his death that kept her on vigil—peering out of the window into the darkness outside. It was the note.

It was almost dawn when she finally fell asleep with the image of the chicken-scratch handwriting in her head.

Getting out of bed, she pulled on yesterday's clothes and went into the garden barefooted.

The garden had been her sanctuary since she bought the house, just as the study was for George. Though it was little more than a backyard farm to a casual observer, it was where she came to work, to think, to escape. She shut her eyes, took a large breath in, opened her eyes, and walked deeper into the garden, her feet mashing lumps of wet sand mixed with grasses and rotten leaves.

She sighted a fluted pumpkin lying on a carpet of withering leaves. The large vegetable cocoon seemed to be one of the few things alive in the garden and somehow, it brought an unexplainable joy to her. Moving forward, she bent down to carefully pick it up, but her fingers sank into its flesh.

It was decayed.

A frustrating groan left her mouth, and she kicked the pumpkin, covering her foot in muck. A sudden seething anger and weariness took over her. The truth was, she was as weary as hell. She'd not had a good sleep for a while now. Presently, her body was swamped in fatigue, but she was too hyped to rest, her nerves jangling, and apprehension dancing through her fiber.

She took a deep breath and let it out slowly, then broke down in tears as the image of Enitan's unseeing eyes jumped into her mind.

And the note Fola found.

"Sweet Jesus."

She grabbed both sides of her dress and waited for the fleeting panic that had just gripped her to pass. It didn't. She squatted and cried some more, then got up and walked out of the garden. She felt a sudden urge to call her father and tell him everything, but the urge passed, overtaken by the dominant voice inside her head that insisted she suppress it. Put a lid on it and wait. This might be nothing. Besides, the old man might do something that would end up putting her in deeper trouble.

A snatch of conversation from behind made her cast a glance over her shoulder. Isa, her gateman, was speaking with someone that looked like a courier at the gate. She stood and watched the man hand Isa a package and walk off.

She retracted her steps and headed towards the gate, realizing as she got closer that there was a red car slowly pulling away from her outside space. A red Nissan Altima—

"For you, ma." Isa handed the package to her. "'Im talk say

I fit sign the paper for you," her gateman defended, giving her a toothy grin.

Ife nodded, turned the package over in her hands. "The person that gave this to you—"

"Na woman, ma. Na because say im wear helmet for head na im make you no know. Her voice na woman voice, and her body. She get long nails."

Ife nodded. "She came with that..." she pointed at the car. "That red car?"

"Walahi. Me sef shock. How person go dey inside moto come wear helmet again? People dey craze for this country, I swear."

"Hmm." One more glance back—the car had disappeared—and Ife returned her attention to the padded envelope, turning it over again. It was small enough—no bigger than A4—manila in color and padded. Her details had been scrawled on the back in a blue marker.

"Okay, thank you," she said and started strolling back to the house, her thumb hooked under the flap of the envelope, forcing it open. Then she stopped. Her eyes stared unblinkingly at the object she'd just slipped out of the envelope.

"Madam, na watin?" Isa asked from behind her.

Ife would have snapped at him for sneaking up on her—a bad habit of his that always dragged on Ife's nerves, but she was stupefied by what she was staring at. She was so stupefied that she allowed the object to slither out of her hand and drop to the ground.

Then she began to feel it again—the notch.

For a moment, she and her gateman were momentarily speechless. They just gazed at it—a bird. There was something fragile about the manner it lay so tiny and motionless. Frail, except for the blood on its feathers and the severe neck wound.

"*Inna lillahi*," Isa whispered.

Ife couldn't speak.

"Wa inna ilayhi raji'un!" The pitch of her gateman's voice betrayed his alarm. Before long, Bashiru and Salewa came running at the same time George honked outside the gate.

"I should call the police," Ife said quietly, still trembling.

"That's not necessary," George argued. "I think it's just a prank."

"Of course it's not," Bashiru impatiently stated in his usual flawless English, glaring at George with his unmistakable dislike. "We must deal with this properly," he added. "Is there a note in the package?"

"No," Ife whispered.

"What about an address?"

George picked the envelope up and squinted at it. "This is crazy," he sighed, reaching out to place his hand across Ife's shoulders.

Ife could feel his apprehension from the weight of his arm on her, even though he was trying to remain calm. It brought back the reality of what was before her. And that realization made her grit her teeth. It was all she could do so she wouldn't burst into tears. The bird was on the ground, almost at her feet —a stern message. But what exactly did it mean?

Instantly, images came tunneling up through memory: the Nissan Altima parked, almost hidden, in Rasheed's office premises. The flutter of wings on the bars of the cage that caught her attention. The twitter. The soft feathers with a flare of blue at the neck.

The bird!

That bird!

But it couldn't be. It was not possible. She tried to shrug off the possibility. Yet the strangeness of the coincidence pressed down on her. It was not a coincidence. The bird. The car. Rasheed.

"Don't let this bother you," George said quietly. "I know you'll want to alert the police or your father but...this happens to rich kids like you. You'd be amazed at the kind of stupid kids out there that have nothing to do with their lives. Fucking idiots who think it'll be great to scare a rich man's daughter," he began stroking her face. "Could be one of those protesters you met at the state house. I told you they are angry and would do anything to rattle privileged kids like you."

"I even hear say person don give Senator Dankwambo daughter shit before," Isa added.

"She is shitty," George said abruptly. Then he picked the bird off the ground and sickness rose to Ife's throat. Without a word, he slotted it into the envelope and walked off to the backyard.

Some minutes later, he reappeared.

"I've set it on fire," he said.

The staff had retired back into their quarters.

"You all right?" he asked, guiding her into the house.

She nodded.

As they sat down, his hesitancy returned, but it was something different now. "Really," she said, trying to smile. "I'm fine."

"You're not going to call Daddy and tell him about it?"

"No."

"You know he's going to ask you to come stay with him. Or even flood this place with armed policemen. Can you deal with that?"

She thought for a while. "I don't think so."

"I'm staying with you, not going anywhere," George said, stroking her arm. "I want to make you feel better."

"Hmm," she bopped her head and leaned on him, while hoping that this wouldn't slip to the media. She wasn't sure she was ready to deal with such publicity.

But words scattered like ash blown by the wind. Before long, her phone was erratically buzzing. It was her father first, howling over the phone as if there was obituary news of her on the TV. He had ended the call with a promise to go see the commissioner of police over the issue. Then there were calls from tabloid hacks, and after a few hours, she got a call from a female police officer.

Do you know who might have sent it?

Have you received similar threatening messages in the past?

Do you know anyone who might have a grudge against you?

Ife thought a little over the last question. While she wasn't sure if she had any mortal enemies, she was aware there were people who would want to hurt her and her siblings to get back at her father. People who thought her father was ruthless and deserved severe pain. But when the police officer asked if there was anything significant that had happened to her—a warning sign or alarm—before now, she was immediately thrown into the nudge of memory again: Fola's notes; the red Nissan Altima. She had felt the tightening around her throat, the pinch of another notch.

"No, there's nothing," she'd answered, desperately wishing it was true.

Something about this made her deeply uneasy. And it was not the dead bird. It began with Rasheed showing up at her party that fateful day, like some portent of doom. Yet she didn't see this whole spiral coming.

Because her brain was overridden by lust.

But now, she could feel herself being sucked into a darkness she wasn't prepared for. And this policewoman's questions, instead of reassuring her, had left her feeling worse. The officer's careful questioning hit her like someone was sticking a finger into her fear and having a good poke around.

After the call, Ife couldn't sit still anymore. George's presence didn't help either, so she picked up her car key and left the house, driving around town with no destination in mind. Sighting the Crushed Mountain Park, she drove her car into a space, turned off the engine, and silence filled the air around her. She could have gone to her father's house, but she couldn't bear the thought of human contact at the moment. She would rather sit alone in her car and watch the evening. Soon, tiredness pulled her limbs, dragging her towards sleep. She could either head back home or give in to her weariness and sleep for thirty minutes.

She chose the latter, letting go of everything: the package, the delivery woman, the red Nissan Altima, all wiped out by the blankness of sleep.

She didn't know how long she'd slept when her phone chimed into her dream. Instantly she opened her eyes, squinted under the glare of the sun from her windscreen, and pulled herself up, head heavy and swimming with drowsiness.

The gadget stopped ringing before she could get it. It started again as she relaxed back in the chair, causing her heart to leap with fright.

Ignore.

Pick.

Ignore.

Ignore...

But the ringing persisted, so she picked.

"Ife?"

Rasheed. Her voice froze in her throat.

"Ife, are you alright?"

"Rasheed..." She tried to keep her voice firm, hoping it didn't betray the myriads of emotions that were pulsating through her now because it was strange hearing his voice so normal. Its soft timbre, low-graveled tone...like pebbles under water, reaching every part of her inside. Though there was a rasp in it that she didn't remember, a kind of scratch.

"I loved the way you called my name the last time we were together."

There was amusement in his voice.

"Listen," he went on, his tone assuming seriousness. "I think we have to talk. Can you meet me?"

"Me meet you?" She tried again to sound firm but failed. "You...you. What do you want from me?" Yesterday he almost had her. He made her lose her head to the pleasure of his touch, his kisses. All the while he was planning to shock her like this? "How did you do it?" she asked.

"Do what?"

"You were with me in your office yesterday, kiss—" Words got stuck in her throat as a nostalgic wave hit her: she remembered his mouth over hers, his tongue sweeping her moist, his hands...his touch. She would have sworn every desire she tasted in his mouth was pure, that his confessions were true. "A dead bird. Someone sent me a bird with its throat slashed."

Maybe it was the sound of his breath from the other end of the phone while he waited for her to finish, or the softness of his voice when he said, *"HasbunAllah wa n'imal wakil"* after a brief silence, that made something inside her plummet.

"I didn't send any dead bird to you, Ife," he said.

She didn't know what to expect, but it definitely was not him denying the accusation.

Or wasn't he the one?

Was there any possibility of...of...No, everything was pointing at him; Fola's notes, the red car, the bird, even his persona aroused suspicion.

"I'll never do anything to harm you, Ife."

"Someone was murdered and...and I saw the hammer... it was there." As she spoke, she pictured the object in her mind's eyes: long yellow wooden handle, its metal head smeared with blood—Enitan's blood. "The same hammer that was inside that car! The red car parked in your premises."

"I know nothing about any of the things you just mentioned."

Jesus! How could he be lying so blatantly?

"I've done some terrible things in my life, but I've never killed. I'll never deliberately hurt anyone."

Deliberately. That was it!

In Fola's note, he said he was pushed, that he wouldn't have done it if Fola had listened and obeyed him. Now he would do another terrible thing because Fola was speaking to Her! "You killed Enitan—"

"I didn't kill anyone."

"You are going to hurt me too."

"I'll do no such thing. Kai! *Inna lillahi,* Ife, what are you on about?"

"That's why you sent it. The bird. It's a message."

"I did not send any damn thing to you!"

"You are going to kill me—"

"I am not a murderer!" he snapped. His calmness had fled, leaving in its wake the shell of a man cloaked in anger and desperation to be believed. "I'll never hurt you."

"Why?"

"Because I—" he paused. "I'm beginning to care so much about you," he said, like it was an afterthought.

She had wanted him to tell her why he wanted her dead. But his sudden confession startled her to silence. There was something sad about the way he said it, the hint of regret in his voice. It was as if he was saying:

I'm not supposed to care about my victim, but I'm beginning to care too much about you.

In the fading light of the day, she breathed deeply, trying to make sense of everything. Suddenly, it occurred to her that he might be close, he might have followed her down here. She watched, from her car, the last of the evening walkers along the park and realized she was looking for Rasheed among them, hopeful of catching a glimpse of him sandwiched between two walkers or hidden behind one while speaking to her.

"Ife, I must see you."

"Are you here?"

"What—where?"

"Tell me, please," she said. "Are you watching me now?" His reluctance to reply stirred panic inside her. "Please, tell me," she whispered, not surprised by the sudden tears that sprang to her eyes. Blinking them away, she swallowed hard and asked again, "I'm losing my mind, please."

"No. I don't even know where you are–But I can come and get you if you want me to."

She hung up, threw her phone onto the passenger seat, leaned her face on the steering wheel, and cried.

It baffled me that you wanted me to meet your family. You were never fond of your mother, and although you spoke to your elder sister on the phone every now and then, you hardly visited her. But your father had your heart. You told me how controlling he was and how much you would love to be free from him. Yet each time he wanted you, off you went, like a good little girl, leaving me for a night—sometimes more—while you ran around with him like his little puppy and, no doubt, flirted with his rich friends. Each time, you asked me to go with you, and each time I refused.

"He knows you are my boyfriend," you said one day. You'd totally forgotten about the smack I gave you across the face on the night you took passion away from me because your puppy died, and the one I gave you a week later when you spent the night with your friends even when I asked you not to. "He wants me to bring you along this time. He's going to think we are not serious if you keep refusing his invitations," you added, smiling to show you were joking, but there was desperation in your voice. "I want to spend Easter with you. It wasn't the same without you last year."

"Then stay here with me," I said. It was a simple choice to make. Why wasn't I enough for you?

"I want to be with my father too. We don't even have to stay the night—we can just go for lunch. Please don't say no. I really want him to see you more often," you begged.

You'd gradually toned down the make-up you used to wear, but that day, you were wearing lipstick, and I watched the red curve of your mouth as you pleaded with me. "Fine." I shrugged. "But any other holidays, it's just you and me."

"Thank you!" You beamed and threw your arm around me. "I suppose we'll need to take some presents along."

Our conversation moved from visiting your father to other things. I mentioned how your things were everywhere and how there was no longer a place in which I felt relaxed. The house hadn't seemed small when I moved in. It was the same size as the one I moved out of, the one that had been sufficient for Fola and I. Fola was quieter than you. Less exuberant. Easier to be with in a way, apart from her lies and threats to leave me which I learned to deal with.

"I'm thinking, maybe I should get a house for myself now that I'll be working with dad," you said.

"What house?" And when did we agree that you would take up your dad's job offer?

"My own place. Dad still pays me allowances, remember? And if I speak to dad, he'll even pay for the whole thing for me."

I hadn't realized you had money left after you loaned me four million to start up a new business. I would have demanded more money from you. After all, you have been living in my house rent-free.

"It's a good idea, honey, but what happens when you need me. You know you always do." I could see you hadn't thought it through.

"I need some space," you said. "If I start working, I'll be bringing work home and you've already seen how disoriented I can be. I wouldn't want to inconvenience you."

"But I like you here." I liked that I could always find you in my house every time I got back home, that you were dependent on me for almost everything—except money. And I hated that you were considering changing that.

"What if I get a bigger house for us? A three-bedroom flat—a duplex even." I didn't mind how much it would cost. After all, you would be paying. I knew how to make you part with money. "I'll find a place with enough space, and we will convert a room into your personal workspace."

"My own workspace?"

"You can make as much mess as you like there."

"You'll do that for me?" A broad smile spread across your face.

"I'd do anything for you, you know that."

It was true. I would have done anything to keep you to myself. Anything.

Fifteen

IFE PRESSED her face against the iron bars, eyes squinted. She felt multiple pains in her ears as if they were pricked by a thousand needles.

"There is nobody there," George said the second time.

She felt his hand on her back, but she couldn't look at him. Instead, she grabbed the window bars to steady her trembling limbs and kept staring. There was someone out there. A hooded figure peeping into her compound from her see-through gate. Why was George trying to make her think that it was all in her head?

"Honey, let's go back to bed, please," George said, gently pulling her by the hand.

Her grip on the bars tightened. "Look! The man is moving. He's walking away!"

"Honey," George muttered, taking her hand again. This time she allowed him to lead her away from the window and made her climb into the bed.

"Oh, God," she murmured over and over to herself. "He'll break into the house and…Isa…I have to call Isa. The police… Daddy…I must call him—"

George grabbed her phone from the nightstand before she could reach it.

"There is nobody there!" he barked.

She tried wrestling the gadget out of his hand, but he pushed her, and she landed with her back on the bed.

"Christ almighty, Ife!" he hissed. "You are losing your mind. How long is this going to go on?"

"I'm telling you the truth, George. Someone is there. A man. I saw him—"

"There is no bloody person there. Christ!"

She felt his fury rising and whipping around the room in a faster revolution than the lazy whirr of the fan standing by the dressing table.

"You know what? I think you are deliberately doing this to create a distance between us. Since you started acting this delusional, we've stopped doing things couples do. It's like you just want to push me away tactfully—"

"That's not true."

"Ife, are you making up this whole bullshit?"

"No!"

"I repulse you so much that you chose to act mad so you can use it as an excuse—"

"Stop, please. That's not true."

"Then tell me what it is! Because you're the only person who sees things. You feel eyes on you when you walk the street. You! No one else."

"Something is happening to me." Her voice broke with the emotion that was lodged in her throat, and tears began to claw around her eyes. "I'm scared. I can't help it.

The last time she left the house—a week after she had that conversation with Rasheed at the park—her determination had faltered immediately when she stepped out of her gate. She hadn't considered where she wanted to go, but had blindly headed to the road on foot. She walked for miles, looking over her shoulders and hugging hedgerows when cars passed, which they did with decreasing frequency as evening drew in. Then, as the cold air began to settle on her, she felt calmer, and was even beginning to forget her fears when she heard a car behind her. She stepped onto the grass verge and turned away from the road so it could pass, but instead of disappearing around the corner like the others, it slowed to a halt about five meters in front of her. Blood had begun pounding in her ears and, without thinking, she turned and ran. She had run so far before she realized she couldn't hear the car anymore, and when she looked over her shoulder—the movement almost unbalancing her—it was gone.

She had not left the house after that.

"Ife, honey." George came to sit beside her.

She felt his arm going around her back, the firmness of his hand on her shoulder holding her against him.

"I'm sorry for snapping at you. I just don't know what to do anymore," he said in a softer voice. "I want you back. I want my woman back."

She nodded. "I understand," she said, lifting her chin to look at his face. "Dad has been calling to know what's going on."

"Is he back already? I thought he extended his medical visit?"

"He's still in India." Unfortunately, her father wouldn't be making it to her brother's memorial service. "But he's worried. He's insisting I move back to the house where his guards will keep an eye on me, since I refused him sending some of them over."

"It's not necessary. I can take care of you," George blurted. "And you should get back to your business because...I mean...why will you allow your salespersons—strangers—to be running it now while you are here hiding like a mouse in a hole because someone is trying to freak you out? Okay. If it helps, I'll be moving around with you from now on.

"George, I don't think it's—" He was right. She should get back to living her life. She shouldn't allow burgeoning fear, like a crack in a windshield that grew with every bump in the road, to ground her. God! She was going to lose everything that mattered to her if she continued like this. "Okay. But you don't have to follow me around. That would be too much trouble."

"Trouble? Ptua. It's my job to protect you. In fact, I'll be attending your brother's memorial service with you today."

"George. That would be nice." She knew how much he hated being around her family, and now he was offering to attend the event—to endure the unabashed disregard just because of her? "Mum would be pleased."

"Cut the bullshit. Your mother doesn't like me. Stop trying to make it look like she would be treating me like anything more than the gold-digger she thinks I am."

"That's not—"

"True? Ifechukwu. You should know better than to patronize me. See, I'm doing this for you."

"I know. Thank you," she said.

"But I have an important business to attend to first. You have to wait for me to come back so we can go together."

"The service starts at eight."

"I'll be back before then."

"Hmm." She took a breath as his hands fell away from her shoulder.

"Now you must go back to sleep," he said, stifling a yawn.

The day Ife learned of her brother's death, she stopped drinking. It wasn't a deliberate choice; she didn't consciously decide to turn over a new leaf. Instead, it was a visceral reaction—a deep revulsion toward herself and the situation. Her grief was so overwhelming that drinking no longer provided solace. She knew she had to change.

But now, sitting on the sofa and nursing a cup of coffee while waiting for George to return, she felt a persisting fear that came with a nudge for a strong drink.

"Did you talk to the police?"

The black and tangy beverage in her mouth made a hurried pass down her throat, almost choking her. Coughing and lifting her teary eyes up, she saw him—Rasheed— standing by the door. He looked tousled. His hair unbrushed, his shirt flew out from his black trousers.

"How did you get in here?"

"You are a wreck."

Same as you, she wanted to say, but the way he looked her over made her imagine how tired and disheveled she must appear.

"Ife, did you speak to the police?" He reflectively moved the bottom of his shirt, maybe to slip his hand inside his pocket, and she saw the pummel of a dagger, that same one she saw on his desk the day she was at his office.

"It's not what you think," he said, concealing the weapon under his shirt again as he read her expression. "It's something...I brought it along just for...I'm not going to hurt you—anyone with it."

"How did you get in?" A brief look down at her cup of coffee and she realized how anxious she was. Her fingers around the chinaware were fidgeting. She leaned forward and dropped it on top of a side stool.

"You didn't instruct your gateman not to let me in."

That was true. She didn't think it was necessary because she hadn't expected he would show up in her house again. Biting her lip, her eyes darted around, then settled back on him.

"So, did you?"

"What?"

"Go to the police?"

"No."

"*Kai! Yanmata.* This isn't a joke!"

"I don't take it as a joke, I just want to understand what's going on! George said it's nothing—"

"George," he scuffed. "Of course, he wouldn't want you running to the police."

"George knows—" Ife paused and took a breath. The truth was she wasn't sure George knew anything or had a plan on how to find out what was happening to her. He didn't even believe someone was after her life! And she didn't want to go to the police yet. They might dismiss her fears like George did. Even if, out of reverence for her father, they chose to carry out an investigation, there was little or nothing for them to work with. This thing required something other than intuition, suspicion and logic. "What are you doing here, by the way?" she asked, her eyes lowering, a second, to the side of his pocket where the weapon was hidden.

"Something happened many years ago, when we were kids." Rasheed said, moving closer, "I've held on to that memory for a long time."

Something about the tone of his voice and the way he looked at her—with a sadness that spoke of a man in love yet unwilling to commit—along with his gestures, made Ife realize, as she stood up, that despite the unpleasant events of the past few weeks and despite his role in the fear tightening around her, she wanted him there. In her space. Even though she was scared of him.

He told her about a man who was dragged to a river by his wife and stepson. He was twelve when it happened. She listened as he spoke of water up to his waist, of pressing his knee into the man's back, and of the man's cries. He had witnessed the murder—had played a part in it.

She listened with a slow-burning shock, too afraid to speak, fearful that any interruption might make him stop. Yet, as he talked, her thoughts kept drifting to the little bird and the shadow of something else: a cage on the seat of the car parked in his premises, the fluttering of wings.

"The last thing you want to do right now is stay here," Rasheed said.

"You killed someone," she whispered.

"I didn't...he was already dead when I got into the water—"

"You murdered a man."

"You have to believe me. Please, try to trust me."

"I can't." She felt the notch around her neck tightening, and her stomach dropped as if she were at the top of a roller coaster. "I can't. I can't!" The feeling didn't go away. It stayed, making her heart race, her thoughts spiral out of control, her chest ache. "You killed someone."

His eyes remained on her face. Then his brows furrowed in disappointment. "That woman was going to kill me. I was scared, Ife. I was only a boy. I didn't want to die."

"You should have run."

"I should have, but I was scared. I thought...I thought...I was never strong enough, Ife."

She didn't miss the hint of embarrassment in his voice as he admitted he'd not always been this man—this stubborn, daring man standing before her. "What are you really doing here, Rasheed?"

"When you told me about the dead bird, I knew I had to talk to you."

"Talk to me?"

She saw his hesitation, the way his eyes passed over her to somewhere behind, the way his mouth bunched into a pensive pout when he exhaled, and she began to feel the quickening of anticipation.

"It's you. You sent it, didn't you?"

"One day," he began, ignoring her question. "A few weeks before Salma was murdered, I walked into her room and saw her sitting at her dressing table, looking like she'd just seen a ghost. She was so pale, her skin almost white. I thought she was ill. I asked if she wanted a pain killer or if I should take her to the hospital, but she sat there, not moving, staring at the table in front of her. And that was when I saw it."

"What?"

"A bird. A dead bird."

Ife's heart stopped.

"Someone had sent us a dead bird in an envelope. It was lying there on the table in front of Salma, this tiny little thing, the claws drawn up like it had rigor."

"What kind of bird was it?" Ife asked, her voice cracked.

"I don't know. I didn't take time to check. I just swiped it off the table and... and... discarded it. I didn't want Salma to think too much of it. But it made me remember eighteen years ago. That night I walked through that bush...there were birds...I didn't see them, but I heard them chirping."

"You think it's connected?"

"I've gotten a similar package delivered to me before. After I... after...that was why I dropped out of the university and lied to my father when he found out. I lost a lot of years, Ife. My father disowned me. And my mother...you can't imagine how disappointed she was. She took ill some months after—my *Inna* told me."

"You-you didn't tell them what really happened. Why?"

"I was so scared. I wasn't supposed to talk about that night or someone would get hurt. That woman threatened me for years and when she died, I thought it would stop but." There was this fear...this regret in his eyes. "Ife, I know who is doing this to you. What I don't understand is why?"

A soft line had formed between his brows as he studied her. Ife could feel emotion roiling within him. She too was jumbled, her inside a total chaos, a mixture of confusion and concern. "This person, you think... you think he killed Enitan, Fola's husband? You know Fola, right?"

"Yes," he said with resignation.

Ife was relieved, a little grateful to him even for finally admitting that he knew Fola. "How? I mean, tell me what is going on with her. Everything. She's been getting threat notes and then her husband was murdered and—"

"I don't know," he interrupted. "See, I made a mistake with Salma. I was so carried away trying to figure out what to do after that bird was sent to us. Salma wanted us to return to France. But I wanted to put an end to it once and for all. She suspected that there was something I wasn't telling her and insisted that I told her. But I couldn't. I wanted to protect her. Then I came home one night and found her—" He closed his eyes and sighed deeply. There was a strange mix of pain and relief etched on his face. "I found her dangling on a rope tied to the roof of our garage." Something had transformed in him when he finally opened his eyes and said, "She was murdered. I can swear with my life. I could have saved her, but I didn't. You don't want to imagine what that did to me."

"Oh God," Ife said, looking around the room. She didn't

want him to see how shaken she was, to witness the fear that was crawling up from her toes, the sickness and panic that were colonizing her whole body.

But she was late. He sensed it and took her hands in his, leaning his face closer to hers. "I don't want a repeat of that mistake with you."

It wasn't only what he said that she was disturbed about, but how irrespective of herself, she could feel the warmth of his hands on her skin.

"I didn't kill anyone. Not that man that night, not this Enitan you are talking about. I have never even set my eyes on Fola's husband."

"I don't know if you are telling the truth." It was still difficult to believe him even though she wanted to. God! She so wanted to trust someone.

"I swear with everything in me, Ife."

"Rasheed, this whole thing—"

"I want you to believe me."

"Why?" It would take more than his plea to get her to believe that he was telling the truth. Yet looking at him, seeing for the first time his vulnerability, she couldn't help but think of the weak boy he described earlier, the boy that walked into the bush and witnessed—was forced to participate in a murder. And just for a moment, she forgot her panic and the weapon in his pocket that had added to it. "Why is it important that I believe you?"

His hands, still holding hers, felt suddenly heavy, and she could feel something changing in the air between them.

"Because it will mean so much to me to have you believe me. I-I'm beginning to care so much about you. I am hoping that you could look at me with a little... a little trust."

"You really care about me?"

He made a sound that was meant to be laughter but came

out strangled and strange. "I haven't given in to romantic feelings in a long time." His hand left hers and moved under her chin, tipping it up. "I've always fought it because I know I'm damaged. Too ruined. I shouldn't be getting emotionally involved with any woman. Not after my stubbornness cost me Salma. But then I met you, and my heart—every part of me—revolted." His expression softened as his fingers brushed her cheek.

His fleeting touch sent an exciting sensation through her, lodging in her heart and, shamefully, in her core. She could tell from the measured way he was breathing, holding himself so carefully still, that he was trying not to let this moment lead to something intimate. She too feigned stillness, yet every inch of her was waiting, poised for what might happen if one of them made a deliberate move to lean even closer.

Be careful, her mind reprimanded her. *Don't be fooled.*

You shouldn't allow him to touch you. Don't allow yourself to feel.

Not now. Your life is in danger.

It was dangerous being alone with him. Isa was at the gate post, Salewa had gone to the market, and Bashiru had stepped out to see some friends. Yet, his presence, the intimacy of his body brushing against hers with every little movement, made it difficult for her to want to escape. "Enitan," she began, breaking the dense atmosphere. "Fola's husband. He was murdered. You know about it, right? What does he have to do with this?"

He shook his head. "I don't know."

"And Fola?"

"Hers is a long story."

Please," she pleaded. "I don't want to die."

"I won't allow that," he whispered, lowering his face to meet hers.

She thought he was going to kiss her, and feared it wasn't the right time—it was wrong, so was the sudden hunger for his mouth that grabbed her.

"All I ask is for you to trust me, even if only a little."

A mild brush of his lips against hers and instantly, her breath caught like a minute grasped instead of recklessly spent.

She let out a small, startling sound that made him draw back a fraction, but his hands remained on her. Inhaling deeply, she pulled in his scent, like a cup of coffee on an empty stomach, making her feel slightly lightheaded and longing for a place where her scattered mind could find stillness. She grabbed his shirt and pressed her lips to his, desperate to draw truth and possibly comfort, from deep inside him. The kind of comfort that might slow down, perhaps even stop, the tornado of her fear.

It was an invitation that thrilled him.

Unlike the first time, he didn't move fast. Instead, he nibbled, moaning her name softly against her lips, as if expecting her to push him away with a scowl. When she didn't, he plunged his tongue into her mouth, seeking hers with a desperate intensity.

She knew she shouldn't be feeling anything but alarmed.

He is a killer

Unconfirmed

A psychopath out to destroy you.

She was not sure now.

He had a dagger!

But he was kissing her like she'd always wanted to be kissed. Hard, soft, moist, hot, and breathy. His mouth, combined with the way his hand was sliding down her arm, was too much. Reasoning was slipping away. She whimpered, and as soon as the sound left her throat, he gently pulled away.

"You have to trust me. I want you to trust me."

"Rasheed, I—" The rest of her words were lost as he recaptured her lips.

She hadn't had time to think about that first time, in his office, where he made her taste heaven from his mouth. But she knew he had succeeded in burying something deep inside her that day. Something that sat almost hidden among the other unsettling emotions that had been raging inside her these past weeks.

Like a man eager to prove something, Rasheed wasn't just kissing her, he was peeling himself layer by layer so she could touch, with her tongue, the brokenness locked out of reach, his fears and regrets buried deep within. He was letting her reach that soft, delicate part of him she was sure he'd kept away from everyone.

He pulled away and his eyes made a quick pass around the room. "I wish things were different."

"Tell me about Fola. Why is she being threatened? Why was her husband killed?" she demanded.

"Ife, I can't—"

"Tell me now."

"Some things are better left hidden for now, until the time is right."

Hidden he said? Yet he wanted her to trust him. To believe everything he told her. "If you are not the one that sent the dead bird, then who did?"

"I can't tell you that either."

"*Eish*, Rasheed! Tell me something."

"I wish I could but...telling you—" He grabbed her face, his eyes searching hers.

"Tell me, damn you!" she sobbed, hitting his chest. "Tell me, please!"

"George! George is the man behind all of this."

Her soul deserted her immediately. She saw nothing, felt nothing. When her soul returned, the first thing she felt was the notch around her neck cinching to a strangling point.

"No." It couldn't be. It didn't make a single sense. George? Her own George? "That's not true." Of course, it was not. She felt laughter pushing its way out of her mouth.

When Rasheed didn't say anything, she sobered up and it was her turn to search his face. This wasn't a joke. He meant it. "You are not joking," she said.

He shook his head.

"Rasheed." she swallowed hard. "You are lying!"

"I will not lie about something like this. It was him eighteen years ago. Him and his mother."

"H-he killed his stepfather?"

"Three of us knew what happened that night. His mother died some years later—drug overdose, I heard. I didn't see George again until I entered the university. It was the same university he was in. I didn't know. I got to know when I started getting threat notes. He wanted to know if I told my father or any other person about that night. No matter how many times I told him that I didn't breathe a word of it, he was never convinced. Unfortunately, I was still the same boy I was that night; weak, a coward. And he knew. He used it against me. Like his mother, he threatened everyone I love; my father, my mom, *Inna*. He told me he and his friends would sneak into my house and slash everyone's throat."

At first, it was impossible for Ife to connect the tall, athletic built man with *the devil may care* outlook, standing before her, to the lily-livered young boy Rasheed just painted. It was ridiculous even to imagine him being bullied. But as she carefully observed him now while he spoke, noticing the tiredness in the set of his shoulders, a kind of fear at the edge of his gaze, she knew he wasn't lying. Something might have happened to change him, something strong enough to make him metamorphose into this man, but there was still that frightened young boy that couldn't stand up for himself eighteen years ago lurking somewhere inside the Rasheed standing before her now.

"Your mother—is she still sick?"

"She suffered a stroke," he said dryly. "Dad wanted to fly her abroad for further treatment when she wasn't getting better, but she refused. Dad had to call me back home as his last resort to convince her to travel. It worked. Both of us left for France. That's where I met Salma. She was my mum's nurse. Five years older than me. Such a great lady... she helped me with schoolwork. She was so good with debugging, so good that I wondered why she chose nursing instead of computer software engineering." He heaved a sigh. "But my relationship with my dad didn't get better. In fact, he blamed me for mum's sickness. If not for mom, he wouldn't bother looking for me. I lived every day of my life with the guilt of that single decision to leave school...that pain of being hated by my own father, of knowing that one single explanation would have changed how he felt about me and yet couldn't say anything because...I simply couldn't."

She watched him pick her cup of coffee, "Can I drink this?" he asked. When she nodded, he twirled the black liquid and brought the cup to his lips. He was anxious, his hand fidgeting. Somehow, she felt he had a lot more to say but wasn't sure if he should continue.

"It was Salma's idea that we came back to Nigeria after our marriage. We got another nurse for mom, and I was overseeing Hantech's Nigerian branches remotely, so..." he shrugged.

"She felt it would be nice to just, you know, she's not been to Nigeria before. I didn't want to come back here, not in a thousand years. But for her, I was willing to put my anxiety away." He sipped again from the coffee. "She liked it here. She even got a job at the teaching hospital." He gave off a sad chuckle. "My anxiety was dispersing everyday as I watched her blend into the environment. At one point, I thought...maybe...coming back wasn't such a bad idea. Then one day, after a year or so, I got an unexpected call that reminded me that I've not escaped him—George. He knew I was back. He knew about my wife. He had been waiting for my return. Waiting, Ife. That bastard was waiting for me."

"What if..." She started as he downed the remainder of the coffee and dropped the cup.

"Mm-hm?" He wiped his mouth.

There was something about hearing a shocking, unpleasant revelation. It knocked you out, Like a sucker punch in the stomach, or a blow on the head. And when you got revived, you wished you shouldn't have probed, that you should have remained in the dark. "What if—" She'd wanted to lay the *what if* cards: what if everything Rasheed told her were lies? What if it wasn't George who drowned the man but Rasheed. The notes, the dead birds, his wife's murder, Enitan, what if Rasheed was behind them all?

What if he wasn't the desperate voice crying wolf but the big bad wolf himself hiding in a sheep's clothing?

Just as she was about to take a few steps away from him, she felt it—the strong nudge of curiosity, of suspicion. "Why didn't you go back to France when George started with you again? After your history together, his threats. Why did you stay even when your...Salma wanted you guys to leave?"

"I was no longer a boy. I've grown into a man and men don't run away from troubles. I was determined to fight him.

To hurt him because he wronged me. He and his mother ruined me. I wanted to get back at him in any way. I was ready to fight. Besides, I had a family, a wife."

"The more reason you should have left. You had a family, a wife to protect."

"A vengeful man thinks of getting even first before any other thing. That was my mistake. I thought it was the right time to make that *Banza* pay." He swallowed and looked away.

"You chose fight over protecting your wife?" When he didn't answer she continued. "Your determination to get even cost you, Rasheed. You lost your wife. And now you are back again. George said you contacted him first. On Facebook. Why? Why did you even come to my engagement party that night?"

"To achieve what I wasn't able to achieve the other time."

"To make him pay?"

"I don't forget the wrongs done to me."

"Why didn't you go to the police?"

"There are other ways of getting justice than going to the police."

His statement rattled her inside and the claws of suspicion that gripped her made her think of the weapon in his pocket for a moment. "Y-you seem like a good man."

He gave off a bitter laugh. "You don't even know me."

No, she didn't. That was why it surprised her that she could think him a good man even when there were a lot of unanswered questions about him. A lot of things she should be worried about.

"I'm no longer the coward I used to be those years, Ife. And I want to prove that to George." he allowed a brief pause. "I want to play his game. This time I lead, and he follows until he steps into my trap."

"I'm the bait I guess?"

His silence settled and hovered and remained for much more than a moment. "No," he said finally.

"Really? Then what is this? What am I doing in the middle of your vindictive plan? Tell me, Rasheed, what are you doing with me?"

"I didn't know I'll meet you—that I'll develop this..." he splayed his hand in exhaustion. "Getting attracted—drawn to an Igbo lady, a Christian for that matter, was the last thing I told myself I would ever do. If there was any faith I had in your tribe and religion, George killed that. But when I set my eyes on you, I couldn't let you go."

"You know what? You are not making sense right now."

"How can I be making sense when you, *Masoyiata,* are the beginning of my insanity?" he said. "Besides, I fear what George will do to you. I've seen him hurt women. What he did to Salma, I don't want a repeat of that."

She turned her back at him. Her heart was pounding like persistent waves against a crumbling cliff, her body swamped in heat. All these years she'd been with George, there was nothing that indicated him capable of murder. In those years, he'd only smacked her twice. No, three times. But those times were moments of extreme anger, and jealousy. He was quick to apologize on those occasions.

"I care so much about you, Ife. And I swear I will rip his heart out of his chest before he even thinks of hurting a single strand of your hair."

Sixteen

IT DIDN'T STOP as she stepped off the taxi with her backpack—the sense of displacement she felt when Rasheed left her house. The same feeling that made her book a ride, pack a few things, and leave for her mother's place without waiting for George. A crack in her form, she must call it. Her mother saw it too.

"Ifechukwu." Her mother had pulled her into a hug immediately she walked in through the gate. "You look a little out of place," she said.

But there was no time to explain what was going on because her mother needed to attend to some guests.

Ife's eyes moved in the direction of the policemen in uniform, guns in their hands, their gazes hard and unrelenting, while making her way towards the entrance porch where Ozioma, her elder sister was waiting.

"It's like a war zone," Ife said, stepping into her sister's embrace.

"Dad's gift." Both women stood in silence, looking around. The security presence was everywhere in the compound and outside where cars and buses lined the walkway. "Typical of him not to show up for his family, but wants to choke us with his affluence," Ozioma hissed.

"You know he would have been here if he was strong enough. He lost a son too. He has not gotten over the grief."

"He would have tried to be here. He can go back to India later. It's his son's memorial we are talking about."

Apart from her sister being swamped by wariness, probably due to the whole drawn-out rigmarole surrounding the memorial service, Ife noticed that something had changed in her sister since the last time they met—which was during her engagement party. And while she couldn't place her finger on what it was, she knew enough to draw back from asking her sister. Not while she bore her own burden of fear.

"Let's get inside," Ozioma took her hand.

Ife glanced over her shoulder and saw three policemen entering the compound. For the first time since leaving the house, she considered Rasheed's suggestion to arrange security guards for her. He also suggested that she confided in her father completely, allowing him to handle the situation from his end. This came after she had declined Rasheed's offer to send her to his house abroad until it was safe to return. However, her father was very ill. She didn't want to worsen his condition. As for Rasheed arranging security guards for her, she was hesitant. What if he was the one who had committed the murder eighteen years ago and was now trying to cover his tracks? What if he was the dangerous one framing George instead?

Ife exchanged pleasantries with a few guests and followed Ozioma up the steps to her room. Ozioma jammed the key into the lock and with effort, turned it. They threw their weights against the sticking door so that they burst into the room.

"When was the last time somebody entered here?" Ozioma asked, panting.

The first thing Ife noticed was that someone had opened the windows, which was a relief. Stepping inside and flicking on the lights. Her Secondary school graduation suit was laid out on the table, wrapped in plastic, cleaned and ironed. "Mom." She smiled to herself at her mother's thoughtfulness.

"She never stopped missing you, Ife."

"She didn't want me."

"You thought she didn't want you, but you are her favorite. You've always been. Sometimes I get jealous of how both our parents could give you so much love while the rest of us have to grapple with what is left."

"You know it's not true. Mom loves you more." There were no more plants in the room, no pets—she used to have a dog Bruno. She took him along when she moved out with her father. Unfortunately, the mastiff died and she got a puppy, May. May died too. Everything in the room was exactly as it was when she left. But it felt different now. "Did you ever sleep in this room when I left?"

"No, mom wouldn't allow me. Not that I stayed longer here anyways. You know I was in school when you left. I did return occasionally. Then I got married the same year I graduated."

"Someone has been cleaning it."

"The housekeeper. Mom must have instructed her to do so. You never visited, Ife."

It had been several years. "I keep in touch with everyone. With Mom." Ife knew now that wasn't enough. How could she have known her mother still cared so much after she sided with their father when things went south between the couple? When Ife declared in court that she wanted to go with her father, her mother didn't contest it or try to convince her otherwise. In all their phone conversations and text messages since then, her mother had never asked her to come back home.

"Mom would have loved that you come around sometimes. But she understands that dad had you, and probably made you think she didn't want you." Ozioma squeezed her shoulders, then turned to leave. "Get ready for Church service. We are already late," she said, pausing for a while, then asked, "are you okay?"

"Yes, why?"

"You look...uhm...off."

Ife slipped her backpack off her shoulders and ran a hand over her face. "Tired, that's all." The tightening around her neck had returned also. "Being here brings back Uche's memories."

"*Eziokwu*. That is ehn." Her sister allowed a few seconds' silence. "What do you think he would have been up to now, if he was still alive?"

"I don't know. Causing mischief and breaking women's hearts, I guess."

They laughed.

Then out of the blue, her sister asked, "How is your fiancé —George? Are you still getting married to him?"

With that question blood came pounding in Ife temple. She wanted to tell Ozioma everything. At least Ozioma would know what to do. Her sister had always known the right thing to do in ugly situations. But something in Ozioma's expression made Ife draw back. "I don't know," she said rather. "We are slowing things down for now."

"Hm," Ozioma said and faced the door. "Get ready fast."

"Will do."

"Don't keep everyone waiting. Mom will not like that."

"I can come later to church."

"Mom wants all of us to be part of the procession."

It happened several minutes after Ozioma left.

An envelope slid beneath Ife's door.

Groggy from a sudden headache that felt like a hangover, she walked barefoot across the floor to pick it up. A brown envelope. It seemed ordinary enough until she turned it over in her hands and saw her name scrawled in blue marker. A lurch of recognition hit her in the stomach.

Sweating as she braced herself for another disturbing delivery, she opened the envelope and looked inside.

It contained a stack of documents—printouts from the internet. Taking them back into her room, she spread them out on her bed. They were images of mutilated, lifeless bodies, milky white limbs stained with crusty blood, and faces frozen in open-mouthed stillness. Some images were blurry and indistinct; others had shocking clarity.

Standing in her underwear, Ife pored over each page, each image, then dropped them onto the bed, fear and confusion washing over her like an unwanted intoxication. Her mind teemed with thoughts, each clambering over the last: Who uploaded this stuff on the internet? Who searched for it? Who were these people whose death masks were being circulated online? And, overriding all other questions, who was sending them to her?

She immediately remembered Enitan's battered, lifeless body, and her thoughts quickly shifted to the story Rasheed had told her about the man who was drowned eighteen years ago. For a moment, the train of thoughts brought apprehension back to her. She tried to convince herself that this had nothing to do with that story or Enitan's death—that maybe this was just a coincidence. There must be some sick person with a mobile phone, angry at the world, who had decided to take out their bile on her because she was a rich kid, just as George had said.

Her conviction deserted her when she turned to the last two pages. These weren't gleaned from the internet; they were photocopies of old newspaper clippings. One featured a grinning Enitan with his big front teeth and bespectacled eyes. Beside it was a more pronounced picture of his mutilated body. Seeing that gruesome image again after many weeks sent a jolt through her, bringing every muscle and sinew alive with tension.

The other clipping showed a beautiful white woman with an amazing smile. Beside it was another horror: details of her suicide. Nerve endings prickled like a rash over Ife's skin as she stared at the woman she didn't recognize until she saw the name, Salma Rabiu Lawal, printed in black.

Scrawled in blue marker on the clipping was another note:

Rasheed's wife.

Until now, Ife didn't know what the woman looked like; she had never thought to find out.

But someone had done that research for her.

Fear now filled the room, like a malevolent presence perched on top of the wardrobe, its fatal gaze fixed on her, watching her reaction. The papers trembled in her hands, and the belt around her neck felt suffocatingly tight. She couldn't move, nor could she look away as her brain began to process this latest "gift" from her anonymous correspondent. Slowly, she started to make the connection.

Someone was after her life for reasons she didn't yet understand.

And that someone had followed her to her mother's house.

***

The service had already begun when Ife got to the church. She joined the others in the hush of the heavily air-conditioned auditorium and sat on a fold-out chair while trying to bring her breathing under control. She didn't know if it was the AC, but she was feeling chilly and strange and jumpy as a cat. Ozioma glanced across at her— a scowl in her gaze— and all at once, Ife's suspicion was aroused. Why was Ozioma looking at her? What did she know?

Staring at her knees, Ife pushed down the paranoia that kept rising inside. Still, it was there. Fear cementing in her gut, lodging itself within her.

The priest was talking now, and Ife tried to keep up, but it was so difficult with this pain in her guts and all these people in the auditorium she barely knew. She was about to return her gaze to her knees when something caught her attention. A familiar hair color mix. The owner turned and...

Rasheed?

W-what was he doing here?

He had his back to her, his shoulders tensed. She thought of the way his eyes narrowed when their gaze connected some seconds ago, the coldness in those dark orbs. Did he know about the package that was slid underneath the door of her room?

Did he send it?

That single thought gave her a kind of floating feeling, like her heart was beating somewhere outside her chest.

God, she needed a coffee. No, something stronger.

Her mother stood behind the lectern, reading a speech from a sheet of paper spread in front of her. Her voice was so low in the mic that Ife had to strain to hear her.

Perhaps it wasn't her mother's voice that was low but rather her mind blacking out as the belt around her neck tightened to the point where she could scarcely breathe.

Her chair scraped against the floor as she stood up. She

was certain eyes followed her, but she didn't stop until she was outside.

"Ife!"

He was following her.

"Ife, hold on!"

She couldn't tell if it was the fear crawling inside her or the confusion over Rasheed's presence that caused her to falter and drop her bag. As she bent to pick it up, it hit her: Rasheed had always shown up at odd moments in her life. That meant he must be stalking her.

With that realization, everything around her blurred.

"Let me," he said.

His hand was under her elbow, helping her up, guiding her out of the gate as she gulped in lungfuls of air. She was acutely aware of him—the steadiness of his hands as he seated her in a car, the calmness of his voice as he told her to wait there. She heard him leave, and a few minutes later, he was back.

"Here." He offered her a cup.

She didn't ask what it was. Taking it from his hand, she closed her eyes, tilted her head back, and drank it all.

"Better now?" he said, and she opened her eyes to him.

"*Kismet*. Arabian tea," he added, cradling a tea flask.

He kept a steady watch on her, his eyes frank and appealing. There was a weariness about him, a premature hunch of the shoulders, wrinkles ran across his forehead as if all the sins he'd ever committed had chosen that day to haunt him.

She looked again at his flask. "Someone sent me a package today. Pictures, newspaper clippings and worse." The words petered out.

He had placed the flask in the car's cupholder and was now staring at the steering wheel, but she could see how stunned he was by this news. The expression on his face was like he had just witnessed an accident.

For a moment, her conviction that he might be the one tormenting her faltered.

He took his *Tangaran* cap off and lowered his head into his hand. She heard his voice, low and choked, saying, "*Hasbun-Allah waa ni'mal Wakil.*" He let his hands drop and she saw the strain of confusion on his face. Once again she thought of that weak little boy he said he once was.

"*Na shiga uku*. I told you to let me help you leave this—"

"How would I have made it out of this country in less than two hours?" she interrupted. "Besides I thought I was safe here. Look around you, there are enough armed-to-the-teeth security men to fight a battalion of bandits, yet I got the package slipped under my door."

"Crazy," he muttered, pulling the flask from the holder and taking a swing. "Ife you should talk to the police. Let me report this to the police. At least that would slow things for a while and buy me more time to conclude what I'm working on."

She couldn't help but feel disappointed with his response. Maybe she was expecting him to say something different, to admit to something.

"How did you get to know about the memorial service?" she asked.

If he was surprised by her question, he didn't show it. Instead, he said, "I found out about your brother. I knew you'd be here—you wouldn't want to miss your brother's memorial service."

Something about his words spiked her suspicion again, and she had an overwhelming desire to leave, to breathe real air, not the purified oxygen from his car's AC. But he held her. His hand on her arm was both strong and gentle, making her forget her suspicions for a moment, though she wasn't sure whether she liked that or not.

"George didn't come," she blurted out, hoping he'd understand her point. "We were supposed to come together, but I left him after... after you made me think... believe... after the story you told me. He should have been here nonetheless."

"He isn't."

"Yes, he isn't." What that meant was there was no way George had slid the envelope beneath her room door. When she returned to her father's house, she would ask the housekeepers and security men if George had been seen anywhere around, just to be doubly sure.

Rasheed bopped his head. "If I'm getting you correctly, George cannot be pointed out as a suspect in today's package delivery. And because I'm here—" he gave her a sidelong glance. "Ife, I'm not heinous. I'll never—" he swore under his breath and placed his hands on her shoulders. "I've never thought of doing you harm. Why will I even think of such a thing when I've fallen in love with you?"

For perhaps a split second her panic was suspended, shock taking prominent.

Rasheed must be joking. Ife understood when he said he was beginning to care so much about her, but this? Falling in love with her? Must be a joke. Of course, it was. Only that there was no cocky grin on his face. "What...what did you just say?"

"Falling in love with you was the easy part. Admitting it to myself was the hardest," he spoke softly, his brow furrowed.

She didn't say anything—she couldn't—though she felt words, questions jostling inside her, pushing upwards, threatening to suddenly burst out and break the shock that had her trapped.

"I am so sorry *Masoyiata*," he said, his voice dropping low, a new urgency spilling into it. "You must understand why I'll never dream of hurting you. I'm not asking you to feel the same way for me as I feel for you. Just trust me, even if it's a little trust." He leaned forward and kissed her forehead. She felt the brush of his beard and with it came a lurch of fear, like a foreshadowing of something unseen but terrible. She wanted to hold on to him then and never let go, but he drew back and gave her a weak smile. *"Masoyiata,* I'll find a way to stop this, *insha'Allah."*

She could feel his eyes on her as she got out of the car.

Back in her mother's house, she was told that nobody came looking for her, nobody received a package on her behalf. Without pressing further, she took the stairs two at a time to get to her room and shoved a few things in her backpack. In less than an hour, she was in the car park, determined to leave for a place she hadn't decided on yet.

She threw glances around. There was a woman sitting on the waiting bench reading through papers. Two words in a page of the papers, written in bold caps caught Ife's attention;

Daura, Katsina.

It sounded like a perfect place to go to.

She had been there only once. She and Fola had followed Habibah to the place for the *Gani festival*.

Seventeen

IFE WAS the last to get off the bus.

The park was almost dark and empty, the adrenaline of her departure a distant memory. She pondered on what to do now that she'd arrived Daura. Spending the night in a hotel crossed her mind, but how would she find one?

She looked around and approached a man slumped on a pavement. The man looked up and gave off an angry mutter that made her back away and started walking out of the park.

A handful of people strolled up and down the road—villagers she almost asked for directions—only to draw back when they looked at her with unsmiling faces and eyes holding secrets. Maybe it was in her head, but everyone seemed suspicious.

She decided to play a game with herself instead: she would take every road on the left, no matter where it led. At each crossroads, she would choose the smallest streets, the least traveled options.

Feeling light-headed, almost hysterical, she began to wonder what she was doing. Where was she going? Was this what it felt like to lose one's mind?

Well, she didn't care.

Nothing mattered anymore. Nothing but safety.

She must have walked for miles because her feet had started to ache, and the weariness of everything that had happened to her, and of things she wasn't aware of, was descending on her like the darkness around her.

There must be a river close by. She could hear waves hitting the shore and birds chirping. She looked ahead and squinted to read the caution, *'a river ahead'* from a signpost. Apart from the sound of birds and waves, there was this quietness that made her feel like she was trespassing as she walked along the road.

She was now picking her way down a winding path, feeling invisible eyes on her that made her panic. Her foot slid on a stone, and she let out a gasp. Unbalanced by her backpack, she missed her footing, and bumped, rolling and sliding her way down the rest of the path, damp sand crushing beneath her.

Ife took a breath, waited for something to hurt. But she was fine. And that made her wonder if she had also become immune to physical pain: if her body was not designed to handle both internal shock and physical hurt together. Her hand was throbbing, but at a distance, as if it belonged to someone else.

Suddenly desiring to feel something other than the emotional distress, sense of betrayal and fear she had inside, Ife took off her shoes despite the cold and felt the grain of sand pressing against the sole of her feet.

"I'm still alive," she muttered. But she was tired of walking. She needed to sleep. Finding a good place would be a challenge she didn't think her body was ready for. She looked around and found a tree and walked towards it. She dropped her bag at its foot and sat on it. Leaning her back on its trunk, she closed her eyes and waited for her strength to return.

She didn't know how long it would take.

Ife slapped her ears and slowly opened her eyes. It was morning.

Eish! For the first time, she had slept outside like a vagabond. She stretched her painful, frozen limbs and stood, watching the vivid orange blush spread across the skyline. Despite the light, there was no warmth from the sun, and she shivered.

This had not been a well-thought-out plan. However, in the daylight, it was easier to navigate the narrow path. She noticed that the area was not, as she had thought last night, deserted. About half a mile away, there was a low building next to neat rows of mud houses. It seemed like a good place to go and ask for help.

She approached one of the houses where a woman was sieving blended grains for *pap*. "Good morning," she said.

The woman lifted a charcoal-dark lacerated face to look at her.

"I'm looking for a place to stay," Ife added.

The woman straightened, dipped her smeared hands inside a bowl of water beside her. "*Ka zo kayi hutun ka anan ne?*" she said. "Funny time of the year to have a holiday maker though." A smile taking the sting out of her words.

Ife tried to smile back but her face wouldn't respond. "I'm hoping to stay here for a while. I need some time away from... from."

"Heartbreak? Men and their wahala," the woman

muttered. Her English, though fluid, was heavily laced with an accent. "But it's okay. I'll help you."

"Thank you," Ife replied. That would do. No need explaining to this woman that she wasn't nursing a heartbreak but extreme fear.

"*Kada ka damu,*" the woman said, getting up. "You'll get over it."

Ife nodded, realizing, as the woman looked her over, that she must be so dirty.

"You must have had a rough night."

"Yes," Ife replied. Also, the cold of last night seemed to have reached her bones.

"You need to warm up." The woman shepherded Ife into the house and made her sit on a worn-out sofa before disappearing into another room.

Alone, Ife's eyes roamed the small space. It was clearly intended for no more than two people, at most four. The walls were painted a watery blue. Hanging on the lintel of a door, which led to the room the woman had disappeared into, was a photo of a bearded man with a turban wrapped around his head. The picture opened a portal in Ife's mind, ushering in a face and a name.

Rasheed.

Ife was furious with herself for letting him invade her thoughts at this moment. She was several miles away, yet he seemed deeply lodged within her, like a weight that inhabited her chest. From the beginning, she had noticed the subtle threads of feelings between them, but she had concluded it was just attraction. Mad sexual attraction.

Now, she was confused. There seemed to be something more—something that made her want to cling to all thoughts of him, so she could dream with his taste on her tongue, even when all she wanted was to stay away because she didn't trust him. She didn't trust the sadness that lay beneath his smile, the softness buried inside his hard shell.

She wondered what he was doing now.

Looking for her?

He must have known that she was gone.

Would he be worried? Would he try to find her?

What about George? Ife doubted if George would even notice her absence till weeks have passed. Maybe he would notice but would choose not to bother, typical of him, until her family officially declared her missing.

The thought of being declared missing brought back to her mind what Rasheed told her about George. An involuntary shudder ran down her spine and made her look around self-consciously.

The woman reappeared with a steaming cup and offered it to her. "This will help you get warm."

"I really don't want to—" Ife began to object, but the aroma of hot chocolate and milk wafted into her nose, and she realized she needed not just to get warm but to get something into her stomach. "Thank you," she said, accepting the tea.

"You'll be looking for somewhere to rent then," the woman said, taking the seat beside Ife. "I know a place not far from here. A family used to live there. An incident made them move. Their father left the house one Durbar night and didn't return. Some said he was murdered. His body was not found. I was a kid then. My name is Kubra, I live here with my husband." The woman pointed at the photo on the lintel, her face beaming with fondness.

"He's out to fix a friend's generator. He will be back before nightfall." She took Ife's empty cup, disappeared into the other room again. "I'll call my brother Dauda. He'll help you get a place." She popped her head out from the door and smiled at

Ife. "Don't worry, Dauda *yayana nekuma yana da kyau kuma mutumin kiri ne*. He is really a nice person."

The woman didn't pause for an answer. She vanished again for a few minutes, leaving the notch around Ife's neck tighter. For no particular reason, Ife began to feel uneasy about the place, about the whole village in fact. She sensed a kind of tension spreading around it, emanating from an unseen source. Suddenly, she began to wish she hadn't settled here, that she'd gone farther.

Yet two hours later, she was walking with Dauda, a man with a face so brown and eyelids so puffed that his eyes almost disappeared into it, to go see the house.

"It is far from the road," Dauda said, shocking her with the shift of sound in his English. "But since you said you want quietness—" he shrugged. "The original owners moved away when I was a boy. Their mother left the house key with my mother and told her that someone would come for it. No one came. My mother died. My sister and I cleaned it and had been renting it out to holiday makers. We've not had any in months."

"That's fine," Ife said, but she wasn't sure. There was a heavy pall of restlessness descending on her as she listened to Dauda. And her legs hurt too.

"We are here," Dauda pointed to a house ahead. More like a modified herdsman's hut. It looked like it was once painted white but had long abandoned its battle with the elements and had now turned to dirty gray.

There was something unnerving about the house and its surroundings. Ife was unsure what it was. Maybe it was her paranoia kicking in, or a warning. How could she tell?

"When are you moving in?" Dauda asked as they got to the building.

"Now," Ife said, looking around, her eyes lingering on the

bushes surrounding the place. "I have nothing to move, so I can stay here now."

Eying her suspiciously, Dauda asked, "you can pay, can't you?"

"Yes." Although she had no idea how long the money in her personal account—the only account she could access without a cheque or a token—would last, or what she would do when the money ran out.

Dauda seemed unconvinced. "Do you have a job?"

Ife thought of her business for a moment. "I'm a businesswoman," she said eventually.

Dauda grunted and began to tell her what to do and what not to do with the house. "There's a well behind where you can fetch water from. Be careful with the footstone, it's tricky. You may slip and fall," he said. "You can go to the river instead. The shortest route is through that bush," he pointed backward.

They settled on a rent which, although ridiculously low, would soon race through the money Ife was putting aside in that account. But the house was hers for the next six months and she breathed a sigh of relief when Dauda called out his account number, waited for her to do the transfer and strode out of sight.

She stepped into the house, closed the door and dragged across the stubborn bolt. Despite the sun that had come with vengeance, she drew the curtains, shut every window—coughing at the cloud of dust from their folds. Then she sat on the floor and listened to the sound of her own breathing. For the first time since her hurried departure from town, the panic that had attacked her earlier when she opened that envelope came back.

Ife pulled her knees up, wrapped her arms around them and

pressed her face against the rough denim of her jeans. Although she knew it was coming, she wasn't ready when the wave of emotion engulfed her, bursting from her with such force she could barely breathe. The pain she felt was so physical it seemed impossible that she was still living, impossible that her heart would continue to beat when it seemed like it had been wrenched apart.

She shouldn't have come here. She should have listened to Rasheed and talked to someone: her sister, her mother, even her father who was sick and out of the country would have done something to keep her safe. But each time she tried, she always felt uneasy and muddled, like someone who had mistakenly swallowed a thick swatch of cloud.

The pealing of her phone made her look up. She'd forgotten to turn it off again after transferring money to Dauda. Staring at the table where she had dropped it, she waited for it to ring out, then reached for it.

It was an unknown number.

Out of her inner prompt, she checked her call log; thirty-seven missed calls. Four from Ozioma, her sister. Seven from her mom. Twelve from her dad. Ozioma must have alerted him. There were two from Fola. Strange.

The rest were from George.

None from Rasheed.

Ife felt a fleeting knot in the pit of her stomach as she checked her WhatsApp for voice notes. She was shocked at how much, irrespective of what she thought about Rasheed, she desired that he tried to reach her, that he made the effort at least. Even though she wouldn't want him to find her.

There was a voice note from Ozioma, and another from George; her sister had called him to ask if she was with him, so he wanted to know what was going on.

The last two messages were from Fola. Her voice was low

and scraping, like nails on a blackboard. Broken, thin, and pained.

"Ife, you asked me for the identity of the man behind the notes and Enitan's death. It's him. You were right, Ife, it's him…"

What started as a whisper rose to a scream so high that Ife had to strain her ears to make out Fola's words.

"I came to your place and they said you weren't home. George said he doesn't know where you are. You need to know the truth before someone else dies. Please, call me."

Ife stared at the phone. She didn't want to contact anyone —not yet. Not until she was calm enough. As she had sat on the bus that brought her to this village, she thought the best thing to do was to lose her phone. Maybe when this nightmare was over—if it ever would be—she would get a new one, a new number too, and start her life over.

But Fola might be the one person to tell her the truth. So, with jittery fingers, Ife dialed Fola who picked up almost immediately.

"Where are you?"

Ife hesitated,

"I need to see you. It's urgent, please!"

I didn't know when you left. I waited for you to come home. It was only when I eventually went to the bathroom that I realized your toothbrush had disappeared. I looked for the suitcases and found nothing missing but a small bag.

Throughout the night I sat down thinking about why you chose to leave. You knew I hated being abandoned. We only had a little fight the previous night: you insisted on going to work for your father. You said the pay was huge, that it would help you buy a house for us. But I didn't want a house from your father, I wanted you, just you to myself.

We argued and I smacked you across the face. The shock in your eyes pleased me, and I hit you again, and again, and again, until I was satisfied. Then I left you to go find a bar.

You were curled up on the bed when I returned. You sat up and pushed yourself to the end, backing up against the headboard. There was a wad of bloody tissues on the bedside table, it was like you had tried to clean yourself up. But despite your effort, there was dried blood on your top lip. A bruise was already forming on the bridge of your nose and across one eye. You began to cry when you saw me, and the tears took on the color of blood as they reached your chin, dripping on your shirt and staining it pink.

I sat next to you, and you shivered. "Are you cold, I asked. "Here. Wrap this around you." I pulled the blanket off the end of the bed and placed it around your shoulders. Picked an unused tissue from the bedside table and began to clean your face.

"You are tired, it's been a long day." I kissed your forehead but still you cried, and I wished so much that you hadn't argued with me earlier. I thought you were different, and that perhaps I wouldn't ever need to feel that relief again: that blissful sense of peace that comes after a fight.

I left you to be by yourself the next morning, only for me to return and you were not there.

How could you?

How dare you?

Next day, I went to your father's house, and he said you were never there. He also refused to tell me where you would likely be. But I knew. From the flatness of his voice and the lack of apprehensiveness in his attitude, I was sure he knew where you went off to. And whom you'd likely be with.

These men that he introduced you to at the many political functions he made sure you attended with him, did they offer you juicy positions in their offices too? Did they tell you they were going to make you happier than you were with me?

You disgust me.

But I chose not to bother.

I told myself I was better off without you, and that as long as you didn't run to your pathetic dad with the accusation of what he would no doubt call abuse, I would let you run off to wherever you wanted to go.

I was done running after women and begging them to stay with me. First it was my mother: several nights I watched over her. Several nights I begged her not to succumb to despair.

But she didn't care about me.

All she wanted was her peace.

Such a selfish thing to wish for when you had a needy son.

I helped her get relief. Seven pills dissolved into her drink—she was too wasted to notice—did the job. I watched her struggle, stood by the door and didn't move a foot when she called out for help.

Second was Fola. Just like you, our attraction was instant. I gave her everything. Loved her just the way I loved you. She almost had me believing that she wasn't going to leave, until the day that 'simpy' son of a cow had his birthday. He didn't want me to come, but because I enjoyed watching him turn into a jumpy cat each time I came around him, I made up my mind to go, and mentioned it to Fola.

"Can I come with you?" she had asked.

I would have loved to take her with me, but because I've seen the way ladies leered at the spineless chicken—the birthday boy, the way they behaved around him, I refused. I didn't want to give Fola that chance.

"Please, I really want to follow you," she begged just like you always did. And I gave in.

That was the first time he saw her. But he made no attempt to hide his admiration for her despite the look I gave him. I was appalled *to see her laughing with him when all I expected was for her to roll her eyes at him. He made her blush.*

Throughout our journey back, she was talking about him as if nothing was wrong, as if she hadn't humiliated me enough. My fist furled without instruction when we got to my room, the skin stretching tightly over tensed knuckles as the bubble of pressure expanded in my chest, filling every available space, pushing my lungs to one side. I looked at her, still laughing, still jabbering, and I raised my fist and slammed it into her face.

Almost immediately, the bubble burst. Calm washed over me, like the adrenaline released after sex, or session in the gym. My headache eased, and the muscles at the corner of my eyes ceased to twitch. She made a bubbling, strangling noise, but I didn't look at her. I left the room to go drink some more.

When I got back later in the night, he was with her. I didn't know how that happened, but when I opened the door to my room, ready to apologize to her, I found him there.

Anger boiled inside me. Grabbing the front of Fola's jumper, I hauled her to her feet. The sound of her scream stopped me from thinking straight. I pushed her backward across the room and held her against the wall, my fingers pressing against her throat. I felt her pulse beat fast and hard.

"Don't! stop it!" I heard the 'son of a cow' yell behind me.

Slowly, gently, I pressed my fingers onto her neck, watching my hand squeeze tighter as if it belonged to someone else. She made a choking noise.

"Stop, you're going to kill her!" he cried again.

"Make me." I was enjoying his fear, his anguish. "You want my woman? Come on, make me stop."

He did. For the first time since I knew him, he struck someone. He struck me. I first heard a cackle, then with a flash of pain that started from my left ribcage, I was on the floor, bewildered. He stood above me, panting, his fingers still tightened in a fist.

But he didn't strike me again.

He left the room with Fola.

Guess how I took my revenge on him. Go on, take a guess. You can't? I made him believe I was sorry for all I did to him. Like the child he was at heart, he believed me. Once again, I had him where I wanted. Once again, I began to plan.

He apologized for making Fola leave me, and I told him I had long forgotten about everything that happened back then, that I didn't care about Fola anymore. But I cared, all thanks to you. You helped me find Fola. Because of you, I found my lost woman. But she was married—another sin committed against me. I should have been married to Fola and not that rabbit-toothed nerd she got herself hooked to.

Anyway, I took care of that, didn't I? Just like I took care of that son of a cow's naïve French wife, Salma.

Did you want to know how I started with Salma? How I frightened her for a couple of weeks: Sending her packages. Stalking her and making sure she knew someone was always lurking around?

Oh, that cat and mouse game, always the best part of my plans.

When he came to me with the news that his wife had received an envelope, a death threat—he called it, and wanted to know why. After all, I promised him it would never happen again. I told him I knew nothing about it. It wasn't me. Maybe someone else did it. Someone who knew the secret, who knew about what happened eighteen years ago.

He didn't believe me this time. He was furious.

I knew it was time to toughen the game.

At first, I didn't mean to strangle the white bitch. But it did happen. And Fola should be blamed.

No. Him. He presented me with that option.

Eighteen

THE SCREAM CUT through Ife's sleep, jolting her awake. The sun wasn't up yet but thank God she had electricity— she couldn't bear to feel the darkness around her. Heart pounding, she concentrated on slowing her breathing.

In and out.

In and out.

The silence around her was oppressive rather than calming and her fingernails carved crescents into her palms as she waited for the panic to subside. Her dreams were becoming more vivid. It always started with Rasheed walking her up a cliff where they would stand and watch the sunset enter raindrops and emerge as rainbows; the way their fingers intertwined, as if their hands held memories of meeting in a thousand other lifetimes, felt so natural and right. Then the exciting moment would evaporate like an episode in a dream, replaced by another scene. A nightmare rather; her body floating, hair spread like weed in the water, and a voice in her head whispering: "You are drowned, dead and forgotten."

The nightmares didn't start the day she arrived and settled into her new environment. In fact, she enjoyed a few days of inner peace and tranquility. But now they were here, relentless and unyielding. Each night, after dragging herself out of the horrors, she would lie in bed, playing scenarios in her head:

Was it Rasheed who pushed her into the river?

What were her last thoughts before she drowned?

Did she plead for her life?

Jesus! She found herself mentally walking through her possible end—drowning, one of the worst kinds of death. If she had the power, she would choose a much easier alternative. Perhaps there was a way to dismiss this feeling of doom and everything that had happened to her as just another nightmare. However, she knew this was her stark reality, shaping her present life.

For weeks now, she had been waking up multiple times a night to the sound of her own futile screams.

Making a fist with her hand, she unfurled her fingers, stiff from the night's sleep. Her palm was numb, and two of her fingers tingled with the same sensation. She repeated the process until the feeling improved. Swinging her legs out from under the pile of blankets on her bed—thankfully, Dauda and his sister had left enough to make settlers like her somewhat comfortable—she gathered her permed hair, plaited it into a single cornrow, walked to the sitting room to slide her feet into her trainers, and headed out for her morning jog.

She had never jogged at home, but here, she forced herself to run for miles, feeling lost without her business, without friends, without family. No one to talk to.

Settling into a rhythm that echoed with her heartbeat, she increased her pace, sprinting along the path. The wind whipped strands of hair across her face, and she shook her head to clear it. Running even faster, she felt alive, awake, and safe from the nightmares.

She stopped when she reached the end of the path and saw

the tarred road ahead. As the adrenaline from her morning exercise began to fade, she watched people pass by, their faces unfamiliar. Some turned to stare at her; others didn't care at all.

She was halfway back when she thought of Kubra and decided to check on her. Kubra reminded Ife of the friends and family she had left behind, and the ache of homesickness was beginning to set in. A few days ago, in a fit of frustration, she had thrown her phone into the river, unable to stand its incessant ringing. Now, there was no way to reach anyone, especially her father, who was undoubtedly worried sick.

She wondered again why she had chosen to run instead of seeking help. The answer hit her—the one she had been searching for. She had been too confused, too traumatized, and too distrustful to reach out or open up to anyone. Even now, she wanted to remain hidden. Although she missed her home, her father, and her business, she just wanted to disappear.

She told herself she would send messages to her family or maybe call them when she felt ready.

As she neared Kubra's house, her resolve to visit began to fade. From where she stood, she could see shapes moving in the window. Narrowing her gaze, she saw more clearly: a man —presumably Kubra's husband—was showering Kubra's face with kisses, pushing her hijab behind her ears to whisper something. Kubra's laughter rang out, a sudden explosion of happiness that stirred a deep longing within Ife, pulling her into a reverie. All at once, she was back in Rasheed's office, her back against the wall as he caressed her lips with his. The rhythm of his heart became the oxygen she needed to breathe as his hands stoke fire all over her body and she feared that any form of removal would leave her empty.

Another shrill of laughter from Kubra jarred Ife out of her *wool-gathering* and she ran back to her house. The door cracked open when she touched it. She tried to recall if had left it unlock. She'd been a lot forgetful these days.

She hissed and pushed the door wider.

She'd only been inside for a few minutes when there was a rustle behind her.

"Ife?"

Ife let out a gasp, turned and her body went rigid with confusion. Fola was standing a few feet away from her. How was it possible that Fola was in her house? Ife remembered telling Fola the name of the village, but...that was all!

"The door wasn't locked." Fola shrugged, looking unsure. "I'm so sorry for showing up unannounced."

The women stared at each other, the old clock on the wall ticking crustily.

"It wasn't too hard to find you," Fola broke the silence. "I only showed a few villagers your picture on my phone. The one I took of you on your engagement night. It's a very small village. Everybody seems to know the stranger who just arrived."

"It's beautiful here," Fola said, wrapping her palms around the mug of coffee Ife gave her, looking down at it.

"It's perfect for me." Ife replied, observing the other woman, and thinking that she looked like a fish lacking water. Dry. Sickly. Her eyes sunk so deep inside their sockets. Ife knew she wasn't looking better either, but she wasn't expecting to see Fola looking like an old hag.

"Tiny and cold." Fola looked around, taking in the sparse sitting room. "But I agree with you, it's perfect," she said with a ripple of forced laughter that slopped coffee over the rim of her mug. She gave an ineffective rub at her trousers and the liquid sank into a dark patch on her thigh.

Both women slid into an uncomfortable stillness while Fola drank her coffee.

"Everybody is looking for you," Fola broke the silence. "Your family is offering twenty million to anybody that knows your way about."

"Is my father back?" Ife couldn't help asking.

"I don't know. I only watched the news on TV. Your sister was live on Channels."

They allowed another moment of quietness.

"He deceived you." Fola bent to carefully drop the mug on the floor. Then she leaned back and stared at Ife. "He has always lied."

Ife would have asked who the other woman was talking about, but then she remembered that since that fateful day Rasheed waltzed into her engagement party to muddle her life, everything and everyone had been lying. Even she had been lying to herself. So, she kept mute, while Fola accompanied her statement with a humorless laughter, shaking her head.

"When we first met, he was so perfect—great body, fierce goodness inside him—and a sense of humor. Of course, the sense of humor. But there was something else that drew me to him, that toughness that came from a place of suffering. I could tell that he was lost and bewildered and distrustful of his place in the world, just as I was. He didn't need to ask me twice to date him. I just felt I should. We were meant to be together. But I was wrong. About everything I thought he was—I was wrong."

Fola paused and Ife wondered if she was supposed to say anything, ask a question maybe?

"I discovered a diary," Fola stated, hesitated and continued.

"I was searching his box for my old sim card. He took it one day we had a fight over a number that had constantly called me—you know, one of those things men don't take lightly. Things he wrote about me in that diary...he called me a gold digging, low level, overused flappy vagina. An overused flappy vagina, that's what he wrote about me. He wished I would choose to commit suicide so he wouldn't do it himself —kill me. He wrote about drowning me."

As Fola spoke, Ife's head began to spin as a familiar wave hit her.

"I didn't know how he found out I read the diary and... and... Ife, he's not human. He's a monster. A psychopath."

"Who is he?" A ticker tape began to run through Ife's mind, bringing a striking clarity. Without Fola having to answer, Ife suddenly knew who this man was. She had always hoped the obvious truth wasn't real, because she found herself drawn, like Fola, to the sadness lurking just beyond the man's smiles, his sense of loss, bewilderment, and distrust. But now, it was time to embrace the truth.

A sigh of resignation escaped Fola's lips. Fidgeting, she scratched her head, and for the first time since she had shown up at Ife's house, Ife noticed her cropped hair. Fola used to have very long hair.

"George." Fola murmured.

"What?"

"He was my ex, the one I told you about."

The ticker tape in Ife's head jammed and twisted into a knot. For a moment, she couldn't speak, couldn't breathe. She could only stare, mouth agape. When her breath returned, a sound escaped her throat, more like a laugh of relief than a shocked sob.

Did Fola just say George was the murderer?

George, and not Rasheed?

Eish, Rasheed was right all along.

"I regret ever meeting him," Fola said spitefully, wiping her face with her hand. "Such a bastard. A narcissistic idiot. He told you about me? I was his girlfriend—the most terrible relationship I'd ever been in. Then one day, I met someone else." She smiled at Ife, a grin tinged with nostalgia and the light that comes when one speaks of a loved one. "Rasheed."

Rasheed? "You...you dated Rasheed?"

Fola sat up a little straighter in her seat. "It's not what you're thinking. I wish we had done more...intimate things. But Rasheed wasn't like that—I mean, he was very charming, shy, and subtly flirtatious. He loved the company of women, but he would never take advantage."

Ife wondered, for the first time, how deeply in love Fola was with Abdulrasheed Rabiu Lawal.

"I think he was terrified of George. The way he shrank when George came at him made me wonder if there was something George was blackmailing him for. But he was a nice guy. Really nice. He knows the right thing to say and the right time to say them." The nostalgic look returned to Fola's face. "One night, when George almost killed me in his room after a party we both attended, he stood up for me. That's the very first time I saw him hit George. It felt so good—the shock on George's face, the way he crumbled to the floor like a bag of shit. That was the day I made the decision to end what I had with George. Rasheed helped me take that decision. But no girl leaves George, I learnt that very late. Soon he began to threaten me, sending notes, waiting outside my lecture hall, in front of the hostel. He threatened to harm my friends if I didn't come back to him." Her voice was thinning. "Two of my friends got stabbed and he blamed me. He said I made him do it."

Ife examined the laminated surface of the desk she was sitting on. Her fingers shifted a table knife she left there the previous day to get instinctively to the edge where it was starting to peel away.

"I had the choice of going back to him or leaving the school. I chose the latter. I went to stay with my grandma in the village."

Years later, George found Fola again. Had she really met him on a plane and willingly follow him to bed as she had claimed? How was it possible that after all those years, he was able to pull her strings and manipulate her like a puppet?

"I went back to school after spending two years with my grandma. I worked my way into the University of Abuja. I was so scared he would find me one day." Fola adjusted herself on the couch, running her hand through her hair. "You can't imagine how many times I changed my number. I dreaded walking along the road, always looking over my shoulder, convinced he was trailing me. When I met Enitan, I was able to relax a bit. It took time, but I finally did. I even started to believe that George was a closed chapter in my life—that I could finally move on. But I was wrong. I met you, and you introduced me to him as your boyfriend. My fear resurfaced."

"Why didn't you tell me?"

"Tell you? What good would that have done? I was afraid for you as well as I was for me. There is no escaping George once he has his claws around one's neck."

"You were in contact with Rasheed all the while?"

"I never set my eyes on him or heard from him until that night. Your engagement party. By then, things had gone bad for me. George had me by the neck, worse than before."

"You knew about his wife?" Ife asked. "Rasheed. You knew his wife was mur...committed suicide?" Ife observed Fola's calmness, feeling like an outsider looking in. She congratulated herself for her current composure. Even as she formed questions in her mind, knowing without a doubt what the answers would be. She prayed she was wrong, that this was all a badly told joke.

"It wasn't suicide, Ife." Sweat had broken out on Fola's forehead. "George murdered her."

Ife felt numbness creeping from her feet up her body. "You knew?" She wanted to scream the question, but it came out as a whisper. That was good, in a way. It was better to keep her emotions in check for now and treat this situation like a case study she was investigating, as if she were a detective. An awful, shocking story that had nothing to do with her.

"He threatened me with it. Blamed me for it. It was his punishment to Rasheed for making me leave him." Fola leaned forward and placed her hands on Ife's thighs.

Staring at the hands on her thighs, Ife asked, "And Enitan?"

Fola lowered her face, tears splashing onto her lap. "You have no idea what he's capable of, Ife," she said. "The day you introduced him to me as your man, I was so scared. We'd already met on that plane, and I was trying to stay away from him because...I couldn't do it anymore. You brought us back together. You made him find me again." She swallowed a sob.

"Salma died because...George said it's a debt Rasheed had to pay. Enitan died so I could...so I could—"

"He killed Enitan." Ife could taste her own bitterness like an acid reflux in her mouth. "It's him. And you let him do it. You let him get away even when you should have told the police the truth about him. Why? You would have saved everyone...saved me, you had the chance to do the right thing, but you chose not. Why?"

Fola left a silence that made Ife shiver even before her answer landed.

"Because it was me. I killed Enitan."

The hand Ife moved must have belonged to someone else. Lifting it to cover her mouth became a struggle; it felt heavy and trembled. Her face must have been drained of blood. In fact, her whole body felt numb and devoid of sensation.

"The night Enitan returned, George came to my house. He had a box with him. He said his car broke down somewhere and he had called his mechanic to check it out. Enitan knew him already..." Fola broke into bouts of coughing, slapping her chest to ease the fit before continuing. "He had dinner with us—those were the most torturous hours of my life. I watched him have a decent conversation with my husband. At some point, I relaxed." She laughed, a bitter sound. "I told myself maybe he wasn't here to do us harm." She laughed again. "A few minutes later, he passed me a note under the table. 'He's dying tonight, and it's because of you.' That's what it said. I tried to stop him. I struggled with him."

Fola sounded robotic, as if reading from a script, oblivious to Ife sitting there, listening.

"He thanked Enitan for the food, then got up to get his box. That's when I saw what was inside—the hammer...the same one I saw inside the red car he picked me up in the day you came looking for me. You remember the red Mazda?" For the first time since she started the horrifying story, Fola looked up at Ife. "George struck my husband with the hammer. The blow knocked Enitan out. Then he carried him into the bedroom, laid him on the bed, and hit him again and again on the head before handing me a pocketknife to...to stab him." She turned away, wiping her eyes roughly. "I wasn't going to do it, but he was in my head, screaming that I should. I felt like I was watching another woman lift the knife. He was in my head, Ife."

It didn't make any sense: the room where Enitan's body was found, the note Fola recovered from his body. Fola said she was in church that night and had returned to meet... Jesus! Lord!

"Each time I close my eyes I see it—my Enitan, the horrible thing I did to him," Fola continued. "You know, if there's anyone that deserved to die that night, it's me. I knew what a devil George is."

She knew what a devil George was, the same way Rasheed knew. They had known all along. Yet they allowed him to walk free?

"What else do you know, Fola?"

"What do you mean?"

"You know what I'm asking. Someone was stalking me—you knew, right?"

Fola said nothing, but her gaze faltered like one who was reluctant to tell the whole truth.

"I don't think you are telling me everything, Fola."

"I swear, Ife, I swear!"

"I saw the red Mazda parked inside Rashed's office premises," Ife said. It was just a hunch, an insistent voice of instinct. Ife was certain Fola knew something. She had to know. "The hammer was inside the car, along with a bird in a cage. I've been getting spooky packages, pictures of dead people. Threats. I think you know exactly what I'm talking about."

Fola held Ife's gaze for a moment, then broke it with a small, sad smile. That gesture—a brief, sorrowful smile—triggered a flood of memories for Ife, bringing her back to the day she received the first package.

"It was you," Ife said.

Fola's attention was snagged by the seriousness of Ife's tone.

"My gateman said it was a woman that delivered the dead bird—it's you!"

"Rasheed was going to tell you some ugly things about George and George didn't want that. He didn't want you to leave him."

"Fola, you have not answered me. The jump scares, the feeling that someone was slipping inside my office and my house—"

"He made me do it. All of it—he made me arrange all of them. He said it was to get you scared enough to stay away from Rasheed."

Ife kept her eyes on the woman, at her features she once thought so beautiful. Feeling the need to turn away, to run, yet there was an itch in her brain—more questions that demanded answers.

"You are in contact with Rasheed too."

"No...yes... okay, George forbade me to speak to Rasheed."

"You called him." Ife remembered that day vividly. It was in George's apartment, and Rasheed had rushed out to answer Fola's call.

"Just once. I was confused. I needed help, alright? He gave me his card that day we met at your engagement party. I've also sent him messages just like I sent to you. But George found out and made me stop contacting him. That day, when he picked up the call, I couldn't go ahead to tell him why I wanted to speak to him. I was so scared George would find out and do something terrible to me, to us."

"Who drove the Mazda to Rasheed's?"

"Ehn?"

"The Mazda, who parked it inside Rasheed's premises?"

"George did."

Ife was confused at first. George was supposed to be on his way back to Abuja from Lagos that day—they had spoken, and she was to pick him up at the airport. Unless he hadn't traveled at all, or he had returned earlier than he said. That made sense now. Everything was beginning to make sense.

"When he picked me up the day you came looking for me,

we drove straight to the place. It's easy to get in because he's been there a few times and they know him. He knew you were already suspicious of Rasheed. You'd been asking questions about him. After our encounter that day, he was sure you'd want to go there, so he did his math. He told me you would want to look inside the car once you spotted it, and from what you just said, you did."

Dragging her body like a deadweight, Ife staggered towards the door that led to the room, ignoring Fola's cries for her to wait. Finding the edge of the door, Ife pushed it open, stumbled in, and slammed it shut in Fola's face.

Fola knocked instantly, her hand never leaving the door as she knocked again and again. With each knock, Ife's panic grew. Jesus! She felt the noose tightening around her neck and her entire body shaking uncontrollably.

"Ife!" Fola called out, knocking again and again.

Ife covered her ears with her hands and curled herself into a ball on the bed. But she could still hear it—the sound of knuckles hitting wood. She got up, paced the length of the room, got into the bathroom to sit in the bath she filled with water the previous day. She sank deep, letting the water get to her mouth, her nose, her eyes, until she began to choke and cough so hard. She let her head up and gave in to the tears that started building in her eyes, crying with all physicality she'd never experienced before, doubling over with the sobs that forced their way from the pit of her stomach. When she was exhausted, she got up and walked back into the room, her limbs stiff and cold.

She listened.

Silence.

Fola was gone.

Now what?

The sharp stab of fear that hit her didn't come as a surprise.

But she chastised herself. Finding comfort in the softness of an old jogging bottom and a faded sweatshirt, she folded her wet hair into a bun.

Just as Ife was beginning to feel, if not better, then more composed, she heard a knock on the front door and froze. She waited a few minutes.

It came again.

Fola wasn't going to give up. Ife could stay locked inside all day, and Fola would wait, knock, and shout. The realization filled Ife with hot rage, piercing through the veneer of calmness she had convinced herself was real. She marched towards the door.

How dare Fola? A murderer who recounted stabbing her husband like a bedtime story. Fola had probably realized that spilling the truth wasn't such a good idea and was now desperate to get back inside and kill Ife to keep her secret safe.

The thought rattled in Ife's head like a pinball, firing shots indiscriminately. As a form of defense, Ife grabbed a pair of scissors—the object was in the house when she moved in—from on top of the wooden locker beside the bed. She unlocked the door and yanked it open.

"Here you are." Kubra said. "I thought you were inside the bath or something. You should learn to lock your door dear. This place is not safe for a single woman like you."

Ife saw Kubra's eyes lowered to the scissors in her hand.

"Mai ke faruwa?" Kubra said, looking up at her. "Are you okay? You look like you've seen a ghost."

Nineteen

I HAD A TEMPER.

I was no more or less out of control than you; it's all about the triggers.

We both had one. Just because you kept yours hidden didn't mean it wasn't there. It was better to come clean about it than to let someone else press your button and unleash the red mist.

'Know your trigger, accept and control it.' That was the theory.

Mine was being abandoned. It always pushed me to drink.

I wasn't a stereotypical drunk. You never found me asleep in doorways with piss-stained trousers and a can of beer in my hand. I never rolled down the street, shouting at strangers or getting into fights.

I was what people call a functioning alcoholic.

Smart suits, nothing out of place. Schmoozing naive ladies like you, making them chatter. Smiling at irritatingly skeptical old men like your father.

Money made it easier—your money. You bankrolled my habit without even knowing it.

Dumb you. You didn't even know I was an alcoholic.

Your money meant fancy bottles of Glenfiddich in my car while I drove around Abuja, instead of paper-bag-concealed Alomo bitters that would have caused an outcry. Your money meant I could drink Bloody Marys, gin and tonics, and Pimm's whenever the sun peeked out, without anyone giving me a second glance.

When I started drinking, it was to forget the sense of loss and abandonment in my head. Later, I drank because I couldn't stop. Somewhere in the middle, I lost my way.

That baby trapped me so badly that I needed to feed it. Not with the local beers and bitters sold on the streets—I didn't want to go back to those—but with the expensive wines and brandies your money afforded me.

That's why I came looking for you after I told myself I wouldn't.

It didn't take much effort to find you—not in the house of another man like I suspected, but in your father's house. I knew that old oaf was lying when he said he didn't know where you were. He had managed to convince you to forget me.

But there was one thing you wanted so much, one thing he wouldn't give you no matter how much he tried.

You wanted marriage, domesticity, family trips with your own kids. Only I could give you that, so I made plans. Even though I hated the thought of getting married at that time, I was determined to give you what you wanted.

I walked the length and breadth of Abuja before finding a jewelry shop with the perfect ring—the most beautiful one you couldn't possibly refuse. I handed over my credit card, telling myself you would pay back the money one way or another.

The following morning, I drove to your office with the small leather box burning a hole in my pocket. I waited the whole day for you to come out. I didn't call you. I just waited patiently. I was good at that, waiting patiently.

You allowed me to beg for a few minutes, your face indifferent, as if I was wasting my time. But when I was about to go down on my knees, you pulled me up and into your embrace, squeezing me so tight that I couldn't wait another moment to propose to you.

"Marry me."

You laughed, but you must have caught the sincerity in my eyes, because you stopped and put your hand to your mouth.

"I love you," I said. "I can't be apart from you."

You looked around for witnesses—sure, there were a couple of workers grinning and making videos. When you returned your attention to me, I saw the uncertainty in your face, and I faltered. This hadn't been how I planned it. I had expected you to fling your arms around me, kiss me, cry perhaps, but above all, to say yes immediately. Scrabbling for the jewelry box, I thrust it into your hand. "I mean it. I want you to be mine, always. Say you will, please say you will."

You gave a tiny shake of your head but opened the box, your mouth falling open slightly. "I don't know what to say."

"Say yes."

There was a pause long enough for fear to grip my chest, thinking you might refuse. And then you said yes.

"But I'll not be going home with you today. I want to tell dad the good news."

I hated that you would consider him in this. It made me bitter, resentful, angry. All of which made me wish I had taken some alcohol before coming. Then I would have told you to go to hell.

My trigger was women not doing as I expected.

My mother, Fola, and now you.

You made me want to drink, to lose control, to let my fists fly.

But I didn't want to scare you anymore.

I was grateful you didn't tell your father about me hitting you, grateful that you didn't upload your battered face on social media with the hashtag #FearMen.

And since you chose to be a good girl and forgave me so easily, I might consider controlling my trigger.

You took the ring off after three days, and it felt like a punch to the face. You said your father hadn't taken the news of our engagement well and that wearing the ring would anger him.

"But don't worry, dad will come around soon," you said.

"You should move back with me, so he doesn't keep influencing your decisions."

"He isn't influencing anything," you replied. "I just feel it's not right wearing it around him."

To please me, you began wearing the ring on a delicate gold chain around your neck. But I wasn't satisfied.

I made you pressure your father to accept me. When he didn't, you gave him an ultimatum: either he accepted our marriage, or you would move out of his house again.

You moved out. This time, you didn't move in with me as I wanted, but into your own house—the one you bought with your money. I was okay with your arrangement.

"I need the space," you tried to explain. "Besides, we will soon be married, and you'll be moving in here permanently."

Yet you still didn't wear my ring on your finger. It was no longer around your neck either. "You know you could wear it now," I said one day while we were out shopping.

"I know. But I'm thinking we should have a proper engagement party." You were holding my hand, and I squeezed it tight as we walked around the mall. "I've been thinking about it for a while, and it seems like a great idea. My family will be there... friends..."

I didn't like it, but it was what you wanted, what would make you happy. "Fine, fine. But I still think you should have a ring on your finger. How will people know you are taken?" I couldn't let it go. I stopped you and put my hands on your shoulders. You looked around at all the busy shoppers, trying to shake me off, but I held firm. "How will they know you're with me," I said, "if you're not wearing my ring?"

I recognized the look in your eyes. I used to see it in Fola's—that mixture of defiance and wariness. It made me as angry to see it in you as it did when I saw it in her. How dare you be afraid of me? I felt tense, and when a flicker of pain crossed your face, I realized my fingers were digging into your shoulders. I let my hands drop to my sides.

"Do you love me?" I asked.

"You know I do."

"Then why don't you want people to know you are mine?"

I hurried off to the jewelry section in the mall, found a small box with a ring in it—something flat and plain—and returned to you. Opening the box, I dropped to one knee and held it out. There was an audible buzz from the passing shoppers, and a flush spread across your face. The moment around us slowed as people stopped to watch, and I felt a burst of pride that you were with me.

"Will you marry me?"

You looked overwhelmed. "Yes."

Your response was far faster than the first time I asked, and the tightness in my chest evaporated instantly. I slipped the ring on your finger and stood to kiss you. There were cheers around us, and someone slapped my shoulder. I couldn't stop grinning. This was what I should have done the first time: I should have given you more ceremony, more drama. Women like that.

I was going to give you everything to make you stay with me. I was going to try to act right with you, even though it wasn't in my nature. I was going to try.

When you told me we should stop having sex, I was mad but didn't fight your decision. I didn't even hit you for it—I stopped hitting you because I was beginning to think you were something different, something special.

But you proved to be no different from all the others.

Oh, you think I didn't know about him? That I wouldn't notice the disgusting thing you both had for each other? When I wasn't watching, you let him touch you. What did he tell you to get you into his bed? How sweet were his words?

He made you trigger me. So, I had to start this old game with you —the cat and mouse game. It was hilarious watching you look over your shoulder while you walked the street, jumping at every little sound. Even your own shadow made you scream like an idiot.

But I wanted you to cling to me. This whole game was to get you back to myself.

Unfortunately, you remained ignorant. You didn't see my efforts, did you?

Now he had convinced you to leave me without a word. That was abandonment. That was a trigger.

I will find you and teach you how wrong it is to leave me.

Twenty

IFE'S EYES followed Kubra around as she talked about a retired civil servant who had just opened a daycare downtown and was looking for baby minders.

"You can try your luck with them, earn some money. Unless you have enough to last your whole stay here. How long are you staying, by the way?"

"Four months. Maybe six."

Balancing her Mahndi-covered hands on her hips, Kubra tisked. "That's a long time to spend alone in this place. The silence in this house will kill you."

The older lady hardly sat still while talking.

"You may not need the money, but you have to go out and meet people. Men. *Ke kinga fita za kiyi akwai maza fa a gari.* We have a lot of men here who can help you forget the one that broke your heart. Some *Nyamiri*, Igbos."

Ife felt the pull to tell Kubra the real reason she had come to the village. In one way, it would be great to share what she carried with someone neutral. Eish, the relief of just letting it out. But there seemed to be a heavy object pressing down on her tongue each time she opened her mouth, and a feeling like she was underwater. Kubra sensed it too. Now and then, she would shoot her a concerned look.

"Have you eaten anything this morning?" Kubra asked.

She didn't wait for Ife's reply before dashing into the mini kitchen. "Oh, I see you've stocked this place with stuff."

Ife heard her searching through the cupboard. "No chocolate...no milk...only coffee and noodles." Shortly, Kubra walked back into the sitting room with a cup of coffee. "You need to take it hot," she said. "Why don't you go back into your room and get a little more sleep? You don't look well."

Ife didn't need to sleep. She needed to understand why her life had suddenly taken a terrifying turn.

"Thank you," Ife muttered as Kubra sat beside her. "Thank you," she said again, sipping the hot beverage.

"Toh, it's okay." Kubra's face became serious. "So, tell me why you choose to stay in here all day...you hardly leave this house."

Again, Ife felt the pull—the urge to tell Kubra everything from the beginning. But then the belt around her neck tightened as she thought of Fola's visit. If Fola could find her here, anyone could.

"I'm fine, it's just—"

Kubra's phone began to ring. Glancing at the screen, Kubra gave Ife an apologetic look.

"I know," Ife said. "I'll be fine." No, she would not be okay. She wished Kubra would stay a little longer.

"Don't worry." Getting up, Kubra patted her on the shoulder and walked to the door. "Hey, I'll be going to town with my husband. Do you want me to get anything for you? *Kilishi* and *dankuwa*...you like them, abi?"

The mere mention of *kilishi* should have excited Ife, as it was her favorite snack. The spicy dried beef jerky always brought her joy, unlike *dankuwa*, a mixture of cornmeal and groundnuts—she hated groundnuts. But at that moment, fear had formed a large bubble in her stomach, leaving no space for food. Even the few sips of coffee she managed to drink were yet to settle.

"No, Kubra," Ife dropped the cup of coffee on the table. "I don't need anything."

Kubra held her gaze, confusion shifting to something else, a kind of worry. "You got any family? A brother or sister?"

Ife's hand, holding a towel she had picked from the pile of clothes on the couch, began to shake violently. She dropped the towel and pushed her hands into her thighs, squeezing them between her knees.

She had a family: a father who loved her, a mother who wasn't always there but who she now knew loved her just as much, and a relationship with George that she thought... she thought... Mentally shaking her head, she took a deep breath and was about to let it out when a face zoomed into her mind and became prominent.

Rasheed.

She had not thought of him for days. Now that she did, nostalgia beaded her skin like dew on morning grass. For a moment, while her eyes stayed on Kubra's face, she thought of him, and a familiar warmth flashed through her.

Abdulrasheed Rabiu Lawal.

Fola said he was not bad. Charming yes, even a little flirtatious, but he was a great guy who never hurt anyone. It was the same thing he had tried to tell her all the while, but she was too scared, too confused to believe him. Now she knew he was right all along. Unfortunately, she wasn't going to tell him how sorry she was for suspecting him. He too had become part of the past she would have to forget. However, she knew she would battle to let his thoughts go: his half-smile, the way his brows came together when he was worried or angry, the sweetness of his voice—like a good wine down the throat—when he switched from English to Hausa, his vulgar way of speaking about his desire for her. She could turn off all the lights in her head and still felt the flame of his lust for her in her soul.

"Are you okay?"

The other woman's voice and her gentle tap on the shoulder snapped Ife out of her nostalgia.

"I've been talking to you and you seem...lost. *Mai ke faruwa?*"

"Uhm...I'm sorry, I had a lot of things on my mind," Ife muttered, wondering when Kubra left the door to come to her? "Seriously I'm fine."

From the way Kubra was looking at her, Ife suspected that Kubra didn't believe her.

"So, why have none of your family members visited you?"

Again, Ife wanted to tell her. Every second she held on to her secret, horror tightened the notch around her throat to a choking point.

Maybe she should.

Yes, she should.

Kubra's phone started ringing again, with an apologetic look, she bid Ife goodbye, promised to return, and left.

Ife didn't go back to bed when Kubra left.

Instead, she sat by the window drinking cup after cup of coffee. Her mind wandered along dark, lonely tracks, all of which led back to the little disturbing things about George she had ignored. He was an angry man. Leaving him to go out with friends, spending the weekend with her father, disagreeing with him on issues—all triggered him.

But he always apologized. And bought her things.

She hadn't thought for once that his attitude, his trigger, was a pointer to something dark. Red flags enough to sail the seven seas, her father had called them. Or maybe she saw them but thought she was the female version of captain Jack Sparrow who could navigate the most turbulent seas. She had dismissed her father's fears with chuckles and sometimes with bitter counter arguments. Now, they haunted her—the warnings. Accompanying them were the salty tears of self-pity running down her cheeks. She wished she had someone with her now, someone she could lean on and cry.

The first image that came to her mind was of her father, but it disappeared as quickly as it came, replaced by another.

Rasheed.

Rasheed was far away, yet as she sat by the open window of the dim room, inhaling the fresh scent of the green vegetation around her, her longing for him resurfaced. She imagined his arms around her, his lips on her forehead, his voice assuring her he would do everything he could to end the nightmare she was living.

She regretted drowning her phone. She should have written his number down somewhere, so that in a time like this, she could call him.

And tell him what?

It was better this way. Better that she was sitting here, drunk on coffee and memories, mentally laughing like a maniac while crying an ocean. Somewhere deep inside her, the thought of him felt like someone was kissing her lips passionately while continuously pushing a knife into her chest. It was as if a door was opening, revealing something both reassuring and confusing. That something wove its way into her heart, a dull, insistent hum running through her body, reminding her of beautiful things—beautiful moments: his smile, the cocky grin that split his face whenever he said something naughty, the seriousness he assumed when he made promises.

"Rasheed," she muttered, her heart aching as she got up to close the window and head to the kitchen with her empty cup. She had tried to put him, along with everything that reminded her of the danger she fled, behind her. But in the dark hours, when she lay frightened in her bed with tears drying on her cheeks, she would turn to the moments she spent with him, allowing herself to peek at them from the distance of time, and wonder how things might have been different if she had accepted what he had offered her, if she had believed him from the beginning.

She wondered if he was thinking about her now or if he was consumed with his revenge on George. Was he still on George's trail? Of course, he should be. He had said he never forgot the wrongs done to him.

He might have even forgotten about her. It had been months. Her heart squeezed at the thought of him moving on. It would be nice if he thought about her occasionally—no, regularly—because she had been doing so too.

Ife thought she was strong enough. She had told herself, since arriving in Daura, that the memory of him would diminish with time, losing its weight and significance. But she was wrong. Closing her eyes, she let him into her mind fully. She could hear him clearly, as if he were a foot away, teasing her.

She had fallen in love with him.

The realization hit her like a bubble burst on the face.

When did that happen? Definitely it didn't arrive slowly—this feeling she had for him. It was a clap of thunder slapping her face like a fling of hair, so rude and shocking. She could run, ignore it, yet she knew her heart yearned for him in such a way that made her feel that her soul might turn to dust in the wind and her body unwilling to live if she didn't have him.

She was halfway to her room when she heard a rasp, like a scratch on the door. Freezing mid-stride, she listened to the unnatural quietness that followed, a silence that seemed like something dangerous might shatter at any moment.

The sound came again. She wanted to ignore it and tiptoed into the room, then she remembered that Kubra promised to return, and walked to open the door.

It wasn't Kubra but Fola sitting on a stone by the door, her hands folded neatly in her lap, two fingers twisting the fabric of the same shirt she had on earlier.

"Why are you here?" Ife asked. "I can call the police."

Fola plucked a blade of grass and began cutting it with her nails. "I'll go to the police after I'm done telling you everything."

"I don't want to hear anymore."

"But you have to know," Fola said, standing up and letting the grass fall. "He's coming for you."

Ife felt the jarring impact of those words like a douse of cold water.

"George knows where you are."

"George… how… you…" A rustling sound came from the bush a few miles from the house.

An animal maybe?

Everything grew still again. In that silence, Ife felt a nudge of fear.

It was not an animal.

It was George.

"You told him," Ife whispered. "You made me tell you where to find me, and you… you betrayed me!"

"He was with me when your call came through. I didn't want to pick it up, but he made me."

There was movement behind them. Ife saw it, and so did Fola, because she turned around and sighed as an old man lumbered out of the bush.

"You have to leave this place, Ife," Fola said. "He could be here any minute."

"He was there with you when I called?"

Fola nodded. "In my sitting room, with a dagger to my throat." Her voice came off as a whisper. "That's why I decided to find you first—"

"Did Rasheed know?" Ife asked, her eyes following the old man who had taken to the right and continued until he was gone, leaving only the suspicion he had aroused in her.

Fola didn't respond.

"Did you tell Rasheed that George is coming for me?" Ife wasn't sure why it mattered that Rasheed knew she was in danger.

"I sent him an SMS when he wouldn't pick up my calls." Fola wiped a shaky hand across her face. "Please, leave this place now, Ife. Let's go before he finds us."

Ife was struggling to think, to move. She had to leave before George found her. She could call someone... anyone... her father... the police?

Move your frozen limbs, Ifechukwu!

She couldn't. Something was happening inside her, squeezing her world smaller and smaller.

Jesus! Time was ticking, and every minute she spent standing there thinned her chance of escaping George.

"You have a phone?"

"Ehn?"

Ife grabbed Fola by the hand, pulled her inside, shut the door, and crossed the bolt. Adrenaline pumping faster, Ife held the waistband of Fola's trousers, drew her closer, and slipped her hand inside her pocket. Excitement wheezed in her ears as her fingers felt the smooth surface of the phone's screen.

"Stay here."

With the phone firmly secured, Ife ran inside the room and locked the door. Something told her she wouldn't find Fola when she returned, but that wasn't her immediate concern. What mattered now was getting help as fast as she could.

Guess where I went to yesterday. Oh, I forgot you were never good at guessing. I paid Fola a visit. I reckoned since your father would snap my neck if I went asking him of you, and with Rasheed after my life, Fola was the easiest route to getting to you.

Rasheed. Blood thirsty vagabond. You must have known about his evil intention. He must have told you he would pay me a visit two days after you disappeared. I barely escaped with my heart still in my chest, but my flesh had the bitter taste of his dagger—that same one he carried around, the one he told me belonged to his father.

Bloody Fulani. I thought he was different. Naïve even. That he had no guts.

You did this to him, didn't you? You healed him of his grief by offering him yourself. You gave him treacherous hope, made him desire you so much that the fiend I never knew he had hidden inside was triggered.

You made him your assassin.

And now, he won't rest until the job you sent him was completed.

I left for a short while—out of his reach—to take care of my wounds. It occurred to me that to get back at him, I must find you and hurt you like I did his Salma. And to find you, I must visit Fola.

The house hadn't changed much since the last time I was there. The rich green snake plants on either side of the front door were still there, as was the irritating doorbell.

Fola's smile faded quickly when she saw me.

"George," she said flatly. She looked so ugly in her black mourning dress. "What a surprise." She never had the courage to tell me outright what she thought of me, not even after what we did to her husband, what I made her do.

"Long time no see," I said, even though it had only been months since we last saw each other. "Won't you let me in?" I stepped forward onto the black-and-white tiles of her front porch, feeling the right pocket of my pants where I had secured the dagger Rasheed left behind after I fled from his attack. She saw it and had no choice but to step aside. I let my arm brush against her breast as I made my way into the sitting room.

She scurried after me, trying to assert herself as the mistress of her own house.

It was pathetic.

I sat on Enitan's chair, knowing she would hate it, and she sat opposite me. I could see her struggling with herself, wanting to ask what I was doing there.

Pulling the dagger out of my pocket, I began to run my thumb around its medieval pommel. "I'm looking for my fiancée," I said, catching a flash of something in her eyes. She was frightened of me; I had always known that. It was peculiarly arousing, especially now that she was grieving. I wondered how she would be in bed now, with the guilt of what she did to her husband still tearing her apart. Would she be buttoned-up?

"You don't happen to know where she is, do you?"

"No." Her eyes were fixed on the weapon I was toying with.

She adjusted herself on the chair, and I let the silence hang between us until she couldn't bear it any longer.

"You have her phone number. You should call her."

"You know, that would have been a great idea, only that she won't pick up my calls," I said, unsheathing the dagger while looking around the big sitting room. "But you know where I can find her."

"I don't know where she is," she insisted.

"Oh really?" I didn't believe her for a second. "But you two got close lately, you told her things—you must have some idea where she's run off to." A muscle began to twitch in the corner of my eye that was marked by Rasheed's furious dagger, and I rubbed it to make it stop.

"We haven't spoken since the day you... Enitan died. Even if I knew where she is, I'm not going to tell you, George." She spat the word with more passion than I'd ever seen her muster. "You want to hurt her. I'm not going to let you do it."

The muscles in the corner of my eye twitched harder as I stretched my legs and leaned back. She had the gall to be protective of you. After what we did, the evil we committed together. Hypocritical swine.

"Are you telling me you haven't heard from her in all these months?" I wrapped my fingers around the dagger's handle.

"No," she said. Her phone began to ring. I saw her eyes flick briefly to the center table where it lay. "I think you should go." Her eyes went again to the phone, and I knew at once it was you.

"Get your phone," I said.

"Ehn?"

"Pick the bloody phone or I'll perforate you like you did your husband," I said, springing to my feet to reach her throat.

You should have been wise and remained incommunicado, Ife. You should have thought a little more carefully before making that call. I only needed to put a little pressure on Fola, and she cracked like an old brick wall under the weather. She told me where to find you.

With a smile on my face and a muscle tightening in my throat, I got up and left.

I began looking online as soon as I got home. Daura was the small village I grew up in. All I needed to search for were resorts, lodges, and possibly hotels where you might be. Again and again, I clicked on to the next page, but all I found were photos of hills and mountains and laughing children. Thinking that maybe Fola lied to me, I changed my search to Kankia, a nearby village.

You knew I would have tried to love you just a little more if you had asked. But you made me mad with confusion. I had to play all these games just to make you see me, to make you love me as you used to before. You used to tell me how much I meant to you. You used to write sweet notes and leave them under my pillow and in my pockets.

Why did you stop?

"I will find you. Wherever you've gone to, I'll find you."

Twenty-One

RASHEED'S NUMBER was the first in Fola's call log. Twelve unanswered calls.

On impulse, Ife dialed it and waited. With each breath, the day's heat and her panic grew like a fireball, and the knot around her neck tightened to a life-snapping point. Choking back a sob, she pushed the window open and fixed her gaze on the distant grasses.

He's there, her mind whispered. *Somewhere out there, George is waiting.*

Redialing the number, she pressed the phone to her ear. "Please, Rasheed," she muttered, her eyes still fixed ahead.

"Fola?"

He answered. Oh sweet Jesus, he answered! She sniffled and wiped her nose. "Rasheed... Rasheed, it's me."

"Ife! *Lahila ilala.* How could you disappear like that? How could you do that to me?"

His voice... that voice... The contours of the trees and bushes blurred immediately, and before she knew it, she was crying.

"I searched everywhere for you, *Masoyiata*. Where are you?" His tone, though warm, was distant. There was a hush, as if a third party was listening, between every word.

"Remember the bird that was sent to me?"

"*Eeh*."

"It's George."

"I know that."

"Rasheed, he's after me."

"I know already. I warned you about him," he said, a hint of irritation in his voice. "He's on the run—I haven't seen or heard from him since I..."

There was a hesitation in his voice that planted a seed of suspicion in Ife—a feeling that led to distrust, doubt, and questions. *What has he done?*

"He'll not be bothering you. At least not for a while. Trust me *Masoyiata*, I'll find him and put a permanent end to all this, *Insha'Allah*."

"He's here!"

"Ife, Ife calm down. I'm sure he'll not be—"

"No, you don't understand—"

"I'll find him, Ife. I'll end this—"

"Rasheed I'm telling you he's here! He found me!"

She sensed him stiffen, his attention sharpen. She told him about Fola's visit and her confessions.

"*Astaghfirullah*," he muttered.

She could picture him slumping in a chair, lowering his head into his hands.

"I am in Katsina right now, heading to Daura."

Hope sprang inside her like the first glimpse of light after a long darkness. "You...you are here?"

"I got Fola's message." Anxiety tinged his voice. "Ife, Daura is... George and I spent our entire childhood in that village."

The ray of hope that had bloomed inside her extinguished like a puff of smoke, leaving her feeling suddenly ill. Her stomach churned as if she were about to be sick. If George spent his childhood in Daura, and Rasheed did too, then it meant... "The murder—the man he... you..."

"Yes, that's where it happened."

She felt dizzy, like someone who had been swimming and needed solid ground, but the water was deeper than she thought. "Jesus," she muttered, staring out the window again.

"Ife, I'm on my way."

"I'm scared," she whispered.

"Calm down, *Masoyiata.*"

"Calm down?" He chouldn't be telling her to calm down when her head was spinning like a carousel.

"Please, love. I'll get you before George does, *Insha'Allah.*"

"I'm scared."

He exhaled noisily with irritation and when he spoke again his voice was lowered. "I wish you hadn't left. Now I don't know how to find you. How do I locate the part of the village you are right now?" Even from a distance, she felt, shockingly, the warmth and safety in the depths of his voice, the goodness that seemed to be at his very core.

"Rasheed," she said, feeling an urgency that was not connected to her present emergency, one she found hard to understand or explain building in her. "There are things I haven't told you, things I'll want you to know about me."

"Ife, love," he said gently, as if her thoughts were playing on a screen before him. "There'll be time enough to lay bare our souls. For now, your safety matters to me. You need to leave where you are now. Do you have anyone you can call around there—anywhere you can be safe until I reach you?"

Kubra. She could move in with Kubra. "Yes."

"Can this person describe where you are to me?'

"I guess she can. She's from here." Her ears picked firm footsteps outside. Feeling the beginning of extreme panic, she put the phone away, wiped the perspiration that had gathered on her face and raised the phone back to her ear.

Rasheed was gone.

She dropped the phone, pulled her backpack from under the bed, and began shoving things.

She was half done when she heard a knock on the front door and her blood began to pound. Fola was still in her house and that meant it could be someone else knocking.

What if it wa s Kubra or Rasheed?
What if it wasn't any of them?

She shoved more things in, zipped the bag, and secured it on her back. Looking around, she found nothing to defend herself with if she had to fight her way out. Regardless, she walked out of the room.

Fola was gone.

Feeling a whisper of fear as she reached the front entrance, she turned back towards her room, but the door flung open, slamming her to the wall. George walked in.

But for his eyes and well-set jaw, Ife wouldn't have recognized his face that now had an ugly gash across it. It was like someone slashed him with a knife without aiming. His lips too were badly torn— whoever did that wanted to make sure there was nothing left of that soft flesh.

He stared at her and shook his head like one would of a rebellious child.

Bracing herself, she counted her heartbeats while he closed the door and slowly drew the bolt across.

One, two, three.

Her heart was banging against her chest.

Seven, eight, nine, ten.

He turned to her again with what was supposed to be a smile but looked like a horrifying smirk because of his torn lips. A smirk that hinted at what he had in store for her, that told her that, although the end was coming, it wouldn't be swift.

"Don't hurt me, please," she begged.

"You've given me a hard time finding you, honey."

"I'm sorry." Ife was certain he heard, but she repeated it. "I'm—I'm sorry."

His face twitched dangerously– something she had not seen it do before. Or had she?

His hands were in his pocket. He looked relaxed and laid-back. But from the darkness Ife saw in his eyes; she knew it wouldn't take long before he—

"You're sorry?"

In an instant, he kicked her feet off the floor, and she fell flat. Then he crouched over her, his knees pinning her arms down. "You think that makes it all right?" He leaned forward, grinding his kneecaps into her biceps.

Ife bit her tongue too late to stop the cry of pain that made him curl his lips in disgust at her lack of control. Feeling bile at the back of her throat, she swallowed it down.

"I thought you were different." The corner of his mouth edged up, and saliva moistened her face as he spoke.

"I'm sorry, please."

"Don't beg!"

The slap he gave her across the face made a sharp cracking noise, like a whip. When he spoke again, the sound echoed in her ears.

"Why did you leave me, Ife? Why?"

"I didn't plan this," she said, tasting blood in her mouth. "I just wanted to…to…"

"Disappear?" he asked. "Rasheed. He helped you. He

asked you to leave me? To come here—did he even tell you what this place is. This house, did he tell you it used to be my home?"

His last words hit her like a baton on the head, and a whimper escaped her throat. *Eish!* She thought all she needed to do was to get out, to stay as far away from him as possible. Now she'd landed here, in this house that had his memories, his demons trapped in it.

"No?" he asked. "He didn't tell you?"

He didn't. But Kubra did. The woman had hinted about someone leaving the house and never coming back. But Ife was too lost to understand.

"He made you come here."

"I came by myself."

"You can't do anything by yourself, Ife." He leaned forward until his face almost touched hers. "You couldn't even think properly, could you? Have you any idea how easy it was to manipulate you all these years? You are a worthless, pathetic, brainless daddy's girl, Ife. You are nothing without me. Nothing. Just like the dumb skull Rasheed who thinks he has grown balls." George gave her a long stare. "You left me for him." His voice thickened with anger. "Why? What did he offer you?"

She shut her eyes and waited for him to hit her again.

He didn't.

"It won't matter, though. You are a slut. All of you. Sluts. Say it!"

She didn't answer.

"Say it. What are you?"

Blood trickled down the back of her throat, and she struggled to speak without choking. "A slut."

He laughed, shifting his weight to relieve some of the pressure, dulling the pain in her arms. He ran a finger across her face, down her cheek, and over her lips.

"We had something good. I changed for you. Yet you denied me what I needed so badly. I was stupid to play by your rules, so stupid to accept it when you said we should stop having sex because I wanted you to stay and not leave like Fola and the others."

Slowly, he undid her buttons. "Do you remember the first day we did this? You eagerly followed me home, and I wondered how many men you had followed home like that."

Peeling back her shirt, he pushed up her bra, exposing her breasts. His eyes ran over her with dark desires. He reached for the fastening on his trousers and loosened his fly. "You let him touch you, didn't you? You gave him sex while I starved. I was lonely and needy. You didn't see me, Ife. You stopped seeing me. You used to be a good girl. You used to love me more than anything in the world."

Not anymore, Bastard, Ife thought. *Not anymore.*

She lifted her knee, kicked him in the crotch with every ounce of strength in her, and he let out a groan, cupping his groin.

She pushed herself up, pulled her bra back in place with one tug and moved past him to get to the door, but he was quick, grabbing her leg before she could touch the bolt, his hands coming up her waist to hold firm while she fought to get free.

She elbowed him in the stomach, and he gave her a punch that took her breath away. The room suddenly became pitch black for a few seconds, and she lost her balance.

She tried to crawl away, but he stood over her.

Ife had to get away from him.

She had to get away.

Bending her elbow as though doing press-ups, she pushed

back, hard, slamming her whole weight against him. He lost his footing and fell backward.

Ife heard his cry and the sickening crunch of the back of his skull hitting something.

Then she held the wall and got to her feet to unbolt the door.

Twenty-Two

AS IFE MADE her way out, someone grabbed her by the shoulders, sending her into a full panic—her body trembling violently, vision blurring.

The person holding her was moving his lips, but the sound coming out of his mouth was drowned by the cacophonic buzzing in Ife's ears. He leaned close and began to shake her. She still couldn't hear anything, only feel: her chest tightening along with the knot around her neck, her heart about to burst. He shook his head and tried to move her aside to get into the house. But she clung to his arms because someone else had grabbed a handful of her hair from behind.

Someone... George?

This man in front of her, this savior, held her tight and began to pull her forward, almost freeing her from George's grasp. But George yanked her backward, and she landed against his chest so fast that she closed her eyes, bracing for the explosion of pain as a fist landed on her temple, and an arm tightened around her neck.

"George, let her go!"

"Why?"

Her senses began to return; she could smell George's scent of blood and fury and see Rasheed standing in front of her.

"Leave her alone."

"You don't tell me what to do," George retorted.

Ife's eyes stayed on Rasheed, who was taking careful steps forward as George pulled her back into the room. She wanted to speak, to say something to Rasheed, to George, anything that could freeze time. But in quick succession, George replaced his arm around her neck with an object.

"You remember this, Rasheed?" he asked.

A knife… a dagger. Ife could feel the sharp edge. Any careless movement, and her skin would be punctured.

"You must have wondered where you lost it. Your father's fine dagger, you told me. Maybe you left it on purpose. You wanted me to find it, so it would remind me of that fight—these marks you gave me." George wrapped another arm around Ife's face, covering her mouth and nose so tightly that she began to struggle for air.

"She can't breathe, George. You'll kill her!" Rasheed gritted, taking a few steps forward before stopping as George aimed the dagger at him.

"Won't that be nice?" George said, moving his hand away from her nose. She greedily sucked in air. "I could cut her throat with your own weapon. I'd love that so much." He pressed his mouth to her ear and whispered, "Wouldn't you love that, honey?" He redirected the weapon back to her throat.

"The police will be here soon," Rasheed said. "Let her go."

"You…you went to the police? When did you start relying on them for justice? The last time we met—the day you attacked me like a crazy animal because you thought I was responsible for her disappearance—you said you had no need for the police when you could get justice yourself."

The tip of the dagger pressed deeper into Ife's neck, and she felt the stinging pain as her skin tore. Soon, she felt blood trickling from the wound. Her stomach lurched, but she dared not move, fearing the blade would cut deeper.

"I was ready to follow you to the police, to make a statement or whatever they do there. Anything that would make you not use the bloody dagger on me."

"Let her go!"

The command in Rasheed's voice and the anger in his eyes told Ife that his calm, calculative self had taken a backseat. Something...someone else had taken the wheel. He inched closer, stopping when George threatened to cut deeper if he took another step. His stare was fixed on George, a warning as clear as a drawn sword.

"I won't allow you to hurt her," Rasheed said.

"She is my woman!" George blurted, shifting his weight from one foot to the other.

"You're one sick bastard. *Dan banza!*"

"Me, sick? Ha!" An animalistic sound escaped George's throat. "I just want to live, to be happy. To own things—things I deserve. Money. Women that would love and stay with me. I deserve them! I fucking deserve everything! I've been the unlucky one while you...you have everything working for you. You don't even have to struggle for anything, you privileged goat!"

"I lost years," Rasheed retorted. "Do you know what you and your mother did to me? Do you have any idea how much I suffered? You murderer!"

"I am no murderer—"

"You killed your own father!"

"We killed my father!"

"That's what you made me believe all those years," Rasheed said. "You and your sick mother who couldn't get herself to finish the heinous thing she started but had to force two little boys to do it for her while she made videos with the camera I dropped that night. A camera my father gifted me. You blackmailed me into silence for years."

A video? There was a video? Now it made sense.

"Blackmail? You were there that night, you let the old man drown," George spat.

"Lying son of the devil! *Shaidan!* For years I blamed myself. Everything about me disgusted me. I wanted to die because I thought…I thought I killed him. It took me a lot of mental playbacks to finally get the clear picture of what happened that night. It was you who held his head down while he fought for his life. I screamed for you to stop but your mother urged you on. He was dead before I got into that river. I had no hand in his death!"

"But you were in that bush when you shouldn't—"

"I overheard your conversation with your mother. I got curious."

"You should have gone home."

"You're damn right I should have. But curiosity got the best of me. I had no choice!"

"You should have gone home, Rasheed," George repeated.

His hold on Ife slacked. She could make her escape now, but she was scared she might not be fast enough, and any wrong move could be her end.

"You had a choice, Rasheed. Even after that day."

"Your mother tormented me."

"You could have told your father everything, and you know what that would have done to us. My mother didn't want that."

"What happened when we became adults—When your mother died?"

"I wanted to make sure you'd still keep the secret, alright?"

George said, his hold on Ife firm again. "My mom was dead, and I had to protect myself."

"You sent me birds. Dead birds."

"Those were nothing," George said dismissively. "Just me having fun with you."

"You murdered my wife!"

"I didn't—"

"Kai, *Allah wadaran ka!* You dirty liar. I knew it was you from the first day, something about your reaction when you came to my house and met me staring at Salma's lifeless body dangling there. You had no reason to show up at my house that day, but you did."

"It was a mistake. I didn't mean to kill her. She was making a lot of fuss."

"You are a murderer. You killed her! You killed Fola's husband. You want to kill Ife too? Murderer!"

George was silent, lost in memory or listening to the evening. Whichever it was, Ife wished she could turn around to see his face. Her feet hurt from standing. Her stomach, ribs, and knees were all on fire. But the sharp sting of pain from the cut on her throat had reduced to pinches.

Then he tossed her aside. "Sit," George commanded, his eyes were still on Rasheed. When she hesitated, he shouted, "Sit your slutty ass down!"

"Don't you use those words on her!" Rasheed's eyes flared with fury, veins strutting in his neck.

Looking from Rasheed to Ife, and back to Rasheed, George sneered, "What is this? Love? You pig—" He gritted his teeth and swung a roundhouse punch at Rasheed's face.

Without thinking it through, Ife shot forward and grabbed George's shoulders, knocking the dagger off his hand. He turned sharply, slammed his fist into her chest, sending her falling back onto the sofa and tumbling from there to the floor.

Now on her back, bewildered, she saw, as though from another body, his hand swinging out and she had no strength in her to scream as his fist was going to connect to her stomach, or her face.

Then she heard a cackle. A flash of pain crossed George's face as he swung his head backward. Another punch from Rasheed sent him crashing down on top of her, and blood—from her, from him, she wasn't sure—found its way into her mouth.

She heard the slight rasp of material ripping as Rasheed pulled George off her.

"You are not going to hurt her again."

There was so much venom, so much rage, so much fury in Rasheed's voice. Everything happened so swiftly: Rasheed plunged the dagger into George and pulled it out violently, making George gasp, eyes bulging in disbelief.

"Not her, not anyone. *Ka gani?*"

George made a gurgling, sputtering sound, as if trying to cry out for help, to scream his agony and fear, as Rasheed raised the blood-smeared blade again.

Balancing her arms on the floor, Ife propped herself into a half-sitting position, staring at the horror scene before her. George, clutching his side—blood running down his elbow and dripping onto the floor—staggered a few steps forward. He didn't get far. Dropping to his knees, then down onto his hands, he dragged himself about a body-length across the floor. With a spluttering gasp, he collapsed face down.

Rasheed took purposeful steps towards George, who had rolled onto his back. Ife could feel the blood pounding in her chest, blackness creeping into the fringes of her vision, her voice hoarse from screaming.

"Please," she heard George say, his mouth involuntarily spilling blood. "Don't...I don't want to die."

"You don't want to die?" Rasheed said, squatting beside George. "You deserve to die a thousand deaths! For all the years you tortured me. For killing Salma—"

"It's a long time ago, I thought you…you…forgiven. You never showed any…sign…any…anger."

"You bastard. You killed my wife and you want me to forgive you? What about Fola's husband?" Thrusting his head towards Ife, Rasheed asked, "What about her?" Grabbing George by the collar, jerking his head up. "You were going to kill her here, in this place." His voice was cold and low, his hand shaking as he lifted the dagger.

"Rasheed!" Ife called.

He turned to look at her and, in a moment, she saw his rage ebb, his face soften. In her mind's eye, he was a boy again—a boy trapped in the wasteland of grief, pain, and regrets. She was almost sure she saw clouds of tears gathering in his eyes.

"Rasheed," Her heart was beating loudly now. "You are not a murderer."

There was a tightening in Rasheed's face, and his mouth crimped in a defiant pout as he turned his attention away from her to settle it on George.

"Rasheed!" she shouted, but he didn't turn. "Please don't!"

His hand clutching the dagger hung mid-air, a frozen instant of indecision. "Why?" he asked.

She could hear sirens in the distance over the heavy breathing coming from George, who was bleeding profusely. George needed medical attention, or he was going to die.

Isn't it better that he died?

"You are not a killer." Every word came out with difficulty. Her stomach hurt, her limbs too. Her breathing was labored, her throat was parched. "I don't want you to be that man…I don't want his blood on your hands, please."

Dropping the dagger, Rasheed let George's collar go and

sat on the floor. He hung his head in his hands. There was something about this moment of vulnerability that cut through Ife to reach a softer place. She wanted to go to him, but her limbs were too weak, so she watched him sob silently for a while. Then he pulled his head up to stare at his hands, examining every blood-smeared finger.

"*Masoyiata.*" He stood up. "I'm not a murderer. I've never wielded that dagger before. I didn't even know I was capable of stabbing anyone until...until he..." he glanced at George, who seemed to be hanging on a very thin thread of life. "When I returned from my self-imposed exile, after Salma's murder, with this burning determination to get vengeance at all costs, rage drove me into my father's study where this dagger had been lying among his other antiques. I decided that, for the first time, I was going to murder someone—George. I was going to drive the dagger into his heart and watch him die. All these years, I waited for the right time."

His tone had reduced to a whisper, and in those hissed words, she could feel the terrible weight of what he had suffered, and the longing within him to face those who caused him the pain, to exact vengeance in his own way. But George's mother was gone. There was only George now, and even though he had brought more pain to Rasheed, killing him wouldn't be the best thing to do.

"Kill him now and you're no different from him," she said. The sirens in the distance were getting closer.

"What they did, him and his mother, was awful. And he...he took so much from me. My sanity, my peace. He killed Salma. I'm sure she begged for her life, but he killed her. Why should I be the one to let go? Why should I let him walk away?"

"Rasheed, please." Ife knew that whatever she said might not be enough. She could tell from the way his shoulders were set that he wanted more from this encounter; he wanted restitution from George.

"He was going to kill you."

"Don't be like him. Don't let him turn you into the killer he is."

"I'm not a killer," he mumbled.

"Then don't do this, please don't." The siren had stopped. She could hear car engines outside, and distant voices.

Glancing at George, "I think the police are already here," Rasheed sighed. "Your father must have tipped them off."

"My father?"

"Yes. When you went missing, I was so desperate to find you that I traced your father's house. I was told he's out of the country. I asked for his contact number, mentioned my father's name, and his staff was quick to put a call across to him. We have become allies since then."

"Is he back?"

"Yes. He took a flight back home the next day," Rasheed said, scratching his arm. "I told him about Fola's message, and also alerted him when you called today. I didn't know he would find this place so fast."

What seemed like mere seconds later, the police burst through the door. Their guns were trained on Rasheed, who stood as still as George's blood-covered body at his feet. A thick man emerged from the cluster of policemen in the room to approach Rasheed. He was the rumpled, grocer-looking man who had walked into Rasheed's office the day they almost made out.

"I told you to let us do our job, Mr. Lawal." There was disappointment in the man's voice. "We would have taken care of this the right way."

The man was with the police? He's a policeman?

"You said you needed to investigate my claim before doing

anything." Rasheed spat as some policemen came to squat beside George's body. "He killed a man many years ago. He killed my wife! You didn't even agree to get him arrested when I told you he was going to harm Ife. He was going to kill her."

The man looked at Ife for a moment. Was that...sadness she saw in his face?

"You didn't provide evidence to back that accusation. For Christ's sake, I thought you were exaggerating things just to get him out of the way so you could have her. We've seen this happen a lot of times." The man wasn't making any sense, and he knew it. There was a hint of uneasiness in his voice. "I wanted to be sure it wasn't another case of a privileged male using the state's security system against someone he feels would be a threat to him getting what he wants.

This is Nigeria and you know things like this happen."

"You've known me for a while now, Commissioner, and..."

"I know, I know. I'm sorry I misjudged you."

Rasheed didn't object when the man handcuffed him. As he was being taken away, Rasheed stopped to look at her. She saw the fear, and the yearning in his eyes. And felt consternation rising like something hard in her throat. What would they do to him? This man capable of volcanic anger and extraordinary tenderness, the man she had fallen in love with. How would they treat him? If George didn't survive, what would become of Rasheed?

He broke his gaze and followed the policemen out.

In a few minutes, Ife felt hands all over her, voices asking if she was okay:

"Miss Ojukwu, can you hear me?"

There was another voice. A very familiar one.

"Dad..." she sighed, closing her eyes.

"*Kai, kawarta.* You didn't tell me you were in trouble?"

Kubra. Ife wanted to smile, but her lips hurt like hell.

Twenty-Three

SIX MONTHS LATER

THERE WAS a light rap on the door. Ife knew who it was.

Since she had returned home, Habibah had made it her duty to be at Ife's beck and call, visiting every day to help with one or two things. Not that Ife needed extra help—her housekeepers were doing just fine—but without Habibah, Ife would have cracked.

"Your mom gave me this for you," Habibah said, holding up a bag of seeds. "I met her yesterday at the farmer's market. She said you can start gardening again. It will help you get your life back." Putting the bag down, Habibah searched through her handbag and came out with a flash drive. "I downloaded a playlist for you," she said, waving the device in the air. "Can I connect it to your speaker?"

"Be my guest," Ife replied. Habibah knelt to connect the drive, and soon, Johnny Drille's gentle voice filled the room, temporarily soothing her troubled mind.

"I'll go make coffee for us," Habibah said, walking towards the door.

"Strong," Ife called after her, wondering why Habibah had turned down the invitation to travel with Ahmed to Cyprus just to be here with her.

"Would I brew anything but strong coffee for you?" Habibah called back.

Ife waited for the door to close before continuing to place George's things into the bag on the bed. Clothes, shoes, some books. She hadn't been able to go through his belongings since she returned from her father's house. She insisted on leaving because she didn't want to endure the mental torture of remembering what it was like with George. She didn't want to think about how she had loved him so foolishly, blind to the man he was and what he had turned her into.

"You are no different from those senseless women in Nollywood romance movies," her father had said to her a week after she was admitted to the hospital.

A knife in her chest would have been faster, cleaner than the deep cut those words gave her. The worst part was that her father was right. She had loved like a fool—blind and unreasoning. Her first boyfriend had turned out to be a worthless fraudster who vanished after two years. The second was no better.

George was the third, and the worst. Thinking of him now, she realized she had loved him way too much. She had loved him enough to call him ten times a day, even though he never picked up when she wanted him to. She had loved him enough to refresh the WhatsApp application on her phone every two minutes to see if he had replied to any of her messages.

She loved him enough to ignore her family's warnings to leave him. Or was it loyalty that made her stay, even when she later found her heart reaching out to Abdulrasheed?

Habibah returned with two mugs of steaming coffee. "Now, what's the order of the day?"

"Moving his things out of this place."

"And how can I help?" Habibah asked.

Ife told her they would need to pack as much as they could.

"I'd rather gather all this and set it on fire," Habibah grumbled. "Why go through the stress of neatly placing them in a bag? Not that he's going to come for them. That *Banza shashasha* is staying locked up for a long time."

She was right. Ife's lawyer said George might be getting a life sentence. Fola could be acquitted if her lawyer put up a good defense like Rasheed's attorney who presented a case of self-defense against the attempted murder charge. As for the man who drowned eighteen years ago, Rasheed's lawyer argued duress, and at the end of the first hearing, he was granted bail on the condition that his sureties would ensure his appearance in court.

"So," Habibah said, picking up a shirt and inspecting the collar. "Have you heard from that other guy?"

Ife knew she meant Rasheed. They had met a few times at her father's house when he came to check on her. On those occasions, Ife barely spoke to him. Not that there weren't chances to talk, but she felt content just watching him. It seemed he was comfortable with it too.

"No," she replied.

"Nothing at all?"

"Nothing."

"I like him, though. I wish he was—"

Everyone liked Rasheed. Ozioma said he looked like a cute child. Her mother got attracted to him the first day they met at the hospital when he came with a basket of assorted fruits. Her father couldn't stop talking about him:

"He's a nice guy, well-mannered and intelligent too. He

knows about everything and can hold a meaningful conversation for a long time," her father had said. "I knew his father, the late Mohammad Lawal. He got me my first job in the ministry. Did you know I once shared a hotel room with him many years ago in Barbados? Amazing man, I tell you."

Habibah finished her coffee and placed the cup on the nightstand. "I think he's in love with you. The way he was always doing things for you at the hospital, calling every minute to check on you when he wasn't there himself."

Ife knew all that. Her mother and Ozioma couldn't stop talking about how often Rasheed called to ask if she'd eaten, if she was sleeping well, if she was still having nightmares.

"He's still apologizing for putting you through all that," her mother had said one day. "Such a sweet soul. Why is he a Muslim?"

"He would have made a perfect husband for Ife. I wish my husband would go into murder mode against anyone that wanted to hurt me," Ozioma had replied.

Charming—that was the effect Rasheed had on people. Fola called it flirtation, but Ife would say he was fascinating. She hadn't seen it before, but now it was like a dark cloak had been lifted from him, revealing an indescribable glow capable of attracting even the most aloof hearts and dissolving the stoniest fortresses.

"I heard he left Nigeria permanently," Habibah said.

"He'll still be visiting. The court case isn't over yet."

"Returning once in a while for court hearings is different, Ife. I think he's gone...like gone, gone. You and him, you know."

"It's for everyone's good."

It had been two months since he left for Brittany. Part of her wanted to beg him to stay, but the other part—the better part—knew they needed time away from each other to think about everything. When he came to say his final goodbye, Ife had pulled herself together for those few hours. She tried to show decency, sobriety, so they could talk, if nothing else.

She remembered leaning against the doorframe, arms folded across her middle, watching him walk around the sitting room, touching everything as if they were great works of art he hadn't seen before. She watched the careful movements of his hands. His composure and self-possession amazed her because she could barely hold herself together. Each time he leveled his gaze on her, smiling like yesterday never happened, she tried harder not to break down, not to fall to her knees and beg him to stay.

They hadn't talked about things—not in any real or meaningful way since she left her father's house—and there were so many questions she had for him, so many confusion that it was hard to know where to start. She was fearful of approaching it. In the end, it came down to one question: "What happens now?"

He had stopped walking around and looked down at the car key in his hand. "I don't know," he said quietly, putting the key in his pocket. "I'll be coming each time they need me for the court hearings, but that will be it. I'm relocating to Brittany permanently. At least, I'll see my mother more often. Someone else will have to take over running this branch of the company."

"Will you keep in touch?"

"Do you want me to keep in touch? I have nothing to offer you, Ife. Besides, you need time alone to heal and decide what you want to do with...with what we had," he said, his eyes gentle. "Do you remember the first day we met? I told you I've seen you before? I have. At Nnamdi Azikiwe International Airport. I was returning to Nigeria after five years. You were the most beautiful woman I'd seen since

Salma. I couldn't stop looking at you, but I couldn't approach you either."

He spoke faster, his voice low but urgent, as if he was reliving an exciting episode of his life. "This cold heart hadn't melted for years, yet there you were with the warmth of sunshine, and I felt my heart softening. I had never felt that awkward staring at a woman. Maybe because it was my first time in years, since Salma's death."

Ife thought of the many times she'd been to that airport, browsing through her memory to see if she could remember seeing him on any of those occasions.

"I couldn't tell you that day how I felt, I couldn't even walk up to you to ask for your name. But the excitement that bloomed inside me made me want to meet you again, even if by chance. I was searching for your face everywhere I went, amidst every crowd. When I finally found you, you were engaged to George! I wanted to forget about you."

His brows furrowed, and she knew he was struggling with his thoughts.

"It was hard. I was so helpless about my feelings for you, and I was angry that you could choose someone as vile as George to be with. However, I persuaded myself that I had to get you away from him by any means possible. It wasn't easy, Ife. The more I tried to get you to see how dangerous being with him was, the angrier I became because I thought you were blinded by the fact that I am a Muslim and a Fulani, not to mention the lies he told you about me," he said, sitting down.

Nodding, Ife remained standing, though she felt herself collapsing inside.

"It took me time to realize that your reluctance to be with me wasn't because of my religion or tribe, but because...because I was no good. My heart was filled with bitterness and a hunger for vengeance. I was no different from George, Ife. I don't deserve you."

"Rasheed, I—"

"It's late. I'd better get some rest so I don't oversleep and miss my flight tomorrow."

He stood up and brought his car key out of his pocket, and something in her rose against his leaving. She had to stop herself from barricading the door. But she knew he had to move on, and she couldn't blame him.

When he leaned in and kissed her briefly on the cheek—not on the mouth—it felt dismissive, somehow final. She wanted to grab his shirt and crush his lips with hers so he would understand how much of her he was taking away by leaving. What was she even thinking? He had her from the day he stepped into her engagement party. He had her as if God put her heart in his pocket with a whisper and a four-leaf clover. She might not have seen him at the airport the day he spoke of, but she could relate to his feelings because, in a way, when she met him, she was stunned. She didn't know her soul had been seeking for so long until he came along and unsettled her.

She loved him.

She couldn't help how helplessly in love with him she was.

He could be brutal when driven to the edge, a typical example was what happened in Daura, yet she still loved him. She knew he wasn't perfect, but she'd follow him into hell if that was what it took to keep him in her life. She'd stay with him if he would stay with her, trust him as he would trust her, and together they would ride through every storm into a new dawn.

But she didn't say any of these words to him. She knew he read them in her eyes and somehow understood because a slow smile crossed his face.

"*Masoyiata*, I'll always love you in mind, body, and soul.

You know why? You are the trap I didn't know I'd been wanting to fall into my whole life. Liberty from you would simply be an infinite prison. You are the softness I seek, the cradle for my head and heart. But I can't be with you. Not now. If I do, I'll end up frustrating you."

"What do you mean?" she asked. "I don't understand."

"I am a battered soul that needs healing. I don't want to heal on you. That will drain you. But always have this in mind, my love. I'll always love you, and when the time is right, and you still want me, I'll come knocking on your door, Insha'Allah."

She didn't want him to leave and come back when he thought the time was right; she wanted him to be with her now. To heal on her.

"Take care of yourself, *Masoyiata*," he said, then opened the door and left her as if they were friends parting with casual smiles. Despite the urge to run after him, she stayed put. But she was breaking inside, and she knew his heart was as torn as a ripped cloth too.

Who said goodbyes were easy?

Oh, Jesus. Watching his car drive off, knowing that was the last time she might see him, was soul-shattering.

A hand on her wrist pulled her out of her reverie.

"You've been staring at that wardrobe as if there's something there only you can see," Habibah said.

"Sorry." Ife sighed. "I guess I'm getting tired of staying indoors all day."

"Let's go out tonight," Habibah suggested, looking at her watch. "I have to go now. I need to see Ahmed before he travels tomorrow. But I'll stop by at, say, seven-thirty. I hope you'll be ready by then."

It wasn't a question, and despite Ife's reluctance, she knew that Habibah would insist.

Twenty-Four

THREE YEARS LATER

DINNER WAS ready when Ife walked in.

It was her father's birthday, and he had made the effort to cook. He mentioned that he hadn't cooked since she moved back into her house after he had helped nurse her back to health. Now, he decided to do it again, and for her. Ife's excitement wasn't just because she was going to eat something made by her father after a long time, but also because it had been a while since they had a meaningful moment together. These past years had seen her falling into life's routine: going to the shop every day, sifting through emails, documents, account records, negotiating with hair companies while attempting to bring calm and order back to her life. It didn't come easy for her—bringing calm back to her life after what happened. But she dug her heels in and locked out unwanted memories when she had to. And yes, it did help to turn her hot coals into cold impotent ashes, all her hot coals but one.

Rasheed.

Forgetting him had been difficult. Since he left, Ife woke up every day with a sense of nervous excitement and hope that he would call. He did, three months after, and had been in touch since then. Their relationship now had maturity to it. She also noticed, each time he spoke to her on the phone, that his voice was quieter, calmer than before, suggesting that he'd accepted their parting and was in the process of moving on.

"George died last week, in jail. I think you should know," he had said when they spoke three days ago.

"Oh." The relief that washed through her on hearing the news took her by surprise. It was as if she'd been waiting for the news.

"They said he slit his wrist," he had explained. "He had already bled to death before someone found him."

"Uhm...I don't know what to say."

She didn't think he was expecting her to say anything. "They've arranged for his burial."

"When?"

"Inspector Wakeel said George's uncle told him it's going to be in two weeks' time. He will be buried in the Baro cemetery."

"I'd like to attend," Ife had said instinctively, and heard him draw in a breath.

"Are you sure you want to do that?" he had asked gently. "You both have memories—good and bad."

"I think I need to be there, Rasheed."

"Okay."

He had said his usual warm but not too intimate goodbye and was gone, leaving her craving for the old Rasheed that could say the naughtiest sweet things to her without shame, that could say words capable of making her frown if there was someone else within earshot, and shuddering with excitement if no one was watching. Those past naughty moments were her most cherished memories of him, and they had become her salve, a kind of comfort in the background of her healing, the elevator music of her soul fire.

Her father pulled the chair beside her out and sat down. "So, how has your day been?" he asked, uncovering the lids of the dishes on the dining table. "Ifechukwu?"

"Huh?" She dipped her index finger inside the bowl of chicken stew in front of her, licked it, and bopped her head.

"I asked how your day went."

"My day was...good, just good."

Her father observed her for a while. "Bad day, eh?" he asked, getting up to serve her—white rice and the stew.

Shrugging, she picked up a spoon and began to eat.

"The police? They are bothering you again?"

"He's dead," she said. "George is dead."

Then she told him about the call and her plan to attend the funeral. She made herself breathe deeply and evenly, not wanting her dad to see how disappointed she was at her loss of emotion. She felt nothing about George's death, and that was scaring her to tears.

Was that why she wanted to be at his funeral?

Maybe.

Maybe not.

"You'll be fine," her father said, kissing her head.

"Dad?" she said, mixing a portion of rice with stew.

"Mm?"

"Can I ask you something?" She pushed a spoonful of rice into her mouth.

"Mm-hm?"

"What do you think about a girl..." She paused to swallow, scoop another spoonful, shove it into her mouth again, and began to talk with her mouth full. "A Christian girl getting married to a Muslim man."

Her father's silence made her uncomfortable.

"I'm asking for a friend."

"That friend is you, I guess," her father finally said. "Who is this guy?" He dropped his spoon and face her.

"Dad, it's not like I have someone...I just...I'm feeling if he should ask me..."

"A Christian girl that decides to marry a Muslim should know she's stepping into an island where she knows nothing and no one. It's going to be hard for her, trust me." Taking her hands, he continued, "Ife, I'm happy you are considering a relationship after all these years. But with a Muslim? I'm afraid, I'm not sure you can deal with the consequences that come with that decision."

"I can still be a Christian." Even before those defensive words left her mouth, her heart faltered with uncertainty.

"That's laughable. And have you thought of him marrying other wives after you?"

That too. Why hadn't that crossed her mind all this while?

"It's allowed in Islam, don't forget. If you choose to marry a Muslim, you should get ready to become a polygamist."

"But...what if he's a one-woman man? What if he loves me so much that he wouldn't want to have anything to do with another woman?"

"A Muslim man being a monogamist in this Nigeria where we have an abundance of beautiful women sounds ridiculous."

But there are Muslim men who are married to just one woman.

Ife knew two of her customers who were the only wives of their husbands. What about Baba Suki living three blocks away? He had only one wife, Mama Suki. And Ahmed, even though he and Habibah were officially divorced, he didn't remarry because he was still in love with Habibah.

Why was she even bothering herself? Rasheed wasn't

about to propose to her. He had not even given her any hint to suggest that he was still in love with her.

Ife spent the rest of the evening in her room, making calls: first to her sister, then her mother, and finally Habibah.

"I'm sorry I've not checked on you for a while now," Habibah said drowsily. Ife's call must have woken her from sleep. "I've been so busy here—study and all. It's not been easy."

"Biba, I understand if you need time to concentrate on your studies." Last year, Biba decided to get a master's degree in France. "So how are you doing?" Ife said, glancing at the electric light that just came on.

"I don't know," Habibah yawned. "This thing is harder than I thought." Another yawn followed her statement. "I'm missing Nigeria terribly."

"You are missing Ahmed."

Habibah laughed. "I am. But he does visit me every now and then, and we talk almost every day."

"Awww, Biba, you are in love with him."

"I never stopped loving him. Hey, guess who was our speaker yesterday, at the school's Advance Technology Conference?"

"How would I know?"

"Your boyfriend."

"I don't have a boyfriend," Ife said. She'd had two casual dates that were dead on arrival.

"Rasheed."

Breath hitching, Ife gripped a handful of the sheet. "Did he…did he see you?"

"Yes. He thought I wouldn't remember him, but I would recognize that face and powerful voice anywhere."

Heart pounding, Ife cleared her throat, hoping that Habibah wouldn't notice her nervousness. "How is he?" she asked. *Is he suffering emotionally like I am? Did he ask you about me? Do you think he misses me? Eish,* she never knew that missing someone could be this mentally stressful.

"You still feel something for him, Ife."

"Don't be ridiculous." Ife laughed. "It's been three years."

"And you still think about him."

"No—I don't."

"When was the last time you went on a date with a man?"

"Uhm...it's on uh..."

"That long huh?"

"Biba. You know I've been busy—" The problem was that Rasheed had raised the bar so high that every other man on earth was now doomed to live in his shadow.

"Busy thinking about him, wishing he never left."

Ife sighed. "It's too late now, Biba. We've moved on."

"Ife, the court case is over, and he has been acquitted. What else are you afraid of? What people will say? You are a Christian and he is a Muslim. Is that it?"

"No, yes...no. See, he may not even want me."

"Maybe he is the one afraid that you may not want him."

"Or he's being careful because of his religion. He may not want to get involved with a Christian."

"Did he tell you that?"

"He didn't say anything." That was why it hurt more. "Now we are talking about it, I think, maybe that's why he doesn't want anything serious. He knows it's going to be hard for both of us."

"My friend. There is a way out of this and both of you will be together. Convert to Islam, simple."

She would have laughed hard and called this suggestion 'outrageous' if she wasn't this insanely in love with Rasheed. So insane that she had even given the idea a thought, not once, not twice. "It's going to be hard. My family—"

"I know, I know. This whole thing is so messed up. You can't be with someone you love because you are scared people will think you are crazy for going out of your religion."

Habibah's statement almost made Ife cry.

"Anyway, I think love is sacrifice. You want something so bad; you go for it no matter what."

"Let's not get over our heads, Biba. For all I know, Rasheed may not even want me at all, religion or not."

"I don't think that's the case. I think he's scared you will reject him. He's not looking good when I saw him—yeah, still handsome, and classy. But he looks lost and out of place with himself, like a horse in a boat. I told him so. He laughed it off and said he's been working more and sleeping less. But I know he's missing something. I think he misses you."

"Did he tell you that?" Ife asked.

Rasheed never said that to her. In fact, it seemed that neither of them could get themselves to talk about old memories, yet she knew she missed him so much. And when the frustration of not telling him and not having him tell her became enormous, she had learned to take a deep breath and channel her energy elsewhere even when what she wanted to do those moments was to call and shout at him, to throw tantrums and beat her hands on the ground like a toddler. She wanted to call him a coward for running away instead of staying so they could work things out, an insensitive fool for moving on so fast without caring if she was coping well without him. Not once did he visit Nigeria in these past years, not even when he was supposed to be present in court, his attorney had represented him all the while the case lasted.

She didn't ask why he didn't visit, and he didn't tell her, but she knew he was avoiding her because he wanted, so much, to move on.

"Ife, you needed to hear the concern in his voice when he

asked me how you were doing." Habibah laughed. "I'm sure he wanted to know if you've gotten a man in your life. Just that he didn't know how to ask me that."

If he wanted to know if she was seeing someone, he would have asked her. But he didn't, not once when they spoke on the phone.

"Hey girlfriend—I think you should come visit France someday. I'd love to see you in person again. We can do some fun things...climb the *Arc de Triomphe,* meet *Mona Lisa* at the *Louvre,* or just wander through *Montmartre.* It'll be fun."

When they ended their conversation, Ife stared at the phone for a while, a conflicting thought nagging in her head. Feeling like she should, she clicked on the Elon Musk's X app, went to Rasheed's handle, and scrolled through recent pictures. He had cut his hair lower. His beard too. And it suited him. It sat well with the crisp suit he was wearing in one of the pictures.

Ife wondered if there was a new love in his life now or if he was still single.

Did he think of her in a more intimate way? Did he spend some minutes gazing at his phone, his mind conflicted about what he felt for her?

After some minutes of going through his pictures and his posts—mostly business and some motivational posts—on all social media platforms, her phone battery screamed low. Hissing, she got up to connect a USB cord to its charging port. She stood with the device in hand, one by one she closed the apps she opened, stopping when she got to X, hesitated a bit, then she slid into his DM.

"Hi," she wrote and closed the app.

Ife was jolted awake by the persistent buzzing of her phone. She stumbled out of bed, squinting against the harsh light of the screen. A notification from X caught her eye—a direct message from @official_AbdulRasheedLawal.

In an instant, any remnants of sleep vanished. Unplugging her phone, she walked back to bed, anticipation thrumming in her veins.

11:27 PM
'Hey'
11:40 PM
'You are awake?'
11:43 PM
'I'm so sorry for not replying earlier, I was working out. Are you okay?'
12:15 PM
'Let me know if you are awake and want to talk.'
'Hey, you,' she typed.

In the darkness of her room, the glow from her phone cast enough light to see the mosquito that had just landed on her arm. She swatted it away. Her bottom lip was caught between her teeth as she waited, fingers drumming on the mattress.

He was typing, and it seemed to be taking forever. Or maybe she was just being impatient.

12:26 PM:
'Yan mata, this one you chatted me up first?'

He had always been the one to call or start an online conversation first.

12:30 PM:
'Oya, talk nau. What's up? Are you getting married?'

She giggled and typed a reply. Deleted it. Typed again. Deleted it.

How could she confess that, all these years, his thoughts had lingered, sometimes so strong she had to push them back, even tried to extinguish them. Yet they remained as persistent as a heartbeat? How could she tell him she still remembered the first day she saw him as if it were yesterday? That even now, her heart had rejected every other guy, despite reminding herself he was far away and might never return? Hearing from Habibah that he still thought of her had thrown her into a state of euphoric nostalgia, like the highest level of a caffeine overdose.

12:32 AM:

'Kai, this thing you are writing that is taking time like this? Are you sure I won't call you, so we can talk instead. Abi you wan do voice note?'

She laughed again, wondering if a voice conversation would be better, but she preferred typing. It allowed her to pour her heart out more clearly. Asking him about her earlier discussion with her father would be too embarrassing to voice out. So, she decided, 'No, I'd rather type,' and hit send.

'Toh,' he replied.

She hesitated, then typed, 'If you meet someone, a woman you really, really love and get married to her, will you marry other wives after her?' She stared at the message for a while before sending it.

Her heart pounded as she waited for his reply, wondering if it was wise or appropriate to ask. When his response didn't come immediately, even though he had read it, she considered deleting the message.

She didn't.

Instead, she typed, 'Forget I asked that,' and sent it. Then she threw the phone under her pillow and lay her head on top of it, reaching for it again when it gave off multiple muffled buzzes some minutes later.

Rasheed had replied.

12:52 AM:

'Sorry, I went to pee.'

12:54 AM:

'Ife, polygamy is halal in Islam.'

Her heart sank.

12:56 AM:

'But it's not an obligation.'

She sat up, folded her legs, placed the pillow across her thighs, and typed. 'But will you marry another wife after the woman you love?' she sent.

He didn't reply immediately. Was he taking his time? Carefully weighing what to say to avoid hurting her? Was he worried she might be disappointed if he answered in the affirmative?

He was typing...

Then he stopped typing.

Typing again...

Stopped.

Typing...

1:03 AM:

'This is a delicate topic to discuss, Ife. But I'm going to tell you what I believe. Love is a sacrifice I would want to make for the woman I love. If I love someone enough to spend the rest of my life with her, it's going to be just her till the end. Three is already a crowd, and I don't like moving with the crowd. When I married Salma, I promised it would be just us, and I kept that promise until her death.'

Typing...

1:07 AM:

'My dad married just my mom. Even when his family wanted him to get another wife because mom couldn't have more kids, he refused. He later told me that marrying another woman would hurt mom, and he loved her too much to allow that. Theirs was the best love I've ever seen. Though they concentrated on each other a little too much—I used to feel neglected sometimes. But he loved and stayed with her until his death. I'm going to do the same with my wife.'

1:10 AM:
'Insha'Allah.'

Relief brought a smile to her lips and excitement to her heart. She believed him. She didn't know why, but she did. Maybe because he didn't seem like a man who would break a promise to his woman. He hadn't broken the one he made to his late wife, Salma, and that was something.

1:12 AM:
'Ife?'

1:14 AM:
'Are you still there?'

'Thank you so much, Rasheed,' she typed and sent.

'And I want to let you know that I love you, like... really love you.' She couldn't help the warmth tickling her neck and the smile stretching her lips as she typed those words she knew she shouldn't be typing. 'It's funny, right? A little bit crazy, I must admit. You must be shocked. But I haven't stopped thinking about you, about us.' She sent and waited.

He read her response but didn't reply.

'Your silence is making me feel like a fool right now. You know what? Forget it. I didn't mean that. Don't take it seriously,' she typed and sent, switched her phone off and went back to sleep.

Twenty-Five

GEORGE'S funeral service took place in a Catholic church.

Ife sat in the front row, the one without kneelers. She had never been this far up in an orthodox church before, and the massive image of Jesus on the cross loomed above her, his glassy eyes seemingly looking straight down at her. She averted her gaze, focusing instead on George's uncle, who was seated alone near the casket.

Two more people entered, familiar faces she couldn't quite place. One of them made eye contact, nudged the other, who also looked her way and raised his eyebrows in recognition.

Wait a minute. She knew those guys—they were newsmen from The Punch Newspaper who had covered George's court sessions.

They must be here to gather some material for their pages. Judging by their expressions, there wasn't much newsworthy things happening yet. The funeral had few attendees.

"Hi," said the older man with a chapfallen look, signaling for her to move over so he could sit at the end. The younger man pushed his way in and sat on her other side. "Sorry for your loss," the older one added.

Two altar boys were processing in with a priest.

"You look well," the younger newsman whispered.

The priest began to speak from the pulpit. Ife tried to concentrate but soon found herself staring at a stained-glass window depicting Holy Mary standing on a green snake with a ruby eye.

"Do you still feel hurt?" the younger newsman asked in a hushed tone.

"Do you have a man in your life now?" the older one added.

Ife turned to tell the latter to go to hell but caught sight of a figure entering the church from the corner of her eye. She looked back, and words died in her mouth, her heart skipping a beat and then resuming in a slow, unsteady rhythm.

Rasheed.

"Why did you come for the funeral?"

"Did you know George was seeing…"

The newsmen's words became a sluggish drone in Ife's ears as her eyes and mind focused solely on Rasheed.

Habibah was right. There was something different about him, something in his features that hovered between grief and longing. Ife kept staring, her brain struggling to process that he wasn't just one of the pictures she often viewed on his Twitter handle, but real and present.

Rasheed had seen her too. She knew because she felt his intense stare even though his eyes were hidden behind dark shades. He slid into a pew, gripping the backrest of the one in front of him.

"Who's the guy?" one of the newsmen asked.

Rasheed sat down, his gaze still fixed on her.

"You don't know him?" the other replied excitedly. "Abdulrasheed Rabiu Lawal. The Hantech guy who stabbed that other guy."

The conversation between the two men served as a perfect distraction. Ife managed to tear her gaze away from Rasheed and focus on the priest who was concluding his speech.

"The last I heard, he relocated to France. What's he doing here?"

"I don't know. We have to find that out."

They fell silent for a while.

A choir member began singing. Ife watched George's uncle approach the altar.

"You think we can get anything from him?" one of the newsmen asked.

"Not now," the other replied.

"But—"

"We'll meet him outside after the service."

"That's if he doesn't disappear."

He won't, Ife thought, feeling her excitement build. *He's here to see me, to speak to me face to face.*

After she had poured out her feelings to him the other night, she woke up to a long, emotional, soul-baring confession from him. He said he never stopped thinking about her and had always hoped to ask her again to be his. In his message, he asked if she would come to France or if he should come to Nigeria so they could talk more. She replied that she would prefer to meet him in France but needed some time to arrange things.

"How long?" he had asked.

"I don't know. Just give me time," she had responded.

And now he was here. Clearly, he couldn't wait for her to get things together.

The choir member started another dirge after George's uncle made his speech and the priest said a short prayer. Four young men lifted the casket and began to walk down the aisle. The priests and George's uncle followed, but Ife remained seated. She didn't look up when George's uncle stood beside her, his animosity palpable.

"We should join the procession," the younger journalist said.

Ife wasn't sure if he was speaking to her or his colleague, but she moved her legs to let him pass.

Once the footsteps and singing voices had faded, she rose and walked toward the exit. Emerging into the sunlight, she caught a glimpse of the black ambulance leaving the premises, watched it disappear, and sighed. She pulled off her headscarf, stuffed it into her bag, slung the leather carrier over her shoulder, and stepped down to the church porch's first landing. Her head darted here and there, searching for the man she had longed to see and touch all these years.

"*Masoyiata.*"

Ife's body convulsed in a sudden jolt on hearing his voice, and she made a sharp turn backward. Rasheed was leaning on the wall, one leg crossed over the other, arms folded across his midriff.

How the ground between them vanished, she would never recall. One moment they were staring at each other, feeling the familiar twinge of what might have been but never was, and the next they were morphed into a single being. The warmth of his body met hers. One of his hands clasped around her lower back, the other stroked her hair as she felt her body shake.

"*Rabin raina,*" he groaned.

With each soft touch, more tears fell. She cried for the times they'd lost, cried to release the tension of these three long years.

He pulled her head back to wipe her tears with his finger, and said, "my Ife."

Feeling his hands on her skin for the first time in so long was like drinking the first glass of cold water after being dehydrated. It was perfect, like the sun warming her body. It felt like survival.

"Rasheed. Call me *Masoyiata*," she said, sounding like an entitled child.

He laughed. "*Rabin raina* sounds better. That's what you are to me, my better half. But I will call you whatever you want me to call you, my love."

He devoured her with his eyes, running his hand through her hair. When he kissed her, it was sweet and gentle, and an all-consuming fire so hot it devoured worry and loneliness and fear and time and being and thoughts. It tasted of years of intense longing. It was so deep and complete that she felt like she was falling, floating, spiraling down, down, down. She wanted to speak, but all she could manage was a croaked, "Don't leave me, not again."

He smiled softly, nodding once before folding her in his arms again. "Some guys are approaching us."

Indeed, the newsmen were walking towards them with a camera balanced on the younger one's shoulder. The older one, looking like a Peeping Tom who had caught two adults making out, had his phone ready and was grinning.

"Let's lose them," Rasheed said, looking around for an exit.

"Great idea. I'm also getting uncomfortable with parishioners walking by and glaring at us like we're desecrating the church."

"Don't blame them. A holy place is not a love nest. I shouldn't have kissed you here. I hope Jesus forgives me."

They hurried down the church porch's steps as the newsmen drew near, left the premises, and followed a road that led towards a reserved park. As they walked, their hands touched and his fingers laced with hers.

"Where are we going?" Ife asked.

"Nowhere. Just walking."

She appreciated his silence, the loud statements made by his firm grip on her hand. She knew he wanted her to feel this moment, to remember how it used to be three years ago. He was deliberate, as always.

"You now deliver lectures at University conferences," Ife said, picking a flower from a shrub along the road. "My friend saw you."

"Habibah," he said. "I didn't know she was in France. It was good to see her again after a long time."

Another silence followed. The park was almost empty.

"Do you lecture often?" Ife asked, sticking the flower in her hair.

"Not too often," he replied.

"When you get invited?"

"And if I'm free. I'd love to teach more, tell my story, and inspire young people to do a lot with their lives. But running the company has not been as easy as I thought. Now I understand why my parents never had time for anything else."

They stopped in front of a fountain, and Ife withdrew her hand from his, slipped it into the pocket of her flared skirt, and stared into the water.

"Come to France with me," Rasheed said after a while. "We can live our lives there freely, without any encumbrances."

"France?" She looked up at him, her face scrunched in confusion. "I thought you were back. I thought you were staying…"

"I have nothing left here. Nothing but you. The company's branch here is in good hands, and my mom is in France with me."

He wasn't here to stay but to ask her to come with him, to pull her away from her roots, from her family. "Why?" she asked. "Why won't you stay here?"

"*Masoyiata,*" he muttered, giving her a sidelong glance before returning his gaze to the fountain. "Nigeria has nothing but unpleasant memories for me. After what happened…" He looked at her again, his face deepening with emotion. "I have so much going on for me in France. My life is there. Please come with me."

As what? His wife? His girlfriend? It was easy for him to settle in France because he had no family here in Nigeria to miss. His mother was with him over there, so everything was perfect for him. He wasn't like her, who had everything—business, family, friends—here. Her life was in Nigeria.

But you love him.

And he loved her too. Shouldn't he be the one making sacrifices? For love's sake, he could easily settle here as well as he did in France.

You can sacrifice too.

It would be a very difficult sacrifice.

"We can get married there if you are comfortable with spending the rest of your life with me. We can get married in court."

She caught her breath, instinctively searching his face. "Abdulrasheed Rabiu Lawal!" she whispered, "Are you…did you just propose to me?"

A smile crept onto his face, and he simply let it sit there. "It's kind of old fashioned and not glamorous but, yes. I am asking you to marry me, Ife."

His smile morphed into a teenager-like grin, filled with part love and part mischief. "Oh, I get it. You would have preferred I do it while you lay naked underneath me and I'm pumping your *labino* so well that you can't even say 'no' even if you wanted to," he said.

And suddenly, memories of those core titillating nasty words he'd said to her years ago, words he taunted and seduced her with, were there in her head and as her breathing pattern changed, he laughed in the same way he did those times he saw the effect his naughtiness had on her. So she laughed too, and then there they were, two beautiful idiots that had missed each other, laughing together on a sunny day.

"I missed you, Ife." His laughter reduced to chuckles.

"Me too Rasheed. Me too."

"So, what do you say? Are we getting married or not?"

"It's really nice. What you're offering—"

"But?"

"It's going to be hard for me."

"You still don't want to marry a northerner, a Muslim who was once accused of murdering his wife?"

"God, no." She flushed. "It's not that. Well, we have to talk about the Muslim part."

"Ife...*Ina son ki.* I love you. And I can do anything for you, I can come to any terms for you."

"Then stay here. Stay in Nigeria."

She detected a note of exasperation in Rasheed's unblinking eyes that were fixed on her face, and she suddenly felt responsible. She didn't want to make him sad.

"Will you... give me time to think about this?" she asked. "To seek my dad's advice and... and I want to be sure I'm doing the right thing."

He relaxed. His lips, though not quite smiling, tilted as though they meant to. "That would be great," he said, inching close. "Of course you can take your time, I'm so sorry if you feel pressured."

She nodded and began to do up the two top buttons of her

shirt that she deliberately left undone while dressing up for the burial service. But he was making her uncomfortable and clumsy.

"Here," he said. "Let me help."

She watched his fingers carefully fit the second button and hole together. She was rigid with anxiety and excitement when his hand came up to do the first top one, and instead of stepping back when he was done, he placed his hand on her shoulder. "Will you promise me you will talk with your father tonight? Or any time soon?"

She nodded.

"As for our different religions, we can sort that out once your father gives his consent."

"I don't know, Rasheed."

"I promise you, Ife. You won't be forced to do what you don't want to do in this relationship, and that includes conversion. Will you tell your father that?" His fingers were stroking her neck. Swallowing the desire that rumbled up her throat, she nodded.

"Or would you want me to come with you to see your father now?"

"Oh... no, no. I'll be fine. It's better I speak to him alone first."

"Okay," he said, withdrawing his hands. Immediately, she missed his touch.

"What are you doing tomorrow?" she asked. "Can I see you tomorrow?"

He shook his head. "Not tomorrow. I'll be leaving."

"What? Where are you going?"

"Back to Brittany."

Ife lowered her face, fighting off a feeling of disappointment. "Work?"

He nodded. "It's just for a few days, *Masoyiata*. There are things I need to do, and I can't delegate them. Please understand."

Before she could reply, he leaned forward and kissed her softly on the cheek, then on her lips. "I'll never leave you, my love. Never. Until the day you think we are over, that you can't take this journey with me."

"We will never be over," Ife said, and Rasheed smiled at her as though she'd said something profound.

"Then it's us against the world."

"Yes. Us against the world."

"The world doesn't stand a chance."

Yes, it didn't.

But she couldn't help the fear that stroked her heart as he walked her back to the church where she would get into her car and drive home to face her father.

Twenty-Six

THREE WEEKS LATER

BRITTANY, FRANCE

IFE PLACED the empty wineglass on the table and walked to the window. Her hands were unsteady, so she began to tap her fingers on the wooden frame.

Tap, tap, tap.

A thin line existed between maintaining objectivity while they played with each other's emotions online these past weeks and losing it completely due to one ill-considered action.

By agreeing to meet Rasheed here, she'd lost every sense of objectivity.

She started losing it the day she, against all the warning hints in her father's reluctant consent, packed her things and boarded a flight to Brittany with the ridiculous excuse that she was going to see Habibah. Then she called Rasheed yesterday and told him about her arrival.

"Ife! *Alhamdulillah*. This is crazy. You didn't tell me you were coming?" he said.

"Is this a wrong time?"

"God, no! Every time with you is the right time, *Masoyiata*." He didn't try to hide his shock and excitement. "But how? I thought you said your father insists you give yourself more time?"

"He didn't say I shouldn't visit France," she giggled.

"Did he know you'd be seeing me?"

"Who—my father?"

"Yes."

"I'm twenty-nine, not nine, Rasheed." The truth was that her father only knew she was traveling for the summer and would be staying with Habibah. However, something told her that her father already suspected she would be reuniting with Rasheed because he knew Ife was stubborn. Regardless of his valid concerns, Ife would go in search of Rasheed because what she felt for him was different, unique, much more than what she had felt for any other man she'd ever dated. And she would never be satisfied if she didn't explore that feeling.

Rasheed had wanted to send his personal chauffeur down to Dinan to get her, but Habibah insisted they make the one-and-a-half-hour trip to Morbihan—where Rasheed was residing—by themselves. Habibah would drive.

"It's going to be fun, I promise," the adventurous Biba said.

The ride was fun, but standing here and waiting for the arrival of this man who made her heart live in her throat was melting her inside with anticipation. Through the dim glow of streetlights that pierced the warm August night, Ife studied the muted outline of the Victorian brownstone opposite. The house looked to be three stories, but it was hard to tell with no lights shining through its windows. Habibah said, when they pulled in front of Rasheed's magnificent medieval building by the time darkness completely covered the sky, after Rasheed armed them with an address and Google helped in finding the place, that the neighborhood was one of Brittany's older ones. The houses were built in the 1940s.

Still watching the house opposite, Ife wondered if there were people in there, family perhaps, or just housekeepers like Rasheed's.

The Nigerian woman who ushered her into this room after Habibah left said Rasheed had left in the morning and had not returned. But he had informed them of her coming and instructed them to make her comfortable.

"What of his mother?" Ife guessed his mother might be staying with him.

"Hajiya doesn't stay here. She visits often," the woman answered. "I think she will come tonight since you are here. They talked so much about you the last time she visited. Ife, right? You are beautiful. More beautiful than Mr. Rasheed described."

The woman talked uncontrollably. She reminded Ife of Kubra, whom she met in Daura.

"We are here," the woman said, pushing the door wider for her to step in. "This is where he receives his important visitors." The woman gave her an appraising look before leaving and shutting the door behind her.

Some minutes later, a male steward came in with a bottle of wine, a glass, and a wide grin.

The only illumination in the street, as Ife stared out, came from the porch lamps in front of Rasheed's building and the one opposite, their beams forming a puddle of amber light that bled over onto a red car that just slowed in front of Rasheed's. Pressing her face to the window, she watched the car door open, and Rasheed stepped out.

Ife shifted her gaze to look around while willing herself to breathe slowly. She wasn't a teenager, and this wasn't her first time going to meet a man. The room had a polished wood floor surrounded by soaring paneled walls. There was a thick-legged table—the one where the steward placed her wine—holding a carved rock on a brass stand with a light in its base, standing against the wall. In-house trees and flowers were beautifully lined on both sides of a bookshelf.

She nudged up the sleeve of her dress and checked the time as she heard voices from downstairs and later footsteps proceeding up the stairs. Her wristwatch's luminous dial glowed eight-fifteen. In Nigeria, after what happened to her, Ife wouldn't dare come to meet anyone at that hour. But here, she was the one who chose this time because Habibah had an all-girls sleepover, and making the journey earlier would mean she would be staying with her at Rasheed's place for a while. The adventurous lady didn't want to do that.

Ife suddenly realized how deceptively small the study seemed when the door swung open and Rasheed stepped in, his lips curled in that cocky grin as his gaze held hers for a long moment before dropping to her feet. She became ashamed of her unmanicured toenails. He let his gaze slide slowly up her legs, upward to the slim-fitted black dress that began from the knees, curved at her waist, and ended in a throat-caressing neckline.

"*Masoyiata.*" he called softly, closing the door. In the room that was twilight and shadow, Rasheed stood close enough for Ife to breathe in his scent. His arms wrapped around her back, and in one gentle pull, their skin touched. His hand in her hair, sliding down her cheekbones, then her lips. In a second, the kissing started and they were moving like partners in a dance. She drank in the need in his shuddering breath, and he drank in the soft, yielding sound that rose in her throat. Their bodies fit together as though they were made just for this, to fall into one another, to feel this natural rhythm.

His hand moved to her back, to the nape of her neck, then forward to the hollow of her throat, and he moaned as he felt the quick, faint tremor of her pulse.

"I've missed you, my love. I've missed you," he murmured into her mouth. His kisses became demanding, aggressive.

Ife's hand rose to settle on his chest as lust whipped through her quietly, painfully. She couldn't remember the last time she felt such a raw need, a need so powerful it overrode her better judgment, her self-control.

Letting out a low gruff groan, he moved his hand to her ass and pressed her hard against his bulge and she lost the iota of control left in her. She needed this man so much. Here. Now. Forever maybe. Her family might despise her for choosing a Muslim, her father might be disappointed, but she had no doubt she belonged with Rasheed. A man that his past was darker than hers, his demons more visible, but his determination to do the right thing and to love properly stronger.

"Tell me to stop now, Ife," he gritted.

"No." She was caressing his face, neck, running her palm down his chest, reaching his... ah yes. He was fondling her breasts in a way that was driving her crazy.

He pulled away. *"Alhamdulillah,"* he murmured, wrapping his arms around her and resting his jaw on her head. "When was the last time we kissed like this?"

"Long ago. In your office."

"That's like forever. You don't want to imagine how much I crave you. These past weeks have been hard for me. I can't stop thinking about you. I blame myself for not...for not—"

"For not what?"

He shut his eyes and sighed. "I've always thought about making love to you. After meeting you again three weeks ago,

I couldn't control it. I asked myself why I didn't take you somewhere...my house in Nigeria—it's still there, I have domestic staff taking care of it now until I decide to either sell or give it away. I had wanted to take you there and make love to you."

H-he had wanted to make love to her that day? Why didn't he? She would have loved that so much. Even now, hearing him speak about it made her cove titillate. She would want nothing more than to have him rut her in such a way that would leave her sore and satisfied.

"I've masturbated with your thoughts in my head," he continued. "It's something I shouldn't tell you because I'm so ashamed of it. But once I pictured you, and the urge came so strong, I couldn't stop myself."

"Rasheed," she moaned, touching his face.

Should she tell him what she did the night of George's burial, after he held her hand and walked her through the park? The sexual numbness he re-awoken was seething. The fire his touch ignited tickled her core as if he had his fingers inside her, stroking and thrusting.

"I would have gone anywhere with you that day, Rasheed. I would have given myself to you."

"Ife, listen to me—"

He smelled of eternal summer in a bottle. Sultry and powerful. As she drew his scent and acknowledged how incredibly good it felt to be in his arms again, her mind rushed forward, she imagined how she would feel beneath him, her naked body, belly and breast, sealed against his flesh. She had been careful in letting her mind run wild with this imagination for the past three years, but now she didn't mind letting it loose.

"Rasheed, Make love to me."

"Are you sure?" he said in a strangled voice, his thumb stroking her cheek.

"You have always wanted me."

His brows knitted in a frown. "Yes, but—"

"Then, I'm here."

A groan escaped his throat. "*Masoyiata,* you don't know what you are saying."

"I do. I want you inside me, here, in your house. Make love to me like you said you would love to." She cupped his face and searched his eyes. He wanted her, it was evident in the rock-hard bulge in his pants that was brushing against her pelvis each time he moved. Yet he was acting unsure. "Don't you find me attractive anymore?" Had he found someone else? Was that why he was delaying? "Tell me, did I waste my time coming all the way to look for you?"

"Allah forbid that I stop finding you attractive," he retorted. Moving his hands down to her hips, he pressed her pelvis hard against his arousal.

She wished she could undo his fly and give his needy shaft the freedom it was craving.

"And if you hadn't come, I would have flown down to Nigeria to get you. I have never stopped thinking about you."

"Then why are you not...you don't want to—"

"I don't want it to look like this is all I want from you, *Masoyiata*. I want you. All of you. Now, tomorrow, forever."

Relief brought tears to her eyes and she rested her head on his shoulder. "You have me, as long as you want me."

"I'll always want you, my love. But I'm worried about your father. He has not approved of me, has he?"

"He likes you."

Shaking his head, "That's not enough," Rasheed groaned.

"He's scared I will be made to convert to Islam. He doesn't

believe you will allow me to make that choice." Ife had thought everything through and had concluded that what mattered was what they felt for each other. Her father would have to accept her decision. The old man loved her too much to hold a grudge. And from what she'd noticed, he loved Rasheed too. His only problem was that Rasheed was a Muslim.

"What matters is us. We can sort other things out later. You and I against the world, have you forgotten?"

That was what he said to her, what he wanted her to tell her father.

"I have a solution," he said after a moment of silence. "I'll convert to your religion if that will please your father. I will do it—"

"No." She crossed a finger on his lips. "You are not going to do that."

"I spoke to my mother about it and she was worried too. But she has no problem with me exploring another religion if I'm sure it's what I want to do."

"Rasheed, babe."

He chuckled. "Babe? You've never called me that before," he said, caressing her face.

Giggling, she lowered her gaze to his neck. "You don't like it?" She was suddenly shy.

"Call me anything you want. I will gladly be that and more to you."

Laughter erupted between them.

"But I'm still not allowing you to change religion because of me."

"Ife, your father—"

"My father will come around eventually. I will not allow you to throw away your religion because of me. I will...I will convert instead."

He shook his head.

"Listen, listen..."

"Ife, no."

"But I want to."

He stared at her in disbelief, then slowly shook his head again. "You have to be sure this is what you really want to do."

"I want—"

"We will find another way, alright?"

She didn't respond.

"Alright? Ife?"

"Alright," she said. "But does your proposal still stand?"

"Proposal? I thought you've already accepted to be my wife?" There was humor in his voice.

Slapping his chest, "Silly you," she said. "So where were we before the issue of my father's consent crept in?"

"I was thinking if we should fuck while my mother wait downstairs for us to come meet her, or we should go meet her first and come back to this later."

Ife gasped and stepped away from him. "Your mother is here? How could you not tell me? *Eish!* Your mother is here, and you didn't say a thing."

He was laughing hard now, dodging her playful punches. "But she can wait. She knows we will take some time before coming to meet her."

"No, no, no, we have to go meet her now."

"Are you sure that's what we should do?" Grinning mischievously, he grabbed her by her waist. "Mom said we should take our time, you know. Coming down earlier than she expected would be disappointing."

They went to meet his mother, a gun-metal gray-haired woman with an angelic smile and eyes gleaming with energy.

But for the almost imperceptible slur in her speech, one would hardly notice the effect of the stroke she suffered. They sat like two mischievous kids that already had their next roguery planned out while the woman gave them a long *chastity before marriage* talk over dinner.

A few seconds after the woman retired for the night, Rasheed was guiding Ife into his room, both laughing in hush tones like two juvenile thieves that snuck into a chocolate factory by night.

With the door closed, every pretense fell. The facade they showed his mother melted away and all they wanted was to make love like it was their last. Every kiss had a raw intensity, every breath was fast, their heart rates even faster. With a laugh, he lifted her right off her feet, carried her toward the bed and let her fall with a soft bounce on the mattress. He brought a sachet of condom from the drawer of his bed stand —he told her he bought some on his way home because he felt…maybe they might be doing this. She refused him using it.

"I'm clean," she said. "I had my last test two months ago."

"I had mine just last month. Just a routine check. I've not had sex in a while," he replied with that grin she'd come to love. "But what about pregnancy?" he asked.

"It's my safe period." Even if it wasn't, she wouldn't mind carrying his child.

They locked eyes for a moment, just enough for them to feel safe with one another. Then Rasheed put the protection away and became all business, undoing her zip, pulling the cloth off, kissing from her toes upward, slowly, his hands on her legs as his mouth found hers again.

"Mom will have a heart attack if she knows we are doing this," he murmured.

Ife felt his mouth on her lips stretching wider than it

should. He was fighting between grinning and kissing her.

She grinned too.

They weren't supposed to be doing this. Not after listening to his lovely mother talk passionately about remaining chaste until the wedding night. *'Premarital sex is haram,'* the woman said. But they were humans—two people madly in love with each other, unable to resist this thick lust whirling around them.

Ife arched her back in anticipation as he continued touching and stroking her skin, knowing where his fingers would soon reach. Her head rocked back against the pillow as he touched her there, the first moan escaping her lips. Then before she knew it, they were totally naked and their skin was moving softly together, like the finest of silk. She felt his hand enter from below, moving fast as their tongues entwined in a kiss. In a breath-second his fingers were inside, changing her breathing with every thrust, making her moans to time his movement as he thrust—like he said he would do years ago. Suddenly, he stopped thrusting, withdrew his hand and was now kissing from her breasts to her stomach. Then he was using his fingers again, watching her reaction: how her legs moved, how her body was writhing with pleasure, laughing and slapping her hand off when she reached low to grab his shoulders.

He knew what she wanted and told her to beg for it. But she just let out a moan, unable to articulate a response.

In seconds he was inside her, rutting her so good, just long enough to intoxicate her mind before he stopped and pulled out.

"Rasheed please." Already, her brain was on fire. "You are killing me." Again, he was sucking and flicking her titillating bud while giving her an out-of-this-world kind of painful pleasure with his fingers buried inside her cove. Painful because he would take her to near climaxing and would deliberately not take her there. Yet he was an angel. Her angel with a mouth and fingers filled with convulsive sparks.

"I'm just taking my time," he said against her tingling clit.

"Abdulrasheed Rabiu Lawal!"

Laughter burst out of his mouth. "Now that's something," he said. "I got to make you call my name in full."

If it was begging he wanted, he had to stop what he was doing to her with his mouth and his fingers long enough for her brain to start working again first...oh...oh...he had the whole of her clit in his mouth now and that was...oh...*Eish*...oh...

"So what do you say?"

"Yes...yes..." she moaned as pleasurable waves after pleasurable waves spiraled through her.

"Speak in clear terms, *Soyyaya*."

Love. *Soyyaya*. This man never ran out of endearing names for her. And she loved it that he was loving her tonight with his words as much as his eyes and his fingers that were buried inside her. Their souls were mingling in the quiet moments between action and stillness. The cool room already felt warm, and it was hard to hold back, to not want the climax of this moment.

"Tell me, Ife. Say it."

"Don't...oh...don't stop please...take me, Rasheed. Fill me, please."

"That's enough, my love."

She dug her heels into the mattress, lifted her pelvis as he entered her again. And when he grabbed her hips and thrust his whole length deeper, she caught a glimpse of his face—his mouth forming the letter 'O' as he shuddered and threw his head backward—before she rolled her eyes up and let out a whimper.

"Ife...Ifechukwu..." he groaned.

She didn't know if it was the fact that he said her name in full for the first time or the way he said it—so perfect, as if he had been practicing—that heightened the maddening sensation his shaft was sending from her cove through the whole of her body. And when he began to move, she couldn't hold back from shedding a few tears.

"Abdulrasheed."

"My love...*Rabin rai na*," he murmured, his voice strangled, heavy with his own pleasure, his fight to control this moment so he wouldn't come faster than he wanted.

"Rasheed, I've not...not done it in three years."

She heard a grunt escape his throat and he paused. "Ife! *Alhamdulillah*."

"I couldn't get myself to do it with any other man. I love you, Rasheed."

"*Alhamdulillah*," he muttered again, grinning widely and resumed thrusting. Slowly at first, then faster, his shaft kissing that place, that place inside her cove that sent her into sensory whirlpools of delirious intensity. Propping her pelvis with a pillow, Ife grabbed his ass and began to guide him in and out, timing his thrusts, guiding him more daringly to that hungry place inside her, building the intensity of sensations until each dive inwards was met with an outward rush of pleasure.

He was grunting as loud as she was moaning, his eyes fused with hers while his hardness kept hitting deep into her pulsating flesh that was about to explode.

"Rasheed, I..." What his shaft was doing inside her...tapping at her secret stores of liquid desire and... "Rasheed."

"Masoyiata..."

He was thrusting with a rabid, focused intensity, sending shock and desire, desire and shock like entwined threads all over her, heightening the pleasurable electricity through her body. He had succeeded in dissolving her into nothing but currents of pleasure, pleasure breathing in and gushing out, breathing in and gushing out. How could she hold such an ocean inside her? "I'm close...oh sweet Lord...I'm going to..." Her orgasm, hot and intense, bursting through the alleyway of her carnal, completed her sentence.

"That's it, *sahibata*, my girl," he said with a smile. "My sweet, sweet girl." Leaning forward to wrap his fingers around her neck, he filled her up again and began pumping and draining her, making her want to live and die at the same time. "Ifechukwu. You are scattering my brain," he whispered. "What is this sweetness?" And then he was making choking sounds. "O... Ah...Ife...*Matata ta kaina*...my wife...my heartbeat...you are so sweet, so soft and tight and sweet."

He was thrusting faster and faster now, mingling the sweet sensation in her cove with a dull ache. She thought her heart would stop and that she would take her last breath there, on his bed, underneath him.

She could have said: "I can't take any more," but she wasn't sure she had gotten enough of him. She was tired and sore but didn't care. She still wanted the ache, wanted him in her. His weight on top of her. She wanted to squeeze him in further and further while watching his face. She wanted his sweat to drop onto her and hers on him.

By the time he was ready to explode, she was already there with him. Their orgasms came with a wild thrill such as they had never known, accompanied by joy, fear, excitement and fate that moved too fast, hope and promises from their hearts.

"Thank you, Ife," he said as he rolled off her, pulling her into his arms. "Thank you for giving me you. I couldn't imagine...couldn't believe you would be here, that you would allow me to drink of your sweetness."

"But you said I would come to you. Three years ago, you had hope." She dipped her fingers in his hair.

"Hope, *Masoyiata*. But that faltered after what happened and I left. You rekindled it the night you wrote to me about your feelings. I couldn't believe it. After all these years."

Shutting him up with a leisure kiss, "I love you Rasheed," she said.

"*Matata...*"

"*Matata—* your wife?" She slapped his chest and laughed. "I'm not your wife yet!"

"Says who? Ife, we will be going back to Nigeria together to meet your father. I'll ask mom to come too so we all can plead for your father's blessings. I don't want you away from me again. And I don't want to have you any other way but as my wife."

They made love again, took a leisure bath together, talked some more and fell asleep. When she opened her eyes some hours later, Rasheed was standing silhouetted in front of the opened wardrobe, and from his perfect outline Ife knew he wasn't wearing a stitch. He gave her one of those corny words he used on her when he was still *chasing* her, and she swallowed a laugh.

"You are up already?" she said, yawning.

"Yes. I have to meet up for a 7 a.m. business meeting in *Guadeloupe*," he replied and walked to sit on the bed. "But I will be back today so we can plan our trip to Nigeria. You'll be coming with me to these meetings when we are finally married."

Ife smiled. She would love that so much. She would also love to continue her business when she finally resettled here. She would have to talk about it with him later. "I'll be leaving—"

"No, love. You are staying here until I get back."

"But Habibah will be worried."

"Give me her number. I'll call to tell her you are in good hands."

He's fresh from the shower, still wet in places, so deliciously attractive, and with one kiss, her sore essence charged with enthusiasm.

"I'll take care of you, *Masoyiata*. I promise. You'll not cry or regret us," he said, lying beside her, taking her reaching out to touch his nipple as an invitation to shift closer so he could slip his hand between her thighs, grab her ass and pull her in.

"Trust me, Ife. I'll dedicate my life to making you happy, and your father will never regret giving you to me."

As he pulled her head back so he could kiss her, not minding her morning breath, she felt again that strong conviction that he was the only man on earth for her, the only one who could breathe fire into her when she was cold.

"*Gimbiyata*, my princess." He kissed her neck, his hands stroking her back down to her ass and up again. "Let's make love again."

"But you have a plane to catch."

"It won't leave in an hour's time. So I can still make love to you and meet up with my flight."

Lifting her leg so he could sandwich his between her thighs, "I need to get out of your room before your mom wakes up," she said.

"You think she doesn't know we did *it* last night?"

Laughing, she rose to kneel astride him, a soft gasp escaped his lips as she guided his ready shaft inside her, and slowly she began to ride him.

THE END

Printed in Great Britain
by Amazon